A FARM IN
THE
AFTERLIFE

A FARM IN THE AFTERLIFE

THE COZY ABYSS BOOK 2

HARMON COOPER

Podium

Copyright © 2024 by Harmon Cooper

Cover design by Daniel Kamarudin

ISBN: 978-1-0394-5499-6

Published in 2024 by Podium Publishing
www.podiumaudio.com

Podium

A FARM IN
THE
AFTERLIFE

CHAPTER ONE

INSPECTION

Sylas Runewulf let out a deep breath. He felt like collapsing. He felt like heading back upstairs and getting into bed, where he would later wake up, be told that there were sixty-four days until the invasion, and get on with it.

After a night fighting cinderspiders, coupled with the pressure of the looming inspection from the Ale Alliance, the overwhelming weight of the invasion message, his hope in finding the men he'd served with, *and* his desire to help his new neighbor, Eleanor "Nelly" Redgrave, Sylas was already exhausted.

And it wasn't even noon.

But he was also alive.

Or as alive as a dead person could be in the Underworld, which had quickly become his second chance at life. This was the reason for the grim smile that stretched across his face as he looked over at Azor, who was frantically sweeping the pub.

"What?" the fire spirit asked, pausing, the flames flickering at the back of her head suddenly tangled.

"Look at Patches."

Azor turned to the piebald pub cat, who had just picked up a broken bit of a chair with his teeth and was in the process of dragging it out of the pub. Patches knew. Sylas didn't know how he knew what was about to happen, but Patches seemed aware that they were trying desperately to tidy up the place.

A knock at the door of The Old Lamplighter swiftly stole his grin.

"I can delay them," Azor told Sylas.

"No, no . . ." Sylas looked one more time at the mess that was his pub.

It was only about halfway cleaned at the moment, and there were still burned bits of cinderspiders laying about, plus pockets of glass, some of it melted, from the pint glasses that the spiders had knocked over in their mad dash away from the well behind The Old Lamplighter. His eyes settled on a curious burn mark on the wall right behind the bar. It was as if a flaming spider had jumped on the wall and used it to springboard in a different direction.

The knock, again.

"I'll get it," Sylas told Azor.

After dusting himself off, Sylas approached the door and opened it to find a dark-haired woman with striking green eyes. A painting wrapped in cloth was tucked under her arm. "Sylas?"

"I'm glad it's you," he told Iron Rose, the owner of The Ugly Duckling pub in the neighboring town of Cinderpeak.

"What happened?"

"A lot. A lot happened."

"I brought you this." She removed the cloth covering to show Sylas a painting of a swan, one set in a nice frame that had been painted with gold accents. "Sort of a pubwarming gift. Did I already give you one? I can't remember," she said as she peeked around his shoulder. "By the gods . . ."

"It's not pretty." He motioned for her to come inside. "And it gets worse."

"Worse?"

"Representatives from the Ale Alliance will be here at any moment. Did you see them coming into town?"

"I took the portal. I didn't see anyone," Rose said as she stepped in. Her nose crinkled. "What's the smell?"

"Hi, Rose." As flames rose off her shoulders, Azor launched into an explanation of what had happened last night, how they had later hunted down a giant cinderspider possessed by a demon known as a Hellrift.

While she spoke, Patches finished taking the bit of wood outside. He stepped back into the pub, saw Iron Rose, offered her a clipped mew, and went back to work cleaning.

"Thanks for this," Sylas told Rose as he continued admiring the painting. "Do you mind if I, um, hang it now?"

Iron Rose glanced at the burn mark behind the bar. "By all means. I'll help—"

"You don't have to," he told her.

"Wait. I'm missing something here." A questioning glance was directed his way. "How did you get down the well? Did you mention that?"

"You're going to love that part," Azor said, excitement causing her to flare up. "Archlumen Tilbud has a power called Shrink. He shrank Sylas, Tiberius, and himself down."

Her face filled with shock. "What?"

"And the spiders came out of the well, and we had to kill them, and they broke into the pub, and—"

Another knock.

"Shoot," Sylas said, the big man now holding a nail with his teeth. "Coming, coming!"

"I'll hang it," Iron Rose said as he handed off the painting to her. "Distract them for a moment."

"How?"

"Charm them."

"I can help," Azor said.

Patches jumped to his spot on the windowsill so he could peer out at the entrance to the pub. His tail bushed up, and he made a low sound with his throat, one that seemed to shake the floorboards.

"That's another story entirely," Sylas told Rose hastily. "Patches is no ordinary cat, let's just say that."

A look of alarm remained on her face. "No ordinary cat? What is he?"

"He's a magical cat," Sylas said as another knock came. "Right. I think . . ." Sylas ran his hand through his dark hair. He fixed his posture. "How do I look?"

"You look . . . presentable," Iron Rose said. "Distract them for a moment so I can finish hanging this painting. I'd distract them, but its best they meet the owner first thing."

"I love the painting, by the way," Azor said. "I always secretly wanted one of your paintings."

"Thanks, I've been meaning to bring it over, especially after how nice my deathday celebration was. Sylas?"

"Yes?" he asked Iron Rose.

"You've got this. Distract them."

Sylas faced the door, gathered his composure, and mentally cranked up his charisma. "Right, let's pass the inspection."

Of the two inspectors from the Ale Alliance, Marty, the sigilist, seemed to be the nicer. The thin man, who wore a vest that was a size too small for his long torso, smiled kindly every time Sylas apologized for the current state of his pub.

Greta, Marty's counterpart, did not.

Equally thin, but without a smile, Greta pursed her lips and noted something on the clipboard she carried every chance she got, including during the five minutes that Sylas took to distract them.

"We shall observe the cellar now," Marty said after an uneasy look around. "Please, stay here. Greta? Care to join me?"

"Just let me note something here," she said as she scribbled something. "Got it. I'll follow your lead."

"Right, come then." Marty led Greta downstairs, leaving Sylas with Azor, Iron Rose, and Patches, who looked from the big man to the two inspectors and ran after them.

"Patches!" Sylas called out, but by this point, the cat was gone. He turned to Iron Rose. "Well? What do you think?"

"Greta is the worst, that's what I think."

"She can't be that bad," Azor said, who now floated behind the counter.

"I saw what she was writing. She even wrote down the presence of a bloody fire spirit, like they've never seen something like that before." Iron Rose crossed her arms over her chest. "Maybe I should head down there and explain to them what happened here last night. I could do so politely."

"I already told them. You heard me tell them."

Another knock at the door caught their attention. "I'll get it this time," Azor said as she zipped over the bar. She opened the door to reveal Nelly, Sylas's new neighbor.

"Oh, my! Wasn't expecting to see you," Nelly said. She had pulled her auburn curls back, clipping them, and seemed to have cleaned up a little. "Azor, yes?"

"At your service." The fire spirit leaned closer to the woman. "We're sort of in the middle of something. It's bad."

"Bad?"

Her flames pressed back. "Inspection."

"Inspection? Right! That's happening now? I figured they would be here later."

"You know who you should see?"

"Who?" Nelly asked.

"Mira. In fact, yes, that's a good idea. Sylas, I'm taking Nelly to see Mira," Azor called out.

"Who?" Nelly asked again.

"She can show you around. Come on." Azor raced out of the pub in a plume of flames that quickly settled. She grabbed Nelly with her gloved hand and turned her away from The Old Lamplighter. "You'll like Mira, she's such a nice woman."

"Is she—"

"Mira is an apothecary. If you're sick, she's the one you want to visit. She's sort of the Ember Hollow mascot. She'll answer any and all of your questions. She did that for Sylas, you know, not that we mind getting questions. Or Sylas, I mean, not that *he* minds. I'm just bonded with him, but we're around each other a lot. Have you heard of the Chasm yet?"

"Chasm? No . . . ? That sounds ominous. Please, Azor, slow down. You're practically hyperventilating."

"Me? I'm fine. I'm not fine. But hopefully, never mind. Mira can tell you about the Chasm. And it is definitely ominous, as you said. Not far from here, actually."

"Please, Azor, slow down," Nelly said as the fire spirit continued to tug at her arm.

"I'm just trying to help. The inspectors are total jerks—well, one is—and Sylas doesn't need any more distractions at the moment."

"Was there another person in there? I heard another voice."

"Her? That's Rose, Iron Rose to her friends. She owns the pub in Cinderpeak called The Ugly Duckling. She's a painter." They turned the lane and passed by another row of abandoned buildings.

"What happened here exactly? You don't have to guide me anymore, you know. I can walk myself."

Azor let go of Nelly. She pulled back as she realized that she had perhaps been too forceful. "I'm so sorry—"

"It's fine. What happened here?" Nelly swept her hand to the abandoned village. "It's so empty."

"I thought the same thing when I first came to Ember Hollow and I think the same thing now." Azor swayed nervously. "From what I've picked up, it didn't always used to be like this. It doesn't help that it's close to the Chasm."

"The Chasm, there you go with that word again."

"Mira can give you a deeper explanation, but you're in the Underworld. Congrats!"

"Thanks?"

"In case you didn't find a map in your general store, the Underworld is surrounded by the Chasm, hell itself. Above"—Azor pointed up at the golden clouds—"are the Celestial Plains, heaven. So you're in between heaven and hell. In between and surrounded."

"And you're from the Chasm?"

"I am. But I bonded with Sylas so, technically, that's no longer a problem."

"Are there many like you?"

Azor touched her chest as if she were flattered. "No, not really. But yes, there are some. You might meet one the next time Archlumen Tilbud comes around. He has a water spirit named Horatio, who never speaks. Anyway, Mira, she loves helping new people. But she lives with her grumpy uncle. So let me do the talking if he answers."

"And which house—"

"This one!" Azor swiveled around and knocked on Mira's door. "She's really nice, trust me."

"And she's the apothecary?"

"Correct," Azor said as Mira came to the door. The apothecary offered the fire spirit and the woman she'd never seen before a tight smile.

"Azor . . ."

"Good morning, Mira! This is Nelly Redgrave. Nelly, Mira; Mira, Nelly. She just died, and as you can tell, she's here with us now, so that's a positive, or negative. I don't know. Anyway, Nelly has a deed to the general store next to The Old Lamplighter."

"She does?"

"I mean, I didn't see it myself, but she's holed up in the place, and you know what I mean. Anyway, we have inspectors from the Ale Alliance at the moment and things aren't looking great. Can you take her around?"

"Really, Azor, I don't need to be *taken* around."

The color drained from Mira's face. "The inspectors are here? I didn't think of that. The place must be filled with rubbish after last night."

"We got most of it out. Patches helped too. But it still needs some work. Anyway, Nelly needs that new person tutorial you seem to pride yourself on."

Mira raised an eyebrow at the fire spirit. "You want me to show her around and answer her questions?"

"Yes! Exactly that. You're the perfect person for the job."

"Mira?" a gruff voice called from behind her. "Who is that?"

"Did we wake Tiberius?" Azor asked with a whisper.

"No, he's been awake. After last night's little excursion, he couldn't sleep."

The second door at the front of Mira's home opened to reveal a short man in a nightcap. He squinted at Nelly with his one good eye. "Who are you?"

"Nelly Redgrave."

"Redgrave, huh?" Tiberius's emerging smile made it evident that he recognized the name. "It is an honor, Lady Redgrave." He shuffled his feet for a moment and bowed his head at the newcomer.

"Please," she started to say.

"No, it is. In fact—"

"I have a deed to the general store near the pub and I'm also looking for my husband. We died together, and I'm still trying to figure all this out."

"Mira, let's invite dear Nelly in and tell her everything she needs to know about the Underworld." Tiberius straightened up. "You weren't busy, were you?"

Mira gazed at him in disbelief. "I was planning to see Miss Barrowsly in an hour."

"Plenty of time. Miss Barrowsly will continue to be feeble whether you visit her or not." Tiberius motioned for Nelly to follow him in. When she didn't, he gestured to Mira's door. "That door will work as well. Leads to the same place." He grinned. It seemed forced to Azor, but at least he was trying.

It was only after Nelly entered Mira's side of the home that Azor took a guess at why Tiberius had been so kind. "Maybe it has something to do with her last name?" She shrugged at her own suggestion. "Better ask Sylas."

With that, Azor threw her gloved hands behind her and exploded into the air, the fire spirit rocketing toward the pub. She landed outside and found the front door wide open. Patches was on the bar consoling Sylas, who was sharing a sad pint with Iron Rose.

"We didn't pass?" Azor asked as an overwhelming sense of doom came over her.

Sylas shook his head. "No, we didn't."

CHAPTER TWO

MAYOR OF EMBER HOLLOW

Sylas set his pint down. He shifted back on his stool and Patches jumped into his lap. "They're going to give us another chance in a week. So that's the good news. That's the *damn* good news."

The worry that had filled Azor's form, causing her flames to ripple and peel back, settled and the color returned to her face. "Really? So there's hope?"

"It's fine," Sylas told her. "And there's always hope."

"Thanks to Marty," Iron Rose said as she finished her pint. "If it had just been Greta, you would have had to pay a lot more for the inspection again. I'm talking double the amount you just dished out. But Marty spent time in Cinderpeak. He knows about the spiders near the volcano and how they sometimes spread to other areas. He likes this area, you know. I think he misses it. Can't blame him, really. Battersea is beautiful, but it isn't as peaceful as it is here. Ember Hollow isn't quite a charming little hamlet nestled in the countryside and brimming with thatched cottages, winding lanes, and a timeless air of tranquility. But it is nice. Dare I say bucolic."

"Aside from the spiders."

"Yes, aside from those," she told Azor.

"Let's get this place cleaned up and prepared to open tonight. I need to refill as much of my reserves as I can." Sylas scratched Patches behind the ear. "We've got this."

Patches mewed.

"See? He gets it."

Iron Rose stood. "In that case, I'll head to Cinderpeak and send Anders over to help out. He'll be useful. Right, what else? Anything planned for tonight? I know tomorrow is your weekly feast, but what about tonight?"

"Maybe music tonight?" Sylas asked.

"I'd offer to whip something up, but there's so much cleaning to still do," Azor said.

"Let's get the pub up and running for now."

"If it's music you need, I'll stop by the volcano and talk to Bart as well. He'll be more than willing to put on a show."

"Thank you, Rose. Tell him drinks are on me, then," Sylas said.

"I will do just that." She tipped a hat she didn't have at the two of them. "Azor, Sylas—"

Patches mewed.

"Patches. I will see you all later."

Iron Rose was just reaching the door when Sylas called out to her, "And thanks for the painting!"

They went to work soon after, tidying up the pub and preparing to open that evening. Anders stopped by later and helped them repair some things, the carpenter happy to give them a hand. Sylas offered to transfer MLus to him, but Anders bargained for free pints instead.

Much to Sylas's delight, Mira showed up that afternoon, just as they were preparing to open. The apothecary wore a tight purple dress, dark enough that in certain lights it looked black. She also had on a black apron, which was folded at the front and tucked into its own band. She seemed several inches taller in the leather boots that she wore, which were laced around her ankles.

"Please," Sylas said as he motioned to a stool at the bar. He wanted to comment on how gorgeous she looked, but caught himself just in time.

Mira sat. She looked from Azor to Sylas. "Was it your idea or hers?" Patches hopped onto the bar and joined her, the cat purring.

"Come again?"

"Who decided to pawn the newcomer off on me?"

"Nelly? Is she that bad?" Sylas poured a pint of the lighter ale and gave it to Mira.

"She's not bad, no, but I have work too, you know. And I'm not Ember Hollow's welcoming committee."

"Welcoming committee, huh? That is something this place could use, especially if we keep getting more newcomers."

"You're still a newcomer, Sylas. Need I remind you?" This was meant to sound hurtful, but it came off as playful.

He placed both hands on his waist and struck a pose. "I've been here for nearly thirty days now. I'm practically a built-in at this point."

"Anyway," Mira said as she took a small sip from her pint, "Nelly is fine, but she'll need to go to Battersea to see about her husband—"

"She said they died around the same time," Azor blurted. "I wonder how. Do you think it was suicide? That's so grim. Sorry, Mira, for interrupting."

"No need to apologize to me. As for how they died, I didn't ask. Best not to ask this early on. But Nelly will need MLus before she can afford the trip there. The poor thing. I told her what I could, but I have no ideas about running a general store."

Sylas snapped his fingers. "The Brassmeres would know. We'll get her in touch with them."

"Good idea. Perhaps Cinderpeak would be a good place for her to go. I would have taken her myself, but she was still a bit shocked. You remember what it was like," Mira told Sylas. "It can be a lot to take in."

He took a deep breath, recalling that first fateful day. "It can be."

"I explained the system, the importance of MLus and not getting too low, gave her a bread roll, and then showed her around town. Not much to see here, as you know, but I told her what I knew and introduced her to my uncle's militia. Henry was especially pleased to see her, the old goat, like he didn't hear the fact she was married. I also took her to the Hexveil so that she could get an idea of what that looked like. That was a bit unsettling for her. She wanted to rest after, and so I took her back to her store when I saw Anders leaving here. Now, he's there making notes of what needs to be repaired."

"See? You really are the mayor of Ember Hollow."

"Please, Sylas, flattery will get you nowhere."

"It got me to Ember Hollow."

Both laughed. Azor laughed as well but started in just a bit too late. By this point, Patches was in Mira's lap, purring as she pet him with one hand. "It did get you here, you are right about that. And somehow, the place is starting to look better. Well, at least we have a pub. I suppose that is something. And we'll soon have a general store. And who knows what the next batch of newcomers will bring."

———

"I can take Nelly to Cinderpeak tomorrow," Sylas told Mira later, once the first round of patrons started to show up. The Old Lamplighter was back to its old self and ready to welcome guests.

Sylas was certain that it would pass inspection next time.

A group of people that lived around Cinderpeak Volcano waved at Sylas and took their seats in the back. Brom the farmer from the Seedlands approached the bar and took a step back. He squinted forward and nodded with appreciation. "Something changed about this place, yeah?"

"It's the painting," Mira told him as she winked at Sylas.

"I knew something was different," Brom said. "Anyway, pints and more pints."

More people started showing up. As Azor raced around handing out fresh pints and telling everyone about the upcoming Wraithsday Feast, Mira returned her focus to Sylas. "Taking Nelly to Cinderpeak tomorrow would be very nice of you. I would go with you, but I had to move my appointment with Miss Barrowsly today, and I shouldn't move it again. That reminds me of something."

"Yes?" Sylas said as he poured up a pint of strong ale.

"I am in need of an herb that grows in the forest between here and the Seedlands."

"Which would be on the way to Cinderpeak. We have to walk there anyway."

"You do, yes."

"Please, Mira, tell me what it is you need, and I will find it. I owe you. After this, I'll still owe you, but at least I can feel like I've done something to thank you for all the times you've helped me out."

"You're certain?"

"I'm doubly certain."

"In that case, I'll tell you what I need. In fact, I'll even sketch it for you."

"How about you make it a quest contract just so I'll remember? That would lead me to it, right?"

"It would, and sure."

[New Quest Contract - Find hyperion tulips for Mira Ravenbane. Accept? Y/N?]

Sylas gladly accepted the quest.

"Good, now the picture."

As more patrons stepped into The Old Lamplighter, Mira traced up a picture of the plant she was looking for. They wouldn't be very hard to find, but it would take venturing into the woods on the outskirts of the Seedlands.

"The hyperion tulip grows year-round. I need the bulbs, which I'll be able to grind into a powder that Miss Barrowsly can mix with water. It won't completely remove her ailments, but it will soothe them."

"Understood. I'll see to the task tomorrow, and I look forward to it."

Later, just as Bart started some songs, Mira took her leave and stepped out into the night, which was never quite dark because of the deep golden glow of the Celestial Plains.

As she turned toward her home, the apothecary hummed the song Bart had been singing when she left, a tune about a man from Windspeak Valley who made it to the Celestial Plains. Unlike the songs Bart normally sang, which came from their former world, this one was an Underworld original.

Mira stopped in front of Nelly's store to find the light on inside. She hesitated. *Just go home,* she told herself, yet she approached the door anyway, knocked, and waited for Nelly to come.

"Am I late?"

"Are you late?" Mira asked her. "For what?"

"Is the pub still open?" Nelly looked next door. "I keep hearing music. I'm supposed to meet people, right? I need to meet people and tell them about my place. I have to get Mill-yous—"

"M-L-yous," Mira said.

"Yes, those. I have to get them so I can have enough power to find out where my husband is."

"I wouldn't worry about that just yet. They'll know about your place once you open, considering it's right next to the pub. Sylas doesn't normally open for lunch, so perhaps there is something of an opportunity there."

"A restaurant?"

"Maybe not in the traditional sense. But what do I know? I'm just an apothecary."

"I was going to ask you about that."

"Yes?"

"Do you have things I could stock? I don't want to make competition for you, but if you have salves and simple items like that, those could be something I sell here. Then you don't have to stay open as much. There's this annex, you know, and I don't need the space. So I thought I could put them there. Or maybe there's another option for that space. This is all so much." A nervous flutter seemed to seize Nelly, evident in her fidgeting. "Am I asking too much?"

"No, that would allow me to make more house calls. But we can touch base on it later." Mira peeked around the woman and saw inside the store. "How was Anders?"

"He's great. Already fixed my counter and some of the shelving in the back once he finished with Sylas. Please, come in." Nelly led her into the general store. She had swept and wiped down some of the floors. It also appeared that she had placed blankets in the center of the space, like she was sleeping on the floor.

"No bed?"

"The room upstairs is locked."

"There's only one room?"

"There are two, but the second room is completely empty."

"So you'll need furniture. You can arrange that in Cinderpeak tomorrow. The locked room will be your portal to Battersea, to the Merchant Guild, at least it was for Sylas. Unfortunately, my class doesn't have the kind of network something like a brewer or a merchant would have. The store didn't come with any pets, did it?"

"Not that I have discovered." Nelly's eyes filled with joy. "I'd love a pet, though. It's already lonely here. I wasn't going to head over to the pub, but it sounds like it'd be a good time to meet people."

"Yes, it certainly is a good place to meet people. If the lamp is on out front, the pub is open. If it's off, the place is closed. Easy enough. That's their system, which is also, I believe, why it is called The Old Lamplighter. Actually, no, that was the pub Sylas worked at when he was a child."

"He grew up in a pub?"

"And was later an Aurumite soldier, yes. Tomorrow, they will have their Wraithsday Feast at the pub, so expect it to be a bit lively. They do it weekly, and they usually have a dinner and drink special. If you're looking to actually meet people and have a great meal—Azor can really cook—that would be a perfect time to do so."

"Wraithsday, got it. And today is Tombsday."

"Yes, but not for much longer. You should tell Sylas to announce your store to the people at the pub tomorrow. I know it'll probably be a week or so before you open—"

"That soon?"

"Things move in mysterious ways here. Sylas opened about a week after he arrived."

"I'll try to be ready by then."

"You will be. And tomorrow, Sylas has already said he'll take you to Cinderpeak to meet the couple who run the store there, Mr. and Mrs. Brassmere. You'll be able to get some pointers."

"Thank you, Mira, really. I would be lost without the things you, Sylas, and Azor have already told me. I can't imagine what it would be like to just randomly appear in the Underworld."

"It can be trying, that's for sure. And it happens more often than not."

"Maybe I'll stay in for the night, then. I can't tell if I'm exhausted or not. I thought about eating the roll you gave me—"

"Don't. While it is food, it's also to replenish your MLus, and you may need that tomorrow."

"Noted."

"But if you do want something, you can come back to my place with me. I was going to warm up some stew."

"Are you sure?"

"I am." Mira smiled kindly at her, and only then did she remember what she'd told Sylas about not being the Ember Hollow welcoming committee. In a way, she was, and now that she thought about it, Mira was fine with that. It would make the village better in the long run.

"You really don't mind?"

"I don't. We take care of each other around here. That said, let's try to keep quiet so as not to bother my uncle, or better, make it so he doesn't bother us. If he joins us for a meal, it will turn into a monologue of war stories and the glory days of the Shadowthorne Empire."

"Spare me."

Mira laughed. "Same."

————

Sylas awoke the next morning to find Patches lying next to him, purring.

[You have 64 days until the invasion.]

"And so I do," he said as he mentally toggled through his stats. He had sold two casks the previous night and had brewed after closing. Since he didn't have a very large deficit, he'd allowed Patches to stay in the room with him.

Name: Sylas Runewulf
Mana Lumens: 2280/2280
Class: Brewer
[Active Quest Contracts:]
Find hyperion tulips for Mira Ravenbane
[Lumen Abilities:]
Flight
Quill

"Good, kitty," he said as Azor whooshed into the room.

"Wraithsday! Wait, I forgot to say *happy*."

Patches hissed. Sylas laughed.

"Feast day, it is," he said. "I made a batch of flamefruit ale last night, so we're set there. Limited to twenty pints. What are you thinking we should eat?"

"Fish-and-chips. We'll keep it classic. I'll prepare twenty plates. I'm getting a delivery this morning from Corlin Tartar anyway."

"Great, that works then. In that case, I guess I should see if Nelly is up."

"She's already downstairs," Azor said. "I made her breakfast and left some for you."

"Thanks, I'll be down in a moment."

Patches mewed at Sylas after he stood. "I know, you probably want to come on my grand adventure today, but someone has to keep an eye on the place, and rumor has it, Azor is making fish. You love fish."

Patches offered Sylas a curious meow.

"Just trust me on this. You *love* fish."

After a quick breakfast of fried potatoes and eggs, Sylas set off with Nelly to Cinderpeak. He gestured toward the portal on the outskirts of town. "You'll need to activate this first. It will allow you to fast travel back here."

"Mira showed me yesterday." Nelly now had a scarf wrapped around her neck, one that was a bit too dark for the clothing she wore. Nelly seemed to prefer browns and yellows, and Sylas assumed the scarf had come from Mira, which was something Nelly confirmed once she saw him looking at it. "She let me borrow this. There weren't any clothes in the general store. Maybe that's something I should sell, clothing."

"People always need clothes."

"And I wanted to talk to you, or maybe, Azor, about doing a packed lunch. I was thinking egg and cress sandwiches, something that people could grab on the go, although I don't know what they would be going and doing around here. I don't want to interfere with your food sales."

"We only sell food on Wraithsday—today, actually—and special occasions. I think Azor would like to sell food more often, but that would only be at night. We aren't open during the day."

"Why not?"

Sylas shrugged. "Because we don't have to be. I can set my own hours, and I like to be open at night, giving me the day to do other things. Like this. A quest to find some hyperion tulips for Mira, and to take you to Cinderpeak."

"That makes sense. Do . . ." Nelly stopped walking and turned to him. "Do you like it here?"

"In the Underworld or Ember Hollow?"

"Both?"

"I love it here." Something brushed against Sylas's leg, causing him to jump. "Hey!"

Patches, who had been invisible up until this point, trotted into the brush. He peered out at the two of them.

Sylas started laughing. "Patches, come here."

The cat mewed.

"Does he normally travel with you?" Nelly shook her head. "What am I asking? How was he invisible just moments ago?"

"He can do that," Sylas said as the cat approached him. "And no, he doesn't normally travel with me. I guess he was bored."

"Or he doesn't like Azor."

"He doesn't *dislike* her, but he was pretty annoyed at her when she kept preventing him from going outside. That's a long story," Sylas told her as he scooped Patches up.

"Is it, now?"

As they walked back toward Ember Hollow, Sylas explained what had happened with the well and cinderspiders. He realized once he got to the part about shrinking and journeying into the well that it was perhaps too much information for a newcomer. "That part will all make sense soon. Mira can explain some of it too, better than me. I'm still sort of new; it's only been a month."

They reached the abandoned market that was just past the portal. Sylas had eyed it several times now, imagining that it could be like the farmer's market on the outskirts of Cinderpeak. All of Ember Hollow needed a facelift, but he didn't know how much he could handle with the looming threat of some mysterious invasion.

Hopefully Nuno Landling, the manaseer he had met on his trip to Battersea, would visit soon with more information on the invasion prompt . . .

"Run back home," he told Patches after he set him on the ground.

The piebald pub cat curled his tail as he looked up at Sylas and Nelly, his whiskers twitching.

"Patches . . ." Sylas placed his hands on his hips. The cat finally gave up and turned away. Sylas kept an eye on him to make sure he didn't simply turn invisible again. "I should probably grab something at the pub myself."

"What's that?"

"My fireweave mace. No bladelike weapons are allowed here in the Underworld. It's best to have something on you, though, if you go venturing into the woods."

———

Sylas and Nelly traveled through a meadow, where they found a pathway that was navigable without having to beat away the underbrush with his mace. "If you take a quest contract, the system will lead you there to some degree," he explained to her. "It's quite intuitive."

"So you know where these flowers are?"

"Yep, and we should be there soon." They came to a natural trail, one that was covered in mossy limbs and grass that had a blue hint to it. Sylas had grown used to the coloring of the Underworld, yet every now and then, it took his breath away to see the way things were illuminated, how the Celestial Plains above gave everything an almost gloomy glow.

It certainly felt magical.

Later, and following the guiding line that had appeared before him, Sylas and Nelly reached a small meadow, one that was blanketed by orange-and-blue tulips.

"Better check them," he said as he got out the piece of paper Mira had given him to verify they were hyperion tulips, not some other variety.

"Oh my." Nelly stopped dead in her tracks. As Sylas turned to her, he noticed an overwhelming sense of sadness come over the woman. "Karn would have loved this."

"Karn?"

"My husband. His mother had a thing for tulips. She had this garden." Nelly placed a hand on her chest. "I can almost smell it. He brought me a fresh bouquet one early spring. I was at the academy and it was so surprising. I knew from that point forward."

Sylas gave her a moment to remember.

He was curious at her mention of an academy, and he'd yet to hear anything about Karn or about how they'd both died, yet he saved these questions. This kind of patience was important.

Giving a person the time they needed to collect their thoughts was a courtesy he hoped others would extend to him. It was something he'd done in the camps on the outskirts of battles, where soldiers would soon face unknown horrors.

A flash of some of these horrors came to him and left.

Sylas knew they were real, that they had actually happened. But now, under the golden glow of the Celestial Plains, they felt like a fever dream, a nightmare that he'd never forget yet could no longer get to him.

Once Nelly was ready, they collected the tulips and placed them in Sylas's bag. "I think we can go this way and eventually reach the Seedlands," Sylas told Nelly. "I should confirm that."

"Confirm it?"

"Watch this." Sylas used his Mana Lumens to float into the air. He rose above the tree line and brought a hand to his brow. He spotted the Seedlands beyond, as well as Brom's farm with its fallow fields on the edge of the forest.

"You can fly," Nelly said after he touched back down.

"There's so much you can do with MLus. Watch this." Sylas used his Quill ability to write a message in the air, one that glittered with gold mana. "The guy that taught me these things is a little eccentric. I think already told you about him. Archlumen Tilbud. He's the one who shrank Tiberius and me so we could enter the well. I don't know if he'll be at the pub tonight, but he does like doing a weekly quiz. So maybe. He's worth meeting."

"A pub quiz? Sounds fun."

"It is fun, and I learn something new every time. Come on, not much longer now."

Sylas and Nelly were just reaching the edge of the woods when they heard barking. A dog with black fur burst out of the thicket and raced toward them. She practically ran directly into Sylas before skidding to a sudden stop.

"What is it, girl?" Sylas asked as he recognized the terror in the dog's eyes. He also realized the dog was trying to tell him something.

She let out a short bark and turned back in the direction she had come from. She glanced over her shoulder one last time at Sylas and took off.

"What should we do?" Nelly asked.

"We follow her. If we encounter anything, let me handle it."

Nelly looked around and found a stick. She broke the small branches off it. "What? You don't think I know how to use a . . ."

"You were going to say 'sword,' weren't you."

She held back a grin. "Yes. 'Stick' just doesn't sound as imposing."

"No it doesn't, but it will do." The dog barked again. "Let's go."

CHAPTER THREE

CORNBREAD, GUARDIAN
OF THE FARMLY REALM

Sylas and Nelly reached the fallow fields around Brom's home. He turned to the newcomer. "I should fly ahead, just in case."

"What do you think it is? You still haven't told me what's going on here, Sylas!"

"There's no telling what it is, but if I was to guess, likely a creature that escaped the Hexveil. Monsters. Or some that already live here, like the spiders. I really hope we don't have to deal with more spiders."

"How big are we talking?"

"Large. Hopefully, that isn't what *this* is," Sylas said as the dog barked again.

"And you know whose dog this is?"

"Brom's. Or I think it's Brom's. He had a dog from what I recall, but I never actually saw her."

Nelly crouched. The dog returned to her and Nelly checked her collar. "Her name is Cornbread."

"Cornbread?" Sylas looked down at the black farm dog, who had a tuft brown around her mouth.

"Looks like it. Let's follow her. Go on, Cornbread."

Cornbread raced toward the home, Sylas having to fly to keep up with the farm dog. Nelly ran surprisingly fast and arrived at the front door with her stick at about the same time Sylas did with his mace. "Brom, you in there?" Sylas called out. He beat on the door. "Brom?"

"Is the door open?" Nelly asked after Sylas had called for the farmer twice.

"No. But there's a back door. Let's check that one. It's okay, girl," he told Cornbread, who continued to bark. "We'll figure it out."

"We could try a window."

"Back door, and if that's not open, a window. Or I charge through the door."

"Can you do something like that?"

Sylas nodded. "It wouldn't be the first time."

"Put a pin in that because I want to know how you got good charging through doors."

"I wouldn't say I was good," he told her as they circled around the home. Sylas checked the back door, and it swung open. "Looks like—"

A darkness rushed past them like a unkindness of ravens. Nelly grabbed Sylas's wrist and pulled him to the side as the darkness circled the house and left in the direction of the forest.

"Thanks," Sylas told her as he watched the dark cloud fade, his skin crawling. "Whew. I was *not* expecting that."

Cornbread bolted into the house, barking furiously, every fiber of her being alight with panic. She reached Brom's bedroom door and started ramming her body into it.

"Easy, girl." Nelly set her stick down and grabbed Cornbread, holding her back.

Sylas approached the door, his mace clenched tightly. "Brom, if you're in there, say something. Otherwise, I'm coming through!" He went for the handle, opened it, kicked the door in, and stepped back.

"What is it?" Nelly asked as Cornbread barked.

Sylas had seen death before. He'd seen dead bodies, gravely injured bodies, and he himself had died. But what he saw in Brom's room was beyond anything he had ever witnessed.

Brom lay on the bed, the man's body shriveled, his skin and bones turned into a nest of what looked like dusty spiderwebs.

The smell hit him next. Sylas turned his head, covering his nose with his arm. He approached Brom and stopped short of touching him.

"Is he . . . dead?" Nelly called from the other room.

Sylas didn't answer. Instead, he returned to her and shut the door behind him. "We'll need to bring Cornbread back with us to Ember Hollow. You met Tiberius, right?"

"Mira's uncle? Yes, I did. So he's dead?"

"Brom is something worse than dead. Tiberius will know what to do."

———

Mira had just finished her tea when she heard a knock at the door. Then she heard barking, followed by a bit of hurried chatter. "What could it be now?" she whispered as she returned the herbal concoction she was working on back to its tin. "Coming."

Mira stood, smoothed her hands over the front of her dress, looked at herself quickly in the small mirror she had on a bookshelf, and headed to the door. "Yes?" she asked as she took in Sylas, the bearded man with a nervous look in his big blue eyes. From there she glanced at Nelly, who held a squirming black farm dog in her arms. "What is the meaning of this?"

Sylas cleared his throat. "Mira, hi."

"Hi."

"I'll explain everything. Where's Tiberius?"

Her eyebrow twitched at his question.

"I'm serious, Mira."

"I can tell. Tiberius is out back with Cody and Duncan. Henry was with them as well, but he has since left. He is fond of saying goodbye every time he does," she said with a hint of disdain. "You could have just headed around the home to find them, you know."

"I try not to do things like that with the enemy. Kidding," Sylas said, showing her one of his palms. He held his mace in his other hand, which he kept facing toward the ground as if it were a sword. "We're all friends here. But we do need to speak to your uncle. It's urgent."

"You wouldn't want a dog, would you?" Nelly asked. "One named Cornbread?"

"Absolutely not."

"So that means I can keep her," Nelly told Sylas. "See? I told you Mira wouldn't mind."

Sylas tapped his mace against the side of his boot. "I wonder how Patches will feel about a dog living next door."

"We'll have to find out. Anyway, your uncle, please, Mira, it's important," Nelly said. "A life-and-death situation."

"More of a death situation," Sylas added, "but—and trust me, I hate to say this—Tiberius will know what to do."

Mira gestured for the two to follow her. "Come on, then. And hold on to the dog. I don't know how my uncle feels about dogs."

"Her name is Cornbread," Nelly told her.

"Cornbread? Huh. I wonder where she got a name like that. I can't say I've ever had bread made from corn. But I suppose it's a thing. Anyhow. This way." Mira led them through her shop and into the main room of the home she shared with Tiberius. She noticed that her uncle had left several of his miniature wooden figurines on their dining room table as well as a scattering of Demon Hunter Guild documents he was reviewing.

"No time for that," she whispered to herself as she stepped out back, where they found Cody and Duncan standing around a dummy made of stuffed leather, both men in armor and holding polished clubs. Duncan, the bigger of the two, turned to them and smiled. "Sylas, Mira, lady-I-don't-know, hello."

"Nelly Redgrave."

"Nelly!" Tiberius said as he came out from behind his shed. Sylas now saw that the former lord commander of the Shadowthorne Empire had been using a rope to control the leather dummy, which had since drooped to the ground. "I was wondering when you'd come by again." He bowed to her gracefully.

Sylas gave Mira a funny look. She merely shook her head.

Tiberius ran his hand through his black hair. He grinned and looked the three over, his one good eye settling on the dog Nelly held in her arms. "I see you have a new pet."

"Not by choice, but she sure is cute." Nelly kissed Cornbread. She squirmed a little, yet it was clear to Sylas that the dog was starting to get more accustomed to Nelly.

"Wait a minute." Cody puffed his cheeks out and nodded. "I've seen that dog before. It's Brom's, isn't it? Need us to take him back to the Seedlands, milady?"

Duncan joined in. "We don't mind helping out, especially on the account that you're new around here."

"If anyone is going to help her, it will be me," Tiberius said. "After all, she is royalty, you know."

"Do what?" Sylas asked.

"My apologies, Your Ladyship," Tiberius told Nelly as he bowed his head to her. "The Redgraves are the Royal House of the Morgan Plains. At least, they were when I was alive."

"Please, just Nelly, as I told you before. And we can discuss houses later. A situation has arisen. Sylas, care to explain?"

Tiberius audibly groaned as he turned his focus to Sylas. "What have you gotten yourselves into now?"

Sylas dismissed his subtle comment with a wave. Thankfully, he was used to Tiberius by now, and Mira was certain that deep down, Sylas knew that the lord commander didn't dislike him as much as he seemed to on the surface. Or so she hoped. "We were getting some tulips for Mira—by the way, Mira, I have your tulips."

She smirked at him and cleared away the quest. "Good, thank you."

"Anyway, we were getting her tulips when Cornbread found us. She led us back to Brom's farm."

A sullen look came over Tiberius's face. "What are you saying? Come out with it, Sylas."

"We found Brom dead in his bedroom, and he clearly died in a gruesome way. The reason we came to you is because I'm fairly certain a demon from beyond the Hexveil did it. We saw it only briefly. I opened the door, and this flash of ravens tore out of the home. There had to be hundreds of them. They merged into a dark, cloudlike creature and disappeared into the woods."

"Ravens?" The words left Tiberius's lips with a shaky tone.

"I'll be honest with you, Tib, I've never seen anything like it before."

"Please, Tiberius."

"It was like Brom's flesh and bones had been turned into spiderwebs."

Mira made a disgusted face. "Ewwww."

"I took Sylas's word for it," Nelly said.

Sylas nodded. "So that's why we came to you. I figured you would know what it is."

"I indeed know what it is. We have to go there now. Not all monsters that escape the Hexveil are reported. I will report this one later, hopefully after we've killed it."

"Why later?" Sylas asked him. "Shouldn't you report it now?"

"And create more competition for myself? Why would I do something utterly insane like that? As for what it is, the creature is likely an A-Rank demon known as a Voidslither. If we get the lads together, we will be able to handle it. Yes, now that I think of it, night would be better, because it will be in its more tangible form at that time. Let me explain *before* you ask. The Voidslither moves as a blanket of darkness, not unlike an Eldritch Horror, but different because its body is nearly invincible during the day, when it doesn't *hold* its form. At night, this is precisely what it does, and no need to correct me and say there isn't a night here in the Underworld. You just haven't learned to recognize it. What else? The Voidslither is a collection of lesser ghouls known as Mana Ghouls, which are commonly found near farmlands."

"I can't go tonight," Sylas said. "It's the Wraithsday Feast."

"Can't your fire spirit handle that herself?"

"I am sure she could, with some help, but I don't want to ask—"

"I'll help Azor," Nelly said. "I mean, if it's just pouring pints and talking to people, I'll be able to do something."

"It is beneath someone like you—"

"I believe I will go with you all," Mira said, interrupting her uncle and secretly basking in the look on his face after doing so. "I haven't seen a Voidslither before."

"This isn't a zoo, Mira. There isn't a checklist of demonic beings that you should see."

"I agree. No, there aren't, but I can't let you have all the fun and besides, you might need my help. You never know."

"Your help?"

"And Brom?" Sylas asked before Tiberius could say anything else.

He threw his hands up in the air. "We'll go there now just to make sure the Voidslither is gone. It will be, but someone should take the body to the Hexveil so it can pass through officially. Duncan, Cody, that *somebody* means the two of you."

"Yes, Your Lordship!" they shouted at the same time.

"There will be his property that will need to be handled, but that's not my realm of expertise. In any event, lads, lady, armor up, and let's go kill us a Voidslither."

Patches bolted upstairs once the dog entered the pub. The beast barked wildly as she ran around, wagging her tail, scratching her nails against the floor, and nervously greeting anyone who entered.

Who let that thing in? Patches thought as he sat in an upstairs window licking his paws, the pub cat feeling utter despair.

The dog continued to bark, but Patches was unable to make out what she was saying. He saw the big man leave the pub wearing armor, a buckler on his arm and a mace over his shoulder.

And where's he bloody going? I'd better find out. Patches scratched at the window until he remembered there was a latch. The only problem was that it was too high up for him to reach.

At least at his current size.

Patches grew exponentially larger, until he could barely stand on the window ledge. Now able to reach the latch, he popped it open, shrank back to his normal size, and hopped onto the roof.

He turned invisible as he listened to the humans speak below.

The big man had joined two of the younger men who often patrolled Ember Hollow. The woman who smelled like medicine was also with them. More men with clubs came, and after some discussion in which the oldest of the group did most of the talking, they set off in the direction of Cinderpeak.

Patches paused before jumping to the next rooftop. It was his job to protect the Tavernly Realm, but he also needed to protect the big man. *The fire spirit can handle the pub for now, and there is that dog . . .*

With his decision made, Patches hopped to the next rooftop.

He stopped at the edge and looked down to a barrel that he had eyed from the window before. After gathering a bit of courage, Patches jumped down to the barrel. From there, it was a quick leap to the ground, where he was able to follow the big man, the medicine woman, and the hunters.

The group paused at the edge of the woods, each member illuminated by a spell someone had cast. Concerned that this could somehow expose him, Patches chose to hang back, staying out of the light.

There was always invisibility, but he wanted to save this for the right time. Plus, it was dark out, and Patches operated better in the dark anyway.

Where are they going? Patches thought as the group moved into the forest.

The older man, the leader with only one eye, took charge. He seemed to know exactly what he was doing, and while he was much smaller, he carried himself in a brave way.

Patches had noticed this about all of them, including the big man. They were certainly brave, especially with what Patches soon sensed in the forest.

His whiskers twitched.

Ah, is that what they're after? It was a couple miles away at this point, but something was coming . . .

The pub cat froze dead in his tracks as he listened to the sound that creature was making. It was like a hundred birds quietly grinding their beaks.

He had to do something.

If anything, the beast needed to be distracted once the humans got to it. *Or before,* Patches decided.

He charged ahead, his sudden movement startling the leader of the group. The man sent a trail of mana after him, but Patches increased his speed and disappeared before it could blow his cover. He continued forward, hopping over root and stone in the direction of the monster.

Patches reached a grotto just as the monster came into being, its form a mass of blackness that blotted out the Celestial Plains above.

There you are! Patches skidded to a halt, hissed, turned, and took off toward the hunters.

The monster gave chase, nipping at his tail as Patches jumped over fallen trees and weaved through the forest, the cat's heart pounding in his chest. Patches moved even faster, his whiskers pressed back as he tore through a pile of leaves and crawled under a root blocking his way.

He came up on the other side, slipped to the side to avoid the monster's next attempt to strike him, and sprinted in the direction of the hunters.

He could smell them now, the smell of the humans.

It was almost time.

Patches split himself in two just as he reached the hunters, who were already in the process of getting ready. This confused the monster, which turned toward Patches's replicant only to be struck by a fiery golden blast of mana from the medicine woman.

The others all attacked with their clubs, beating the monster back as it roared with intensity. It never got its bearings as they continued their assault, and Patches watched proudly as they soon overwhelmed it.

They would never know he was the one that helped, and Patches was fine with that.

A monster like that was capable of quite a bit, especially once it was able to focus its attacks. But with Patches's maneuver, the big man, the medicine woman, and the hunters had been able to take advantage of its momentary confusion.

Satisfied with what he had done, Patches slipped back into the forest.

Once he was far enough away that he was certain they wouldn't hear him, he picked up his speed and soon reached Ember Hollow. From there, it was straight to the Tavernly Realm, where he went through the cat door to find a black dog just about to bark at him.

Don't do it, Patches told the dog. He was suddenly oblivious to the people in the pub, who all watched with excitement at how the dog and the cat would react to one another.

Someone said something, a two-syllable word, that sounded like *Cornbread.* But Patches didn't pay attention to them. He was entirely focused on the newcomer.

Who are you? the dog asked, her voice a bit scratchy.

The Guardian of the Tavernly Realm.

She glanced around quickly, barked once, and licked her lips. *Is this the Tavernly Realm? You have good food here and nice humans!*

It is, which means you're in my territory.

I noticed your smell . . .

What are you doing here? Patches asked her, already annoyed with the dog.

My human died, killed by a monster. Her ears flattened. *Why do you smell like that monster?* she asked with a growl.

Because, unlike you, I just joined the humans in the forest, and helped kill the thing. While I was doing that, you were enjoying the attention and, dare I say, food, which is generally saved for me.

The dog relaxed to some degree, her tail lowering. *It killed my human.*

It's dead now. Patches raised his tail and held his head high as he took a step closer to her. *Now, if you will please move, I will be on my way.*

Where are you going?

To the cellar, where I can have some peace and quiet. Where are you going?

She started panting. *What do you mean?*

The big man didn't adopt you, did he? Because there is only one Guardian of the Tavernly Realm, and that's me.

I don't know where I'm going. The woman seems to like me. She has a home next door, but I don't care for it. I want to be back on the farm. Someone has to watch after the place. Maybe I'm the Guardian of the Farmly Realm? Yes, we are both guardians.

Patches considered this. *Perhaps we are.*

Can I sniff you?

Are you serious?

Yes.

Patches sighed miserably. *I suppose I will allow it, but after that, it'd be best if you move on.*

Through the door you came in?

Patches looked back to the cat door. *I don't know if you can fit or not.*

She charged toward the cat door and pushed through to the other side. Then she returned and the patrons clapped.

Oh, bother, Patches told her.

Looks like I fit. Can I . . . sniff you now?

Patches glanced at the fire spirit, who placed a plate on the counter with a bit of fish on it and smiled at him. *Fine, but make it quick. And absolutely no licking.*

CHAPTER FOUR

ONE FARM AND A FUNERAL

Sylas ignored the invasion warning the next morning as he took a look at his overall stats. As it had been before, the Douro flamefruit ale, which glowed orange and had a particularly interesting taste, had been a hit. So much in fact that Sylas had already made the decision last night to replace two of his regular casks of ale with the special ale going forward, for which he'd charge ten Mana Lumens per pint.

In total, Sylas had brewed six casks last night, costing him close to five hundred Mana Lumens. With the four hundred Lumen bonus he had received from the hunt, plus his ale sales, Sylas had surged past the three thousand Mana Lumen mark, which had been topped off due to Patches, who purred next to him, the cat with an adorable look on his face as always.

Name: Sylas Runewulf
Mana Lumens: 3375/3375
Class: Brewer

Yet again, Sylas was reminded of his advantage in being the owner of a pub. Most classes, at least most he was familiar with, couldn't simply jump hundreds upon hundreds of Mana Lumens ahead in a single day. But that was possible as a brewer. After his initial investment of twelve casks, the numbers always went up. Adding flamefruit at the same price point as his strong ale would mean that each cask would bring him a hundred and twenty Mana Lumens after the cost of production, which was much better than producing regular ale at a twenty Mana Lumen profit. It also served the same purpose as the regular ale, because the flamefruit was not as intoxicating.

A barking dog downstairs caught his attention. "Looks like Cornbread is here."

Patches tensed.

"Azor told me last night that you were friendly enough," Sylas said as he petted the pub cat. "Is that true?"

The cat's ears twitched.

"I know, I know, cats aren't supposed to like dogs, but Cornbread isn't so bad. Let's head down and see about the commotion." Sylas dressed, yet Patches remained on the bed. "Fine, have it your way."

He reached the main floor of the pub to find Azor racing around as always.

"Morning," Azor told Sylas as she placed a bowl of food out for Cornbread, "And Happy Thornsday! Cornbread came through the cat door, which is quickly becoming a dog door. I hope you don't mind."

"Why would I mind?" Sylas said as he took a seat at the bar.

"Mira was just here too. Now, she's over at Nelly's place helping her move things around. Everyone is going to the Seedlands today to pay their respects to Brom."

"Actually, I have another question about Brom."

"Yes?"

"Since this Voidslither killed him in the Underworld, that means he goes to the Chasm. This may sound stupid, but what's that like?"

Azor slid a plate of food over to him and he thanked her, Sylas promising under his breath that he'd make breakfast next time.

"I don't understand your question," Azor said.

"I mean, what is it like when people from here go there? I guess that's a weird way to phrase it. Once Brom arrives, will he be given a pub, or a farm, something like that? What is it like for newcomers there?"

"Not great. There aren't system-generated deeds, or anything like that. If you want something in the Chasm, you'd have to take it from someone else. That, or just join one of the numerous factions that fight for more territory. There are campaign cities too, but that's just part of the war. It's a constant battle there, one waged by higher-level demons that inevitably draws everyone in because of their power and territory."

"Huh. I was hoping it'd be better for Brom." Sylas shook his head. "That's really too bad."

Cornbread barked.

"Will she be coming with us today?" Azor asked.

"I would guess so, yes. We're holding a funeral for her owner, after all."

Azor zipped around the counter and crouched in front of the dog. She carefully petted Cornbread and smiled up at Sylas. "I like her. And I think she likes me more than Patches does."

Sylas laughed. "Patches likes you; he's just a cat. They can be ungrateful little bastards sometimes, but he's *our* ungrateful little bastard. And I think he was there last night."

"Where?"

"In the woods. You should have seen that thing. The Voidslither was coming right at us and then it shifted to the side, like it was confused. Tiberius heard some sounds early on in the hunt, something moving ahead. Pretty sure I know what that was."

"You really think it was Patches?"

"You said he was outside last night, right?"

"When he met Cornbread? Yes, he came from the cat door." She slapped her gloved hand against her forehead. "I can't keep track of that cat."

"I think that is sort of the point of cats. I also found the window open upstairs."

"Patches can go through the window?" Azor sighed miserably and Cornbread made a whining noise.

Sylas looked down at the dog, nodded, and gave her a bit of bacon off his plate. "I didn't open the window, did you?" he asked Azor.

"I most certainly did not."

"Then it was Patches."

"Great. He can open windows now."

As he was waiting for the perfect time to enter, Patches came trotting down the stairs. He took one look at Cornbread and his disposition soured. Patches sat and began licking his paw with disdain.

Azor laughed. "I think they'll be friends soon enough. They just have to get used to each other."

"I don't think Cornbread is who we need to worry about . . ."

————

Sylas didn't know what to feel about attending what was the equivalent of a funeral in the Underworld. The farmers he recognized from the pub were there, as were some select people from Cinderpeak, like Rose, Anders, Mr. and Mrs. Brassmere, and their assistant, John. On the Ember Hollow front there were Tiberius and a few of the militiamen, including Duncan, Cody, and Henry. Azor, Nelly, and Mira were also in attendance. Nelly excitedly told Sylas that the Brassmeres had made plans with her help her get her shop up and running.

Finally, there was Constable Leowin with his short silver hair and his ironed cape, who gave a baffling sermon from Brom's front porch that was mainly about his own life, what it had been like to become constable of Cinderpeak, and the good things he had done upon taking the role. Mira gave Sylas a few looks during Leowin's speech, but she didn't said anything about it.

As Leowin was wrapping up, a man Sylas didn't recognize tapped him on the shoulder.

"A word?" the man said, who was dressed in a dark purple suit that had a hint of gold lining. Beyond the man, Sylas could see Godric the fireweave tailor and Bart, both of whom were looking at Sylas and the man in the suit.

"Can I help you?" Sylas asked.

"My name is Shamus, and I am an estate manager that deals with certain trusts here in the Seedlands. I'm part of the Management Guild, out of Battersea, one of their subbranches, if that matters."

Sylas looked to those who had gathered to honor Brom. "I hate to say it like this, Shamus, but we've barely covered his grave."

"We mourn every day in the Underworld. It is part of life here. *Afterlife* here, I should say. Anyway, a word? I've already spoken to other interested parties."

Sylas caught Mira looking at him. She stood next to Azor, who hovered near Cornbread, the dog resting on the ground with a sad look on her face. "This better be good."

"I assure you, it is good," Shamus said. "Or should I say, it is necessary. Please, right this way." Shamus led Sylas to the start of what should have been one of Brom's fields if he'd been a better farmer. At the moment, nothing was growing and the field was parched and fissured, a testament to its fallow state. "It has come to my attention through a discussion with the other farmers and a group of people that live around the volcano that call themselves the Lava Boys—"

"The who? Oh, their pub quiz team. Got it. Sorry. Continue." Sylas glanced back at the people gathered around the house. None of them were looking at him, yet he still felt judgment for stepping away.

"Let me ask you, Sylas, do you know what happens when someone dies in the Underworld?"

"I was just talking about that with my fire spirit. I don't. Aside from the fact that they go to the Chasm, which is an insult to injury if there ever was one."

"It's quite rare, but they can go to the Celestial Plains too." Shamus squinted up at the golden sky. "I've seen that happen a handful of times. To further explain what I do: when someone passes here in the Underworld, their deed is passed to a trust. That trust is able to sell the deed to someone else, depending on the stock available, or the trust can sell it back to the system so it can be assigned to a newcomer. The problem with selling it back to the system is that it could take years for that role to be filled."

"I have more questions about that."

"I'm sure you do but let me see if my explanation doesn't answer some of your questions first. If possible, we prefer to sell it to someone interested in the property, with the caveat that no single person should own everything. How often have monopolies worked out for humanity?"

"Not really my area of expertise. So what you're saying, Shamus, is that because someone claims I've expressed interest in the farm before, I am able to buy the deed if I so choose."

"Yes, there will be an auction for it tomorrow."

"What would . . ." Sylas massaged his forehead for a moment. "Fine, I'll ask. What would a farm like this cost?"

"A farm with ten fields would normally start at twenty thousand fixed MLus, and that is before bidding takes place. But this one is in poor shape, and as you can see, the fields have seen better days. The farms here can only grow certain things, and Brom clearly didn't get it right. Look at the farms beyond."

Sylas could see the other farms, which were green. Many things remained evergreen in the Underworld, something he attributed to the fact that the realm didn't really have seasons.

"Did you say I would bid for the farm?"

"Yes, there might be others interested, and that can drive up the price at auction. Or no one is interested, and you might get it for a steal. A sad farm in this condition, I'd estimate, would go for ten to fifteen thousand fixed MLus."

"I have three thousand and some change."

"Yes," Shamus said, still maintaining his smile. "That is to be expected. Before the auction starts, you will have a chance to meet with a bank loan officer, who will take a look at your overall earning potential and decide what kind of loan they will offer you."

"How do the loans here work?"

"They are generally fixed at ten percent, but if you have a high earning potential, this can fluctuate in a good direction. For you, anyway. The payment is taken out of your daily total earnings, your Mana Lumen revenue, until the loan is paid. The interest doesn't compound either. Whatever loan you take out, the interest is added at that time. While a bit steep, it's not a bad deal, and it would allow you to purchase more in the future at your leisure. With some limitations, of course." Shamus folded his hands together in front of his body. "Having more than one property generating MLus is a surefire way to grow stronger and accomplish whatever goal you may have. Or just grow richer, also a goal of many."

"I see."

"Anyway. I won't take any more of your time. If you are interested, come to my place in Cinderpeak tomorrow before the auction. If you'd like, I can set it up as a quest contract so that you won't forget, and you'll be led directly there."

"Please do."

[New Quest Contract - Travel to Cinderpeak to take part in the auction. Accept? Y/N?]

Sylas nodded.

"Excellent," Shamus said as he patted him on the shoulder. "And I'm sorry to bother you with this during such a trying time. But your friends pointed you out and told me you would be interested. Good luck in tomorrow's auction."

———

While Nelly headed to Cinderpeak with the Brassmeres, and Mira and Azor returned to Ember Hollow, Sylas decided to stay in the Seedlands for a bit with Cornbread. The dog didn't seem to want to leave the farm, and Sylas figured that he could visit a few of the farms near Brom's estate and ask about farming.

"I can't believe I'm even considering this," Sylas told the farm dog, a smirk on his face. But it was worth exploring, and he knew that he needed to grow stronger if he was to take on whatever invasion would come.

As he headed to a farm just down the lane, Sylas recalled what Nuno had said about the invasion: *The warning message is not about the Chasm. I know that much. But I don't know much else. This might take me some time to decipher. And I'll need to visit another manaseer that I know, my teacher. She can be very hard to locate.*

How long would it take Nuno to find this manaseer? Would he just show up with life-altering information? Likely.

Sylas would need to be prepared at that point for whatever was to come next, which would require more power and more abilities. At least he assumed this was the case . . .

After a short walk, he approached a quaint, single-story wood home painted with a nice mauve trim. Beyond, rows of tomatoes grew on vines that ran along thick wooden stakes. He heard a dog barking inside.

"Do you know the person who lives here?" Sylas asked Cornbread, who was looking up at him with her tail tucked between her legs. She let out a squeak of a bark, one that sounded almost nervous. She tried again, louder this time.

Sylas heard movement behind the door before he could knock. "Cornbread?" a male voice called out. "Is that you?"

The door opened to reveal a man Sylas had seen at the pub before, yet had never been properly introduced to. The man quickly stepped out, shutting the door behind him. He had a thin mustache and his wispy blond hair was parted to the right. The man wore overalls, which did little to conceal his rotund stomach. "Ah, Sylas," he said, the man instantly biting his lip. There was more barking behind him. "Don't mind that. Just my dog. How can I help you?"

"I never got your name."

"Me? I'm . . . I'm Edgar," the man said as he touched his chest.

"Brom's neighbor."

"That's right. How, um, how can I help you?" Edgar's eyes shifted to the side, as if he were hiding something. Since there was little to hide, Sylas interpreted this as something else. Perhaps Edgar was shy.

"I was approached by a trust manager about buying Brom's farm."

"You mean Shamus?"

"That's him."

"He's not so bad. He has sold several of the farms around here. Lucille's leafy greens farm, just down the way. He sold that one to her just a few months back. Big one too. Over fifty fields. Are you thinking about buying?"

"I don't know. I wanted to ask you about it, what you thought. I also don't know if I'd need to change my class or something. Someone told me something about that before, but I forgot what they said."

"You wouldn't change your class, you'd *add* a class with a lumengineer in Battersea. I guess you could see if they're available at their branch office in Duskhaven, but you'd do best to travel to Battersea."

"So I would have two classes?"

"You would. It's not so uncommon, but you'll need something that triggers your right to add the class, like a farm deed."

"We'll circle back to that. I guess I should start with this: What can you tell me about farming? Why would I want to add a class? I'm assuming that it isn't like farming in our world. Brewing ale is certainly faster."

"Oh, it's faster, but farming has its rewards as well. There are several things you'll need to be aware of. First, the cost. To start your field, you'd need a power known as Mana Infusion, a type of fertilization skill. Someone classed as a farmer, like me, already has this power. You'd need to purchase it with fixed MLus, that, and Mana Saturation. You would also want a power called Harvest Silos, which I had to purchase as well. The class doesn't come with that one because you could technically harvest by hand or hire people. But believe me. You'll want it, and you could get it baked into your farm loan."

"How long would it take to grow a crop?"

"It depends on the crop. Some can take up to two weeks, others around seven or eight days."

Sylas wanted to ask him something along the lines of *What kind of numbers are we talking here?* but he decided to be a bit more couth about it. "And what kind of yield would I anticipate?"

"Again, that depends on the crop. There's something else you should know about that as well. You won't be able to farm anything already farmed here in the Seedlands. This was Brom's issue. He kept trying things, but we have a particular type of soil, and he should have grown something with that in mind. If you ask me . . ." Edgar swallowed, as if he were suddenly aware he was talking too much.

"Please, go on."

"If you ask me, Brom should have gotten a loan to purchase the leafy greens farm when it became available. The only problem is that those fields are separated from his fields by a little ravine. That ravine could be moved, however, and these plants don't need water anyway. But Brom didn't want to pay the price to remove it, and so he kept his fallow fields, always saying he'd figure it out. I don't want to speak poorly of Brom because I liked the man, but he wasn't cut out for this. He wanted to be an adventurer, from what he told me. He should have taken a second class, but he never got around to it. Too bad, too."

"I remember him saying something about wanting to move to Battersea."

"I wish he had, for his sake." A sudden sadness came over Edgar. "He didn't deserve to die like that. But back to what you're asking: if you were to buy his farm, you'd need to plant something that isn't already here. We've got my tomatoes, legumes and other beans, onions and garlic, leafy greens . . . what else . . . we have peppers from a farmer named Sterling."

"What about varieties? Could I plant varieties? Like varieties of peppers?" Sylas also made a mental note to visit Sterling about the peppers. It seemed like something Azor would be interested in, and maybe, just maybe, there would be a limited ale he could make that had a spice to it.

"Nope, you'd need to find something that we don't have here."

"Any ideas?"

"Not off the top of my head. You could visit the Farm and Field Guild in Battersea and pay them to help you figure it out. I can tell you this: while it might not look like easy work, farming is one of the best ways I know of to gain MLus. Ten fields like Brom had could net between two thousand and three thousand bushels, and each bushel can sell between two and five MLus. It will take time to harvest, depending on what you grow, unless you have other means. So you do the math."

Sylas ran the numbers in his head. He had been told that brewing was one of the fastest ways to wrack up MLus, but this seemed even better. Two thousand bushels selling at two MLus would net him four thousand additional MLus, and that was the lowest Edgar had mentioned. If he sold two thousand at five MLus a bushel, it would be ten thousand total. If he sold three thousand . . .

Naturally, Sylas stroked his chin.

"Not bad, right? And you can just keep planting again, creating something like a passive MLu income. Not a lot of upkeep, just funding the spells and making sure your crops are protected. Now, there are some things you'll have to consider. You'll need to consider the cost of the loan, whatever the interest rate is. You'll also need to consider the MLu cost of Harvest Silos, Mana Infusion, and Mana Saturation when you cast them, which varies based on the crop. This is unlike most powers, which don't have a fixed cost to cast. Still, worth it in the long run. Plus, you'll need to learn the abilities as well, which would take an archlumen. The Farm and Field Guild could likely recommend someone, but you'd need a farm first. So after you have the spells, and you have something to plant, you can get going. Harvest, collect your MLus, and pay the tax you'd owe to Cinderpeak."

"A tax?" Sylas asked. This was the first he'd heard of something like that.

"A tax of five to twenty percent of your farming revenue depending on the size of your farm. At ten fields, your tax will be seven percent, but it goes up from there. The reason Ember Hollow doesn't have taxes is simple. You all are next to the Chasm. No one wants to live next to the Chasm. Personally, we're not far from the Chasm, and it could be argued that we shouldn't pay taxes as well, because, well, look what happened to Brom, but I'm not about to change that overnight."

"So taxes, and the costs of using the spells to start my field, continue it, and harvest the crops."

"Correct." Edgar scratched the back of his head. "I think that about covers it. Do you know what you're going to do? I'd love to have a neighbor that actually gave a damn. Judging by the way you got The Old Lamplighter up and running, you are definitely the man for the job. But only if you think you have the time and the start-up costs."

CHAPTER FIVE

BUYER'S REMORSE

Patches could ignore the barking, but he couldn't ignore the sound of the neighboring dog entering the Tavernly Realm late at night, her tail beating, her joyous attitude, and her nails scraping against the wooden floor like she couldn't retract them.

Hi! Cornbread said. It was late, and the fire spirit was now up, speaking to both of them. Patches ignored the dog and she barked again. *Hi!*

How did you get out?

Of the nice lady's place? Easy. I just scratched at the door until it popped open. I might have slammed my body into it too.

She didn't stop you?

I'm here, aren't I? She's actually the reason I came. I wanted to see if you had something I could bring back to her. She doesn't have anything I'd call food. Just a bunch of grains. Cornbread wrinkled her nose. *I thought that the fire spirit might have some bones.*

Have you ever seen a human eat a bone?

Cornbread considered this as the fire spirit kindly lowered closer to the dog. She said something in a soothing voice and petted the dog with a gloved hand.

She's nice too, Cornbread said as she looked up at the fire spirit.

You can't just show up unannounced. This is the Tavernly Realm. It is not a place for dogs!

So . . . no bones?

As if she could understand Cornbread, the fire spirit zipped away and returned with a bone.

Good! Cornbread took it in her mouth and exited through the cat door. *Bye!* she called over her shoulder, her mouth full.

Patches watched in disbelief, until the fire spirit started to laugh at him.

I don't need your mockery. Patches fluffed his tail up and headed down into the cellar, where he paced back and forth, annoyed, hoping that a rat would appear so he'd have something to kill.

Nothing came, and eventually Patches went upstairs, where he gave the big man some of his power before falling asleep at the end of the bed.

————

After talking with regulars the previous night and having a long conversation with Mira about running two businesses, Sylas had come to a decision.

[You have 62 days until the invasion.]

He needed more Mana Lumens, even if he didn't quite know what he would do with them all yet. But he knew more power meant more options in the Underworld.

Sylas now had close to four thousand Mana Lumens after gaining a little over five hundred the previous night through ale sales. He had brewed four casks, a regular, two strong, and one flamefruit, and had a feeling that he would be able to sell even more tonight, especially with the buzzing gold words that hovered in front of his door.

Sylas, my dear, dear, dear pub friend. It's Fireday, which means quiz night at The Old Lamplighter. Do get excited, and do see if Azor is in the mood to whip something delicious up, as I am already famished. Sorry for such short notice. To be fair to myself, I left this message a few days ago, and I could have told you then, but I wanted to be able to cancel it in case there was something happening for me in Duskhaven. Rest assured, there isn't. I wouldn't say Duskhaven is as boring as Ember Hollow, but . . .

See you tonight!

Archlumen Octavian Tilbud

"Just the man I wanted to have a conversation with," Sylas said. Patches let out an angry mew. "Sorry to wake you."

His door swung open and Azor appeared. "I heard you talking. Is everything—" She saw the fading message from Tilbud. "A meal tonight? Um, sure. Sure! You were going to Cinderpeak anyway. We can pick up some supplies. Wait."

"Yes?"

"I was going to tell you about how cute Cornbread looked when she came in through the cat door last night and begged for a bone, but now I'm wondering how Tilbud got this message up here."

"He must have snuck up to my bedroom."

"But how?"

"He's an archlumen. He can do all sorts of crazy things we probably couldn't imagine. But I need him and his expertise. Anyway, I'll be down in a minute. Has Nelly stopped by?"

"She did. She is having Anders do a few things before she attempts a soft opening tomorrow. She isn't fully stocked yet, but she was able to get a loan for her initial supplies."

"Huh." Sylas realized something important in what Azor had just told him. This was, yet again, why he had advanced so quickly as the owner of a pub. There was little Sylas needed to do before he was able to open, and he certainly hadn't needed a loan.

"She wants to talk to you about doing a lunch thing. I already told her to do whatever she wanted because we're not open for lunch anyway. Unless . . . ?"

"No, we won't ever be opening for lunch. She's just being extra cautious before launching her sandwiches. But no competition here. Not having lunch gives me time to do things during the day, and I'm certainly going to need that time here in the near future. I appreciate your help as always, Azor, and I'll be down in a bit. Before you go," he said as the fire spirit turned away. "Has Mira stopped by yet?"

"Not yet, no." She left.

Sylas knew why Mira hadn't come by, and he wasn't ready to deal with it. He was well aware that he was biting off more than he could chew, and that she was only looking out for him. But this was also his choice, and she needed to understand that.

Azor returned just as Sylas was about to slip his shoes on. "Never mind. She's here."

"Really?"

"It's like you summoned her. I'll tell Mira you'll be down shortly."

Sylas headed downstairs to find Mira seated at the bar. Her dark hair was pulled into a tight ponytail this morning and was held in place by a purple ribbon.

"I didn't think you'd be stopping by," he said as he took a seat next to her.

"I didn't think I would either, but I've said my piece, and the least I can do is help make sure you don't screw things up."

"You really should be mayor of Ember Hollow, you know that?" he said.

"To have a mayor, we would have to be incorporated into a county or start our own. Aside from the *beautiful* silver wall of magic protecting us from the Chasm, we don't pay taxes this close to the border, and if we had a mayor, we would. Then again, if we did, things around here would certainly be different, perhaps for the better."

"Are there any other benefits of living here?"

"Besides the great apothecary, a pub called The Old Lamplighter, and a new general store set to open any day now? Not really. But it is quiet, and we don't have the clutter or the rush of the city. Anyway, whenever you're ready."

Azor flared up behind the counter. "Would you like to have breakfast, Mira?"

"Not today, but thank you, Azor."

"I'm making it tomorrow," Sylas told Mira. "So you should come by. Tilbud will be here tonight, so that will be another mouth to feed if he stays. And he usually stays."

"A pub quiz?" Mira's eyes filled with delight. "I wonder which team I will be on."

"You are definitely the secret weapon on any team."

"Am I, now? In that case, I'll be here tonight, and of course I'll come for breakfast tomorrow, and you know what, Azor? Sure, I'll have something. Just a small plate, if you will."

"Coming right up!"

After a quick meal of boiled eggs and toast, Sylas and Mira took the portal to Cinderpeak. "I actually have a quest contract from Shamus," Sylas said, "just in case I get lost on the way to the auction house."

"I'm sure you do, but I know where it is so no need to worry," Mira told him.

They were halfway through the small city when Azor left them, the fire spirit headed to a different food market on the side of town closest to the volcano. "I'll catch up with you all later," she said as she trailed away.

"Not much farther now," Mira told Sylas with an uncertain smile on her face.

Soon, the pair stood in front of a two-story building with intricate woodwork above the windows.

[Quest Contract Complete - Travel to Cinderpeak to take part in the auction.]

"This is it then, huh?"

"It certainly is," Mira told him. "Let's head inside."

As they entered, they were greeted by a woman wearing a dark dress with white stitching. "Welcome, and what are your names?"

"Sylas Runewulf and Mira Ravenbane. We are here for the auction," Sylas told her.

Mira placed a hand on his arm. "We're here early to talk to a banker."

"Great. The auction will take place here." The woman swept her hand toward a set of pews in front of a dais. "A few bankers just arrived. We have a representative from the MLR Bank and the Cinderpeak Credit Union."

"MLR," Mira said.

"I'll let her know you are here."

"Thank you."

"Why not go regional?" Sylas asked Mira once Shamus's assistant was gone.

"If we didn't live in Ember Hollow, I'd recommend going regional because you'd get a better interest rate, but we are truly in no-man's land, which means you'll have to go national. There is another bank we could go with, but they don't seem to have a rep here at the moment. So MLR."

"That's not great. It gives us less leverage."

"Ha! We never had much leverage to begin with, Sylas, so I think we'll be fine."

Shamus's assistant came out of one of the offices. She took her place next to the door, her hands behind her back. "She's ready to see you now."

Sylas stepped into the office along with Mira. He took a seat in front of a woman in a pressed jacket, black shirt, and a bow tie around her neck.

"Good morning," he told her.

The woman looked both of them over. "Elena," the woman said as she continued to examine them over the glasses she wore. "Are the two of you married? If so, I'm not seeing any of that in your statuses."

"You can see our—"

"We're not married," Mira said, cutting Sylas off.

"I see. And who will be taking out the loan?"

"I will," Sylas told her.

"In that case, if you aren't married, then you aren't required to be part of this conversation." The banker smiled at Mira. "If you have something you would like to discuss, we can do so after."

"She can stay, Elena," Sylas said.

"Are you certain?"

"Yes, we're . . ." He was about to lie and say *engaged*, but thought otherwise. "We're good friends."

"I see." Elena continued to look at them in a strange way, as if she were looking right through Sylas and Mira. "In that case, I'll be servicing your account if you decide to take a loan today."

This statement struck Sylas as odd. It implied that he already qualified for the loan . . .

Elena folded her hands together on the table. "Let's discuss the terms you can expect from MLR Bank. I am assuming you are interested in the farm that will be up for auction in the hour, yes? If this is about something else, I'm afraid we may need to return to my branch in Duskhaven to better serve you."

"Brom's farm, yes."

"We believe it will go for ten to twenty thousand fixed MLus. I don't see it going over that amount. You are classed as a brewer, which means you will need to add farmer as a second class. To do so, you would need to visit Battersea."

"A lumengineer, yes," Mira said.

Elena cleared her throat in a way that indicated she did not like to be interrupted. "There would be an additional charge for that, and once you added a second class, you would need to learn the abilities that are commonly gifted to the farmer class. In the same way that you are able to magically brew ale, they are able to grow crops. Finally, you would need to have an approved crop for your farm."

"How do I pay you back, when do I pay you back, and what would my interest rate be?" Sylas asked, cutting to the chase.

"Your interest rate would be ten percent of the loan. This does not compound. With what you earn already at the pub, you qualify for a thirty thousand MLu loan. Your payments start the day after you agree to the loan, which would be tomorrow. On top of whatever it costs to buy the farm, we will set you up with a lumengineer at a fixed cost as well as an archlumen in Battersea. You can travel to Battersea, yes?"

"I can."

"I ask because it is far easier to facilitate things there at the Farm and Field Guild. If not, it will take a bit more arranging on our part, and we will have to negotiate the prices in advance for you and adjust your loan accordingly. Aside from travel costs, everything you need to purchase, from the loan principle to the powers you will need, are fixed MLus. And they will be deducted as such."

"Even the lumengineer?" he asked.

"Yes, that as well because you are adding a class."

"Couldn't someone just take out a loan and use it to learn any power they want or, I don't know, take any class they want?"

Elena blinked twice at his question. "You are new at this, I forget. The reason that isn't possible is because the bank already covers the preset amounts you need for the cost of the farm, the class change, and the powers. A loan like this has a very specific intention and the MLus can only be used to purchase the agreed upon products. They won't even be listed in your status, in case you were wondering. But you will see what you owe every morning and through the system, if you choose to access it."

"Ten percent."

"Ten percent is the rate for this loan, yes, and it is also what will be deducted from your daily net revenue of MLus as calculated in the morning."

"Before or after I brew? Generally, I only brew after I have closed for the night, to maximize MLus."

"It would take place when you wake up in the morning. Let's say you end the night with two thousand MLus after a five hundred gain. So you had fifteen hundred before, you didn't brew, and now you have two thousand total. That morning, you'd wake up with fifty less MLus than you otherwise would have. I have paperwork with examples as well."

"No, it makes sense. I'm just wondering about Patches."

"Patches?"

Sylas exchanged glances with Mira. "Never mind," he finally told Elena. "So everything would be covered in the loan, from the purchase of the farm to the skills needed, with a flat ten percent interest?"

"Yes, and your payments would be deducted from your total MLus at ten percent of daily earnings until the loan is paid. There are other things that you should know about, which are listed in the paperwork. Things like deferment and forbearance, and what happens if you are already low on MLus. You should read it all, but I can tell you now that this system isn't designed to kill you. Why would anyone want to take out a loan that would kill them, and why would a bank want that for a client?"

"You're the banker," Sylas reminded her. "You tell me."

"Right. If you are low on MLus, the payment won't happen." She slid several papers over to him. "We try to keep things as simple as possible. On these pages you will find the terms of the loan, a detailed breakdown of how the payment works, examples, as well as an itemized list of what the loan will cover. If you agree, and once you're ready, you may sign here."

A hovering golden line appeared in front of Sylas. He exchanged nervous glances with Mira.

Elena smiled. "You can sign it with your finger. Because you're doing so in front of me, I will also notarize the contract, and you will be good to go. If you decide during the auction that you would like to nullify the contract, or the farm's purchase price exceeds your expectations, please visit me after."

———

Sylas didn't know how to feel after easily winning the auction, especially since there were no other bidders. "Sold," Shamus said as he pointed his gavel at Sylas. "You will now return to Elena to finish the paperwork, in case you didn't know how something like this goes. Normally, there are more people. It's quite fun."

Shamus's assistant approached Sylas with the deed held tightly in her hands.

"That was . . . anticlimactic," Sylas said told Mira as his heart settled.

"Maybe you should take that as a warning." Mira, who sat next to him on the pew, flattened her hands over the front of her dress. "I didn't mean it like that. Not harshly. I just mean no one wants the farm for a reason. It's not easy being a farmer."

"I talked to Edgar about it. Once you get it all set up, it requires a lot less effort than being a pub owner. Besides, you know why I'm doing this."

"The invasion warning," she said under her breath so Shamus, who still stood at the podium, couldn't hear her.

"Exactly. I might need the mana, and I'm capped with what I can do at the pub. Well, sort of, but this gives me another stream of income, and maybe I'll get someplace else after."

"Another place?"

"Shamus, the market in Ember Hollow, is it up for auction?" Sylas called to the man.

"The market?" A puzzled look came across his face as if he were examining something. "We can circle back to the market later. You don't want to bite off more than you can chew. After all, you still have to figure out what it is you plan to farm."

"I'll get it figured out," Sylas assured him. "It's what I do. And tonight, there's a pub quiz at The Old Lamplighter. Prize will be MLus and a round or two. It depends on how many people show up."

"Thank you, I'll see if I can—" Shamus's eyes lit up. "You know, we are always trying new ways to reach the community and to let them know that properties are available, that they aren't stuck with a class—you can even have one removed!—and that loans are available. Our guild has a budget for advertisement, and I believe, yes, I believe this would be a perfect way to continue to get the word out. I will be there with my assistant. I'll also invite some of the bankers. You never know, they might want to come see Ember Hollow for a night. Is there an inn there?"

"There is not," Mira said.

"Right. I should have known that. Most unfortunate, but we can see about the deeds and whatnot for Ember Hollow later. They are likely sealed, which means it will take me a little time, and who am I kidding, under-the-table mana, to get an answer. But we'll be there tonight, and we'll match whatever the prize pool turns out to be, doubling it. Good luck with your farm."

Sylas and Mira entered Elena's office to find her still having a conversation with Shamus's assistant. The other woman left, so Elena could go over the details once again:

"Your total loan amount is nineteen thousand MLus. Ten thousand for the purchase itself—what a steal—seven thousand for the abilities you will need to use the farm properly, and finally, two thousand for dues to the Farm and Field Guild to facilitate your membership. With the ten percent flat rate loan, the total amount you have borrowed is . . ." She waved her hand and the numbers appeared in the air in front of Sylas.

[20900 Mana Lumens]

Sylas nodded as he took in the number. It seemed like a lot, but he hadn't had to put anything down and the interest didn't compound. All he needed to do now was get the farm up and running. "The guild can help me figure out what to grow too, right?"

Elena hesitated. "Who told you that?"

"Edgar, the tomato farmer, suggested it."

"I would have to check to be sure, but I'm nearly certain there are additional fees associated with something like that, which aren't covered in your loan. We can amend the loan, if you'd like," but by the way she said this, Sylas had a feeling Elena didn't want to go through this process.

"I'll just figure it out," he said, feeling a bit crestfallen.

Sylas had never had a lot of money in his world, but he did recall a time where he had received long overdue pay and had spent most of it in a single weekend in a city on the coast of the Aurum Kingdom called Joysville. He had a similar feeling after that, but this was somewhat different. At least with that experience, Sylas had enjoyed himself.

"Great." Elena offered him a firm smile. "You will make your first payment in the morning. Your system will be updated then, and it will tell you what you owe, and how much you've paid the previous day. Should you need me, I'll be at the branch in Duskhaven." She stood and extended a hand toward Sylas, which caused the floating numbers to vanish. "Good luck to you."

————

After parting ways with Mira and reconvening with Azor, Sylas and the fire spirit headed to the Seedlands.

"You really did it," the fire spirit said after they reached the portal.

"I did." Sylas grimaced. "I hope I haven't overextended myself."

She laughed nervously. "Who? You? The guy that hasn't been here thirty days yet and who has tasked himself with solving some mysterious invasion that is yet to come while still running a pub and now a farm? No way."

Sylas scratched the back of his head. "When you put it like that . . . anyhow. Tell me about the meal you're planning tonight."

"I hope you're hungry."

"I hope you bought enough for me to make breakfast tomorrow. I'm planning to do that, you know."

"Only if I can help."

"I'm making it for you and Tilbud, if he stays the night."

"And Mira."

"And her."

"Tilbud will stay the night," Azor said as flames swelled around her. "I think he secretly likes visiting Ember Hollow. He strikes me as sort of a magical playboy who needs to escape Duskhaven from time to time on account of whatever it is he has gotten himself into. Trysts. I mean something like that."

"So I'll be making breakfast for him too."

"Sylas, I can't eat."

"You can burn the food. I'll count that as eating."

"Fine. And yes, to answer your earlier question, I have a recipe in mind for tonight that will certainly have leftovers. I'm planning to make sausage, mashed potatoes, and a sort of onion gravy."

Sylas licked his lips as they turned onto the lane that led to his newly purchased farm. "Sausage will be great."

"Cornbread will like it too. All of the food should be there by the time we get back. It didn't cost much either. My guess is I'll net at least two hundred MLus if not more tonight, and that's with the cost of food."

"Not bad, not bad at all."

They reached Sylas's new farmhouse, which sat on a small hill overlooking his property, his porch with two rocking chairs on it. "That's odd."

The exterior was bare, but seemed sturdy. It didn't look new, but it did look as if someone had stripped the place to transfer ownership. Sylas approached the front door. Golden mana swirled around his fingertips as he touched the doorknob.

He heard a lock click.

"Here goes nothing," Azor said as Sylas stepped into the place.

All of Brom's shabby furniture was gone. At least, Sylas assumed this was the case until he cautiously opened the bedroom door to find a different bed than the one that had been there before. "It's like the place reset," he said to himself as he was trying to forget what he'd seen in the house, how gruesome Brom's death had been.

"It's sort of cozy, right?" Azor floated over to one of the windows. She pulled the drapes aside to reveal the farm beyond. "Just think, you could lie here in bed watching your crops grow. Are you going to stay here, or the pub?"

"The pub, for now. I think. I'm not so certain how much I want to stay here after what I saw."

"You'll be protected. I'll be here with you. Or you could get another elemental. I'd say a water spirit would be helpful, but the plants don't take water. Perhaps a terra spirit could be useful."

"Where would I even meet someone like that? We just sort of met each other, you and me."

"It was a good day too," Azor said as the smile on her face deepened. "Elementals are around, but we might have to adventure somewhere new or less explored to find one. If you got together with a good adventurer, they might know a place. You could also hire someone, maybe someone from a bigger city who is looking for a bit of solitude. The only problem there is that the house is really small, so it wouldn't hold a family unless you did renovations."

"And the place would need to be furnished. All it has now is a bed and some drapes. I'll have to check the cabinets too."

"There's probably more in the storage shed outside, but that would be farm stuff, not furniture."

"True. I'm guessing it's the same as the cellar of my pub, the supplies I need to get started. Maybe there's a hint in there as to what we should grow here. Let's check it out."

They left the home, heading straight to the shed. Sylas found a variety of tools he'd need for the farm, from work gloves to shovels and stakes, but he didn't find anything like a seed packet. "Still, it's a start," he told Azor.

"That's a positive way to look at it, over the way I was looking at it when I first saw the place." She pretended to take a deep breath, which caused the fire at the back of her head to strengthen and settle. "And the air is fresh here."

"There is something less dreary about it compared to Ember Hollow, but that's because Ember Hollow needs work. It needs work, and it needs people."

"People come for the pub."

"And they'll come for the general store once it's open. But that's just the start," Sylas told Azor, even though it was a bit premature. He laughed. "Before I start planning my next purchase, maybe I should learn how to be a farmer first . . ."

————

"Sylas, good man, you should have spoken to me *before* you agreed to pay seven thousand MLus to learn harvesting skills. To me, I tell you!" Archlumen Tilbud said as soon as he'd heard what Sylas had done. He was seated at the bar having a pint before the pub quiz was set to start, Patches in his lap and purring. "I could have gotten you those skills for, five, no, three thousand MLus. Maybe four. Perhaps somewhere between four and five, but closer to four. You, good sir, my good man, are the victim of highway robbery. But not to worry."

"Yeah?" Sylas asked as he arranged pint glasses.

"As you very well know, I just so happen to live in Duskhaven, and I just so happen to be, ahem, an acquaintance of Elena's. Dare I say more of an acquaintance?"

Mira groaned. "You're not serious, are you, Tilbud?" the apothecary asked. She sat next to Tilbud and had just finished a cup of tea.

"I am serious. I am always serious, and as a serious man, I should tell you that I am one of Duskhaven's most eligible bachelors. Now, this isn't due to some nefarious skill I was able to pick up with my class which is entirely possible, mind you. No, this is with my own charm, my own wit, alone." Tilbud raised an eyebrow at Sylas. This looked comical, especially with the strange hat he wore, which was made of a teal velvet material that matched his cravat and his suit.

"Yes?"

He leaned in closer. "Correct me if I'm wrong, Sylas, but didn't you say something about wanting to find a friend of yours. Yes, it was you. Or was it? Perhaps that is another client? What can I say? Everyone wants to find a friend in the Underworld. I really should be keeping a journal of other peoples' problems."

"There are a couple people I'm looking for, the first one being a man I served with named Quinlan. Nelly, the woman who owns the general store next door—"

"Yes, her, Nelly. I still need to meet her."

"She'll be here later," Sylas told Tilbud. "She needs to visit a lumengineer to view the Book of Shadows so she can find her husband, who died with her."

"Come again? Did you say he died *with her?*"

"Apparently."

Tilbud shuddered. "That sounds traumatic. And viewing the Book of Shadows isn't cheap."

"I need to go to Battersea anyway to get to Geist to find my friend. She could go with us."

"Does Nelly have enough MLus?"

"Definitely not, but I figured I could cover them."

"And what about your loan?" Mira asked Sylas. "Have you already forgotten they will be deducting MLus from you daily?"

Tilbud laughed. "Really, Mira, you act as if we aren't dead and our debts will never be settled. I have a better idea, Sylas. You could just let me take you all from Duskhaven. The portalist there owes me a favor, and I'm always looking for new clients."

Mira turned to him. "You'll rip off Nelly in the same way you did Sylas, charging him twice the amount normally charged to fly."

"Rip off?" Tilbud twitched at the comment. "I have the best methods this side of the Chasm. And since, as you know, we are, indeed, *surrounded* by the Chasm, what I'm saying is that I'm the best in the business."

"No one is questioning that," Sylas said. "If you want to journey past Battersea, and you don't mind taking Nelly and helping us find her husband, then that's fine by me. Like I said, I need to go to Geist, which I've heard could be Ember Hollow's sister city in the east."

"Geist," Tilbud said as he ran his hand down his mustache. "It has been ages since I've been out there. And who are you looking for again? The name, I mean."

"I'm looking for a friend of mine named Quinlan Ashdown, an adventurer. And hopefully his younger brother, Kael. I served with both of them. The other person I'd like to find is named Raelis Sund, but he is a demon hunter now on whatever it's called when people go to the Chasm."

"A Hallowed Pursuit," Mira said.

"Oh my," Tilbud said with a big drink of his ale. "Well, we won't be going on anything like that anytime soon. Now, as for these skills you need. You were planning to visit the farm guild, yes?"

"The Farm and Field Guild."

"Right. Sylas, believe me, I'll be able to get you these skills at a much lower rate than whatever nonsense they will charge you there. How about this? Tomorrow, after an absolutely legendary pub quiz, we go as a group to Duskhaven with Nelly, and I will visit with Elena personally and have your contract amended. Then, we speak to this portalist and head out from there. I suppose there is the issue of getting to Duskhaven, for our dear Nelly, since she's never been before. But we can address that issue in the morning. Also, I might know a lumengineer that owes me a favor, so hold off on giving her the MLus she needs to find her husband."

"I'm not even going to ask," Mira said.

Tilbud chuckled. "Perhaps it is best that you don't, my dear."

They heard barking. Patches, who had remained resting calmly in Tilbud's lap, stood, arched his back, jumped to the ground, and headed upstairs.

"That's Cornbread," Mira said. "The dog that came with the farm that Nelly has since adopted. The dog, not the farm."

A look of concern traced across Tilbud's face. "That's not going to work."

"You don't like dogs?" Sylas asked.

"What? No. Good heavens! I love dogs. The only people that don't like dogs are monsters, and that is precisely why this isn't going to work. Sylas, if you plan to have a farm, you have to protect your farm from monsters that come to feast on the mana. That is why Cornbread came with the farm. He—"

"She," Mira said.

"She is a watchdog. And it is something else you will need to think about now that you have decided to add another class. Once you have crops growing, you will need to stay there often so you can be alerted if there are any issues."

A question came to Sylas as he stood there dumbfounded. The image of Brom dead in his bed was still fresh on Sylas's mind. "Why didn't anyone tell me that?"

"Which part?"

"About the monsters and the need to protect my crops."

"Who have you spoken to about this besides me?"

"Mira, Nelly, Azor, and the people at the auction house, including Elena."

"Well, that would be why," Tilbud said as he slowly took another sip of his ale. "None of those people run farms."

"Wait, I spoke to Edgar too, he's a tomato farmer who lives near Brom's place, ahem, my place."

"Perhaps he was waiting to see if you would actually go through with it. In Douro, just as an example, the flamefruit farmers all work together to deal with any monsters. They have a system setup. I can't pretend to know this system, but I believe it is paid for by the taxes they pay. Did this Edgar mention taxes?"

"He did, but he didn't mention them going to protect anything."

"Then that would likely account for some of it. What kind of farmer was this Brom?"

Sylas remembered his first encounter with Brom, the quest in which he had fetched Mr. Brassmere's hammer. Thinking back now, Sylas was certain he'd heard a dog barking, which must have meant Cornbread was in one of the rooms.

But that wasn't important.

What *was* important was that from the moment he'd met Brom, the man hadn't been a great farmer, to the point that he'd been looking to get rid of his farm.

"I'm going to guess by your silence and the longing glance you just gave Mira that he wasn't great. If this is the case, perhaps the other farmers in the Seedlands let him die so someone else would take the farm. It sounds gruesome, but it won't be the first time that has happened here in the Underworld. Did any of them bid against you?"

"I only know Edgar, but he mentioned a woman who had a leafy greens farm and a guy with a pepper farm. No one bid against me at the auction, though."

"I see. And you paid what for the farm again?"

"Ten thousand MLus."

Tilbud nearly spat his ale out. "Sylas, why would you pay that much for a farm without a crop? Is the home particularly nice?"

"No," he said, thinking of the two-room place on the hill. "It has a porch."

"Well, I suppose that is something. Wait a minute. Wait a bloody minute. I see what happened here. You were there with him, yes?" he asked Mira.

"How did you know?"

"You two go well together, that's how I know. Anyway, I believe—and I could be mistaken here but we will know tomorrow once we pay a visit to Elena—that you, my dear friend, my dear friends, were duped. Not duped badly, but someone had already made an offer on the farm and you bid over it."

"Why didn't they bid against me then? No one was there."

"Maybe it was just a lowball offer and the auctioneer wanted to see if there were other options, so he poked around, told some people, and you are the man that happened to show up. Anyway. I know this sounds grim, but it isn't. And it was still a steal if the porch is nice. Not to worry at all. Tomorrow, we will get everything cleared up. We will also look to greatly reduce your loan amount. I believe I will be able to get you the skills you need for five thousand, maybe even four thousand MLus. That will save you some. You said the total loan included the farm, the spells you'll need, and what else?"

"That was pretty much it."

"Ha! Just like our world, these banks do not have your best interest in mind. I will negotiate directly with Elena tomorrow. Rest assured, Sylas, by tomorrow night, a good chunk of your debt will be wiped away and we will be in Battersea on our way to bigger and better things. Nelly will know of her husband's fate, and things will be looking up. But first, a pub quiz. I need to go over my questions and make sure that they are just difficult enough to stump people." Tilbud raised his pint to Sylas and Mira. "Cheers, mates. Cheers."

CHAPTER SIX

POCKET-CLASS TICKET TO BATTERSEA

Sylas ignored the doomsday message the next morning as he focused on his status.

Name: Sylas Runewulf
Mana Lumens: 4556/4556
Class: Brewer

A new prompt came to him:

[**A loan payment of 81 has been deducted from your total Mana Lumens. Your total loan balance is 20819 Mana Lumens.**]

This registered with what Sylas had made last night at just over eight hundred Mana Lumens. It would have been more had it not been for the two rounds of flamefruit ale that went to the winning table of the pub quiz, which happened to be the Lava Boys, but only because Mira had joined them. She remained the deciding factor in the weekly pub quiz.

Sylas had been too busy to hear most of Archlumen Tilbud's questions during the quiz or Shamus's pitch to the patrons afterward, the man also buying a round for everyone. The Old Lamplighter had been packed, and before everything had truly kicked off, Azor's sausage dish had been well received. Music played late into the night from Bart, who brought a lutist from Cinderpeak named Mary, the pair creating such a lovely environment that Sylas hadn't wanted to close.

Now lying in his bed, petting Patches, Sylas remembered the night of merriment and pondered something he wasn't quite ready to decide yet: perhaps he *shouldn't* have purchased the farm.

Too late now. He shook his head, which caused Patches to sit up. The cat meowed at Sylas, concern in his eyes. "I'll be fine. Just overthinking things. Invasion, we can't forget the invasion."

"Happy Specterday," Azor said as she floated into the room.

"That's right, and I promised you breakfast."

"You don't have to, Sylas."

"But I insist!" Once Sylas was up, he headed downstairs to the cellar and whipped up a breakfast that consisted of slightly charred potatoes diced with leftover sausage.

He was just finishing up when he heard the door open upstairs, followed by barking. Sylas went up to the main floor of the pub to find Nelly and Cornbread. The dog charged at Sylas once she saw him standing there with the plates of food.

"Happy to see you too," Sylas told Cornbread. "Morning, Nelly."

"Good morning, Sylas," she said cheerfully. Nelly hadn't made it to the pub quiz last night, but Sylas was certain she'd heard the commotion.

"Sorry for any late-night singing," Sylas said as Cornbread continued to circle him. The dog sat, looked up at Sylas, and started to whine.

"There was singing?"

"You didn't hear it?" Azor asked Nelly.

"No. It was almost too quiet."

"Huh," Sylas said. "Maybe there's some sort of magical barrier. Heh. I have no idea what I'm talking about, but we do have someone who does. He should be down any minute now."

"What are you talking about?" a tiny voice asked. "Why, I'm already here!"

Sylas glanced at the bar to see Tilbud sitting there, the tiny archlumen in a lime green vest and matching pants, a cloak over his shoulders and a complementary hat that was cocked off to the side.

Nelly jumped. "He's that small?"

Azor burst out laughing. "I was wondering how long it would take the two of you to see him!"

"Ha! That's good," Sylas said as Tilbud quickly reverted back to his normal size. "It's a spell called Shrink," he told Nelly.

Tilbud, who now stood next to the bar, turned to Nelly. "A pleasure to meet you," he said as he took her hand and kissed it.

"Um . . ."

He smiled warmly at the newcomer. "Well, what are we waiting for? Let's see the general store, my dear. I've been dying to meet you, ah, but I suppose I should properly introduce myself first. The name is Archlumen Octavian Tilbud, and yes, in case you're wondering, I'm the very same fellow that taught our dear Sylas to fly and to use a very useful power called Quill. But these are just a taste of the spells I am capable of teaching. But a taste."

"He'll be joining us on our trip to Battersea, where we'll be able to learn more about your husband's whereabouts," Sylas said.

Tilbud placed a hand on his stomach and bowed slightly at Nelly. "This is indeed correct. I'm sorry if I came off as a bit intrusive."

"It's quite all right. As for my store, I've almost got everything set up."

"Let's look at it after breakfast," Azor suggested.

"Right," Sylas said. "I made breakfast for everyone this morning, including you, Cornbread."

The dog started barking again.

Nelly looked Sylas up and down again, as if she were just now noticing that he wore an apron. "And Mira, will she be joining us for breakfast?"

"I'm afraid not. She had a last-minute appointment."

"Will she join us later, then?"

"I tried to get her to come with us. Really, I did. But she wanted to stay here to help Azor with the pub tonight."

"So we will be staying in . . . what was it, Batter-y?"

"Battersea," Tilbud told Nelly. "And yes, we will be staying there tonight. Sylas and I will then continue on toward the other side of the Underworld in search of some of his friends. We'll also figure out the spells our dear Sylas will need to get his farm up and running. Which brings me to another issue, the banker. But don't you—"

"Hold on. I thought you knew the spells yourself," Azor blurted out, who had been privy to yesterday's conversation.

"I do not, but I know where to learn them, and it's much cheaper for me, for *us*, to go this route. And if I learn the new spells, which I will be able to do at my guild in Battersea, then it will be yet another trick up my proverbial sleeve, a win-win if there ever was one. Now, a meal, a grand meal of the most breakfasted variety cooked by Sylas, the pub owner himself, and then a tour of Ember Hollow's new general store is in order. Please"—Tilbud motioned Nelly toward one of the barstools—"Sit. Let's see how good of a chef our dear Sylas really is."

———

Nelly felt a bit nervous as she opened the door and let everyone into her general store. The interior was cleaned up, and a new counter had been built, but the shelves were still empty and she'd yet to repaint the walls.

All of this was new to her. She was the daughter of a regent, which Tiberius had already revealed to everyone with his "Royal House of the Morgan Plains" comment. Running a general store didn't come naturally to her.

Her husband, on the other hand, would know what to do.

Karn Redgrave had grown up the son of an innkeeper who later added a general store to their inn. If anyone should have received a deed for a general store, it should have been him, not her.

Now, as Sylas, Azor, and Tilbud complimented her on the work she had done in the shop, Nelly thought of those precious last moments with her husband, how they had died looking at each other's eyes . . .

This rush of memories was the main reason she hadn't heard Tilbud's question. "Come again?" she asked.

Cornbread barked again and Azor lowered to pet the dog, who seemed to enjoy the fire spirit.

The mustachioed magician gave Nelly a funny look. "I'm asking if you are ready to fly," he said again. "Are you?"

"Did you say fly?" she stammered.

"You haven't activated the portal to Duskhaven, and while we could go on foot or horseback, that would add too much time to our journey. Luckily, I have a solution for this, and that was precisely why I shrank myself earlier."

Azor looked up at Tilbud. "You're not suggesting putting her in your pocket and flying like that, are you?"

"I most certainly am. I would say we can portal, but I have yet to try that with the Shrink ability. Flying, on the other hand, works. That's right, Nelly, you can ride here, in this pocket." Tilbud tapped the pocket on the front of his overcoat. "I suppose you could stay in the pocket on my vest, but this one will give you a view of where we're going."

"I never thought of doing something like that," Sylas said. "We could also activate the portal in the Shadowstone Mountains with her. I need to visit the man who runs the inn there anyway and discuss selling ale to them."

"I agree it would be smart to activate that portal for Nelly," Tilbud said, "but perhaps you should decide whatever deal you plan to work out with this fellow once we return to Ember Hollow. We have important matters in Duskhaven with your loan, and later, with the lumengineer—I still have to call in that favor—not to mention the Farm and Field Guild in Battersea."

"Hold on," Nelly said. "I'm still not sure I heard you correctly. You are saying that you will shrink me and put me in your pocket?"

"Why, yes. That's exactly what I'm saying. Keep up, darling. Then, you can activate the portals along the way, and you will be able to travel more easily to Duskhaven, the Shadowstone Mountains, and, later, Battersea. Do note there is a fee for traveling to two of those places, but we can address that later. And that fee would be nullified once you make contact with your guild and fulfilled whatever requirements they have."

"I have money?"

"No, no, you do not," Tilbud told her. "You most certainly do not. None of us do. You have MLus, Mana Lumens, which are a bit different from money. You must think of it that way."

"I took a loan."

"You did?" Sylas asked her.

"That's what Mr. Brassmere said I needed to do, something about our class not being the same as yours, someone who can just get started."

Tilbud's eyebrows raised. "Did your loan happen to originate with MLR Bank and a woman named Elena?"

"How did you know?"

The archlumen smiled. "Ah, Elena strikes again. She is good at what she does. In that case, I'll have to review the terms of both of your loans because there might be some savings I can get the two of you. I'm assuming you need to visit whatever guild runs general stores."

"Yes," Nelly said as she recalled her conversation with Elena. "But I think I would need to have the place up and running first."

"Same with my situation," Sylas added. "Then again, the guilds and alliances operate differently."

"So your loan doesn't have any of their dues baked into it, hmmm?" Tilbud asked Nelly.

"No, it doesn't. It is just to cover getting initial supplies and travel associated with those supplies."

"I see, then you would need to do that before you can portal to Battersea for free," Tilbud told her.

"I don't understand."

"Ah, let me explain more clearly: once you are a member of the guild, you'll have a private portal in your shop. Did you see Sylas's upstairs? He has one that just hasn't been activated yet."

"I have not, but I do know the room you mean," Nelly told the archlumen.

"Otherwise, it can cost three hundred MLus to portal to Battersea. However, at the moment, all of this is speculation. Travel costs are included in your loan, and we'll see what they say at your guild. Besides, we have a more important mission: find out about your husband, find the poor fellow, get the store running, then set all of that up. It will be worth it in the end. You'll get much better deals in Battersea with your class, and then your items can be delivered via portal too. Why do you think we don't see a load of carriages around here?"

"I haven't really thought of that," Nelly said. "Tiberius did show me his horses, though."

"Of course he did. If you don't mind me asking, what sort of spell do you get with being classed as a merchant?" Sylas touched his chest. "For me, I'm able to magically brew."

"She's able to get better deals than you can imagine," Tilbud said for Nelly. "Think of it as a boost to charisma, the likes of which you've never experienced before, especially when purchasing in bulk. She also has unlimited storage of said items through her Storage Inventory system."

"Her what?"

"I can access whatever I want, as long as I have it in stock. It just appears. Watch." Nelly turned her palm around and an apple appeared. She took a bite of it. "This is from a sample I picked up yesterday."

"Now that is a skill!" Sylas ran his hand through his hair. "I might need to consider a general store next time I add a class just for that ability alone."

Tilbud laughed. "You need to figure out what to plant first."

"Yes, there is that." Sylas wasn't quite crestfallen, but he did lower his shoulders to some degree. "I have a ways to go."

"We all do, my friend, but before we go wherever it is we need to go, we need to catch Elena *before* she leaves her home. I will not let the banking industry get the best of the people I care for!" Tilbud slammed a fist down onto the counter, startling Cornbread.

Nelly scooped the dog into her arms. "What about Cornbread?"

"She can stay with me while you all are gone," Azor said. "I'll be watching Patches anyway."

"That's fine." Nelly registered a look on Sylas's face. "What's that look mean?"

"Ugh, about Cornbread. I've recently been informed that Cornbread is, I don't know how to say this exactly—"

"Cornbread is a farm dog," Tilbud said, coming right out with it. "And because she's a farm dog, once Sylas's crops have started, Cornbread's services will be needed on the farm. Her job, believe it or not, is to act as an alarm and a deterrent. We don't have pests here like you are used to in your world, our *former* world, but we do have low-rank monsters—some from the Chasm and others simply around because, well, who knows why—and they are particularly drawn to the mana from farms."

"So Cornbread has to go?" Nelly's throat suddenly felt dry as she hugged the dog even tighter. She glanced from Sylas to Tilbud.

"I'm afraid so, yes, at some point. Like Patches to the pub, Cornbread has a mana link to the farm. But that doesn't mean we can't find another pet for you."

"But I . . ." Nelly set Cornbread down and nodded. "I understand. And sure, Azor, if you don't mind watching Cornbread, that would be much appreciated."

"I don't mind, but Patches might."

"He'll be fine," Sylas told them.

"Right, in that case, my dear, dear Nelly, are you ready to change sizes?" Tilbud asked gently. "And in case you had any worries or doubts, it won't hurt. But it will be fun, a first-class, no, a *pocket-class* ride if ever there was one." The archlumen glanced around. "But perhaps we should do this outside of the pub, and Azor, please keep Cornbread in the pub with you. I don't want her to get the wrong idea and think Nelly has suddenly become a bite-sized snack."

"She didn't eat you when you shrank yourself," Azor told him.

"Yes, but she was too distracted by actual food. Which was quite excellent, Sylas, I must say."

"Thank you."

"Come on, Cornbread," Azor said, the black dog following her down into the cellar.

Once Cornbread was downstairs, Nelly grabbed the scarf Mira had given her, wrapped it around her neck, and joined Sylas and Tilbud outside. "I can't believe I'm letting you do this," she said as she spread her arms wide.

"No need for that. Just step over here. Yes, there," Tilbud said.

Nelly saw a flash of gold. The world grew in size around her so quickly that for a moment, she felt like she was going to be sick. She now stood on the ground, huge blades of grass around her. Nelly was about to say something when a big hand reached down to her.

The first thing she noticed, aside from a growing shadow, was Tilbud's fingerprints followed by his nails, which were well-groomed. "Come on, then," he said, his voice booming loudly as he turned his palm around.

"I can't believe I'm doing this," Nelly said as she stepped into his open hand. He carefully brought it up to the pocket on his vest and let her climb in. Sylas leaned forward to look at her, his blue eyes each as big as the sun.

"You'll be fine," he told her with a grin.

"Yes, she will." Tilbud placed a hand on his pocket to make sure she was in place. Nelly felt the muscles in his chest move as he turned to Sylas. "Shall we?"

"Lead the way."

The enormous world around them grew smaller, the golden, cloud-filled sky larger as Sylas and Tilbud took to the air, Nelly in the archlumen's pocket. "That's your store," Tilbud told her as they circled once over Ember Hollow.

From there, he picked up speed, moving ahead of Sylas, who Nelly could no longer see.

Below, she caught glimpses of forests and small lakes, outer settlements that were mostly abandoned. She could also see the enormous wall that was the Hexveil, where Mira had taken her on her first day.

To be dead was quite the experience, and she may have feared it less had she known this was where she would come after what had happened. They had done what they could to survive, her and Karn.

Those memories would be ones that she would never live down. Hopefully, they would be reunited soon.

————

After activating the portal near the Shadowstone Mountains, the three continued on toward Duskhaven, Sylas trailing behind Tilbud. The archlumen was a much better flier than Sylas and was able to flit through the air like a diving bird. Occasionally, Sylas would catch Tilbud saying something to Nelly, but he generally wasn't part of their conversation.

It took more Mana Lumens than Sylas would have liked to fly to Duskhaven, but at least they reached the city, and now, Nelly had access to another portal.

"Right," Tilbud said once Nelly was normal-sized again and fixing her slightly frizzled hair. "This way. Elena should still be home. If she's not, I'll have to call Horatio to find her."

"Horatio?" Nelly asked, her hands a bit shaky. Sylas knew how disorienting it could be to go from small to large, how he didn't feel normal in his body for a few minutes after.

"Horatio, my bonded water spirit. He's not chatty like Azor, but he's useful in situations like finding people. Or if we need to take a boat somewhere. We will certainly take a boat in Battersea," Tilbud told Sylas. "A boat ride is the best way to get to the other side of the Underworld, well, aside from portaling. Anyway, Elena, Elena, Elena—let's pay our dear banker friend a visit. And by 'we,' I mean let me do all the talking."

They reached a brick home with a well-maintained walkway leading up to a grand front porch. There were flower beds on either side and a nice bench beneath a tree covered in purple flowers.

"This is wonderful," Nelly said.

"Quite. Bankers do have MLus, generally," Tilbud said as he rubbed his hands together, clearly hatching a plan. "In any event, this bench will be the perfect place for the two of you to wait."

"You don't want us to talk to her with you?" Sylas asked.

"No, that's fine. I'll do all the talking," he told Sylas. "If the two of you are involved, it may complicate things. Well, it won't complicate them that much, but it could put us in a situation where there are further negotiations, and I certainly don't want that. I want what is best for you, which turns out to be best for me too. Toodles. And please, if you hear anything out of the ordinary, don't come running."

The archlumen departed, leaving them near the bench.

"What does he mean by that?" Nelly asked after she'd sat down next to Sylas, both facing away from the home.

"Which part?"

"The 'best for him, best for us' part?"

"He means that he wants the MLus for teaching me the skills I need to know to run the farm. For you, I don't know what that means."

"I don't understand."

"It costs fixed MLus to learn something like Shrink, or this," Sylas said as he traced up the words *The Old Lamplighter* with his Quill spell. "An archlumen buys these skills at a fixed price and then sells them to us. In this way, he is very much a middleman, but that is how the system works. With my farm situation, these fixed MLus would have been paid to whoever the Farm and Field Guild recommended, seven thousand to learn three spells: Mana Infusion, Mana Saturation, and Harvest Silos. Tilbud is going to negotiate a cheaper price, which I'm guessing will be paid to him."

"He knows the spells?"

"Not exactly, but he knows where he can learn them in Battersea."

"Where exactly?"

"He didn't say. I'm assuming his guild, whatever that may be called."

"And you trust him?"

They heard some yelling in the home, but Sylas couldn't quite make out the words. This was followed by the sound of something smashing on the ground. It sounded like a vase. "Tilbud is unorthodox, but he will get the job done."

"Are you certain? It sounds like they are physically fighting in there."

Sylas suppressed the urge to get up. "Let's hope not."

Nelly jumped as a flash of golden mana exploded out of the chimney. It burst into fireworks and sizzled by the time the motes of mana hit the rooftop.

Sylas looked back at the home just as it rocked. "What are they doing now?"

"Still yelling, it seems. Had I known this was how to negotiate with a banker . . ." Nelly laughed.

"Tilbud is unorthodox, as I said. Your flight. You never said how that was?"

"Pocket class was interesting, I'll say that."

"Tilbud can teach you how to fly."

"Yes, I'd like that. It seems like it would be a great way to get around—"

They heard something that sounded like a window breaking. Then a door slammed, followed by what Sylas was certain was a table scraping across a stone floor. Repeatedly. Then more yelling. Some thumping. Then yelling that sounded like moaning. Then a sudden spell of quiet. Then shouting and a bit of stomping.

"Please tell me they're—"

Smash!

Nelly was interrupted by what sounded like a bookshelf being pushed over.

Tilbud stepped out of the banker's home, the archlumen a little worse for wear. His lime green hat was cocked off to the side, his mustache ruffled, his shirt untucked, his cape ripped, and his vest unbuttoned.

Sylas never saw Elena, but he did see the door slam behind Tilbud.

"Right," the archlumen said as he approached, the man blinking a few times to steady himself. "Negotiations are complete. As I said, Elena and I have a past. Perhaps we now have a future, likely not. But that is neither here nor there. Well, it is here, but it's not there, *there* being Battersea, where we need to go next. I suppose I should visit my home first as well to tidy up and change clothing. But that won't take long. I'll explain the status of your debts along the way. Trust me," Tilbud said with a grin, "you are both going to like the new terms."

"Thanks," Sylas said.

"Yes, of course, anything for a friend. And, what can I say? It gave me a reason to visit Elena." Tilbud removed his hat and smoothed down his hair. "Who knows what will come of that. Anyhoo. Let's continue on." He gestured toward the Duskhaven street and offered Nelly a tight smile. "Grand old place, isn't it?"

According to Tilbud, Sylas would see the new amount he owed the MLR Bank starting tomorrow. The archlumen had been able to lower his debt by three thousand Mana Lumens with the promise that he would visit the archlumen guild in Battersea, known as the Archlumenry, to obtain the spells Tilbud needed to train Sylas.

This still left the issue of what Sylas would farm, but he would be able to tackle that soon enough.

Later, after changing at his curiously spherical home with a door that resembled a porthole, Tilbud struck up a deal with the Duskhaven portalist, a deal that ended up involving Sylas. "That's right," he told the man, "a free round of drinks the next time you visit The Old Lamplighter, that, ahem, on top of what you already owe me for the you-know-what."

The portalist, a younger man who had a little cap tied under his chin, grimaced. "Fine, Tilbud, but this is your last free trip to Battersea. Last one, mate. I mean it."

"Is he always getting in trouble like this?" Nelly whispered to Sylas, who stood next to her.

"Tilbud? Always. But there's a method to his madness, or perhaps, a madness to his method."

"And she has never been to Battersea before, yes?" the portalist nodded to Nelly. "Well, Tilbud?"

"I'm afraid she has not. Is that a problem?"

"You know I'm technically not supposed to do that."

"And I'm technically not supposed to use my powers to—"

"Fine, fine," the portalist said with a scowl as he showed the archlumen his palms. "But this is the *last* time."

"I believe you said that already, but I could be wrong. In any event, thank you, and please, Nelly, Sylas, let's continue on."

Nelly seemed reluctant until Sylas stepped onto the runic circle and turned to her. "Come on then, it's not as crazy as it looks."

The three appeared in Battersea, where they were instantly greeted by seagulls twisting in the air above, the wind carrying an almost briny scent. The archlumen smiled faintly. "Welcome to Battersea, the City of Seven Hills."

"It's near the ocean?" Nelly asked.

"No, an enormous lake. Lake Seraphina is the name," Tilbud said as he continued to adjust his light maroon clothing, the archlumen now in a three-piece suit. His hair was still a bit ruffled on the sides, which he had yet to smooth out, and he wore a pointed hat two sizes smaller than it should be. "Anyhoo. Welcome, my dears, to the capital of the Underworld."

"It sure is something," Nelly said, her eyes widening as she looked around.

Sylas agreed. From where they currently stood, he could see down a hill where there were homes with tiled roofs. Another hill rose in the distance, one currently blocking the view of the lake. People moved up and down steps cut into solid stone, carrying goods. There were also a few elementals performing various tasks that Sylas would have paid more attention to had it not been for Tilbud, who was already leading them away.

"Off we go! First, let's deal with the lumengineer. We are, after all, at the edge of the Sigur District and The Distinguished Society of Lumengineers and Etheric Constructs isn't so far from here. Then, guilds— No, then, we find a place to rest. A place with a view, mind you. Later, or perhaps tomorrow, guilds. I didn't come all the way to Battersea to stay at a bloody boardinghouse and *not* go out for a night of revelry."

"Let me guess," Sylas asked as he caught up with Tilbud, "someone owes you a favor."

"No, not this time. I'm afraid we will have to start paying at that point, but I may be able to weasel my way into a free session with a lumengineer."

"How?"

"A friend of mine double-classed as an archlumen and a lumengineer. It wasn't easy either. They no longer work at The Distinguished Society of Lumengineers and Etheric Constructs, but they were quite influential there, and their name still holds some weight. Trust me. There is no way we will be paying full price, or any price, for something like this. I will make a scene if I have to," Tilbud said.

In the end, no scene was necessary.

Tilbud was able to use his leverage to get access to a lumengineer, who just so happened to be the same woman Sylas and Mira had visited on his previous trip to Battersea. Catia, who now had her orange hair pulled back and tucked behind her ears, seemed a bit surprised to see Sylas.

She wasn't surprised to see Tilbud. "Ah, you."

"Ah, you," he told Catia with excitement. "I believe we've met before."

"I can't say that we have."

"No, I'm sure of it. I suppose that is beside the point. This is Eleanor Redgrave, and she is *gravely*—I'm sorry—in need of your assistance. Now, as lumengineer Sir Scott Reid has made it known several times to me, there is a charity program here to reunite couples that sadly passed together."

Catia eyed him with a bit of contempt. "Yes, I'm aware. But that program ended well over a year ago with the change in leadership here at—"

"And who, my dear, who do you think helped end that program? Why, it was Sir Scott Reid, himself! He didn't end it out of cruelty, he ended it to expand this service to people who didn't benefit from the program in an effort to unite lost souls, *shadows*, as I believe it is written in the bylaws of The Distinguished Society of Lumengineers and Etheric Constructs, ahem, to reunite lost souls with their lost souls. Now which section was it in? Nelly, be a dear and let me see that book I gave you to put in your inventory."

"This one?" Nelly asked as she summoned the book Tilbud had given her back at his home in Duskhaven.

"Ah, yes, that would be it." He flipped through the pages. "Would you look at that, here it is. I'll make it easy with Quill." A flash of mana was followed by a string of golden text:

In the matter of the Reunification Program of The Distinguished Society of Lumengineers and Etheric Constructs

Pursuant to the powers vested in The Distinguished Society of Lumengineers and Etheric Constructs (hereinafter referred to as "the Society") and in accordance with the ethical and operational mandates governing the Society's engagement with the

Underworld's populace, the following bylaw is hereby enacted as an update to the existing Reunification Program protocols (Version 4.2).

Section 1: Scope and Intent

1.1. This bylaw is promulgated to facilitate the reunification of familial individuals who have died together, upon entry into the Underworld, have been separated from their immediate familial entities, including but not limited to spouses, progeny, and direct kinship relations, hereinafter referred to as "Family Members."

1.2. The bylaw is crafted to ensure a structured and equitable process for reunification, adhering to the Society's core principles of compassion, fairness, and ethereal integrity.

Section 2: Eligibility and Application

2.1. Eligibility for reunification under this bylaw is contingent upon the applicant(s) demonstrating a preexisting familial bond, as defined by the criteria set forth in Annex A, with the sought Family Members.

2.2. Applicants must submit a formal request for reunification to the Society, accompanied by relevant documentation, as stipulated in the Reunification Application Procedures—

"I get it," Catia said as she swept the code away. "Please, no more."

"I'm with you," Tilbud told her. "I hate when bylaws get in the way of me making rash decisions, but these are the rules and regulations, and without them, well, we would be no better off than the monsters of the Chasm, now would we? I believe that is the common argument for the reason these kinds of rules are created. In any event, you can check for familial evidence, can you not? We can obtain the information we need, get whatever we need to add an additional class for Sylas here—"

"What?"

"—and get on our way. I don't know if you have plans for tonight, but you could join us."

"Is he serious?" Nelly whispered to Sylas.

"Tilbud works in mysterious ways."

Catia folded her hands together and offered the three of them a tight smile. "Right this way. We will view the *Book of Shadows* and locate your husband, Mrs. Redgrave. Regarding Mr. Runewulf adding a class, I will need to see that he has obtained property that would warrant such a change and he will then need to go, with the paper I give him, to the appropriate guild to fully activate it as part of our new two-step authentication system. As for joining you, please, don't flatter yourself, Tilbud."

"I'm not trying to flatter myself, I assure you. I'm just saying that it would be good on your end to get to know some of the newest citizens of Ember Hollow," Tilbud told Catia as he followed her. "I heard that that village is up and coming, you know."

"You heard, did you?"

"Yes, I not only heard, I can confirm, my dear Catia. And what's not to like about an outer village on the cusp of the Chasm? There's a sense of wildness there, you know, and it's invigorating. Plus, there is such a wonderful pub there. Ember Hollow is nothing like the big city, mind you, but there is a charm, and I believe it's a charm that people from here will enjoy. You could come to the next pub quiz. I am the host, and it is quite challenging. Or visit on Wraithsday, when they host a weekly feast."

"Stop here," Catia said as she approached a large wooden door. "And for the remainder of this session, I ask for your quiet and respect. We are about to enter a very unique space."

"And about joining us later tonight?" Tilbud asked her. "You'd be more than welcome."

"Sorry, I have other plans."

"And the pub in Ember Hollow?"

She paused again. "I'll think about it," she said, surprising Sylas.

"You will?" Tilbud asked.

"Yes. Now, please keep quiet. I need to focus."

———

Sylas didn't know what to tell Nelly. "Sorry," she said, as a wave of emotion came over her. "My apologies," she told Tilbud. "He didn't deserve that. Karn doesn't . . . what can we do?"

"Please, Nelly, let's find somewhere we can regroup and come up with a strategy before we are all reduced to tears. The hallways of the Society are hardly the place for waterworks. It's not comfortable, my dear." Tilbud swept his hand toward a set of wooden chairs. "They don't aim for comfort here, especially comfort for someone needing to shed a few tears. If they did, everything wouldn't be made of wood and stone. They aim to treat us like cattle, brand us, and push us on our way," he said loudly as two guards slowly approached.

"This isn't the place—" one of the guards started to say before Sylas cut him off.

"Out of the way."

It was a simple phrase, only four words, but in those words and the way he tilted his head, Sylas meant to convey something that any man who had spent time in the trenches, time spitting in the face of death, would understand. Sylas was not to be trifled with.

And it worked. The two guards exchanged nervous glances and stepped aside.

"I think Tilbud is right," Sylas told Nelly. "Let's find a place and come up with a plan."

"And we do have a plan." The archlumen motioned them toward an exit. "You're not out of luck yet."

Sylas recalled the way Catia's face had changed once she opened the Book of Shadows and the book spoke through her, detailing Karn Redgrave's journey. It was a slight twitch of her eyebrow, followed by a sympathetic, "Oh." A pause, and then Catia had delivered the bad news: "I'm sorry, Mrs. Redgrave, your husband arrived outside of Geist and was tricked by an evil spirit from the Chasm. I have seen this happen before, and once it takes place, this person generally falls off our map due to being enslaved."

"Enslaved?" she had asked.

"Yes, that is generally how these demons, known as a Nox, use newcomers."

It was at this point that Sylas had remembered his first encounter in the Underworld, the shapeshifting man-demon, how Mira had saved him at the very last moment. Would this have been his fate? Would he have been enslaved?

"Karn has been possessed by a demon," Nelly said now as they reached the street outside the Society. "After all we've been through—"

"What have you been through?" Tilbud asked. "I won't be able to better help you until I know the details of your death."

"Why?"

"Why? Your question to me should be *how*. And to answer that question, I will first need a bit more information. You are dead, my dear, and the possibilities of what are possible—huh, 'possibilities of what are possible,' I like the sound of that—are endless. I didn't say anything back there because Catia declined to dine with us tonight. I joke, and I know I shouldn't, but I must. I didn't say anything because these sorts of system exploits are frowned upon by establishments like the Society."

"I'm with Nelly," Sylas said as they turned onto a bustling street. "How could knowing how they died help?"

"Because it will help me better understand the situation. Once I can do that, let's just say I know a few people who might be able to help us further, or better, you may know a few people. But I need to know the right person to go to, and we'll likely, at some point, need MLus."

"I have my loan," Nelly said.

"You won't be able to use that for this. But one step at a time. First, let's find room and board for the night. We can then discuss what happened, and once I know more, I will be able to go from there."

"And you are certain?"

"I assure you, Nelly, all hope is not lost. Yet. We still have enough hope to go around, and once we do have the information we need, I'm sure a demon hunter like our dear Tiberius would be interested to know about this shifter. There are rituals that can be done, ones that are frowned upon legally, and I will get to them later. But someone will be able to help us find Karn."

"Good luck getting Tiberius to do something illegal," Sylas said.

"He'll do it for me," Nelly told them as she wiped more tears away. "I am confident of the fact."

Tilbud nodded. "Likely. And who cares of legalities when we are all dead? Ironic I say that considering I just used legalese to get us what we needed back at the Society, but you know what I mean. The two of you need to wake up. The system and its classes are helpful for the common folk, but those who know the intricacies of it are able to exploit the system in ways that make being dead better than being alive. At least that is generally the case. Let's not touch on insane power creep and how that can push you toward the Chasm—"

"Is Karn in the Chasm?"

"What? No, who said that?" Tilbud asked her.

"Catia hinted at it."

"That's where he'll eventually go if and when this evil spirit sees to their nefarious plans, but we have time. More time, likely, than we do for the invasion message."

Nelly stopped. "The what?"

"That is a story for another day," Sylas said.

Nelly stopped walking. "If I'm to share the innermost details of my life, details that might turn you away from me, you should be willing to share something as well."

Sylas and Tilbud exchanged glances. The archlumen spoke: "It is your message to share, Sylas."

"Fine, let's find a place to stay, have a drink, perhaps a small meal, and hash all of this out. What do you say?"

"I know just the place," Tilbud said, "and it is rather comfortable. The price isn't so bad either. For three rooms, it should be three hundred MLus or so. I know the owner, of course, so it's a bit cheaper."

"I'll cover the rooms," Sylas said. "It's the least I could do."

"Then I'll cover the meal and drinks," Tilbud said. "After, I have a few spots I need to visit based on the information I receive."

———

The three found the place, called the Dragon's Whisker, which had a restaurant and lounge downstairs and a dozen rooms on the second floor. In seeing the setup, Sylas understood more of what was possible when two or more classes got together. They even had a small general store called the Dragon's Trinkets, which meant that an innkeeper, a merchant like Nelly, and some sort of pub class had gotten together to form the establishment; that, or someone had taken out the loans necessary to gain the advantages of all three classes.

Once they had their rooms, Sylas and Tilbud met downstairs while Nelly freshened up.

"Are you sure it's smart to tell her about the invasion message?" Sylas asked the archlumen as he took a seat at a round table. A waitress came by with a woven basket of various hardbreads and a spread. She set it down, smiled at the two of them, and left.

"Well, you're the one that volunteered that information, not me."

"Yes, because you mentioned it."

"Nelly is your neighbor. I assume she would like to know. Wouldn't you if it were the other way around?"

"I suppose I would," Sylas said as he took a bite of the stick of bread.

"Please, don't be an animal. Use the spread." Tilbud deliberately showed how to put the spread on the bread. "Front to back, not side to side—"

"You're good at this."

"I had a fling with a fellow who was part of a society of manners. It was quite tedious. Who would have thought eating and enjoying food could be that complicated? It was a bloody ritual, if you ask me, totally unnecessary. And the functions we would have to attend. You remember when I said anything is possible when you're dead?"

"That was only about thirty minutes ago, so yes."

"Just because it's possible doesn't mean it's necessary, Sylas. The tension is what ultimately thwarted our budding love affair. Not only did I laugh at the wrong time, I yawned without covering my mouth, and well, here we are." Tilbud motioned to the table. The two glanced up just as Nelly came down from her room. "And there she is. I have gone ahead and placed an order—"

"You did?"

"I did while you were upstairs," Tilbud told Sylas. "Why do you think we're getting bread?" He stood and Sylas followed suit so Nelly could take her seat. "Yes, as I was saying, manners are important. Now, let's do exactly what we came here to do, feast and tell secrets." The archlumen grinned, the ends of his mustache curling to some degree. "Nelly, you first."

———

Tea came in tall ceramic mugs without handles, which made them hot to the touch. Nelly hesitated as she looked at the two men, one of whom, Tilbud, seemed eager to hear what had happened and the other, Sylas, who looked like he felt bad for prying.

"You aren't going to like this," she finally told Sylas.

"I'm sure I'll be fine."

"You are an Aurumite, Sylas."

"I *was* an Aurumite. The longer I'm here in the Underworld, the more I believe that wherever you were born doesn't need to follow you. I could have been born in any kingdom. I'm not an Aurumite here, I'm an Underworld . . . ian? Underworldian?"

Tilbud considered this. "Perhaps Underworlder. No, Underworldian sounds better. If we're being honest, neither sounds good, but I get your point. Please, Nelly, continue."

"So as an Aurumite, you are familiar with the Gold Guard?"

Sylas, who had just taken a bite of bread, chewed it quickly and swallowed. "I am. A sorry lot, those ones."

"The Gold Guard is a term I, myself, am unfamiliar with. Do tell," Tilbud said to Sylas.

"The Gold Guard were recruits taken from an Aurumite prison colony, mercenaries, sent to new parts of the front line to ravage our enemies," Sylas said. "Imagine combining the worst of a kingdom, putting them into several brigades, and sending them ahead to seed destruction and turmoil in ways we are forbidden to do as normal soldiers. The name itself is meant to cover the things that they typically did, actions that don't bear repeating here because you all know what a man at his most savage is capable of."

"Oh my," was all Tilbud said as Nelly took it from there.

"A new wave of these Gold Guard came, and my husband and I decided to work with them so the people in our village, namely women and children, could escape. We had some sway as the regents, and we secretly ordered all of their food be poisoned. Most of the mercenaries died that night, but those that survived came for us. We were taken prisoner and executed shortly after, executed together. Right next to one another. He was the last person I saw before I died." She wiped a tear with her scarf. "Right in front of one another."

"Well," Tilbud said after an excruciating pause. "We asked, did we not?"

"I'm not proud of what we did."

"No, I wouldn't assume so, Nelly, but now that I know that, I believe I may have a way to gather more information regarding your husband's possession. Your scarf, please."

"My scarf?"

"I'll need it, yes. A manaseer I know has an ability that could help here. We'll still need someone classed as a demon hunter later, for the tracking part. But this is a good start."

Nelly removed her scarf, folded it, and gave it to Tilbud.

"Right. Good, this is good. Well, not good, but good to know."

She returned her focus to Sylas. "That's also why I didn't tell you initially. I didn't know you were an Aurumite, but once I heard your name, I was certain you weren't from the Shadowthorne Empire. I have since learned from Mira that you were a soldier."

"I was, yes, but I wasn't a fan or supporter of the Gold Guard. They made our job hell, and destroyed trust between us and anyone we met after they moved through an area. What I said earlier stands though: I may have been an Aurumite then, but I am not one now. I'm merely trying to live the life I couldn't live in our world, which brings us to the invasion message."

Nelly, who had just taken a sip of her tea, paused. "Invasion message?"

"Go on, then, Sylas," Tilbud said as he smoothed the scarf out and flattened it.

"It's peaceful here. Generally. Well, we do have the fact that we live so close to the Chasm, but generally, it is nice. And I'm not conscripted, nor are we at war with anyone, nor is there anything too pressing that can't be solved through basic life skills. Is it strange that our mana system, our very life force, acts as capital? Sure, that's a bit odd."

"But is it any different where we all came from?" Tilbud chimed in. "Weren't we basically paying to stay alive and working to do so?" He drew his hands together on top of the scarf. "I suppose that is neither here nor there, and if we're being honest, I hate these kinds of debates. It's clearly better here because we can fly. And do other things, of course, but flying is fun. Please, Sylas, continue. Ignore me. Invasion message."

"I started receiving it after my first day here. *You have eighty-nine days until the invasion.* That's what it said. I thought initially it had something to do with the Chasm, being so close to hell itself, you know. But according to Nuno the manaseer, the message isn't about the Chasm."

She took another sip from her tea. "Then what is it?"

"I don't know yet. Nuno hasn't reported in."

"So you get a message every morning, telling you that you have roughly three months before the invasion."

"I do, yes," Sylas said.

"And what day is it on now?"

"Sixty-one days."

"Huh."

"Huh?" Tilbud asked Nelly.

"What else is there to say? I suppose we could shore up the village defenses."

Sylas sat back and crossed his arms over his chest. "We'd need to shore up the entire village and get more people there, people with skills."

"In two months."

"Yes."

"Have you been to Ember Hollow?" she asked with a smirk. "Not much to shore up."

"It is quite sleepy."

"If we're being honest, and is there anything one can be *but* honest over tea, I like the sleepy nature of your town," Tilbud told them. "I stay out of trouble when I'm there. I'm not a troubled man, but I am a trouble magnet and, I should confess, part of the appeal of running the pub quiz, aside from testing my knowledge, the knowledge of my peers, the free pints, and how it makes me feel smarter than everyone else, *is* that it allows me to get away from Duskhaven. And I only moved there to get away from here." He motioned toward the nearest window.

"You used to live in Battersea?"

"I certainly did," he told Sylas. "My old stomping grounds, as it were."

"Yet you are going out tonight?" Nelly asked.

"Why, of course, I am. Someone must be around to make sure the grounds are properly stomped, and in my absence, I'm afraid the haunts and dives I frequented will be without a purpose." The archlumen grinned at Sylas.

"Keep telling yourself that, Tilbud."

"I think I will."

CHAPTER SEVEN

CHARMED

Cornbread liked the attention she got at the pub. There were plenty of people to pet her, and there was the fire spirit, who made sure she was always fed. She also liked the cat, even if he was pudgy and a bit curmudgeonly. It was a life she could get used to if she didn't have a lingering feeling that something was missing.

The farm dog thought about this later that night as she rested on the ground near the pub's hearth, the fire spirit fast asleep, and the cat prowling about.

Being here was nice, but it wasn't the farm, and Cornbread missed the farm.

She got to her feet and turned to the small door that the cat liked to use. She was just approaching it when the pub cat slipped in front of her.

Where are you going? the cat asked, his tail swishing against the ground.

The farm. Someone has to protect it. That was my duty until I came here.

The Farmly Realm, huh? How far is that from here?

I don't know. I should have paid better attention, Cornbread said as one of her ears flopped down. *Have you been on a farm before?*

I try to stay around here, the Tavernly Realm. Does your farm have a name other than the Farmly Realm?

Not that I know of.

Typical dog behavior.

Cats name things?

Patches arched his body. *If it needs naming, yes.* He then relaxed. *If you were planning to leave, don't let me stop you—*

Both of them heard a scratching noise outside.

Cornbread turned to it, her lips pulling back as she exposed her teeth. She sniffed the air. *It's a raccoon. I'll do something about it.*

Patches's tail continued swishing back and forth as he did everything in his power not to turn immediately to the sound. He had to make sure the farm dog respected him.

Don't you hear it? Cornbread asked impatiently, the farm dog nearly to the point that she was whining.

Outside? Yes. Near the well. Not the first time that well has given us trouble.

What happened with the well? I noticed a smell there that I have only sensed when demons are near.

Patches's ears pressed back against his head. *Spiders and demons. The raccoon is probably here to investigate.*

We take the raccoon?

We try to run it off, and if we must do worse, we do that.

I've seen some nasty ones, Cornbread said, getting excited. *Possessed ones.*

I'll bet. You have powers?

I do. You?

I can turn myself invisible, split myself into two cats, grow exponentially larger, and use my hairballs as weapons. Among other things.

Cornbread nodded. *I have a magical bark, but that would wake the fire spirit.*

We don't want that. Patches tilted his chin toward the fireplace. *The fire spirit isn't bad, but this is our problem, our realm to protect.*

Yes, our realm to protect, Cornbread said, now even more excited. She still missed her farm, but this was invigorating, Cornbread loved battling monsters, and she could tell by the sound of the raccoon that it was no ordinary beast.

And your other powers? Patches asked.

Healing drool is one, um, barking, howling. My howl can alert the entire village if I wanted it to—

Let's not do that. Stealth first, always stealth first. I don't know what it is with dogs and wanting to alert the cavalry. The best way to handle most things is silence and efficiency. I'll turn invisible, sneak out, and slip around the raccoon so we can corner it.

Cornbread nodded enthusiastically. *Good. Once you're in position, I'll rush out and attack.*

Try not to bite me.

Try not to scratch me, Cornbread said.

I'll try.

I'll do the same.

Patches turned invisible. Cornbread, who could still smell the pub cat, stuck her snout out and touched Patches.

That's incredible!

Let's deal with this raccoon. The cat door quietly opened, letting in a bit of chilled air from outside as Patches left.

Once the cat was gone, Cornbread closed her eyes and took an even deeper inhale through her nostrils.

Suddenly, she could see it all.

An outline of everything that was happening outside took shape in her mind's eye. Cornbread now had a spatial understanding of where Patches was located, how the cat was slowly making his way around to the back of the well. She could also see the raccoon, which was *twice* as large as any she'd encountered on the farm.

Oh, that's a big one. A really big one.

Another deep breath added a touch of color to the scene. It also reinforced something that she could already smell. The raccoon had a dark influence, something Cornbread had experienced before on the farm.

It wasn't possessed by a demon, but it had been—she sniffed again—it had been *influenced* by a creature possessed by something from the hell beyond the wall of magic that kept this world safe. The raccoon would need to die before it could fester and turn into something that could create more trouble.

There you go, Cornbread said as Patches made it to his position behind the raccoon. The cat was crouched low now, his rear up, ready to pounce.

Cornbread had the notion to explode out of the small door. That would definitely be dramatic, and it would scare the raccoon right into the cat's clever trap. But doing it like that would also wake the fire spirit, and the cat didn't seem to want that.

Quietly then, stealthy, like the cat said.

Cornbread squeezed through the small door and was just placing her back feet down when the large raccoon looked up. It hissed and bared its teeth.

Here I am, Cornbread growled, her fur standing to attention, eyes locked on the raccoon.

She approached slowly, growling and snapping her teeth as the raccoon did the same.

Screeeeow!

Patches exploded toward the raccoon, catching it off guard. The raccoon, which had been perched on the well, swiveled to face the incoming attack. It tried to bite Patches, but was quickly taken down by the pub cat, who landed on top of it just as Cornbread rushed forward.

Cornbread managed to clamp down onto the raccoon's tail. She shook her head, ignoring the rank smell of the creature, the dark energy radiating off its fur.

The raccoon scratched at Patches and bent forward to bite Cornbread, who quickly let go.

Patches jumped for the raccoon again, his form doubling in size. He landed on top of the creature and bit down onto its neck.

The raccoon tried to scratch him away, and managed to get a few good cuts in, but Patches held strong.

Good! I'll help! Cornbread bit down onto the raccoon's tail again, preventing it from using all of its body as Patches continued to bite into its neck.

Soon, the raccoon gave up the fight, dead. The fire spirit was still inside.

We did it, Patches said as he swayed back and forth, bleeding.

Just stay still. I can handle this. Cornbread approached Patches and began licking the cat, whose wounds instantly healed up. Once she was done, Cornbread turned back to the raccoon and sniffed it.

At least it is dead, Patches said, who now licked his own healed wounds in an effort to clean the dog slobber off.

What about the body?

The cat grinned at the farm dog. *I could take care of the body myself, but I know a better way to handle it.*

Yeah? What did you have in mind?

Let's wake up the fire spirit. You're going to want to see this . . .

———

Sylas was only awake for a few moments before the doomsday message appeared:

[You have 60 days until the invasion.]

This was followed by a blue box with details about his loan.

[A loan payment of 62 has been deducted from your total Mana Lumens. Your total loan balance is 17757 Mana Lumens.]

Sylas checked his base stats and had to think again as he focused on his loan payment of sixty-two MLus.

"That's based on ten percent of my daily gross, which would mean . . ." He squinted a few times as he went over the various scenarios of what Azor could have sold back at The Old Lamplighter. It had to be several casks, probably four if it was a mix of regular, strong, and flamefruit. One thing was certain: Sylas would have to brew more once he got back home. Hopefully, that would be today. Sylas knew that brewing requirements could add up quickly, and he didn't want Patches to bear the brunt of recharging his powers.

Now lying in the bed of the inn they'd stayed in, Sylas thought of Patches, the way the cat always curled up next to him. He found himself missing the cat and was ready to get back to Ember Hollow.

Once he was ready, he went downstairs to find Tilbud seated with Nelly, the two enjoying coffee over a tray of pastries. It was quite the spread, everything from lavender-colored scones to eclairs painted with pale pink fondant icing and miniature sponge cakes covered in strawberry jam with dollops of cream on top.

Sylas yawned and the archlumen smiled up at him. "You'd think that you had been up with me last night."

"Come again?"

"He didn't get any sleep, can't you tell?" Nelly asked Sylas.

"Sleep is for the wicked. Is that how the saying goes?" Tilbud winked at the two of them. "I'll be fine. As we're fond of saying at the academy, *There's a spell for that.*"

"A spell so you don't have to sleep?" Sylas asked.

"Yes, but to be used most sparingly. Well, as sparingly as you want. Anyway, good news and bad news, I'm afraid."

"Yes?"

"The good news is we get to go on a boat ride today across Lake Seraphina. The bad news is that before we do that, we'll need to visit not one, but two guilds. Nelly will at least register with hers, with the promise to pay dues later. While she's busy at her guild, you and I will get the spells we need at the Archlumenry: Mana Infusion, Mana Saturation, and Harvest Silos. In that order. Hopefully. And yes, I'm being frank about numbers here, but I've been up all night and I consider you, and you," he told Nelly, "to be friends. If I can blag it, and I do intend to do so, I would like to get each of the spells for one thousand, so I can make a profit of a thousand. Four thousand total. Nice and tidy."

"Do you know what they will cost?" Nelly asked.

"I have an idea of what they will cost, yes. And the farming spells are much more than that. But there are package deals, and I might be able to swing a bargain." Tilbud took a bite of one of the eclairs, the icing remaining on his mustache as he chewed.

"Do you know someone that works there?" Nelly asked.

"Ah, at the Archlumenry? I used to, but Andrew has since moved east to work at an academy. Good fellow, that Andrew. Alas, we will have to be on our best behaviors, Sylas. While I'll likely know the people at the front desk, a little charm will go a long way."

"Would it now?" Sylas smirked at the archlumen.

"When in doubt, and when you find yourself in an impossible situation that could use a little charm, use my Charm spell." A spark of golden mana spiraled around Tilbud's finger. It formed a semitranslucent web between the three of them and flashed away in a scatter of glitter. "We could all use a little charm, could we not?"

Sylas turned to Nelly and noticed something different about her.

There was a change in the glow about the woman, his senses suddenly heightened. She seemed warm and inviting, familiar in a way she shouldn't be, considering they were still getting to know one another. Sylas couldn't be certain, but something had also changed about her facial features as well. Nelly had always been a pretty woman, but now she seemed downright gorgeous, appealing in ways he hadn't noticed before.

"What in the—" Sylas turned to Tilbud.

The archlumen, who had looked tired and a bit manic earlier, now appeared as if he had just gotten out of a fresh shower. His clothing seemed crisper and as he spoke, his voice felt truly genuine and crisp. "Ah, it has worked. It truly is a pleasure to know both of you, truly, and I'm sorry if I wasn't clear already, my, dear, dear, lovely friends, we have all been charmed."

Sylas turned back to Nelly, who had a hungry look in her eyes now as she observed him.

"Rather strong, isn't it?" Tilbud said, interrupting their shared gaze. "Do remember that we are all charmed, so for the next hour or so, we will be charmed by each other, *and* we will be able to charm others. We must be careful! I don't use the Charm spell very often, even though I should. There are certain spells, you know, that are to be used sparingly, and while I may seem like the type to simply enjoy my life, my afterlife, and live it how I see fit, I do take the maxims of the Archlumenry quite seriously. Sylas, you are a very handsome man. Nelly, you are an absolute goddess. Sorry, perhaps it is best we get on our way, use our, ahem, *charming* personalities accordingly." He glanced down at the pastries. "Even the delicacies are charming here. Such a lovely place, no? I do wish we could stay another night, but business is business."

Tilbud wiped his mustache and stood. Sylas and Nelly exchanged glances and he looked away.

Seeing her was too much.

Sylas didn't want to feel attracted to the woman, especially since he was planning to help her find her husband, and because she had a shop directly next to his pub.

Like a horse with blinders on, Sylas kept his head down as Tilbud led Nelly and him to the Merchant Guild, which was set in a towerlike building covered in well-manicured vines.

"I believe this will be goodbye for now," Tilbud said as he turned to Nelly, the man's gaze shaky.

"Do what?" she asked.

"The guild will activate your portal, and you'll be able to travel cheaply back to Ember Hollow."

"But I haven't paid my dues."

"Different guilds work differently. And with how charming you are at the moment, I'm certain a polite request will go a long way. Good luck to you, dear Nelly. And do not worry, love, before we leave, I'll check to make sure you made it back to Ember Hollow safely."

"Are you sure I can't come with you all?" There was now a pleading look in her eyes.

"You can. You *can* do whatever you'd like, my dear, and I'm certain Sylas and I would enjoy your company further. That said, you have a general store to get to, and we have an old friend of Sylas's to find. I also have your scarf, which I'll use to locate your husband."

"You never explained that part," she said.

"Ah, that's an easy explanation. I know a manaseer who, as you can probably guess by now, owes me a favor. You think Mana Lumens are the only thing traded in the Underworld? Think again. Favors go a long way, but if you need a deeper explanation of the Quest Contract System, perhaps another time. Now, where was I? Right, my friend. Or my acquaintance. Probably best to call her that. She will help me find the region your husband is in, and we'll need a demon hunter with tracking abilities to locate him from there. My word, Nelly, you are an absolute vision, a timeless beauty, an absolute treat. My apologies for feeling so charmed by you!" He shook his head. "Right. Right! Focus, Tilbud. The Charm spell is stronger than it was last time. Ah, yes! We'll be back to Ember Hollow tonight, I believe. That is the plan, is it not? Go to Geist, find Sylas's friend, activate the portal, and be back at the pub for a night of libations."

"That's right," Sylas said, trying not to stare deeply into Nelly's eyes.

Tilbud clapped his hands together. "I'm sure it will be solved soon, and by solved, I mean we will do everything we can to reunite Nelly and her husband, handle the invasion message, get the farm up and running, and live happily ever after. Anyhow, I'm slowly falling in love with you, Nelly, you charming devil. Sylas, I am resisting my urges for you as well, and will do my best to remain professional. It's best we move on and forget I ever cast this spell. Goodbye for now, dear Nelly."

Tilbud turned and Sylas did the same. It was only after they were several blocks away that Sylas realized he hadn't said goodbye to Nelly.

"I should go back—"

"No, no, Sylas, it is best we move on. We'll check to make sure she made it home later. That said, if you ever need to Charm someone, I do charge to have access to this spell. I can't teach it to you, but you can pay to use it."

Sylas considered this for a moment, his thoughts settling on Mira. He shook his head. "It's best we just keep moving."

They reached the Archlumenry, which was constructed from shimmering stone that seemed to absorb and refract the light around it, including the dark golden glow from the Celestial Plains above. They entered through a pair of towering oak doors and were greeted by a man and woman seated on stools that were three times as high as a stool should normally be. The pair shared a table, which they peered over as they looked down at Sylas and Tilbud.

"Morning," Tilbud said as he took off his tiny hat. "Archlumen Octavian Tilbud, A-Rank Sovereign of Arcane Mysteries and Paramount Luminary of the School of Echelons and Enchantments, my good sir, my good lady, here for, oh, what was it? Ah, yes, a trio of spells for a dear and especially near farmer-to-be. Him, Sylas Runewulf. Ah, I just remembered we need to visit the Farm and Field Guild as well to activate the class. How could I forget?" He laughed in a jovial way. "You know how it goes being an archlumen with the weight of the Underworld on your shoulders."

"Oh, no, not you," the man seated on the stool groaned.

"Is that?" The archlumen squinted up at him. "Meldon? My dearest Meldon! How are you, old chap? I hardly recognized you seated on such a pristine wooden stool wearing such flowing golden robes. Is that angelwood? I do believe that's angelwood. Has anyone ever told you that you look like the Celestial Plains themselves? Surely you mustn't have much longer in the Underworld with such a handsome and fantastic demeanor as that. And who is this lovely lady?"

"Get on with it, Tilbud," the man said.

"Yes, on with it, right. How is your wife, Meldon? Last I heard she was doing fantastic. You adopted a child, no?"

"A . . . a boy, yes."

"Wonderful. And how is he?"

The man tensed up and then relaxed. "Actually, Robert is not doing so badly. It was quite the shock coming here to the Underworld, but Sarah and I have been able to raise him right—he will always be a child, as you know—and he'll be an archlumen someday. We're using the Archlumenry discount to pay for his class upgrade. I'm quite proud of him, really." Meldon nodded to the woman next to him. "This is Andrea. She's new."

"Hi," she said, the silver-haired woman said, her eyes transfixed on Tilbud.

He bowed deeply at the woman as if she were royalty. "My lady. I am so very grateful to meet a silver vixen such as yourself. I do not want to take any more of your time than I have to, so I'll cut right to the chase: I am in search of three spells for a person who recently classed as a farmer. That person would be my dear friend, Sylas." Tilbud gestured to Sylas. "He's not normally this quiet, but don't mind that. The spells we seek are Mana Infusion, Mana Saturation, and Harvest Silos. My budget is three thousand MLus, and because I know this will likely fall under the asking price, I can read up on learning the spells myself rather than having the two of you wonderful archlumens doing it for me."

Meldon blinked as if he were doing the math in his head. "Three thousand MLus?"

"That is correct, yes. Would it be possible, from one humble archlumen to another?"

The archlumen exchanged glances with his counterpart. "I believe we can make that work, Tilbud. But before we can give them to you, he will actually need to have the class activated."

"Right, I do have the form from our dear lumengineer. We will just need to take it over to the Farm and Field Guild. We will return on the hour, my dear Meldon, my dear Andrea, and we both look forward to seeing the two of you at that time. Come, Sylas."

———

The people at the Farm and Field Guild were equally charmed by Tilbud and Sylas. Soon, after checking to make sure Nelly had indeed portaled back to Ember Hollow, they were back at the Archlumenry with the approvals they needed, where they were greeted by Meldon, who was now down from his stool and holding a small binder of papers.

"Good," Tilbud said. "I will study these pages tonight and I should be ready to transfer the power tomorrow. Sylas, the payment."

Sylas was about to ask how to transfer the MLus to Meldon when a prompt appeared.

[Transfer 3000 Mana Lumens from your MLR Bank loan to the Archlumenry? Y/N?]

He selected yes.

[Transfer 1000 Mana Lumens from your MLR Bank loan to Archlumen Octavian Tilbud? Y/N?]

Sylas selected yes again.

"Great. In that case, we have a boat to catch. Meldon," Tilbud tipped his hat at the man, "give my regards to Andrea as well, wherever she may be."

"I'm here," the woman said as she peeked out from the back room. "Good luck on your farm, Sylas."

Still in a daze, the two left and headed toward the top of a hill, away from the water. Sylas was just about to say something to Tilbud when he pointed at the skyway tram above them. Sylas had noticed them before but had been so enamored by the sheer beauty of Battersea that he hadn't paid much attention to them.

"It will be much easier to take that to the shorelines. It shouldn't cost much either. There might even be a package deal that will come with boat access across the lake to Geist."

"Geist is on the other side of the lake?"

"Yes and no. Yes, it is geographically there, but not directly across from Battersea. We will still need to do some flying once we arrive. But we're almost there, and the Charm spell is wearing off, thank the heavens. I'm sorry if I said anything that made you uncomfortable. I will have to apologize to Nelly later. What is your friend's name again? I meet too many people, you know. It makes remembering them all difficult."

"Quinlan Ashdown."

"A grand name, really. Do you know his class?"

"He's classed as an adventurer. I'm looking for both Quinlan and his brother, Kael."

"Was he possessed by a demon like Nelly's husband?"

"Not to my knowledge. She just said his whereabouts were unknown."

"Really? It sounds as if Catia isn't so good at her job. Any lumengineer worth their weight in MLus would never give an answer like that. There may be a case in which I am forced to visit the Society again to check in with her via her superiors, but I'm also not a meddler. So I won't. But I want to. I want to for you, Sylas."

"Thanks."

Tilbud shook his head. "Damn this Charm spell. I thought its effects had worn off, but here we are, or rather, here I am, charmed again." He shook his head. "It can do that, coming in waves like that. But we should be good in the next thirty minutes. I hope. Anyhoo. Let's get to the sky, get to the water, and get to the sky again."

The ride in the tram was shaky, but Sylas wasn't too scared because he could fly if he wanted. The only reason they'd traveled this way was to conserve Mana Lumens, something that Tilbud encouraged. "The more we have, the easier this all becomes. Besides, Sylas," he told him as they approached the docks, "you have a world to save."

"Come again?" Sylas asked, his statement drawing him away from the golden clouds above and grounding him firmly in the Underworld.

"To my knowledge, you are the only one getting this message. When we get closer to this doomsday event, perhaps we will be able to loop in more people and build a proper coalition. But likely not. The Underworld doesn't work that way. We don't have governments or kingdoms like our world did. Just townships and guilds. Wouldn't you know, people get along surprisingly well without a national identity and a need for religion. We truly are all stuck in it together, for better or worse. Anyway, my dear Sylas, enough babble from me, let's find a boat!"

CHAPTER EIGHT

A ONE-HANDED ADVENTURER

The wind was strong, easily able to push the sailboat toward the other side of Lake Seraphina. The lake was filled with other sailboats of varying size with colorful masts, which added a touch of the divine when coupled with the gold light shining down from the Celestial Plains.

"Tea?" a waitress asked as she came by them with a cart.

This was another thing Sylas hadn't expected. The sailboat was much larger in person. Sylas and Tilbud were seated below deck near large portholes looking out on the lake. The two had already been up top, where they were able to take in the sights.

Sylas hoped to go up again, but first, he had a question.

"I've been thinking about something," he said to Tilbud as he took a small cup of tea from the woman. "Thank you."

"My pleasure," she told him before pouring up a cup for Tilbud and moving on.

Tilbud blew onto the hot water, puckered his lips, and took a sip. "Yes?"

"So Azor already halfway runs the pub. If I'm gone, like I was last night, I can't brew. Is it possible for a contracted spirit to take a class? Could she become a brewer like me?"

"Could Azor class as a brewer?" Tilbud set his teacup down on the table, next to the documents from the Archlumenry he planned to review. "I don't see why not. Actually, yes, yes, I believe that she would be able to. This has happened between bonded spirits and other classes, you know, namely merchants. But you'd have to appeal to the Ale Alliance. They would approve it—likely, hopefully—and then Azor would be able to help you out around the pub as you work on your, ahem, green thumb. Although you would have to figure out how this actually worked in terms of the cost of brewing and sales of said brews from the bonded spirit. The guild would know."

"So I wouldn't need to go to Catia?"

"No, the Ale Alliance would use their lumengineer. And really, if we're being honest, it will be easier that way. You could go to Catia, but then it would create more expenses for you."

"I just need to pass inspection to officially join the Ale Alliance."

"And when would that be?"

"Tombsday."

"And you failed inspection last time because . . . ? Right," Tilbud said after he saw the way Sylas looked at him, "the pub was overrun with spiders. What a dreadful day that was!"

"We'll pass the inspection this time."

"I agree. In fact, I'm certain of it. If not, then we will appeal through a barrister I know. See? Do you see it now?"

"See what, exactly?"

"The reason for paying me what you paid me to learn to fly. I've since become your best friend here, well, perhaps aside from Mira, and I've introduced you to a world of contacts. Plus, I have helped make your pub the most happening spot this side of Battersea. Or that side, because we are on the *other* side now. You get what I'm saying."

"Thanks, Tilbud," Sylas said with a chuckle.

"It is a duty and an honor. Now, if you don't mind, some quiet, please. I need to review these documents so I know exactly how to give you the powers to become a farmer."

Sylas looked at the stairs that headed above deck. "I'll head out then for some fresh air."

"It is certainly that."

———

They arrived in a port city known as Everscene, one that was much smaller than Battersea and built around a long strip of docks. As soon as they were off the sailboat, Tilbud led Sylas to the portal, which they quickly activated.

"It's only one hundred MLus to portal here," the archlumen explained. "And you might think of this as a work around *not* to pay the fee to get to Battersea, but do note you'd either have to take a boat or fly over the lake, which will cost you four hundred MLus, give or take. At least if you go first class like we just did. Just something to be aware of. Next, we'll fly to Wraithwick."

"I believe Mira mentioned that before."

"It's not far from here, on the way to Geist. Wraithwick is a city that has grown due to its access to this port. But, if we're over here, it's best to activate any and all places possible. That will make traveling easier in the future. Right, follow me."

The two took flight, Sylas trailing behind the archlumen, who always moved swiftly through the air. They later landed in Wraithwick, where the roofs were all red and the homes made of a light gray stone. The farms beyond mostly had livestock, Sylas seeing an assortment of cows, pigs, goats, and sheep.

After activating the portal, they continued on.

Sylas and Tilbud passed over a dense forest of trees with blackened leaves that made it look as if they were flying over a bed of coal.

"It's a wonderful type of wood, you know," Tilbud called to him over the wind. "If you ever have the chance to own something made of Geistian wood, do so. It's sturdy, beautiful when polished, and it will last a lifetime. Ha!"

They later touched down in Geist, and the town was much larger than Sylas expected considering how far out they were. It was practically the size of Cinderpeak and was surrounded by the same black trees they had been flying over for some time now.

"Now, to find this Quinlan, fellow," Tilbud said after he smoothed the ruffles out on his shirt. "Perhaps we start at the town square. Are there any features I should be looking for, anything that will set this man apart?"

"Now that you mention it, there is one thing. His hand."

"His hand?"

Sylas nodded. "Quinlan is missing his left hand. Lost it in a battle. Those kinds of injuries transfer over, right?"

"They most certainly do. A one-handed adventurer. Should be easy enough!"

Geist's town square was bustling with activity, the citizens out in force as they perused a market that looked to have been hastily constructed at one point in the town's history and never dismantled. The market was a permanent fixture now, where some of the stalls had morphed into robust structures made of wood while others remained makeshift, as if they could be taken down at any moment. Canopies in a kaleidoscope of colors stretched above the stalls, reminding Sylas of the sailboats he'd seen out on the lake. The pathway between the stalls had been paved, allowing the Sylas and Tilbud to follow a trail through the market as they asked people if anyone knew a man named Quinlan.

"Quinlan the adventurer?" an older man who ran an armor shop asked. "One-handed fellow? Yeah, I know the bloody fool. He still owes me for some leather faulds I made him two weeks back."

"He has a home here, then?" Sylas asked.

"Pfft. He has a home, all right. Quinlan *lives* in one of the inns, and I'm sure he owes the proprietor enough MLus to buy himself a ticket to the Celestial Plains. If he wasn't so damn useful at times—"

"What do you mean?"

The merchant gestured around. "Look where we are. This close to the Hexveil, you need someone willing to risk it all to save the town whenever a demon decides to come around. And they do come around, bloody demons."

Sylas smirked. "That sounds like Quinlan to me."

In all the time Sylas had known the man, Quinlan had been in debt, yet never in debt enough to get himself in trouble. Along with Raelis, Quinlan was one of the bravest men Sylas knew. Kael, Quinlan's brother, was also brave, but he was quiet, antisocial, and monk-like in his behavior.

"The name of the inn?" Tilbud asked, cutting off the merchant, who had continued to rant about Quinlan.

"No name, but you can't miss it. Just outside the square, looks like a building that should be in Wraithwick. You know the type. Red roof, gray stone. And if you visit Quinlan, tell him Vistian is still awaiting his payment! Don't be surprised if he's hungover."

––––––

"May I help you?" A young woman with a scar running across her throat asked. It was jarring to see someone for the first time and know exactly how they died. At least Sylas felt this way upon initially seeing the woman that ran the inn. He then realized that if this were the case, he would have puncture wounds all over his body from his final battle against the Shadowthorne Empire.

This meant that the woman's scar was from before, that she had *survived* having her throat slit.

Sylas gathered his wits. "We're looking for Quinlan."

"Not again. Bloody hell."

"My dear," Tilbud said, taking over. "We're not here for any debts owed, nor have we been sent by someone, perhaps Vistian, the man who runs the armor shop, to send Quinlan to the Hexveil. Nothing like that, no! Quinlan is an old friend." Tilbud gestured to Sylas. "A dear old friend from *back home*."

"I see," she said, her demeanor changing. "In that case, Quinlan is asleep upstairs, first room on the left. If you do bring him with you, wherever you're going, make sure he settles his bill one way or another."

Tilbud and Sylas exchanged glances. Rather than say anything, Sylas turned to the stairs and climbed to the top.

"Your friend sure has a reputation," the archlumen said, "but so do I, so I will refrain from judgment."

Sylas knocked on the door on the left, and once there was no response, he knocked again.

"Quinlan. It's me, Sylas. Open up, or I'm taking this door down."

Scrambling on the other side of the door followed.

Soon, the door swung open, Quinlan wide-eyed, his hair a mess. "Sylas?" he asked, the color draining from his face.

"Quinlan!"

He came forward and hugged Sylas, beating the stub of his hand across Sylas's upper back. "Bloody Sylas, I can't believe it! No, my god, man. How did you, mate? Of course, that makes sense, a lumengineer tracked me down, but why? No, not why, I know why, of course. Of bloody course."

Quinlan, who wore a set of robes that were barely concealing his lower half, squeezed Sylas even tighter. The ragged-looking man smelled of musk and alcohol, with an undertone of body odor that Sylas had grown used to in the trenches with his men. Quinlan, who was a head taller than Sylas, finally let go and stepped back. He nodded to Tilbud. "Who's he?"

"Archlumen Octavian Tilbud. Please, if we must have this conversation here, tighten your robes, good man! You're swinging like a donkey's tail and it's unbecoming."

"Right," Quinlan said as he did just that. He grinned at Sylas, his teeth a shiny white behind a scruffy beard. "I'm in utter shock, mate. Sorry."

"I figured you would be. I'm the same."

"You don't look it. You look put together, especially for a newcomer." Quinlan scratched his belly. "Took me a good year to get used to being dead. But it's not so bad, really. Anyway, I guess I should put some clothes on and join you downstairs. Tell Priscilla—you saw her, right? Gal with the scar across her throat?"

"We saw her."

"Aye. One of ours did that to her, not our unit, but an Aurumite. Gold Guard, the bloody mercenary bastards. Anyway. Tell Priscilla that we would like lunch, to put it on my tab. It should take me a moment to get ready."

"I will do just that," Sylas said. "See you in a few."

Quinlan shut the door behind him and let out a burp on the other side.

"Interesting fellow," Tilbud said.

"He's not as bad as he seems. Quinlan is one of the most loyal men that I've ever served alongside. Bravest too," Sylas said as they headed down the stairs. "He and his brother, Kael, are quite the pair. But they do both have their, um, idiosyncrasies."

"Sent you away that quickly, did he?" Priscilla asked once they were downstairs.

"Quinlan would like us to stay for lunch. Please, whatever you have available, and I'll pay for it," Sylas said.

"Fine by me." The woman pointed at a round table near a large window. "That seat will do. He likes to sit there and look out at the streets."

Sylas and Tilbud sat. Soon, Quinlan came down, the adventurer in thick armor as if he were preparing to join a battle. He did a spin in front of the table, his club, which had protrusions jutting out of its tip, on his shoulder. "I double-classed, you know."

"Did you, now?" Sylas asked.

"Adventurer and demon hunter. It wasn't cheap either. You?"

"Brewer."

Tilbud looked like he was about to say something but didn't as Quinlan sat and placed his club next to him.

"A brewer, huh? I can't imagine you slinging ale," Quinlan said.

"I grew up in a pub, remember? I double-classed as a farmer."

"A farmer? Ha! Now hold on. Did you say you grew up in a pub?" Quinlan peered off into the distance, like he was trying to catch a memory. "Honestly, I can't remember. But that's not saying much. I can barely remember anyone's backgrounds. Or they've all blurred together. I just remember the things I'd like to forget."

"Don't we all."

"You seem good though, Sylas, happy. There's a lot to like about the Underworld. I have my complaints, of course, but no one really cares to hear them aside from Priscilla."

Sylas looked over to the woman behind the bar, who was currently moving in and out of the kitchen preparing food. "It's been nice so far."

"A brewer, a bloody brewer. I bet you get a lot of MLus doing that, not like a damned adventurer. I had to double-class just to get my cut, and so I could be notified when hunts are available. That has helped some, but it's never enough to really get things going and have some semblance of a social life."

"Is that what you have here?"

"In Geist? More or less. It's quaint and I seem to stay out of trouble unlike my time in Battersea."

"I hear you there," Tilbud said. "The big city was a weight on my heart and my wallet."

"Same, mate. Now I'm living the bucolic life if there ever was one. Doing hunts and clearing out new territories. You know the life."

"What's that?" Sylas asked Quinlan.

"What's what?"

"Clearing out new territories. Are there new territories in the Underworld?"

"Ah, that," Tilbud said as he took over the explanation using Quill. He drew an illuminated circle in the air. "As you know, we are surrounded by the Chasm with the Celestial Plains above. For the Underworld to gain more territory, we must push back against the Chasm. When the Underworld was created, the Chasm was much closer to Battersea."

The magic circle decreased in size.

"Then, new townships and villages were settled, but they can't just point at an area of the map and move there. Like a terrible bramble, the Chasm must be beaten back."

"What about the Hexveil?" Sylas asked.

"The protective barrier remains when this happens, it just moves backward. This unleashes a load of monsters that adventurers, demon hunters, and others are able to handle. Consider it something like a scheduled slaughter. This is what I believe you are referring to, yes?"

"That's right," Quinlan said as soup came. He winked at Priscilla. "Thanks, love."

She rolled her eyes playfully and moved on.

Sylas leaned forward. "How long have you been a resident here?"

"Me? Heh. Too long. A month or three? Don't look at me like that. What I don't pay in rent I pay in other ways. Oi, I'm serious. I run people out if they're not supposed to be here. I do the fixing, and if someone doesn't pay their tab, they can expect a visit from me."

"A visit from a man who hasn't paid his tab," Tilbud chuckled to himself. "No judgment, I assure you. It's actually a rather brilliant arrangement."

"See?" Quinlan told Sylas.

Sylas had been Quinlan's commanding officer so he was used to the ways that the man would work things out. While troublesome at times, Quinlan was loyal to a fault, and the way he had died proved that. The man's death came as the result of a suicide mission, one in which he purposefully acted as bait so the flank Sylas was commanding could flee.

Quinlan had sacrificed himself to save others.

"What about Kael?" Sylas asked later, after they had started on their soups. "I came looking for him as well. And Raelis, but I know what happened to him already."

"You have news about Raelis?"

"Not really. Only that he is in the Chasm doing a Hollowed Pursuit."

"Ah, that. I wondered if he was still there. I saw him, you know, back in Battersea before he left. Always was a patriot, that one. But that's what made him such a good guy as well. As for my younger brother, Kael is at a monastery in the mountains outside of Wraithwick. You know how he was, always praying. Well, he arrived here, found out those prayers didn't matter, found me, and then moved on so he can become a manaseer."

"He can't buy the manaseer class?"

"No one can," Tilbud told Sylas. "It's a class retained through meditation and strict practice with mana cultivation."

Sylas was reminded of Nuno the manaseer, how the world had shifted all around him.

Quinlan continued: "So that's where Kael is, doing some retreat that finishes in two months or so."

"How many days exactly?"

"Why?"

"Just tell me," Sylas said.

"Well, I set myself a quest contract to meet with him when he finishes. Fifty-eight days from now. Why?"

"So I have been getting this message . . ." As their meal came, which consisted of roasted chicken thighs and twice baked potatoes, Sylas detailed the countdown he had been receiving every morning.

"Sixty days until the invasion then," Quinlan said. "And Kael gets out two days before it's all set to go down. Can't be a bloody coincidence, can't be. Kael can still fight, you know. He was an adventurer as well. A better one than me. I get easily distracted, you know."

"We all do."

"Sure, but not like me. I'll just wander off, and poof, it will have been a week and I've lost out on a ton of opportunities. But I still take care of my responsibilities. Opportunities come and go, but responsibilities don't. Speaking of opportunities, there are plenty here, you know, this close to the Hexveil. That's one reason I like the area. I'm glad you came looking for me, though. I always wondered what you were up to. I didn't know when you'd come here either."

"I don't think anyone does, Quinlan."

"I had been meaning to head back to Battersea to view the Book of Shadows, but that's not cheap, I don't like people, Battersea gives me the willies, and I sort of didn't want to know either if you were dead or not. I guess that doesn't make sense. What I'm saying is I didn't want you and Raelis to be here anytime soon. But here you are, and he's there in the Chasm."

"He is. Is there a way we would be able to get in touch with him?" Sylas asked Tilbud, who was working on a chicken thigh.

The archlumen finished his bite, wiped his mouth with his napkin, and nodded. "You could always go to the Chasm. I have been before, you know, but it is dangerous, and there are certain permissions you would need to get before you did it. That, or do things . . . a different way." Tilbud and Quinlan exchanged knowing glances.

"My father is there too," Sylas told them.

"I wish they let people in for that reason. If you have someone that you'd like to find from the Underworld or the Celestial Plains, it is possible. Just difficult and bureaucratic if it's done through proper channels. If, however, they were born into the Chasm or went there after appearing here, like what could happen to Nelly's husband, then that changes things considerably."

"Who is Nelly?"

"The woman that lives next to me," Sylas told Quinlan. "A newcomer. She runs a general store."

"You fancy her?"

"No, and she's looking for her husband, even if I did."

"What happened to him?"

"Possession upon arrival," Tilbud told Quinlan. "They died at the same time."

"Terrible thing, that. But luckily, heh, I took on a subclass as a demon hunter, a tracker."

"I was hoping to hear that," Tilbud said. "Truly, I was. I have Nelly's scarf and I will use it to find her husband through a manaseer I know."

"How will her scarf help you find him?"

"That, I cannot explain, Sylas, but I can tell you it is entirely possible to locate someone this way. I've seen it done before. Something about the essence of remorse. You'd have to ask a manaseer."

"And knowing their lot," Quinlan added, "they wouldn't tell you. But this makes it all easy. If you can get the details for me, I can take them from there."

Tilbud. "Good, very good. We should probably loop Tiberius in regardless, depending on the evil spirit's class, but this is wonderful news."

"When are you going back to Ember Hollow?" Quinlan asked Sylas.

"Today. I have a guild inspection I have to get ready for."

"When's that?"

"Tombsday."

"Then I'll be there Tombsday afternoon. How big is Ember Hollow? How many pubs we talking there?"

"Only one, and it is much smaller than Geist. My pub is called The Old Lamplighter. You can't miss it. There will be a light on outside come dark."

"Got it. I wish there was such a thing as night here, but I'll take what I can get. I'll be there Tombsday, and we'll see about Nelly's husband. It feels good, really, to get the old team back together. Or at least the two of us. But Kael will be there for whatever comes of this invasion. And you know I will. Maybe we'll visit the Chasm too and find Raelis," he said as baked potatoes and grilled meat came. Quinlan smiled up at the woman. "Thank you, Priscilla."

CHAPTER NINE

THE FALLOWEST FARM
IN THE SEEDLANDS

Sylas finished brewing eight casks, fully replenishing his stock after a slow night. He would need to visit Douro the following day to grab some flamefruit to make more of his special brew, and he also had a delivery scheduled from Malcolm, the grain supplier from Cinderpeak, which would hopefully put him right where he needed to be for inspection.

He had to pass this time, especially now knowing that passing would enable him to give Azor access to the brewer class. This would allow him to work more with the farm, which Sylas still felt would be worth his while once he got everything up and running.

Cornbread, who had followed Sylas up to his bedroom, looked up at him and whined.

"What is it, girl?"

Cornbread ran to the window and looked out. She barked.

"You want to go outside?"

She whined some more and Patches entered. The cat, who had seemed averse to the dog before, wasn't bothered by her whining now. He circled around Sylas, moving in and out from between his legs as the fire spirit appeared.

"I really wish Nelly would keep her at night," Azor said. "But she says it's not a good idea to get too close now that it's clear Cornbread is a farm dog."

"Yeah, she is," Sylas said as he petted the dog. "And that's probably for the best. You want to go to the farm tonight, girl? How does that sound?"

Cornbread's tail beat back and forth.

"Tonight?" Azor asked. "But it's late."

"I'm going to have to go back and forth late at night sometimes. I'll be fine.

I'll bring my mace. And—" Patches scratched at Sylas's pant leg. "Who is going to protect this place if both of you come with me?"

"I'll stay. I can keep an eye on everything."

"I wanted to talk to you about that." Sylas had yet to mention to Azor that he hoped she would class as a brewer so she could help him when he was out. He didn't think she'd mind, yet he was surprised to see just how excited she was once he made the offer.

"You really would put that much faith in me?" Little fiery tears appeared at the corners of her eyes. They were blue and stood out against the red-hot nature of her face.

"Of course I would, Azor. Having you around is great. I know I don't say it enough, but you have made this transition to the Underworld so much better."

"I do what I can," she said. Patches approached her, looked up at the fire spirit, and mewed. "You just don't know how it was on the other side."

"About that." The appreciative grin on Sylas's face faded. "We might need to go there at some point."

"To the Chasm? Why would we do that? You aren't trying to do a Hallowed Pursuit are you?"

"No, nothing like that. As crazy as it sounds, meeting Quinlan today has reminded me why I need to find Raelis. With him, Quinlan, and Quinlan's brother, Kael, the four of us should be able to do something if and when this invasion starts, depending on the scale. That is one of the problems here. I don't know the scale. If we're talking about an invasion of Ember Hollow, that would be something we could easily see to given time. If it's larger than that, there are other options. Perhaps. I don't know. The fact that we don't have kingdoms or centralized leadership makes the Underworld both appealing and challenging."

"But you'll figure it out."

"I intend to, yes, and something is telling me I will need them to do so. My father is over there as well, in the Chasm. I'd like to think that Raelis is with him somehow, but that would be too convenient. If I could reach him, that would be a good thing. My mother is in the Celestial Plains, and perhaps my father could get word to her. Perhaps she would be interested in doing something, especially if it affects all of us. I don't know. I don't know, and it's late. I think I'm going to go to the farm." He stood.

"Sylas?"

"Yes?"

"You take on too much."

"Do you mean the farm?"

"The farm, the pub, the end of the Underworld."

"We don't know if that's what is about to happen here, but I want to be ready regardless. And we'll know more soon, once Nuno comes. That's another reason someone needs to stay here, in case he appears."

"I want to help on the farm too."

"You do more than enough here, Azor. And before the farm needs help, I still need to figure out what to plant. That is sort of an issue. But I'll visit the neighbors tomorrow and poke around. I get this feeling that they're withholding something. I can't quite put my finger on it. Maybe it was just the vibe that Edgar was giving off."

"I guess I'll be here tomorrow then. Will you still want breakfast?"

"You don't need to cook breakfast for me."

"Sylas, stop telling me that. I like cooking breakfast. Besides, Mira said that she would be by in the morning."

"She did?" Sylas had yet to hear from Mira that day. He had hoped she'd stop by the pub that evening, but she never did.

"Maybe I'll send her to the farm with breakfast. Or, better, maybe we'll both go."

"In the morning?" Sylas scooped Patches up into his arms and turned back to the fire spirit.

"That works for me."

He looked down into the cat's eyes. "Do you think he'll follow me or should I carry him?"

"Patches is pretty smart. He'll follow you."

———

I think we're going to the farm! Cornbread told Patches. The cat trailed behind Sylas and the farm dog, keeping some distance. A system message had just flashed before him, one he didn't quite understand.

Mana Lumens: 2215/2415

Even so, Patches felt strong, and he could tell that his power was growing. Perhaps the dog being around was helping because people seemed to really like her. Patches couldn't quite understand why. The dog drooled, she was loud, and she was clumsy, but humans seemed to adore that.

Are you coming or not? Cornbread asked.

Someone has to be on the lookout.

I'll be on the lookout at the farm. Cornbread barked excitedly. The big man said something to her in a calming voice. *I really missed him, you know. Did you miss him?*

I suppose . . .

Come on, you missed him!

"Shhhhh . . ." The big man made the noise again, a finger pressed to his lips.

He wants you to be quiet.

But I'm so excited!

They reached the portal and the big man scooped Patches up yet again. Patches didn't like being held, but he also didn't *not* like being held. The Guardian of the Tavernly Realm was supposed to be a warrior, but it did feel nice when the big man scratched him, and he was warm at night.

With this in mind, he didn't struggle as the three portaled away and appeared somewhere entirely new.

Patches immediately got a sense of where they were.

He was certain they were somewhere near the forest, but there were a host of other smells here, from fresh soil to plants similar to the ones that the fire spirit liked to cook.

Home! Cornbread took off running.

Patches, who had been set on the ground, watched her go. The dog was fast, and at full speed, Patches was fairly certain she would be able to beat him in a sprint. But Cornbread couldn't climb, she definitely didn't have claws, and she was far from agile.

The big man said something to Patches. He looked up at him and mewed back. *I don't know why you brought this dog into our life, but she's not so bad. I am worried about the pub . . .*

Patches stopped walking.

The big man turned back to him.

Are we staying here for the night?

The big man said something that sounded positive, his tone calm as always. Patches knew that he was also a warrior, and the two were similar in that regard. Patches had seen what he could do in the battle against the spiders and it was impressive. It was also why he liked him so much. Warriors were brethren regardless of their species.

The big man picked Patches up again and hugged the cat. He carried Patches to a home on a hill, one surrounded by dead fields. The dog barked at the front door and did little circles.

Home!

The big man opened the door and the dog spilled inside. She checked the two rooms and quickly returned.

Home!

Patches wasn't impressed. *This is the Farmly Realm?*

Sure! I'll show you around. Come on.

I'm good.

Come on, Cat. This is exciting.

I need to take care of something first, Patches told Cornbread as the big man set him down.

After a yawn of exhaustion that made Patches feel for him—the big man really needed some rest—he got onto the bed and placed his hands behind his head. The big man seemed like he was about to fall asleep, but he ended up moving the bed instead so that it looked out the window.

Soon, he was snoring and Patches could go to work.

What are you doing? Cornbread asked as Patches sat on his chest, radiating mana.

The big man needs my help. Every night I give him some of my power so he can brew and make the Tavernly Realm better than it was the day before.

You do that every night? That's so kind of you!

I sure do. Watch.

Patches transferred power until he started to feel a bit weak. Now it was his turn to yawn.

Are you going to sleep?

I was planning on it, yes.

But I wanted to show you something . . .

Is it important?

It is!

I think I still have a little energy left. Patches hopped down from the bed. He joined Cornbread at the door.

I don't have my own door like you, but I learned to do this. Cornbread jumped and was able to use her paws to twist the door handle. It came open with a slight creak.

Impressive.

Come on. I'll show you around.

Patches followed behind the dog as she proudly showed him around, going from row to row of a nonexistent field.

What kind of food should be here? He later asked her.

Corn. That's what grows best. My previous owner never figured it out. I tried to tell him.

How? Did you communicate with the human?

I barked it every time he failed at growing his crops. Corn! Corn! Corn! I even brought him some, but he just cast it aside.

Patches stopped. *We have to tell the big man. He won't cast it aside.*

How? Cornbread cocked her head toward him. *I can't speak their language.*

I know you can't. Is there any corn around here? Kernels? Maybe if we just brought him some, he would get the picture. He's pretty smart.

We would have to go to the market to get kernels.

How far is that? Patches asked.

Far. I walked there before with my previous owner. If we left now we'd make it there by morning.

The pub cat considered this. *Let's give him a day or two and see if he figures it out. If he doesn't, we'll intervene.*

Sounds good to me. I have something for him as well.

You do?

My previous owner never wore the stuff, but I know where they are.

Clothing, then? The pub cat yawned. *I don't know about you, I'm ready to call it a night.*

[You have 59 days until the invasion.]
[A loan payment of 40 has been deducted from your total Mana Lumens. Your total loan balance is 17717 Mana Lumens.]

Sylas moved to his stats next to see that they had been topped off by Patches. He was sitting at just under forty-five hundred MLus due to his loan payment and the fact he'd had to make up for all he'd spent yesterday in travel, food, and brewing.

"Thanks for the MLus, buddy," he said.

The cat looked up at him and mewed. Before Sylas could say anything else, Cornbread charged into the room holding a straw hat with charms hanging from its brim. She set it on the ground and barked.

"You want me to wear the hat?"

Cornbread left. He heard scrambling in the other room. The farm dog returned with a pair of reading glasses that had tinted lenses.

"What are those?" Sylas wiped some of the slobber off. He was just about to put them on when he heard a knock at the door. Cornbread took off.

Once Sylas was up, he approached the door wearing the straw hat. He opened it to find a woman he hadn't met before. "Hi," she said as she handed him a fresh baked pie.

"What's this for? Hi, I'm Sylas Runewulf. Sorry, just woke up."

"I'm Lucille. I run the leafy greens farm down the way. I saw the light on last night and wanted to come over and introduce myself. I've heard about you, and been to your pub, actually. But just once. Edgar said you had bought the farm."

"I sure did," Sylas told her.

Cornbread burst passed him and circled around Lucille's feet. "Oh, she's so cute," the older woman said. Lucille wore overalls and a hat similar to the one Sylas had on, yet hers was green and had a flower sticking out of it. No charms either. She had a sweet grandmotherly vibe about her, and Sylas instantly liked her company.

She smiled at him again. "Anyway, I made you a fireberry pie as a farmwarming present. Happy Moonsday."

"Happy Moonsday to you," Sylas told her as he took the pie from the farmer. "And you didn't have to."

"I was going to make one anyway this morning, so I decided to make two. Tell me where you're at."

"In . . . the Underworld?"

She laughed and Cornbread barked. "I mean where you are at in the farming process. Have you visited the guild?"

"I did."

"And do you have the powers you need?"

"Not yet. The archlumen who will grant them to me has promised to do so by Wraithsday. He had to figure out how they worked himself."

"Really? You didn't just do it at the guild?"

"It's a long story, but he's a friend, and it will save me some MLus to learn it through him."

"That makes sense. Have you decided what you are going to grow?"

"I have not. I don't really know what I am even allowed to grow considering the farmland rules here."

"Yes, they can be tedious, but once you decide on a crop, you will literally reap all the rewards. So there is that to look forward to. They have a library at the guild in Battersea, and they can assist you in finding an appropriate crop. You might have to dig back to see what they have grown here previously. I suggest looking through the tax records, but be warned, that may take days. If I'm being honest with you, ever since I arrived, this farm has been fallow. The fallowest farm in the Seedlands is how some have described it. But maybe you will turn things around. Anyway, I'm at the far end, if you just head along this road until you see my name over the entrance."

"Great. I appreciate the pie."

Lucille bid farewell and Sylas shut the door. He set the pie on the table. Patches jumped up to examine it.

"I don't know if you would like pie," he told the cat.

Sylas sat there for a moment, making plans. Once he was an approved member of the Ale Alliance, he would be able to portal to Battersea for free. That would cut down on costs while he figured out what he was supposed to grow. It was Moonsday, and he wanted to have the first crop going by Fireday.

Another reason he sat there was because he was agitated. Lucille likely didn't mean anything in the way she had wished him luck. And she had brought him a pie, after all. Yet he couldn't shake this feeling that there was more to it, more to the way she had spoken to him, and how reluctant Edgar had been to reveal any information.

It wasn't like they were actively hoping he would fail. But maybe he was reading too deeply into it.

Another knock at the door drew his attention. It was prefaced by Cornbread, who stood at the door barking her head off. "You sure are a good guard dog," Sylas told her.

———

Mira heard the dog barking as she stood on the front porch, waiting for Sylas to open up. She was with Azor, who had whipped up breakfast. To say that she was surprised to see Sylas open the door wearing a straw hat with dangling charms that had seen better days was an understatement. It was truly comical, and it had her laughing as soon as the two locked eyes.

"You aren't being serious with that hat, are you?" she asked after Azor greeted Sylas.

The fire spirit rushed past him and examined the pie. "Who made this?"

"Someone gave it to me."

"That was nice!"

Mira was happy to see Sylas, especially with the argument she had gotten into with her uncle earlier that morning. She could feel the weight lifting off her shoulders just being around the handsome Aurumite.

It was time to move her shop, and she knew it. Mira had a plan for this, especially with what Nelly had revealed to her.

Only a matter of time, she had told herself earlier on her trek over to the pub. But she wasn't sure she wanted to talk to Sylas about it yet. She wasn't sure what he'd think.

"Come in," he said as he fully stepped aside. "Also, you've spent more time with the farmers than I have at the pub quizzes. Are they always nice, but slightly standoffish?"

"I hadn't thought to describe them that way, but I suppose there is an element of that. Maybe it comes with being rural."

"How was sleeping here?" Azor asked, the fire spirit zipping up next to Sylas. She was smiling, but there seemed to be a hint of sadness in her eyes. "Was it better than the pub?"

"It's different. Peaceful, and I moved the bed so there's a pretty view. You know, the way the Celestial Plains reflect down at night is something else. Makes me wish the pub had a balcony."

"A balcony?" Mira asked. "You could always make improvements."

"Maybe."

Sylas sat down at the table and looked at the plate Azor had prepared. "I feel like I've already bitten off more than I can chew, if we're being honest."

After their meal and several slices of fireberry pie, Mira joined Sylas in his attempt to meet some of the neighbors. While they did so, Azor returned to the pub with Patches, so she could start preparing for the next day's inspection.

They started at Edgar's home, but he didn't answer his door. They turned in the opposite direction and came to a farm that grew a type of berry. The farmer was out in the field, moving through them.

"This is a fireberry," Mira told Sylas. "The same thing in the pie that the woman brought you. They only grow in volcanic ash."

"Like the flamefruit?"

"Similar, yes," she said as he waved the farmer down.

A young man with broad shoulders approached. He had a flat face and his eyes were just a bit too far apart. The man was muscular, which made Mira wonder what he had done before he died.

"You are the one who bought Brom's farm," he told Sylas. "I'm Trampus."

"I sure am. I also run The Old Lamplighter in Ember Hollow."

"So I've heard. I was there a few weeks back."

"We've only been open a few weeks." Sylas raised an eyebrow at the man, as if he was trying to place where he'd seen him.

"Well, I was there."

Sylas approached one of the plants. "Fireberries."

"Indeed," Trampus told him.

"I've been experimenting with various brews. I recently made an ale out of flamefruit."

"Did you now?"

"Do you have some riper berries? I'd love to figure out something new."

Trampus scratched the back of his head. "I'm just about to saturate these ones. They'll be too bitter at the moment. But I have some from the last batch. You know what? Sure. I'll bring you some."

"I can pay you."

"Consider it a farmwarming gift. And if you do come up with something, I'd like to try it."

"Certainly."

Trampus left and Mira turned to Sylas. "An ale made with fireberries? That sounds rather odd."

"Yeah, why not? You like fireberries, right?" He grinned at her. "It's fun to try new things."

"The berries are good in a jam."

"I haven't tried it."

Mira made a mental note to make him some. She had made the jam before, and it was delicious. "Well, you have done wonders with flamefruit, so I suspect you'll do the same here."

"Speaking of which, you and me, Douro. I figured we'd head there and have lunch at a café. I need to secure some more flamefruits. It would be useful to find a supplier, but I don't know if it will always be the special ale so I'd rather just get it when I need it. Listen to me, telling you my plans out loud."

"It's fine." Mira almost told Sylas her plan of moving her shop into the building attached to Nelly's store, how her deed was transferrable now that Nelly had opened up, but she stopped just short of doing so as Trampus returned with a pail of the berries.

"Thank you," Sylas said. "I'll be sure to have something by Wraithsday, when we do a weekly feast. Please come hungry. Your meal and ales will be on me."

"I'll do just that."

"One more question, if you don't mind," he asked as Trampus was turning away. "What should I be growing? I know it sounds a bit stupid to ask a farmer that, and I'm aware of the rules governing farmlands, but clearly Brom never got the formula right."

"He never got the formula at all."

"And he was here for how long?"

"He didn't make it until his first deathday, if that's what you're asking." Trampus shook his head with disappointment. "But to your earlier question, Brom asked me the same thing, and he tried all of my suggestions."

"And they didn't work?"

"They didn't."

"Well, perhaps we start there. What *shouldn't* I grow?"

———

Sterling, the owner of the last farm on the lane, wasn't home. Yet it was clear what he grew. His fields were full of yellow, green, red, and orange peppers of varying sizes. There were a lot of them too, which gave Sylas the feeling that the man would be harvesting his crops soon. Sylas picked up a pair of peppers that had fallen onto the ground.

"He won't miss these."

"Maybe you could make a spicy ale," Mira suggested.

"Spicy ale?" Sylas considered this as they turned toward the portal. "That would be something."

"I'd try it, but I've always liked spicy foods."

"That makes sense considering where you're from."

"Yes, we always did have spicier foods than they had across the border."

"I had some of it, you know. We were stationed near a town on the border that traded frequently with your side. Their food was a mix of what you'd expect to find in my kingdom and yours."

"It's *yours* now, is it?"

"You know what I mean. The food was good. A spicy ale. Huh. What about some kind of spicy medicine? That one older lady you're always tending to might like something like that."

"Miss Barrowsly?" Mira laughed. "Please, Sylas. Anyway, this concludes our 'meet the neighbors quest' that we didn't quite set for ourselves, yet have been seeing to for the last hour."

"We should have given ourselves a quest."

"True. Back to Ember Hollow, then? Or did you want to go to Douro first?"

"Let's take the berries that Trampus gave me and the peppers to the pub, and then go to Douro."

———

"Oh, that's right," Mira told Sylas as they approached the pub. "Nelly's General Store opened."

"Easy enough name to remember, yeah?"

There was a painted sign above her store and people were actually walking in the streets of Ember Hollow. This second observation took Sylas by surprise. The village was usually empty, and to see even a few people moving about caused him to stop dead in his tracks. He had a vision of Geist and Wraithwick, how lively they were compared to Ember Hollow.

"What is it?" Mira asked.

"I've been so distracted."

"What? Sylas? Why do you look as if you've seen a ghost?"

"The invasion message, opening the pub, the spiders, now the farm. I've been so distracted by everything around me that I'm just now realizing what is actually happening here."

"Where exactly?"

"Ember Hollow. Breathing new life into it."

The hard look on Mira's face softened. "You're just *now* realizing that? It's been that way since your pub opened."

"You think?"

"I know. I live here."

"The community is starting to grow. That's what I'm saying. But with all the other things going on, it's hard to know what needs to be done. I guess I'm just appreciating it more now. And it's mostly because of you."

"Me?" She touched her chest and took a step back.

"I know I was joking when I said you were mayor of Ember Hollow, but you've been the one leading the way."

"Sylas."

"Yes?"

"I believe there is some news that will make you happy."

"You believe? Come out with it then," he said, barely able to contain his smile due to the look of both shame and excitement on her face.

"I am going to move my shop to the space next to Nelly's."

"That's wonderful!"

"I worried you'd feel crowded if I moved in so close."

"Crowded? Absolutely not. I welcome it. Ember Hollow needs a reason for people to start coming here. I'm not saying we need to start giving tours to the Hexveil, but that is always an idea."

"Tours? You joke too much."

"Just another of my many business ideas."

"Perhaps you stick to brews and whatever it is you're going to farm. Kidding, I'm sure a tour to the Hexveil would be enjoyed by someone. I don't know who exactly, but someone. As for my shop, I just can't bear having it at my home any longer. My uncle drives me mad, and while I don't mind his 'recruits,' they do have a way of distracting me and taking my attention away from my own work. So I'm packing the shop up and moving."

"Ember Hollow will have three shops now, a general store, an apothecary, and a pub. We need restaurants. We need a market. We need a smithy and—"

She stepped back. "What about the message you keep receiving? What if we do all of this work just for it all to come burning down."

"That's not going to happen."

"We don't know that."

"That's why." Sylas gulped. "You'll meet him tomorrow. A soldier, Quinlan. He's coming here. Kael, his brother, will join us later. That leaves Raelis."

"Who are these men exactly?"

"The men that I served with. The men that will help me protect the village. With your uncle's militia, we'll have a fighting chance."

"Against an unknown enemy, an invasion that we know nothing about?"

"The unknown is always an enemy, regardless of how well you know your opponents. But it's the only plan I have at the moment, at least until Nuno returns and tells us what he has learned."

"But you have no idea when that may be."

"No, I do not." Sylas looked out at the village once again. "But I'm not going to sit here and let Ember Hollow burn to the ground. Not a damn chance."

After touring Nelly's shop, which was coming along nicely, Sylas assured her that he had a tracker coming that would help them find her husband. "My mate, Quinlan. He's unorthodox, but together, likely with Tiberius and Tilbud, we'll find him, Nelly."

After a quick trip to Douro to secure the flamefruits, Sylas and Mira parted ways. He joined Azor in The Old Lamplighter, where he helped scrub down the place in preparation for the next day's Ale Alliance inspection.

"Will you sleep at the pub or at the farm tonight?" she asked.

"I'll sleep here, just in case the inspectors show up early like they did last time. Plus, I want to make sure Patches and Cornbread are around, just in case we have any late-night intruders. Hopefully, we won't. The well hasn't acted up since clearing out the spiders. Although I still don't think we should get water from it."

"I've been getting water from the well in the town center. It's not that far."

"There's probably someone we can talk to who can check ours to make sure it's fine. Can someone be poisoned here?"

"We can always try it." Azor laughed. "Sorry, morbid."

"Morbid, but funny."

The pub was quiet that night, which was exactly what Sylas hoped for. He netted nearly five hundred from the sale of about half a cask of regular ale, a cask of strong ale, and nearly a cask of the flamefruit ale. He would need to brew three casks, but to do so Sylas would also have to empty what was left of the flamefruit cask to fully renew it.

"Looks like I'm drinking these ones tonight," he said as they turned off the lantern outside.

"I'll finish up in here," Azor called to him.

Sylas and Cornbread headed down to the cellar, where he poured two pints of what remained of one of the flamefruit ales. He drank one, thought about his day, and brewed the two casks he needed to brew, a regular ale and a strong ale.

He drank the other pint and examined the fireberries yet again, running his thumb along their smooth-textured skins.

Sylas had already tasted them. The fireberries were sweet with a sourness that lingered in his mouth. They seemed like the perfect thing for a lighter ale, something that was crisp and less filling than his strong ale. They wouldn't have an orange glow to them like the flamefruit ale due to the deep red color of the berries, which bordered on purple.

Sylas closed his eyes and smelled the berries again. Cornbread came to him and he looked down at her. "I'm thinking about how this will work."

She whined.

"Can dogs eat berries? Well, just one should be fine."

He gave Cornbread the berry and she gladly took it. Something out of the corner of his eye caught his attention. Sylas glanced to the stairs to see Patches coming down, a curious look on his face.

"Glad you could join us," he told the piebald pub cat. "Just getting ready to brew something interesting here, something that will knock the socks off the inquisitors, I mean inspectors, tomorrow." Sylas finished most of the second pint. "What would be interesting . . ." An idea came to him, and he immediately set to work.

———

Patches decided *not* to take care of the big man's power levels just yet, not until he could see what Cornbread was planning for the night. He headed downstairs to find the dog sitting in front of the cat door, her body stiff with anticipation.

Are you ready? Cornbread asked.

Are we going to that other city you mentioned?

No. Cornbread got to her feet. *I don't know how to get there from here, only from the Seedlands.*

I think I could get us to the Seedlands if we cut through the forest.

I have a better idea. Cornbread approached Patches. *We can use the portal near the farm.*

The portal?

I know how to use it. I promise. You go there, make a selection, and appear somewhere else.

Patches started licking his paws. *So then we go to the farm.*

No, not just yet, but soon. Let's see if the big man stays there tomorrow.

Do you think he will?

I don't know.

What do *you know?* Patches asked, already slightly annoyed with the dog.

I know it will be easier to get to the town from the farm and back. There's something else we need to do. Cornbread quietly approached the cat door. She turned back to Patches, nodded, and jumped out.

Too loud, as always. Patches looked over to the fire spirit to see she was still resting, her flames faintly blue. Even though Cornbread wasn't there to watch, Patches quietly tiptoed to the cat door and let himself through without making a sound.

Cornbread turned to the pub cat and sniffed the air. *Do you smell that?*

What? Patches tried again.

Another raccoon. It was here and I think . . . Cornbread started sniffing at the ground. *This way!*

The farm dog kept her nose to the ground as she moved to the front of the pub. She stopped, listened, and put her nose to the ground again. She raced past the store next door. Patches paused for a moment to look at the store. He had yet to explore the place and had the urge to now.

The notion to let Cornbread continue on her own swelled within the cat. Patches didn't like being led around, especially by a dog, but he was also curious what she had smelled. Especially after he got a whiff too.

It was definitely a raccoon, but it was something else, that familiar scent Patches recognized from when he had first seen the demonic spirit. If there were more foul creatures about, that meant the Tavernly Realm was in danger, and Patches wasn't going to have any of that.

He did, however, let Cornbread go nearly a few hundred feet ahead before he decided to finally catch up to the dog.

It's here, she said once they reached the abandoned market. Patches couldn't remember a time when the market was in action, but his memory of the village was spotty at best, especially with all the time he had spent protecting his home.

I smell it now.

Exactly, Cornbread growled. *We've got to do something about it.* She looked like she was just about to run in, pushing back onto her hind legs.

Wait, let me go in first. When you hear me, you come in ready to rip them apart.

You go in first? She cocked an ear at Patches.

I am stealthy. You are bigger than me and your teeth are terrifying.

Thank you.

Patches paced back and forth. *Stay here, and make sure they don't smell you. One more thing. Don't bark when you hear me. Just come running, and be ready to use your teeth.*

Cornbread bared her teeth. *Ready.*

Patches got low to the ground.

He crawled forward and hopped up onto a fence that was missing some of its posts. From there, he jumped down into the shadows of the market and turned invisible. Each step that followed was calculated, Patches moving around leaves, discarded items, bits of wood, and detritus that had collected over the years.

The pub cat came to a shop filled with wooden furniture, Patches squeezing through some of the pieces, a sixth sense telling him the best way forward. If he sat there and thought about it, he'd make a mistake, but if he trusted his instinct, he would always find the perfect place to sift through, duck under, or lightly run across.

He heard the noises now, a low, garbled sound with a whispery overtone to it. It reminded him of human speech.

Patches hopped onto the top of one of the buildings. He crept forward, stopping just before a loose shingle. He looked down at it and shook his head. *Close,* he thought as he stepped over the loose shingle, which would have certainly rattled. *Too close.*

Patches came to a halt at the edge of the roof. He peered down over the side, his worst nightmare realized.

There were three fat raccoons here, one of which had been possessed by a demonic spirit. It seemed to be instructing the others, who stood entranced by the larger raccoon.

Still invisible, Patches slowly doubled his size. He steadied his breath as he prepared to leap down at them. His goal wasn't the raccoon possessed by the demon; his goal was the smallest of the bunch. Take that one out, and there'd be one less to fight once Cornbread came tearing through.

Patches counted off in his head. *Three . . . two . . . one!*

He jumped down from the rooftop and landed on the smallest raccoon. The other two leaped backward in surprise as Patches twisted around with his target, his big claws locked in. He yowled and then bit down onto the raccoon's throat.

The two smashed into a wooden column and crashed through a crate. Patches applied more pressure just as Cornbread came on the scene, the dog leaping once it saw the leader of the pack.

The possessed raccoon actually shrieked.

Patches would remember that later, the shock on its face as Cornbread appeared out of nowhere and attacked it with one of her most epic bites. It seemed as if Cornbread's jaw itself had enlarged, that she had been able to fully unhinge it and clamp down on the demonic raccoon in a way that would soon spell its doom.

It's yours! Cornbread said as the third raccoon took off, even though her jaw was clenched around the lead one's throat.

Patches shrank to his normal size and bolted away. As he neared the fleeing raccoon, Patches hit it with his supersonic purr, which immediately disoriented the creature. He lunged into the air and landed directly in front of the creature, where he enhanced the size of his claws.

The two stalked one another, the raccoon shaking its head, its movements now drunken, due to the cat's sonic attack.

It tried to bite Patches; he swatted at the raccoon, cutting across its snout.

The raccoon pushed back onto its hind legs to scare Patches, who responded by splitting in two.

If the raccoon was confused before, it was now beside itself as it tried to track both Patches *and* his clone. Using this to his advantage, Patches cut forward and drove his claws into the raccoon's sides. He clamped down with his jaw and applied pressure until the raccoon finally gave up the fight.

Patches dropped its dead body to the ground. He turned to the second version of himself, watching as it fizzled away.

Barking from Cornbread drew his attention.

He returned to the farm dog to find Cornbread seated, waiting for Patches next to the possessed raccoon's dead body. *We got them.*

We did.

Cornbread barked, *Hurray!*

Quiet.

Cat's like quiet, don't they?

They do.

But we make a good team, you and I. Deadly, she said, panting.

We are that.

What was that noise you made?

I forgot to tell you about that power. What about you? What was with your jaw?

That's the attack I use on the farm to hunt things. There's a lot to hunt there. Cornbread licked her lips. *What now?*

We head back. I have to make sure the big man is ready for tomorrow.

What happens tomorrow?

I don't know, but they were cleaning pretty hard today, so I think there will be visitors.

Then I'll be on my best behavior. Are you hurt or anything?

Patches turned away from Cornbread and held his head high. *I'm fine. Come on.*

CHAPTER TEN

BEYOND THE VEIL

Sylas let the information linger for just a moment as he slowly came awake.

[**You have 58 days until the invasion.**]
[**A loan payment of 48 has been deducted from your total Mana Lumens. Your total loan balance is 17669 Mana Lumens.**]

As it faded, he briefly skimmed his stats.

Name: Sylas Runewulf
Mana Lumens: 4866/4866
Class: Brewer
Secondary Class: Farmer

Sylas noted that his power wasn't growing exponentially in the same way it had before, but it was still increasing daily. Once he had the farm running, he'd get a weekly boost as well with his crops. He knew it seemed incremental now, and there was still the question of what he should grow, but he had to trust the process.

Doing so had gotten him this far.

Azor rushed into his bedroom. "Happy Tombsday."

"Happy Tombsday, indeed. I'm guessing there haven't been any knocks at the door, have there?"

"None that I've noticed. If there were, you would have heard Cornbread. They're so cute, Patches and Cornbread. I love seeing them play together."

"Yeah?" he asked the fire spirit. Her flames looked different, more yellow, like she had freshened up or something for the inspection. Her fiery hair had changed as well, matted to her head and smoothed back.

"They went out on a little adventure last night. I didn't follow them or anything, but they were trying to be all quiet about it. I know animals can communicate, but you should have seen it, Sylas."

"Through the cat door?"

"Yes, Cornbread first, who was loud compared to Patches. Patches made a point of showing Cornbread how to do it quietly even though she was already outside. So funny. And so cute. I wonder what kind of adventure they got into."

"Hopefully nothing well-related."

"Not to my knowledge. I checked that part, actually, once they were gone. I think they just went exploring. Cute, right? Just imagine those two exploring Ember Hollow and getting into trouble."

"No idea, but I know Patches can hold his own, and Cornbread knows what to do, considering her role as a guard dog on the farm. I do wonder what they're getting into, though. They didn't bring anything back, did they?"

"You mean like a dead animal? Nope, none that I saw."

"That's good. Last thing we need." Sylas placed his feet on the floor and rubbed his hands together. "Let's see to this inspection, pass this time, and prepare for Quinlan's arrival."

"Do you think he'll stay?"

"I'm assuming he'll stay at least through Thornsday."

"So he'd be here for the Wraithsday Feast?"

"Yes, which will hopefully be a celebration of finding Nelly's husband."

"Isn't Tilbud supposed to come?"

"He is. He should be here today or tomorrow to teach me the spells I need. He'll show. As to when, who knows? He's Tilbud. His middle name should be *unpredictable*."

"Where will Tilbud sleep if he stays?"

"I didn't think about that part." Sylas considered the layout of the pub. There was a guest room, but if it was already occupied, and he was staying in his room, the only other free space would be the portal room. "We would have to get bedding, but he could use the portal room. I suppose that's something to pick up in Cinderpeak later. Or Duskhaven. I wonder where it would be cheaper."

"You have to pay to portal to Duskhaven, though."

"Yes, I would need to take that into consideration." Sylas snapped his fingers. "The portal will be activated if we pass inspection, so we can just get it in Battersea later."

"Weren't you planning on staying at the farm tonight?"

"I was, but that was before I remembered that Quinlan would come. In that case, I'd need to stay here. He could get a bit rowdy."

Azor went as pale as a fire spirit can go. "Rowdy?"

"Just a bit rough and ready, that's all."

Once he was good to go, Sylas headed downstairs and did a few last-minute touch-ups. While Azor wiped the tables, he swept the floors, adjusted Iron Rose's painting, wiped down the sign outside with the poem carved on it—*When the lamp is lit, come in and sit. If it's dark, best to depart.* He then performed a final, slow inspection of the pub from top to the bottom.

Marty and Greta arrived just as Sylas was heading up from the cellar with his cask of fireberry ale. "Let's hope they like it," he said as he went to answer the door.

As she had last time, Greta instantly scrutinized him, and as he had last time, Sylas turned up the charm. "Greta, you look dashing as ever. Marty, such an honor to meet you again. As you both know, I had a little mishap the night before your last visit. Being this close to the Hexveil has its disadvantages, you know. But The Old Lamplighter is ready for your inspection, and once you finish, or if you would perhaps like to try something *before* you get started, I have a new ale."

"A new ale?" Marty asked, his interest piqued.

"We will do our inspection first, as is tradition." Greta stepped in with her clipboard and immediately started looking around. "What's this?" she asked as Cornbread approached, wagging her tail. Beyond her, Patches sat in the window, staring at the two inspectors. "You got a dog?"

"Yes, I did. This is Cornbread."

The stern look on Greta's face melted as she swooped down to pet the farm dog. "She's so adorable. I love dogs! I have five back in Battersea. Their names are Bobby, Robby, Nobby, Lobby, and Peter. Little terrors, all of them, but they're my little terrors." She leaned forward and let Cornbread lick her face.

Sylas exchanged glances with Azor, who gave him two flaming thumbs up.

"I can continue the inspection alone if you'd like," Marty told Greta.

"Please, do. I have to spend some time with Cornbread here. Yes, you are. Yes, you are so bloody cute I could eat you right up." She continued to let Cornbread lick her face, now her lips.

Patches made a disgusted face and turned in the opposite direction. Sylas was able to withhold his laugh, but only barely, and only because he made the split-second decision to move away from the woman and pour up two pints of his latest ale.

He was just finishing up when Marty emerged from the cellar. "All looks well down there. Everything looks great, actually. You really cleaned it up. I can tell how cozy this place is too. Some of the other pubs are nice, but they aren't cozy. I don't know how you've done it."

"Yes, our little incident last week was a most unfortunate event." Sylas gestured for him to take a seat at the bar.

"I just can't stop petting you! No, I can't!" Greta squealed. Cornbread was now lying on her back with Greta stroking her belly. Beyond them, Patches continued to breathe heavily, the cat annoyed at the way the dog was hamming it up.

But it worked, and that was all that mattered.

By the time Greta approached the counter, Marty was finishing the paperwork to officially register The Old Lamplighter with the Ale Alliance. "There will be the small activation sequence I'll need to see to upstairs with the portal, but you are an official member. Cheers," he said as he lifted the pint Sylas had poured him.

"Before you drink that, and please, Greta, you should try this as well, I wanted to tell you about the new ale I developed last night. You'll notice it has a purple tinge to it."

"I saw that," Greta said as she examined her pint glass. "It's pretty. Peculiar, but pretty."

"And the foam is white. Plus, there is much more of this foam than there normally is with something like rye ale. Take a sip, and you'll notice that the foam tastes like it has a hint of sweet cream to it, yet the ale itself has a unique flavor profile, light, like a summer ale, and just the right balance between sour and sweet from the foam."

Greta took a sip and blinked a few times. "That is certainly something. It's quite good, actually." She took another sip. "Amazing. And this was what kind of fruit?"

"Fireberry. I'm assuming other pub owners experiment with flavors."

"Not as often as you'd think," Marty said as he finished his first sip. "My, that is something. The sweetness of the foam is natural? It seems like you whisked sweet cream or something and added it to the top."

"I assure you, I did not. And yes, it's natural."

"You are quite the brewer," he said as he took another sip. "A clever ale, actually."

Cornbread barked in celebration.

"I can't give you any," Greta told the dog. "Sorry, but I can give you more pets, yes I can."

Marty savored another sip. "People don't experiment as much, and they really should. There is, in my opinion, a lot of staleness here in the Underworld. Someone discovers something that works, and finds that it works every time, and they stop there. Guilds are formed, but there is little innovation, and because most people tend to consider this a form of retirement even if they do have a job, it's not as serious here as it was where we're from."

"He's right, you know." Greta drank a bit more and smacked her lips. "I wouldn't describe it as stale, the Underworld, but it can be rather stationary. It's safer that way, more comfortable. Most will never make it to the Celestial Plains, and the Chasm is just beyond the veil, as they used to say. It is nice to see innovation. The Ale Alliance certainly needs some, and it will attract attention to Ember Hollow."

"You think?"

"I do, yes. There are people in Battersea who follow the Ale Alliance and its newest offerings. I write the newsletter they receive, and I will most assuredly mention this wonderful ale and the adorable pub pup you have. As for the cat, does he have a name? I remember seeing him last time and thinking he was a bit chubby."

"Yes, that's Patches," Sylas told her. "The patrons like Patches a lot. He might be seated by the window looking a bit grumpy at the moment, but he's a lap cat if there ever was one."

"That's good to hear. And the fire spirit—"

"Azor," Sylas said, keeping his tone firm but also still inviting. "She's crucial around her, and responsible for our weekly meal, the Wraithsday Feast."

Azor, who was hovering behind the two inspectors, turned to the back of Greta's head and grew purple devil horns. They disappeared and she smiled at Sylas.

"Food offerings, innovative ale, and a location that feels utterly rural, briskly bucolic, near the Hexveil yet cozy," Greta said. "This article truly writes itself. I'll pen it up soon, and it will circulate around Battersea. Don't be surprised if you start having more visitors. Is there an inn?"

"Not yet, there isn't."

Marty puffed his cheeks out. "That could be a problem. Is there a building for an inn?"

"I don't know. There is no central leadership here in Ember Hollow, and we aren't part of a county or anything."

"Which means no taxes," Marty said. "That is certainly an appeal, even if it is a bit off the beaten path."

"Yes, *a bit off the beaten path,* I will add that to my article as well." Greta finished her pint. "Sylas, I'm glad that we were able to visit The Old Lamplighter again and that you managed to impress us. Marty will activate the portal before we leave, and I do wish you the best of luck."

"We also have a weekly pub quiz, but that date seems to vary," he told Greta almost as an afterthought. "An archlumen out of Duskhaven runs it."

"An archlumen running a weekly pub quiz? Intriguing. Very intriguing, and worth mentioning in the article. Marty?"

He finished his pint. "Ready. Do you want to come up with me or stay here?"

Greta glanced down to Cornbread, who stood beside her, looking up at the thin woman. "I think I'll spend just a little more time with this absolutely adorable dog."

———

Once the pub inspectors were gone, Sylas turned to Azor. "Let's go."

"Where exactly?"

"Battersea. We can portal there now."

She seemed to sink into herself. "You really trust me to brew while you're gone?"

"You've seen me do it before."

"But I never really paid attention."

"I'll show you everything you need to know. It would just be for long trips."

"Do you think you'll be taking one of those soon?"

"No idea. But I know I'll be going somewhere with Quinlan, and as we get closer to this invasion, who knows where I'll need to go."

She nodded. "I can do it."

"Yes, you can. Now, come on." He tapped the fire tattoo that signified their bond. "I'll bring your gloves and apron."

Azor's body melted into a pool of flames that reformed, her fireweave clothing now lying on the ground. "Good," Sylas said as he packed them in one of his shoulder bags. They headed upstairs to the portal. Cornbread and Patches came rushing into the room after them, just as the portal was starting to glow.

The dog barked, and the cat circled Sylas's legs as he looked up at him with big wet eyes.

"Patches will be fine, but what about Cornbread?"

"We could ask Nelly to look after her," Azor suggested.

"We could. I'll head next door. Come on, Cornbread." Sylas scooped Patches into his arms and headed back down, the dog following them out of the pub. "Would you look at that?" Sylas stepped back to admire the paint that Anders was using for the trim on Nelly's windows. There were hints of hazelnut and chocolate. It looked perfect next to The Old Lamplighter.

"Hey, Sylas," Anders called down from a ladder.

"Is Mira in there too?"

"She is. She's setting up her studio. Or annex. She has called it both. I'm going to add a front entrance through that wall there." He pointed at one of the inner walls. "It's not load bearing or anything. She picked out some Geistian wood for it. Then, we have to do some work at the entrance, turn it into more of a cased opening rather than the door that is currently there. The general store had a lot of storage, but Nelly can store things in her inventory list too. Wasted space. Anyway, how goes it?"

"It goes. I'm off to Battersea for an hour or three. If you see a big rough-looking guy come around, and he tells you his name is Quinlan, let him know I'll be back."

"Quinlan. Rough-looking guy. Got it."

Cornbread barked.

"Come on," Sylas told the farm dog as he let himself inside the store.

It had changed even more since he had last seen the place. There were now shelves filled with various items, from food to household staples, all organized and put together in a clever way. An additional room at the back looked like it would soon have clothing, and there was a door with a translucent glass pane, the entrance to Mira's shop.

Sylas spotted Mira in her new space, the apothecary hard at work as she cut leaves off a flower.

"How did it go?" Nelly asked as she came around the counter and started to pet Cornbread.

"Well enough. We passed the inspection."

"Really? That's wonderful, Sylas."

"It sure makes doing what I'm about to do next easier. I need to portal to Battersea, and I'll be back in a couple hours. Azor is coming with me. I was wondering if you'd watch Cornbread. Don't feel obligated—"

"Of course I'll watch Cornbread." She continued petting the dog, who wagged her tail excitedly. "I got a little bed for her here and everything."

"Did you ask Mira about getting a dog?"

"I did, but I think I'd rather get a husband first. Kidding. Karn was always more of a cat person, so let's see what he thinks about Cornbread. Maybe we just become a neighbor who babysits lovely Cornbread." She crouched down to pet the dog, who began licking her hand.

"I appreciate it, Nelly. I told Anders already, but if a man named Quinlan shows up, he's the old friend of mine who is going to help find your husband tomorrow. When I'm back, and once Tilbud arrives, we'll loop Tiberius in. That should be interesting." Sylas glanced again to Mira's door. "I should probably tell her that."

"Why? Do you think she'll need to run interference?"

"She'll *definitely* need to run interference. Tiberius didn't like me at first, and he likely doesn't like me much now, but Quinlan is going to be more of a handful for him."

"Maybe I should be part of these mediations. Tiberius still has respect for the title I held in . . . our world. I still don't know what to call it, *our world*. But I don't think I should call it home. This is home now." She motioned to her shelves. "It's quite cozy, even if it is the afterlife." Nelly placed her hand over her mouth. "I hope that didn't come off as morose."

"Not at all. And sure, maybe it'd be best if you are there as well."

"You're all doing this to help me; I'd be lost without the help, and I will certainly be there to smooth out any issues that may arise. That reminds me, I made egg and cress sandwiches. Please, take one, Sylas, I insist."

"Do you mind if I eat it here then?"

"By all means."

———

Sylas stepped out of the portal and back into the upstairs room of The Old Lamplighter. He placed the bedding he had purchased for a hundred Mana Lumens, which he'd bundled up and held under each arm, on the floor.

It hadn't cost him anything to give Azor a class, but the explanation of how her brewing would work had surprised him.

"If she brews, it pulls from your mana, wherever you are," Marty at the Ale Alliance had explained. "She will need to have an understanding of what she has sold that night, and if it covers what needs to be brewed. She doesn't want to take too much of your power while you are gone, wherever you may be. Luckily, she can't use all your MLus to brew, meaning that she will hit a point where she can't continue any longer if you're somewhere else and without the necessary MLus to brew a cask."

It made sense, and Azor already knew enough about the price of brewing and what Sylas made from sales to manage any brewing costs. Once Sylas taught her a few things about brewing, she'd be ready to do it herself.

After dealing with her class, Sylas had spent some Mana Lumens on a fresh set of pints which had the words *The Old Lamplighter* etched into them. These would be delivered tomorrow, and Sylas was excited to see how they turned out. If they were as good as he hoped they would be, he would order pint bottles, so he could distribute brews later.

Slowly but surely, his business was taking shape, solidifying in a truly magical way. Considering the nature of how he "lived" and brewed, this made sense. Yet again a reminder of why he needed to get to the bottom of the doomsday message . . .

Azor formed into existence. She looked down at fiery hands and back up to Sylas. "I can make food and ale."

"That you can." He removed her fireweave apron and gloves from the bag he had slung over his shoulder and tossed them to her. She spun twice and caught them before they could hit the ground, flying into the individual pieces.

"Ta-da! If Bart ever needs some fire dancing with his songs, I'm his girl."

Patches appeared at the door. The cat stretched, yawned once, and then raced toward Sylas. He scooped the cat into his arms. "I guess this is his way of saying he missed me."

"Soooo cute. Wait." Azor looked around. "Isn't your friend supposed to be here?"

"Quinlan, yes. We should check on Nelly next door."

Sylas carried Patches down to the first floor of the pub, where he set the cat on his favorite windowsill perch. "Remember," he told Azor as he turned to the door. "Quinlan can be a bit rough around the edges."

"And the beds upstairs. Which should he get?"

"Tilbud will want the bedroom. Quinlan won't care either way, so he can take the bedding in the portal room."

"He won't care?"

"He most certainly won't. Quinlan has slept in worse places, believe me. So have I. Weird to say it like that, but it's true."

In a single blink, Sylas saw himself in some of the trenches that the Aurum Kingdom had built up in a particularly nasty fight against a famous group of Shadowthorne archers protecting an important pass. The trenches allowed them to cover themselves at night, and they had used a flame-retardant plant on the wood so they wouldn't catch fire. But that never stopped the archers from trying.

One of the soldiers had described it as similar to being struck by falling stars, the *thunk* and flash of fire continuing through the night. Then the rains picked up, which helped stop the archers but made the trenches damp, even with the drainage they'd hastily built. It had been Kael and Quinlan who had rallied them through that experience, Quinlan with his humor and Kael with his determination to make every last archer pay.

Later, Raelis and Quinlan had led the charge on Sylas's orders. Many men had died that night, and Raelis had taken the wound that would later kill him after driving him mad with infection.

"Sylas?" Azor asked.

He tensed up and then let the memory go. "Sorry, just got lost in a thought."

They heard some loud laughing outside and barking.

"Quinlan?"

"That would be him," Sylas told Azor. He opened the pub door to find Quinlan running around as Cornbread jumped after him. The large man had a bone in his one good hand, which he waved around, Cornbread playfully frustrated to get it by this point.

Mira and Nelly stood in front of the pub watching the two of them, Mira with her hands crossed over her chest and Nelly with an uncertain look on her face.

"Sylas!" Quinlan shouted as he continued to play with the dog. "I was just wondering about you, mate. Go ahead and say hi to the ladies while I finish up here. Oi! Cornbread."

The dog barked.

Quinlan tossed the bone, but rather than let Cornbread chase after it, he used his super speed to race her to the bone.

"How long has he been here?" Sylas asked Mira and Nelly.

"So this is your friend, Quinlan," Mira said in lieu of an answer.

Sylas grinned at her. "That bad, yeah?"

His grin had the same effect it always had on Mira, causing the corners of her mouth to twitch as she fought a smile. "He's loud, boisterous, vitriolic about the Shadowthorne Empire, clumsy, enormous, and—strangely enough—charming."

"He also smells," Nelly said.

"He could probably use a proper bath," Sylas said as he watched Cornbread and Quinlan chase each other up and down the street. "I'll let him know privately."

"You should send him to the bathhouse in Cinderpeak, the one that is heated by the volcano. Don't let him use yours," Mira said. "They have people there that will scrub him as well."

"Now that's something he'd probably like a bit too much." Sylas stroked his bearded chin for a moment. "But I'll send him along after we talk to your uncle and let him know what is happening. They are both demon hunters. How bad could it be?"

———

"A lord commander?" Quinlan asked as they approached Mira's home. His demeanor changed. "Her uncle was a bloody lord commander and you didn't tell me?"

"It doesn't matter. He's good at what he does, and you're good at what you do. We're all in this together now."

Quinlan stopped. "You act like you don't remember, Sylas."

"I remember damn well."

"Everything we've done. Everything they've done. You're not asking me to be cordial with a Thorny who has served on the front lines like us, you're asking me to cozy up with a bloody lord commander whose only job was to send blokes like us off to the slaughter."

"He wasn't like that," Mira said. "Tiberius was always with his men."

"Yeah? Were you there? Who told you? Him? Because if he told you, then I've got a bit of property beyond the walls of the Hexveil that you might be interested in."

"We all have our past lives, and we have our new lives," Sylas told him.

Quinlan pointed a finger at Mira's house. "How do you know that that man in there *wasn't* standing across from us, sending his soldiers or archers or spearmen or mounted cavalry to kill ours? Did you go over the battles he fought? Did you ask him about the Night of Raining Arrows? No, you didn't. Always were too quick to trust, Sylas. It's why I have always liked you, mate, but it is naive to think that this lord commander wouldn't have done whatever it took to snuff out our lives back home."

He said it, *home,* and Sylas saw Nelly twitch at the word. Quinlan didn't always have a way with words, but he did have this way of getting to the point of the matter in ways that would linger.

Sylas sighed. "I understand where you're coming from, but that is not going to change the meeting that is set to take place. We're doing this for Nelly—"

"I don't mind doing it for her. Anyone that has someone here deserves to find them. And I like hunting demons anyway."

Sylas hesitated. If Quinlan knew how Nelly had died, he might think differently.

Nelly and her husband had been executed by the Aurum Kingdom after poisoning members of the Gold Guard. Sylas and Quinlan had dealt with the Gold Guard before, the regiment of swords-for-hire made up of prisoners, and neither liked them. But Quinlan was a patriot, and information like this could set him off.

With this in mind, Sylas tried a different approach. "Do you trust me?"

"I do."

"Have I ever asked you to do something that I wouldn't do myself?"

"No, you haven't."

"Would I ever do something to intentionally put you in harm's way?"

"No, Sylas, what are you getting at?"

"Do you trust me?"

"Dammit, mate, I already told you I did!"

"Then trust me now. I don't like Tiberius either. He's the least agreeable person I've met in the Underworld. But he's powerful, he's loyal, and he'll likely prove useful."

"I understand, but I can track this demon myself once we get what we need from your archlumen. I've done it before. What makes him so special?"

"I want him to help," Nelly said suddenly. "He knew my family."

"And why is that?"

"Because I'm a Redgrave."

Sylas exchanged quick, horrified glances with Mira.

Quinlan took a step closer to Nelly as he cocked an eye at her. "Redgrave, huh? That's one of the Royal Houses, yeah?"

"It is."

"And how did you get here exactly?"

"I died."

Quinlan laughed, breaking the tension. "You're not wrong there, Nelly, but *how* exactly? Was it our people?"

"It was."

"Then I'm sorry to hear that."

"My husband and I poisoned members of the Gold Guard, killing them. We were taken prisoner and publicly executed, hanged at the same time after being tortured for several days and kept in a trapdoor dungeon. You asked, and I told you. Everyone here has blood on their hands in some way, including you. Now, you don't have to help find my husband, that was Sylas's idea. But your reputation proceeds you, and your friend says you are a good man."

"I'm a bloody great man."

"Tiberius is as well, in his own way. Good remains in the eye of the beholder, and here in the Underworld, we're all given a clean slate. I don't want you arguing with Tiberius. I want you behaving, and when the time comes, I want you to do what it is that has made you one of the best men Sylas has served with."

"He said that?" Quinlan asked, almost entranced by the harsh way Nelly spoke to him.

"He did. He said you, your brother, and one other fellow will turn the tide of the war that is to come. Do you know who else will help with that?" She motioned to Mira's home. "Tiberius and his militia."

Quinlan turned to Sylas. "Didn't you tell me about the militia? Some funny name."

"Yes, the Esteemed Coalition of Ember Hollow Defenders."

Quinlan chuckled. "By the gods that is such a Thorny thing to do, bloated titles and whatnot."

"They're good men, Quinlan," Sylas said. "They've kept Ember Hollow safe. Now, are we going to do this, or are we going to stand here in the streets and continue arguing about this? What say you, old friend? Shall we show these Thornies—sorry, ladies—just how strong we are, or should we let them think that we're too afraid to go after a simple demon?"

Quinlan slowly nodded. "We absolutely will show them, but we should be clear, Sylas."

"Go on."

"These kinds of demons are not simple. Noxes are devious, smarter than the others, and . . ." He slowly glanced over to Mira's home. "It's best to tackle them with more than one hunter. So you were right about that. Not that I couldn't do it myself, but it's better this way. I didn't want to say it, but there it is." He sighed audibly. "This is the right thing to do, but I don't like it, mate. I really don't."

"Just remember that Tiberius was a lord commander. He still thinks that way."

"Like he's bloody in charge of the world?"

"Yes. What?" Sylas asked Mira when she gave him a look.

"You aren't wrong," she finally said.

Nelly, who remained beside her, stepped up. "I will use my sway with Tiberius because of my last name. That should do the trick, and it's why I'm here. It's also why I brought this." She showed them the contents of her picnic basket. "Sandwiches for Tiberius and his men. Small gestures like this can go a long way." A rare firmness came to Nelly's voice as she looked up at Quinlan. "Let me do the talking."

———

The pub buzzed with activity that night, especially once Bart tuned his lute and prepared to play a few songs. Duncan, Cody, and Henry sat in the far corner with several of the other militiamen. There weren't any farmers, but there were people from Cinderpeak who had been planning to go to The Ugly Duckling only to find that Rose was closed for a few days to vacation somewhere south, a retreat of sorts.

That was fine by Sylas. Iron Rose's schedule wasn't great for her business, considering she opened and closed on a whim, but it was perfect for his.

"I still can't believe Tiberius actually behaved himself, let alone Quinlan." Sylas nodded toward his old friend, who sat with the younger militiamen, a merry look on his face.

Mira placed both elbows on the bar and leaned forward, her head cupped in her hands. "I really wish I knew more about it myself. It can't be attraction. He knows that she is looking for her husband."

"Maybe he thinks her husband won't make it through the possession."

"That is rather grim, Sylas."

"Sorry."

"We can just ask Nelly if you'd like. I'm sure she'd tell you. I'll grab her."

"Where's she going?" Azor asked as she came to the front counter with a tray of empty pints.

"To fetch Nelly. We're curious about earlier."

"I'm curious about earlier myself."

"Sorry, with Quinlan around, it's hard to get a word in at times," he told Azor, referring to the back-to-back stories Quinlan had told earlier, just before the pub opened up. "His drinks are on me, yes?"

"He insists on paying for them."

"And I insist on covering them, Azor."

"He refuses to take the ale if he can't pay for it."

"The old dog," Sylas said as he grinned over at his friend.

Mira returned without Nelly and took her seat at the bar. "I'm back."

"Are you missing someone?"

"She's open right now."

"She is? And there are customers."

"There are."

Sylas nodded, impressed.

"But I did get some information. It's actually a bit lively out there."

"Where? Ember Hollow?"

"Is there another village on the edge of the Underworld? Let's go for a walk."

Sylas did a quick head count before motioning Azor over. "Do you think you could cover for a bit? I'd like to take a walk with Mira."

Azor seemed enthused by the prospect. "Sure, this is nothing. If it becomes something more, um, don't take too long?"

"We won't."

Sylas finished pouring a few pints and then stepped around the bar. He petted Patches, who mewed in curiosity as he left the pub. Cornbread watched him leave, her ears popping up, but then she nuzzled up next to Quinlan again.

"I'm glad Quinlan didn't see me," he told Mira as they turned in the direction of the general store. A couple that Sylas had seen before in Ember Hollow was just stepping out with a few household goods. He waved and they waved back, but nothing was said.

"Not exactly friendly," Mira said, "but to be expected. There are people in the town square. Do you hear them?"

"I do," Sylas said. "Laughter."

Mira slipped her arm into his. "Let's see what it's all about and I'll tell you what Nelly said."

They started toward the town square, Sylas surprised that Mira was so close to him. He nearly fumbled his next two steps, but soon found a rhythm that would work walking arm in arm. As they walked, Mira spoke of Nelly and the Redgraves, the Royal House of the Morgan Plains: "Tiberius worked with several lord commanders that served the Redgraves. He gained a lot of respect for them that way."

"Enough that he agreed to work with Quinlan?"

"Apparently, yes."

"In that case, we just need for Tilbud to show up."

"I'm sure that will happen sooner rather than later."

They reached the town square and found a few people gathered in front of a makeshift stage.

"It can't be," Sylas said as he recognized the person putting on the performance, a man wearing a turquoise three-piece suit with yellow accents.

Mira turned to him and smiled. "I told you it would be worth the trip. Nelly said he stopped by earlier."

Archlumen Tilbud enthralled the small crowd with a story about an epic encounter he'd had with an Eldritch Horror. He used his Quill power and a few spells Sylas hadn't seen before to create noise, visuals, and other flashy effects. By the time he finished, several of the onlookers were clapping and asking for more. Tilbud spun, bowed, and tipped his hat to them as the people clapped. "If you want more, come with me to The Old Lamplighter. The music should be starting soon."

As the people turned toward the pub, Tilbud approached Sylas. "Just the man I was looking for."

"You are a wandering performer now?"

"I do wander, and certainly wonder, and I do perform. I was going to stop by earlier, but then I saw people leaving Nelly's, and I figured I could provide a little entertainment. One thing led to another and, well, you know how it goes," he said as he removed his top hat to reveal another, smaller turquoise top hat.

"We should probably get back to the pub," Sylas said, thinking of Azor. "A sudden rush of people might be a bit too much for her to handle on her own."

"Yes, a good idea. Brilliant, even. Shall we fly?"

Mira started to laugh. "You really can't do things the normal way, can you, Tilbud?"

"What do you mean? I always do things the normal way. It is others who are abnormal. Anyway, come on, let's head over. You can start pouring pints, and I'll put on a show after the music. You don't mind if I spend the night, do you? I would portal back to Duskhaven but, alas, my home is in need of some repairs, and you and I, and I hope some of your hunter friends, have things to do in the morning anyway. Plus, there are the farming spells you need. A busy day awaits. You'll be planting in no time. Do you know what you want to plant now, yes?"

"Not exactly."

"Well, that's not good now, is it?"

"I'll figure it out."

"Perhaps we wait then." Tilbud nodded. "As things often do, they'll come together in ways we haven't foreseen. That's how I prefer to live my life, anyway. Now, what were we about to do?"

"The pub," Mira said.

"Right!" Tilbud exploded into the air, the man gone in a flash.

Sylas turned to Mira. "Sorry our walk was cut short."

"Maybe we can do another one soon, a longer one."

"I'm always interested in spending more time with you." Sylas blinked in response to the words that had just come out of his mouth. They were true, so he let them linger.

———

A whirlwind of activity at the pub had Sylas open much later than he normally would, The Old Lamplighter a place of merriment into the wee hours of the morning. The fireberry ale was a smash success. Sylas had also gone through a cask of the flamefruit ale, a cask of strong ale, and more than two casks of his regular ale. He'd given away some drinks, but none to Quinlan, who insisted on paying.

In total, Sylas had gained over eight hundred MLus from his sales that night. It would cost four hundred to brew five casks, but his total MLus would still be higher than the day before, an advantage to the way the system worked in the Underworld.

Azor watched over his shoulder as Sylas replenished his casks, while Quinlan settled into his makeshift bed upstairs, and Tilbud finished up a story he was telling Henry and Godric in a booth at the back.

Sylas would later fall into a deep enough sleep and awaken with the prompts that now ran his life: the invasion message and his loan payment.

———

Cornbread paced in a nervous circle before the cat door. *Are we going out or not?*

I thought we'd go back to the farm tonight. But apparently, the big man will stay here with his friends. Patches sat. *I have met the wizard before. I do not know the other.*

His scent is uncertain to me, but I have smelled it before.

I have as well, Patches told Cornbread. *The scent of a monster.*

He's not a monster. It's the scent of someone who battles them, or perhaps struggles with them. A warrior.

The one-eyed man has that smell.

One-eyed man . . . ah, him. Cornbread sat and bit at something on her foot. She stood again. *Well?*

Patches stared at her curiously. *You think you can make it there to the city with the market?*

I'm certain I can. We just need to reach the farm. I can portal from there. I've done it before to bring my owner food.

Patches tilted his head as he looked at the dog. *You brought your owner food?*

My previous one, yes. He didn't feed himself properly, so I helped. Come on. Cornbread charged through the cat door, causing Patches to tense up. He glanced up to the fire spirit, who lay in a puddle of flames. She watched the two of them, a sleepy smile on her face.

He took one step forward. She didn't move.

Patches reached the cat door and looked back at the fire spirit. She whispered something and motioned for him to go.

You're giving me permission? He sat. *I don't need your permission. I am the Guardian of the Tavernly Realm, not you.*

Patches remained seated in front of the fire spirit, defiant until Cornbread poked her head through the cat door. *Are you coming or not?* she asked, just a bit of slobber flying from her mouth and nearly reaching Patches.

He huffed and ultimately turned away from the fire spirit, his tail raised so she could get a good look at his rear.

Once they were both outside, Patches led Cornbread to the start of the woods.

I've got it from here, Cornbread said, her nose to the ground. She paused, nodded, and took off running. *Try to keep up!*

Argh, Patches mumbled as he ran through the brush, Cornbread always a few paces ahead.

Patches was certain he could accelerate faster than Cornbread, but once the dog was going, she was nearly impossible to catch. And her stamina was impressive. She charged through the woods with bold precision, leaping over stray branches, ducking beneath overturned roots, and whisking through small streams until she came to a stop.

Cornbread waited, Patches catching up with her about a minute later.

You are fast, I'll give you that.

Cornbread nodded. *You have to be fast to chase the things I chase.*

What do you chase?

When our owner—

The big man? He doesn't own me.

He doesn't?

Humans don't own cats. They own dogs, but not cats.

Cornbread shrugged. *I never really thought about the distinction. Anyway, I chase the monsters that come for the crops that, um, my owner, will later grow.*

Patches reconsidered what he'd said just moments ago. *For our purposes, you can call him "our owner," but know that he does not own me. What kind of monsters? Do they eat the food?*

They don't eat the food like you and me. The ghouls eat the mana.

Patches looked ahead at the Seedlands. *Will we encounter any now?*

If we do, they aren't our ghouls to deal with. I might bark at them, though. Cornbread showed her teeth.

If they bother us, I'll do more than that. Lead the way.

Cornbread took off again but ran slower this time. She headed down a dirt road, one marked with wagon tracks, and came to another.

Patches noticed movement in one of the fields. His claws instinctively grew as he saw a being draped in black cloth with a mouth of shining energy.

Cornbread barked. The being vanished. *That's one of them, a ghoul. There can be many. When they join forces, they turn into a very powerful creature.*

Is it made of birds?

Cornbread thought about this for a moment. *When it moves, it looks like that. Anyway, we're close to the portal. This way.*

The two reached the portal a few minutes later. As they approached, text appeared in front of Patches. *You can read this?*

No. But I can do this. Cornbread used her paw to tap the top option presented to them. She turned to Patches and offered the pub cat a toothy grin as they vanished.

They reappeared in a place Patches had never been before. He could instantly see the signs of humans, the lights on in their homes beyond in a town. He also recognized the smell of humans, of the food they cooked and the fires they created to keep warm.

Cornbread stiffened and brought her snout up. *This is the market. Now, we find some corn.*

And then we portal back to the farm and go through the forest from there?

Correct. We will hold the corn in our mouths. The farm dog turned to the market and started sniffing the ground. *Follow me.*

I can deliver it to the big man, Patches said as he caught up to her.

That would be most excellent. He seems to like you if he lets you sleep in his bed.

He would let you sleep there too if you wanted.

Cornbread stopped sniffing the ground. *He would?*

Possibly. Try it out tonight.

I think I will. Cornbread brought her nose up, closed her eyes, took a sniff, and nodded. *Found it.*

They came to a booth that sold grains and produce. The food was covered by patchwork blankets. Cornbread grabbed the ends of one of the blankets with her mouth and was just about to tug it when Patches stopped her.

I have a better idea.

You do?

A little finesse can go a long way. Patches gracefully hopped onto the table. *Tell me which one it is.*

Cornbread moved toward the middle of the table and her ears stood to attention. *It's this one.*

Patches returned to the start of the blanket and bit the edge. He pulled this back until he got to the middle section of the table, where he revealed a stack of corncobs still in their husks.

The farm dog barked. *That's what I'm looking for!*

Quiet, Patches hissed down to her. He placed his mouth around one of the cobs and tossed it to the ground. *That one is for you. I'm going to find a smaller one.*

Patches examined the green husks until he found one that would better fit in his mouth. He tossed it to the ground as well, and then carefully dragged the cover back over the produce. From there, Patches hopped to the ground. *You're in charge again.*

Right! she said, corncob in her mouth.

Soon, they reached the portal and were transported back to the Seedlands, Cornbread once again using her paw to select their destination. The two were traveling toward the forest when the same blanketed Mana Ghoul swelled in their direction.

They heard a terrifying bark. A muscular white dog with clipped ears exploded out of a field, reached the monster, and tore into it.

The two hit the ground and the dog shredded the monster to bits. He turned to Cornbread and Patches. *What are you doing here?* he growled.

Let us pass, or you will regret it, Patches said, corncob still in his mouth.

Cornbread dropped her corncob. *We are just passing through to deliver something to our, um, my owner.*

The muscular white dog barked. *This is my territory.*

It won't be for long if you don't get out of our way, Patches hissed.

I can handle this, Cornbread assured the pub cat. *We are passing through and we will be going now.*

You best be going.

Cornbread picked up her corncob and continued on, cautiously, her tail tucked between her leg.

Patches did no such thing. He wasn't afraid of most things, especially the muscular white dog. He shifted around Cornbread, his ears pressed back, Patches prepared to strike if he tried anything.

I better not see you around here again, the dog growled.

Come on, Cornbread said again. *We have to think of the big man.*

[You have 57 days until the invasion.]
[A loan payment of 83 has been deducted from your total Mana Lumens. Your total loan balance is 17586 Mana Lumens.]

Sylas placed his hand on Patches. He then noticed another warm body on his other side, Cornbread. "You are both here?"

Cornbread looked up at him, her big eyes softening. She licked his hand and then hopped out of bed, where she grabbed something from the floor.

"What?" Sylas asked as she dropped a corncob on his bed. Sylas picked it up and examined it. "Where'd you get corn?" He quietly shifted out of bed and placed his feet on the ground. There was another corncob by the door. "You brought two?"

Cornbread barked.

Sylas stared at the dog for a moment. He couldn't shake this feeling that she was trying to tell him something. "What is it, girl?"

Patches hopped off the bed and walked over to the smaller corncob. He picked it up in his mouth and brought it to Sylas as well.

Cornbread barked again. She rushed toward Sylas and nuzzled her nose against the cob. She licked it and then licked his hand.

"The farm," he said. "You're telling me to grow corn. Your name is Cornbread. Cornbread, the farm dog, comes with a farm that is supposed to be growing corn. I get it! Brilliant work!"

He hugged Cornbread and she slapped her tail against him. Patches hopped on the bed and rubbed against Sylas as well.

"But where did you get the corn?" he asked the two of them. "I haven't seen anything like it around here. Maybe at the market in Cinderpeak. You didn't go all the way to Cinderpeak, did you?" Patches meowed, Cornbread barked, and Sylas burst out laughing. "What are the odds!"

Sylas headed downstairs, where he found Archlumen Tilbud and Quinlan seated at the bar, speaking with Azor. They had empty plates before them, Quinlan leaning back to some degree as if he had eaten his fair share.

"Happy Wraithsday, Sylas!" Azor said.

"Morning, Azor. Good news, all!"

The archlumen turned to him. "Yes?"

"I have it."

"Have what?" Quinlan asked.

Sylas showed them the two corncobs. "I have it. Cornbread and Patches brought it to me. Think about it," he told Tilbud. "Really think about it."

It took the archlumen a moment, but soon, his eyebrows rose and his eyes darted left and right. "They are telling you to grow corn on the farm. And it has been here all along in the name of the farm dog! Absolute madness. But it checks out, it makes sense, and now, we just need to head to your farm, learn some new powers, and make it all happen. What a glorious discovery!"

"We have to hunt first," Quinlan said, his voice transitioning to a more serious tone.

"Any idea how long it will take?" Sylas asked his old friend.

"Not a clue. I will have to pick up the scent first, and I won't be able to do that until we reach Windspeak Valley based on what Tilbud learned."

"Near Battersea, yes?" Sylas asked. "We will portal there first."

"We certainly will. These things can go relatively quickly, but they can be drawn out depending."

"Depending on what?"

The light in Tilbud's eyes dimmed. "The severity of the possession."

CHAPTER ELEVEN

CHAOS AND CHASE

Tiberius paced back and forth in front of the pub, where he had agreed to meet Sylas and the others. He wore his armor and held his best club. And the former lord commander was annoyed to see Nelly Redgrave and his niece approaching, also armed with clubs.

"Absolutely not," he said. "This hunt is already dangerous enough."

Quinlan stuck his tongue in a gap in his teeth and spit. "If you can't handle it, Tib, it's fine. I can take it from here. I'd wager they are better fighters than you, anyway."

Tiberius whipped around and pointed a finger at the man. "We've already agreed to do this my way!"

"I'm the tracker. Don't forget that."

"And I'm the one that is going to kill the Nox."

"*Nox* me?" Quinlan asked, a joke he'd already made the previous day.

"That wasn't funny then, and it isn't funny now. Mira—"

"Uncle, you are truly hoping to make an ass of yourself. It's Nelly's husband we're talking about here. She can go if she wants. I also have abilities that may help."

"I agree with Mira," said Sylas, who stood beside Quinlan. The pub owner was dressed in armor and had his mace resting on his shoulder and his buckler on his arm. Next to him was his fire spirit, who had a concerned look on her face as always.

Tiberius couldn't understand what she nervous about, especially with the powers she possessed. "Of course you do. Of course, you bloody agree with Mira. Well, anyone else, then? Anyone else coming? Perhaps the dog?"

Cornbread barked and Tiberius threw his hand up in exasperation.

"The dog could be useful," Tilbud, who had been quiet up until this point, said.

Quinlan seemed to agree. "Got a better sense of smell than me. You know, I've got a bond with these sorts using my tracker abilities that I've yet to fully explore. I reckon Cornbread will be helpful."

Tiberius looked at Duncan, Cody, and Henry. The two younger militiamen didn't seem to mind that so many were joining them, but Henry certainly did. He stepped forward. "Hold on, now. If all of these people are coming with us, and we got bloody Fido tagging along, does that mean everyone is getting a cut? Because I didn't sign up for that."

"No one is getting a cut," Tiberius said. "Not yet, anyway. Neither Quinlan nor I have officially reported this Nox. Until we do, it isn't registered, meaning no cut."

"And you'll report it when? Right when we're staring down the ugly bastard?"

Tiberius felt a rush of shame. He had already briefed Henry about this particular demon and was not in the mood to do so again. "Nelly, is your husband ugly?"

"What?" she asked.

"Answer the question, dear."

"Uncle!"

"Mira, I'm making a point here. Answer, please."

"No, he is not. Karn is a strikingly handsome man."

"Good, I figured as much. The reason I asked this is to drive my point home," Tiberius told them all. "The 'ugly bastard' we will be staring down will look exactly like Nelly's husband, meaning he won't be ugly at all. Some of the people we encounter may be ugly, but that will have nothing to do with the demon's powers."

"You anticipate several?" Azor asked. "Several . . . Noxes?"

"No, one Nox. It is a two-headed parasitic demon that takes possession of one person, and then uses their control over that person to create acolytes in the people that their host meets. We do not know how many acolytes Karn may have by this point."

"Could be half of Windspeak Valley by now." Quinlan was crouched now, and he appeared to be brooding. He held the scarf that Tilbud had borrowed from Nelly. "This is going to be a fight."

"Which is where you come into play, our dear tracker," Tilbud said. "You will find Karn."

"We can't all find him?" Mira asked him.

"No, we will stick together. The Nox can jump hosts if it feels like it is being threatened. This is also why I think we should reduce our numbers."

Tiberius did a quick head count. "If there are ten of us, and the dog, we will stand out."

"Well, in that case, you can reduce those numbers by one." Henry crossed his arms over his chest and leaned against the outer wall of Nelly's store. "We don't yet know the reward anyway. Duncan, Cody?"

Duncan exchanged glances with the much smaller Cody.

"That isn't a bad idea," Tiberius said. "We could shed a few. No more than five, *six* because the fire spirit can disappear."

"Seven," Tilbud reminded the demon hunter. "Do not rule Horatio out. He will be there in force."

The water spirit bubbled into existence, offered them a firm nod, and vanished again.

"Seven, then. Cody, Duncan, I want the two of you to stay behind with Henry. Do we have another volunteer to stay?"

The two groaned, but ultimately followed the direct order.

"I suppose I will stay as well," Mira said. "But whatever it is, I'm going next time. That leaves you, Sylas, Quinlan, Tilbud, Nelly, Azor, and Horatio. A good team, yeah?"

Cornbread barked.

"And the dog," Quinlan said. "Right, let's get this little show on the road then."

———

They arrived in Battersea through a variety of ways. Sylas took Azor with him, while Tiberius brought Nelly, and Quinlan brought Tilbud, the group traveling through Tiberius's portal on the account that they were both classed as demon hunters. To get to Windspeak Valley itself, they portaled there from Battersea after Tilbud called in yet another favor with a different portalist, which would unlock the option for Sylas the next time he visited the portal.

"We'll have to walk or fly from here on out," Tilbud explained. "There was once a town known as Solyphia in the center of Windspeak Valley, but its portal has long been abandoned, even though people live near there. Expect something different." A crooked smile formed on his face. "Yes, something different. Peculiar lot, these ones. Not a bad place for a Nox to set up shop."

"One last thing," Tilbud told Sylas. "Don't summon Azor just yet. It would be best to use our bonded elementals as a surprise. And don't mind the fog. It is common in this area."

For once, Sylas couldn't see the golden glow of the Celestial Plains. He only noticed it now that Tilbud mentioned the fog, yet it was quite striking, a visual reminder that they were in new territory, one that could prove dangerous . . .

They came to the start of a cobblestone street, one that had seen better days. The buildings hugging the road had been abandoned, shells of their former selves. But they did reach a larger structure covered in ivy, one with a glowing lamp, not unlike the light outside of Sylas's pub in Ember Hollow.

"This place almost reminds me of Ember Hollow," Tilbud said.

"Nonsense. Are you picking up anything?" Tiberius asked Quinlan.

"I'm picking up a lot. Everyone, closer to me." Quinlan took a deep breath into his nostrils. "Half the town are acolytes."

"Karn is close then, yeah?" Nelly asked.

"Likely so."

"Will he recognize me?"

"He will not. Not until we break the enchantment."

"Horatio," Tilbud said, summoning his water spirit.

The spirit appeared, his translucent form barely visible. It was the best look Sylas had of Horatio yet. The water spirit had a swelling chest, broad shoulders, and what could be construed as hair pulled back into a ponytail. "Find the man, the Nox, named Karn. Work with Quinlan."

Horatio started to fade. He stopped. "And when I do?" he asked, which was the first time Sylas remembered hearing him speak.

"I want you to keep him at bay and let us know where he is. Tiberius, you will know what to do at that point, yes?"

"Is that even a question?"

Tilbud didn't take the bait. Horatio ahead, Quinlan keeping behind him.

A man stepped out of one of the buildings. He wore dark robes and a veil completely covered his face. "How may I help you?" he asked in an unsettling rasp.

"Just passing through," Tiberius told him. "Is there a place that we can stay?"

"There isn't much here." The man shifted away from them and paused. He slowly turned back, and as he did Sylas felt his skin crawl. He also felt Azor's presence, the fire spirit ready to flare up whenever she was called upon. The man lifted his veil, so only his jagged teeth were visible. "A room just opened up."

Whoosh!

A flash mana from Tiberius's fingertips lashed at the man, stripping a ghastly creature from his body. The naked beast, which had a tail with a spike on it and charcoal gray skin, died instantly, evaporating into smoke.

The man who had been possessed lay there, cowering. "I'm free," he whispered, his inhales causing the veil over his face to partially suck into his mouth. He spit it out and got to his feet. "Thank you," he said, his voice cracking. "How . . . ?"

"Attacking it with mana put the acolyte seedling in its tangible form," Tiberius explained as he glanced around, scanning the fog. "The Nox will be much harder to kill. Hide. Hide where they can't find you." He pointed in the direction they had come from. "Go now."

"Why do they wear veils?" Sylas asked as the man took off. "Is that something to do with the Nox?"

Tiberius shook his head. "It was the custom in the northern parts of the Shadowthorne Empire, an area an Aurumite like you would have never reached. They practiced it here long before I came and they still do, but mostly in the valley. We had culture, you know. The Shadowthorne Empire was a place of innovation and culture."

"Yeah, you did," Sylas said, "an innovative culture that liked to torture and imprison people. I suppose that is a form of culture—"

"Gentlemen," Tilbud said, but the two kept arguing.

"I've had just about enough out of you." Tiberius was just pointing his club at Sylas when swarms of possessed men and women reached them, all with veils covering their faces. Sylas had been so distracted by their conversation that he barely managed to get out of the way in time.

Nelly, who had a club, struck a woman just as she lunged for her with her fingernails drawn.

"Fly!" Tilbud shouted to Sylas. "And bring her with you!"

Sylas pulled Nelly into his arms and took off, but not before she beat back another one of the possessed townsfolk.

Cornbread leaped toward one of the people only to be scooped up by Tilbud as he whisked into the air.

Tiberius joined them above the people, who crawled on top of one another, kicking away their veils in an effort to get to the hovering group.

"Easy," Tilbud told Cornbread. "Easy, girl!"

She squirmed in his arms. He released her, and the dog floated in the air next to the archlumen, under his control. Cornbread continued to bark until he placed a hand on her head.

Below, some of the younger acolytes climbed onto a roof and tried to jump to them but ultimately landed back in the crowd.

"This is good," Tiberius said.

"How is this bloody good? We have drawn all of them out." Tilbud pointed the palm of his hand at one of the acolytes on the roof and blasted the roof with mana.

"Stop, you fool. It is good because they are distracted, which means Quinlan can do his job, rooting out the Nox. Keep them distracted."

"What about the acolytes?" Sylas asked.

"If you kill the parasite, the Nox, they will all die with it. It is staying alive by feeding off Nelly's husband and the acolytes. If they don't die, Quinlan and I can handle them."

"Summon Azor," Tilbud told Sylas. "Have her make a ring of fire around the acolytes to keep them contained."

Azor flamed into existence, Sylas instantly feeling her heat. She zipped toward the ground and made a ring of fire around the acolytes. She picked up her speed as she twisted around them, drawing the ring in tighter. While they were possessed, the acolytes weren't stupid; they knew that fire would burn them. The only problem now was the few that were still on the rooftop.

"I can handle them," Sylas said. "Tiberius, Tilbud: do what you must."

Tiberius nodded. "I just need to find out where Quinlan is now—"

A sudden mist appeared. Horatio's face was several times its normal size and floating in the mist as he spoke. "We have located the man in a barn. Quinlan has prevented him from escaping."

"Lead us there," Tilbud told Horatio. "We will see to this Nox! Sylas, good man, keep them contained. Nelly, you're with us, my dear. Um . . ."

It was only then that Sylas realized he was still holding her in his arms. "She's all yours!"

Tilbud was able to extend his mana to Nelly and suspend her in the air. For a moment, Sylas felt foolish for holding her for so long, but then he focused back into the action as he lowered himself to the rooftop and grabbed the first acolyte.

The man tried to punch him; Sylas hoisted the small guy over his head and tossed him into the crowd below.

"That's how you do it!" Azor said as she maintained her fiery perimeter around the acolytes.

There was one more person on the rooftop, a woman, who was crouched now, prepared to attack. It wasn't the first time Sylas had seen things play out in his mind before they actually happened. It had saved his life on several occasions, this uncanny knowledge of what was to come.

She charged, and he merely stepped aside at the very last moment, grabbed her by the back of her clothing and launched her off the rooftop, where she was caught by the others. They weren't happy, the acolytes hissing and screaming, but they never got close to Azor's fire.

Sylas remained on the rooftop. He didn't know quite what he should do until Azor spoke. "Go to them," she said. "I've got this."

"Are you sure?"

"This is easy for me. It's like walking in a slow circle for a human. I think. And I'm deciding on what needs to be cooked tonight anyway for the Wraithsday Feast. Not them. Don't get the wrong idea. Maintaining the ring of fire is sort of meditative to me is what I'm saying. I've got this, Sylas, don't worry."

"I appreciate it, as always. I couldn't do without you," he told the fire spirit as he hovered back into the air.

Sylas turned in the direction that he had seen the others go. He picked up his speed, cutting through the fog until he spotted a large barn, one with its front doors open.

Sylas landed just as Quinlan and Tiberius moved in on a man who wielded a pitchfork. They blasted him with mana, much to Nelly's chagrin. She was being held back by Tilbud.

A golden flash of mana lit up the inside of the barn, where dark pools dripped from the ceiling.

"That should do it!" Tiberius said.

Karn, tall and thin to the point that it looked as if skin had been painted over a skeleton, dropped to his knees and gasped.

"Horatio, please check on Azor and make sure she's handling things," Tilbud said.

His water spirit formed, nodded, and departed.

"Karn?" Nelly said, her hands over her mouth. "Is it safe?" she asked Tilbud.

"It should be."

A ghoulish being with two heads tore away from Karn's body, screeching as it raced toward Tilbud and Nelly. Tilbud fired a bolt of mana at it but missed, the demon too fast. It slammed into the archlumen and burrowed into his skin.

"Blimey!" Quinlan said, his eyes locked on Tilbud as the archlumen threw both his hands out. A dark look came over his face.

"Don't—" The rest of the sentence never had a chance to leave Sylas's lips.

Rather than fire at Tiberias and Quinlan, Tilbud shrank until he was a fraction of his normal size. He took off running, with Cornbread chasing after him.

"Get him, Cornbread!" Sylas said as he too started to run.

Sylas was quickly surpassed by Quinlan, who ran with superhuman speed.

Quinlan bounded over a low stone wall and kicked up more dust, barely visible with the fog. Sylas picked up his pace. He listened for Quinlan's shouts, for Cornbread's barks, as he veered down into a ravine filled with farm debris.

"Argh!" Sylas struck his knee on an overturned cart. It was just the edge, but he could still feel his knee pulsing as he picked up his speed again.

He dragged his foot up the other side of the ravine and continued his pursuit. A flash of mana exploded out of the fog. It would have hit Sylas had it not been for Tiberius, who had run up beside him, the former lord commander blocking the mana with a shield of energy.

"Eyes on the prize, Sylas!" Tiberius moved faster than him as well, the two coming to another stone wall, and from there to a grazing pasture where Quinlan stood, the man catching his breath over Tilbud's downed body.

Sylas felt a sudden pang of anguish as he dropped to Tilbud's side.

The archlumen reached up and grabbed his hand. "I'm fine, I'm fine, really. A bit rattled, no, dazzled, no, frazzled. Yes, frazzled. A bit frazzled, razzled, and perhaps, dazzled, but fine, fine enough. I could use an ale. Help me up, mate."

"Damn bugger," Tiberius said as he glared down at the Nox. The demonic creature resembled a two-headed bat, but both heads were human in nature. Sylas had only briefly seen it earlier as it had scampered toward Tilbud.

"Let's turn it in, then," Quinlan said.

"Already a step ahead of you." Something flashed across Tiberius's one good eye. "It is worth . . . quite a bit, actually. To be split seven ways."

"Nine," Sylas said. "Azor and Horatio."

"Right, your bonded spirits. Shall we make it ten and cut Karn in as well? He could likely use it."

"We should," Sylas said, surprised that Tiberius was being so generous.

[You have received 800 Mana Lumens.]

"As you can see," Tiberius said, "it is not as much as we were hoping for, but it will still do, still a good amount."

"How much were you hoping for?" Sylas asked as Tiberius torched what was left of the Nox, mana flowing from his palm.

Quinlan answered this one: "If it is an S-Rank Nox, it would be worth close to twenty thousand MLus. But this was a B-Rank."

"It did that much damage as a B-Rank?"

Cornbread barked.

"What she said." Quinlan winked at Sylas. "All in a bloody day's work, isn't it?"

"That was something," Tilbud said as he found his small hat. He placed it on his head, and for some reason—perhaps it had something to do with the farm setting—Sylas was reminded of the hat he'd found at Brom's home.

As the group headed back to Nelly and Karn, Sylas figured it was worth discussing. This would also help cool the adrenaline pumping through him, Sylas still feeling the chaos and chase that had just taken place.

"There was a strange hat at Brom's place," he told Tilbud as he helped the man over the first stone wall.

"A strange hat, you say?"

"It had corks hanging from its brim."

"Those might be charms, something made by a haberdasher."

"Is that a common thing?"

"No, it is most uncommon."

"Do you know a hatmaker?"

Tilbud looked at Sylas with a hint of mischief in his eyes. "Of course I know one. Where do you think I get all my hats? Well, not from him, from a different one, but I do know a good one. Would you look at that, a new adventure presents itself. We will get your fields up and running tomorrow, and then see about this hat and its properties. I haven't seen it yet, so I could be wrong, but something tells me if this hat was left there, and it came with the farm, in the way that Patches came with the pub, it might be a custom number. Hence the charms."

They climbed over the second stone wall to find Horatio and Azor hovering beside Nelly and Karn. Nelly and her husband were seated on the ground, Karn's head in Nelly's lap, looking up at her, tears in his eyes. "I found you," he said.

"No," she told him, "I found you."

CHAPTER TWELVE

ONWARD AND UPWARD

Cornbread was as excited as ever later that night. Not only had she helped the big man find the demon, but the fire spirit had also whipped up something so good, so tasty, that Cornbread licked her lips again just thinking about it.

Minced beef in gravy with onions, fresh carrots, and mashed potatoes, she told Patches. *Absolutely delightful. Stellar. Brilliant. Please, give me more.*

The pub cat sat across from her, licking his paws. *You keep saying that.*

You should have been there today.

I don't often venture out during the day. I prefer night.

Cornbread sniffed the air. *There doesn't seem to be anything bad out tonight, at least not near us.*

The two were seated on the front porch of the farmhouse, the big man in a rocking chair near them. Like last time, it seemed to be a last-minute decision to go to the farm. Cornbread had already watched him rock back and forth for a while, the man deep in thought. She wondered what he was thinking about; she hoped he wasn't too stressed.

He sure has a lot going on, she told Patches.

He has been like that since he came to the pub.

Do you remember the previous owner?

Only a little. It was quite long ago. Patches approached the dog and examined her.

Do you want to sit next to me?

I guess. Patches found a space next to Cornbread and relaxed, his body pressed into hers.

You don't remember anything about the person?

No, I do not. I wish I did. But the memories of past Tavernly Realm owners fade. Do you remember yours?

Cornbread cocked her head. She hadn't entirely forgotten her previous owner, especially the way he smelled, but some of the details were starting to leave. *I think I'm forgetting.*

That's what happens here, Patches said as he swished his tail left and right.

Where is 'here'?

Here as in 'now'? The Farmly Realm. Here as in 'where are we'? I do not know, but the sky is always gold, and trouble is always close.

Cornbread nodded. While the cat could be a bit stubborn, and he certainly thought he was better than he actually was, she thought he was often wise. *The Tavernly Realm and the Farmly Realm.*

Indeed. The big man stays busy.

Yes, he does. And tomorrow he'll start his crops, which means I will be busy.

You will protect the corn.

The first few nights will be fine, but toward the middle, the ghouls will come in force.

Then I will help you. Patches lightly lashed his tail against her. *You helped me at the Tavernly Realm. I will help you here.*

I always try to be helpful. It's my best trait.

And I will help you. We will help the big man.

We will. And we will get more of that delicious food. Minced beef in gravy with onions, fresh carrots, and mashed potatoes. More please.

Patches purred. *It was good, I agree.*

Cornbread turned and licked his face.

Hey!

Sorry. There was just a bit of gravy on your nose.

No, there wasn't. Your tongue is . . . too wet.

What do you mean? she asked.

Feel my tongue. With a reluctant huff, Patches jutted his head out and licked Cornbread's snout.

That was rough! Mine is much softer than that.

Regardless. We're not going to be that friendly. And I don't like slobber.

I don't slobber.

Then I don't purr.

Yes, you do.

Patches twitched his whiskers. *You're finally catching on.*

[You have 56 days until the invasion.]
[A loan payment of 150 has been deducted from your total Mana Lumens. Your total loan balance is 17436 Mana Lumens.]

Sylas briefly checked his stats and saw that he was moving closer to seven thousand Mana Lumens. He had made a considerable amount the previous night, even with the special that he'd put together with Azor that saw his special fireberry ale reduced to five Mana Lumens so it could pair with the shepherd's pie she made and sell for ten.

There was also the bonus from the hunt, a hunt in which Sylas had barely used any power because the hunters, Azor, and Tilbud, had done most of the heavy lifting. This did raise a few questions for Sylas, ones that he planned to ask Tilbud once the archlumen appeared at the farm.

Cornbread burst into the room holding one of the corncobs.

"I know, I know, girl," he said as she hopped on the bed, startling Patches. "Today is the day."

Once he was up, Sylas boiled some water and used one of the tea bags Mira had given him to make himself a nice cup of tea. As he sipped the tea, he sat on the front porch and thought about Mira and what had happened between the two of them two nights before. Even though he had just seen her last night, a part of him missed her.

A romantic relationship on top of running a pub and a farm, and dealing with the impending invasion was probably a bad idea. It was likely a terrible idea. But Sylas enjoyed her company, and was there anything wrong with seeking out love in the Underworld?

Sylas glanced down at Cornbread, who rested near his feet. Patches and the farm dog had been extra cute late last night, cuddling and being playful with one another. Sylas was glad to see them getting along. He'd never really had a pet in his previous life, and to have two smart and loyal ones was an added bonus of living in the Underworld.

It really is a better life here, he thought.

As Sylas looked out at his fields-to-be, and as he thought about the days to come and seeing Mira again, he was yet again reminded of why the Underworld was worth protecting.

Cornbread barked, drawing him back to the present.

Sylas looked up to see Tilbud approaching the farm, the archlumen wearing a mustard-colored suit and a matching wizard's hat, albeit a few sizes too small.

"Ah, Sylas, just the man I was looking for. Like the suit? I wore it in honor of our corn-planting session. I don't quite have corn yellow, but this is close. Bloody nice morning, isn't it?" Tilbud looked around. He had a small package in his hand, which he handed to Sylas once he stepped onto the porch. "From Azor. Wee bit of breakfast. Good one, that fire spirit of yours. Horatio never makes me breakfast."

Sylas opened the package to find potatoes that had been boiled, diced, formed into two mounds, and fried. There was also a boiled egg and sauce from Tartar the fishmonger. "She's too good to me."

"Yours is a particularly caring bond. They all have their personalities, you know. I've met nasty ones before. You got lucky. You seem to keep getting lucky. It makes me think you have some charm or something that I don't know about." He blinked twice. "Charms, that's right! Didn't you say there was a hat that needed investigating?"

"A hat and a pair of tinted glasses."

Sylas retrieved the items from the home and gave them to Tilbud, who now sat on the rocking chair next to his. The archlumen first observed the glasses. He placed them on and nodded. "Nothing out of the ordinary here. Wait. Oh, my."

"What is it?"

"Why, I know exactly what these are. They aren't glasses for a farmer. They are glasses for a demon hunter. They are an augmented item that allows you to see creatures that have gone invisible."

"Really? How can you tell?"

"Look for yourself." Sylas took the glasses from Tilbud and placed them on his face. He looked out at the fallow fields and saw Patches seated, the cat looking back at them. Sylas removed the glasses and didn't see Patches. "He's invisible right now."

"Yes, he is. Patches the invisible pub cat."

"And the glasses are allowing me to see him."

"Indeed."

"These could be incredibly useful."

"And this hat," Tilbud said as he looked at the hat, observing each of the charms that hung from its brim. "It's definitely enchanted. But the enchantments are locked."

"Locked?"

"I have a skill that allows me to see certain types of enchantments, common ones, really. The more complex ones, like the ones on this hat, need to be unlocked by a person who handles these sorts of goods. In this case, a haberdasher would be ideal. As I stated previously, I do know one. But it has been ages since we spoke."

"Is this another of your old flames?"

"Fires can be reignited, Sylas. And yes, yes he is."

Sylas nodded. It didn't bother him in the least that Tilbud had a variety of lovers. He had suspected as much by this point.

Tilbud continued: "But it has been ages, and Rufus will probably tell us to go to the hat's maker, who appears to be a woman, at least by the name. We will still need to visit him; I have no idea where *Liza's Haberdashery* may be. It could be anywhere."

"Rufus wouldn't be able to unlock the enchantments?"

"Not these ones. They are known as Legendary Locks, which can only be seen to by the originator."

"And if she has moved on?"

"In that case, we would destroy the hat and Rufus would be able to bring the charms back to a starter level. But we absolutely shouldn't do that, not until we look for Liza."

"And where is Rufus?"

"Battersea."

"Could we head there later today?"

"We could, depending on how long Mana Infusion takes. We might be cutting it short, however, especially if you want to spend time at the pub tonight."

"I was wondering about that, the planting part."

"You really have no idea what you're doing, do you?"

"Not exactly. My father had a small herb garden, but that's about it."

"You can't be serious, Sylas."

Sylas placed the hat on. "Not in this hat, I'm not."

"Well, wonder no more. Where is the corncob?"

"Cornbread had one of them earlier. The other is on the table. Let me get it." Sylas returned with the smaller of the two cobs.

"Now, what do your instincts tell you to do?"

Sylas examined the cob. He plucked one of the kernels and information appeared.

"Well?" Tilbud asked.

"Mana Infusion is fifty; Mana Saturation is seventy-five."

"I see, and there are how many fields?"

"Ten."

"So it will cost you five hundred to seed the fields, and later, saturation will cost you seven fifty. Good. There is also the Harvest Silos spell, but that wouldn't be listed in the base information."

"Why not?"

Tilbud stroked his mustache. "Because it is an add-on, a spell that isn't necessary. You could, theoretically, harvest yourself or pay someone to do it. But Harvest Silos will be much easier. If this is related to spells I've learned and taught in the past, I would estimate that it would likely be the same cost as the initial spell, in this case, Mana Infusion."

"So an additional five hundred MLus?"

"Correct. Bringing your total cost to under two thousand MLus spread out over a week. How much did you say you could sell a bushel for? Did you tell me?"

"Edgar said between two and five MLus per bushel."

"Ah, right. Then that would likely be what the charms on your hat would be about. They will increase the quality of the field, or they could—we will still need to get the hat checked. They may also speed up your growing time depending on how good the charms are. I suspect if they are legendary, they are good. There's a tax, yes?"

"Seven percent."

"On yield, then. Right. Right. Even post-death, one still pays taxes. But it isn't much, and that is to be expected a bit farther away from the Hexveil."

"Should I hold off planting until I have the hat?"

Tilbud sighed. "Yes, yes you should. That would be the smart thing to do. But I can still teach you the powers you will need."

"So then I will plant tomorrow, Fireday."

"Yes. That would be correct. And that was an excellent question, Sylas. It is always best to do whatever it is you need to do *with* any charms equipped."

"I wonder if there is a brewer's charm."

"That would be something you could ask a haberdasher, but not Rufus. It is best if we just go in and out there. We didn't—"

"Exactly end on good terms."

"How did you know?"

"One more question: I need to learn more powers, what do you recommend? And would I have to be classed as a demon hunter to do some of the things like Tiberius and Quinlan can do? Speed, some of the spells, and dealing with demons—I'm interested."

"Very good questions indeed. You would need to be classed as a demon hunter to have access to their system, which allows you to turn in demons for reward and to join hunts. But there are workarounds for some of the skills. How much, my friend, are you looking to spend?" Tilbud grinned. "If we're going to Battersea, we can get the best deals at the Archlumenry, but I would need to know what you are interested in learning."

"I was going to ask you: What do you recommend? What are my options?"

Tilbud rocked back and forth for a moment. "What are your options? A question with endless answers. Let's boil it down some on our way to Battersea. I suppose we can just portal there. In that case, let me take you to a quaint little coffee and tea shop I know of there. How delightful. We'll narrow down what you need, visit the Archlumenry, visit Rufus, and, hopefully, find Liza and her haberdashery. It will be a grand day, Sylas."

"A potentially expensive day."

"Yes, it will be that as well, but most grand days are."

————

Sylas certainly recognized the area: it was the Brenham District, where he had first met Nuno the manaseer ten days ago. The water of Lake Seraphina glistened beyond a pier currently being enjoyed by numerous people. While not a sunny day—it was never a sunny day in the Underworld—it was a nice day, and the golden glow of the Celestial Plains added a warmness to their surroundings.

"This narrows it down," Tilbud said as he finished his notes.

"Correct."

"And your budget is no more than four thousand MLus."

"Preferably less."

"Here is the thing, Sylas, while you won't be able to get all the skills a hunter may have, and you certainly wouldn't have access to their system, there are certain workarounds, exploits, if you will, that will allow you to operate alongside them. First, you'll need some sort of mana firing ability. That should be easy."

"How?"

"Your farmer class makes that easy. You need to be able to defend your farm, so once we reach the Archlumenry, we will ask about ways you can do just that. Our friend, Meldon, at the front counter, will certainly help in that regard. If he's not there, we will ask to ping him."

"Ping him?"

"They have a way for archlumens connected to the Archlumenry to communicate using the system already in place. So an attack spell, that should be doable, especially with your farmer class. My estimate is that it will cost you about a thousand MLus."

"Should we go to the Farm and Field Guild instead?"

"That is an option, yes, but we will have better luck going to the Archlumenry on our own. You see, Sylas, not many people can count an archlumen as a close personal friend like you can. Most just go to the guilds associated with their classes. So an attack spell. And you can fly, and you have Quill, which is useful at times. What else, what else?"

Tea came in a ceramic pot. The woman pulled her sleeve back and made a show of pouring it into tiny cups for Sylas and Tilbud. "She is quite handsome, isn't she?" Tilbud said after she was gone.

"Sure," Sylas said as he took a sip of his tea, which had an incredible, bright flavor. It was like he had cut a lemon and squeezed it directly into his mouth, yet it was also sweet, and just the right temperature. "What about the Shrink spell?"

"Yes, Shrink. It is a good one to have, but, as you could see yesterday, there are, ahem, some issues that can arise."

"It wasn't your fault that you were possessed."

"Certainly not, but I could have been eaten. I believe Shrink is a good skill, but perhaps not the best for what you need. Whimsical Drift is a fun one, and I don't mean that just by its name."

"What does it do exactly?"

"That's how I float other people around me. However, it has an important usage for the kinds of things you may be getting into considering the company you keep. The power allows you to blow someone backward. Imagine if some arse-faced demon from the Chasm was close to attacking you or someone you cared for. You will be able to force it away."

"Whimsical Drift isn't so whimsical."

"No, it is not. But it is useful. So I believe that will help round out your abilities. Whimsical Drift, some sort of mana attack power. That should put you at close to two thousand MLus. Now, these are estimates, and they could fluctuate higher or lower. They aren't the strongest of spells, nothing like Dreamwalk, which would cost tens of thousands of MLus, but they are useful. Or Phantom Feast, which is more of a parlor trick."

"Dreamwalk? Phantom Feast?"

"Phantom Feast allows you to create illusory, but convincingly real food and drinks. It serves no purpose but to confuse and anger, which, if we're being clear, has its own purposes and usefulness. Dreamwalk gives you the ability to enter and influence someone's dreams. Not as nice as it sounds, and expensive, not to mention harrowing and unpredictable. Besides, people mostly forget their dreams anyway. The whole notion that someone can plant a thought isn't exactly the case. At least not from my experience."

"You've tested this?"

"Sylas, I've tested many things." Tilbud took a sip from his tea. "Many, many wonderful things. It is something I excel at."

"How long have you been here in the Underworld?"

"Asking someone how many deathdays they have celebrated is personal. I believe there is a phrase about *long enough to know better, but still not long enough to care*, but I'm saying it wrong. Back to you, the focus of our current conversation. You have been given a unique message, one that we still don't know the answer to. It is best that we give you plenty of options for what may come. In fact, perhaps Meldon would be best to round out these suggestions, and suggest another exploit. We don't have a lot of MLus to work with, especially since you're likely going to have to pay to have the charms unlocked."

"Yes, the hat." Sylas patted his hand on his bag. That was inside, carefully wrapped in a cloth.

"Precisely. Rufus's hat shop is on the way to the Archlumenry. I suppose we could stop there first, see if he doesn't know of this Liza woman, and continue from there. The grand adventure continues. Drink up, good man. Excitement is in the air. Hopefully, it won't suffocate us."

———

After their tea, Sylas and Tilbud traveled up the hills of Battersea, passing a variety of shops. It continued to dawn on Sylas that all these shops were part of multiple guilds, that they all had their tricks, and if Tilbud was right, their exploits.

For Sylas, the exploits of being classed as a brewer were baked in, considering how many MLus he could make in a relatively short amount of time. Or, perhaps, the exploit was having Patches attached to his pub.

Having his Mana Lumens topped off each night was a game changer. It was the reason Sylas had been able to grow his power so much quicker than those around him. There was something else that he had noticed in Ember Hollow. Many didn't seem to want to expand their power. Was this different in the city? Was being so far away from civilization affecting peoples' motivations?

Maybe things would be different if Sylas didn't have the weight of the invasion message on his shoulders. He hadn't been that entrepreneurial when he was alive, but that was also due to the fact that he'd been a soldier at war with the Shadowthorne Empire.

This reminded him of something else, a thought that brought a smirk to his face. He still needed to see Shamus about the abandoned market in Ember Hollow. There was also the question of an inn . . .

"Here we are," Tilbud said, which pulled Sylas out of his thoughts. The archlumen stood with his hands on his waist, looking nervously up at a sign shaped like a wide-brimmed hat. "How do I look?"

Sylas looked the man over. Tilbud still wore his mustard-yellow suit, his matching hat just a little crooked. Sylas fixed it for him. "Looks good."

"No smudges or anything? I tried to be careful back there at the tea shop. I was eyeing those scones, you know. The fireberry ones are a treat to be had and celebrated! But I didn't want crumbs. And they can be oily there. So much butter."

"When was the last time you saw Rufus?"

"Ages. Well, I guess that term is relative. Sometime around my last deathday. It was only briefly. We will see what he has to say and move on from there." Tilbud stepped to the door. He turned back to Sylas. "You know, perhaps it is best if *you* speak with him. You may get a better result. Just act like a clueless newcomer. Say something along the lines of *I got this farm, and it came with this hat, do these—*"

"Tilbud?"

The archlumen spun around to find a short man, a bit heavyset, with hair that had been dyed blond. "R-Rufus?" he stammered.

"Hi," Sylas said, taking over. "I got this farm, and it came with this hat. Tilbud, who is helping me with the magic aspect, recommended that you should take a look at it. He said you were the best of the best."

"Did he, now?"

"Do you have a moment?"

Rufus slowly nodded. "Come in, both of you. I do have a client coming soon, but this shouldn't take long." He opened the door to the shop and stepped aside to let them both in.

The shop itself was clean, with dozens of mannequin heads, each wearing a hat. There were numerous kinds, from gaudy numbers with feathers sticking out of them to simple caps meant to cover bald spots. There were hats for men and women, and a few caps made of tweed that were small enough for children.

Sylas carefully got the hat out of his bag and set it on the counter. As soon as he started examining it, Rufus gasped. "You have one of Liza's?"

"It came with my farm."

"I see," Rufus said as he delicately turned the hat over again. "Well, for one, you shouldn't put a hat such as this in a bag. Let me get you a box to store it in. I have an extra, one that a customer didn't want. I'll be right back."

Once he was gone, Tilbud turned to Sylas. "Ahem, thank you for the save back there. Truly. I don't know what came over me."

"Not a worry."

"You are a true friend, Sylas. And while I have many acquaintances, I can't say I have many friends, especially true ones."

Rufus returned with a wooden box. "It's a bit bulky, but believe me, you want to protect a hat such as this. If you ever encounter Legendary Locks on an object, it means that object has been enchanted to its maximum capacity. It is worth preserving. Now," he said as he carefully placed the hat in the box, "regarding Liza. She lives in Ghostford."

"North of Wraithwick, yes?" Tilbud asked. "In the mountains?"

Rufus nodded curtly. "Correct. But Liza stopped making hats years ago."

"Yet she remains in Ghostford?"

"As far as anyone knows, yes. That doesn't mean she won't see to these Legendary Locks and reveal what powers this hat holds. But she may not. I'm not her. I can't speak for the woman. I've only ever seen her once, at a lecture at one of the academies in Gloombra."

"Ghostford. Well, that's easy enough," Tilbud said. "As for convincing Liza, I'm sure, ahem, Sylas's charm will do us well. Or his dilemma."

"Dilemma?"

"Nothing to be concerned about, Rufus." Tilbud picked up the hatbox. He noticed it was a bit heavy and handed it to Sylas. "I do believe we should be on our way. It was nice seeing you."

"Yeah?" Rufus asked, a sullen look on his face. "Same, Tilbud. Stop by again later and let me know what Liza says, if she says anything."

"Most assuredly. Sylas?" Tilbud spun around awkwardly, mumbled something under his breath, and left the shop.

"Thanks again," Sylas said.

"Wait," Rufus called to him as he reached the door.

"Yes?"

"Do make sure that Tilbud is taking care of himself. I worry, you know. He can get in over his head and he likes to concern himself with the problems of others, especially when he's feeling overwhelmed by his own. I don't wish ill on him, you know. I think quite fondly of our time together."

"I will keep an eye on him, Rufus. And thank you again."

"Bloody glad that's over with," Tilbud said once Sylas joined him outside. "It was tense in there, yes?"

"I liked Rufus. He seemed nice."

"He's a joy, really. I suppose I shouldn't say it was tense because he wasn't tense, I just felt tense and . . . and you know what? Let's just focus on the task at hand, which is getting you powers and then making a quick trip to Ghostford. I'm sure we'll be able to convince Liza to help us, especially if I use my Charm spell."

"Let's try *not* to use that. Although, it did help us at the Archlumenry."

"That it did. But there are residual effects of the spell, so any help we had then would likely work in our favor now. We'll just need to get to the Guild District and we should be good from there. Eyes on the prize, Sylas!" Tilbud stuck a finger in the air and walked even faster. "Onward and upward, mate. Onward and upward."

CHAPTER THIRTEEN

LEGENDARY LOCKS

Sylas and Tilbud took to the air outside of Wraithwick, Sylas feeling three thousand Mana Lumens lighter.

Tilbud had struck a deal with Meldon at the Archlumenry for Whimsical Drift; a spell known as Field Warden, that would allow him to fire a horizontal burst of magic from the palm of his hand; and a spell called Soulfire, which Tilbud had insisted would work well with Azor, considering their bond. Since Sylas was there, he was able to pay the Archlumenry directly, but only because of his association with Tilbud.

Tilbud would formally teach him the spells tomorrow, when they also dealt with planting Sylas's first crop of corn.

"Gorgeous day, isn't it?" Tilbud called back to Sylas as he twisted ahead toward mountains on the horizon. They passed over forests and fields along the way, and Sylas had also spotted a few small settlements, villages much smaller than Ember Hollow. In the distance, he could make out what he assumed was Ghostford, a town nestled among hearty pines and built along the slopes of a mountain. The buildings had yellow roofs that stood out against the dark stone beyond.

Sylas could immediately see the appeal.

They landed and both of them activated the portal.

"Good," Tilbud said, his hands on his hips again as he looked out at the town beyond. "Never been here before. Well, I have actually hiked on the eastern slopes of these mountains, but never thought to head over and activate the portal." He took a deep breath in through his nostrils, which caused his mustache to twitch. "I like it. Quaint and peaceful. You there," he called to a man who was carrying a pail of pig feed. "Liza the haberdasher. Where might we find her?"

"Never 'eard of 'er," the man called back in a thick accent.

"Let's check the market or the pub," Sylas said. "Always a good place to start."

"Agreed."

As they headed up a flight of stone steps, Sylas figured he'd ask about the inn. "I was wondering something."

"Yes?"

"I'm going to have to sleep more at the farm, at least when I have active crops. Would it be possible to either turn the rooms I already have at the pub into rooms for rent, or add rooms on?"

"So turn the pub into more of an inn?"

"It would still be a pub. I just figured if there were better places to stay in Ember Hollow, more people would come."

"Which would make everyone there more MLus, which would build the town, which would turn it from a sleepy village into a bustling hub of civilization. I do like your thinking, Sylas, I do. But to have rooms for rent, at least more than the single room you have upstairs that *isn't* yours, you'd need to class as an innkeeper. You should also know when you add any class beyond a third, the cost rises significantly. So you may want to hold off on that until you are certain."

"Good to know. I was also thinking about the abandoned market there, maybe picking that up one day. Would that be a merchant class?"

"If you had a shop there, yes. If not, you'd class as a landlord. If we're being honest—and we are always honest with each other, something I like about our relationship—you'd make more as landlord because you could later acquire other properties. You could even own an inn that is run by someone else, someone classed as an innkeeper, or you could pay the exorbitant cost to add an additional fourth class. If you want my opinion—"

"I always do."

"Karn or Nelly should class as innkeepers, more likely Karn, who does not have a class. Not everyone gets one, you know. This works well with the merchant class because the inn can be an addition to the store, or the store an addition to the inn. I believe you've seen something like this in Battersea."

"Where would they build the rooms? Behind it?"

"Precisely. There is an old shed there that could be struck down and converted into the foyer of a new building. I can draw a sketch of it, if you'd like, using Quill. Or better, I should probably pitch this idea to Nelly and Karn. Town-building is exciting, and the planning is something I've always wanted to help with but never had the chance to in Battersea or Duskhaven."

They reached a small restaurant with outdoor seating on a deck, where they saw a woman bringing food out to an older couple enjoying the view.

"Excuse me," Sylas called to her. "Do you happen to know of a haberdasher named Liza?"

The waitress paused. "Liza? Yeah, I know her. She lives in a home closer to the top. There's a statue of a pelican near her house, one with a hat on it. I think that used to be her favorite pet, but the bird died."

"Familiars can die?"

The woman gave him a funny look.

"Never mind him," Tilbud said as he placed a hand Sylas's shoulder. "I'll explain everything as we make our way to the top." They continued through the town. "Familiars don't die in the same way pets would have died in our world. But they can pass to the Chasm, which is another form of death, as you know. So, I guess that is sort of the same. How tragic! I hate thinking about death, even if we are death incarnate to some degree."

They climbed a few more steps and found the statue of the pelican wearing a wide-brimmed hat, one with fresh flowers sticking out of its band. Upon closer examination, Sylas saw that it was designed to work this way, with grooves cut into the band to allow for flower stems.

"I believe we have found our haberdasher," Tilbud said as they came to a woman kneeling and clipping flowers from her garden. "Liza?"

"May I help you?" she asked as she looked up from beneath a bucket hat that had charms hanging from it. "If you're looking for the trailhead, it's just a few more houses down. Can't miss it, really. There's a sign there, you know."

"We aren't looking for the trail, my lady, we are looking for you." Tilbud motioned to Sylas. "My dear, dear friend here has recently come to acquire a farm. That farm came with one of your hats, which, as I suppose you can guess by now, has Legendary Locks. Since he isn't the original owner of the hat, he will need you to unlock the charms."

"Is that so?" Liza reached her hand out to Sylas and he helped her up. "Thank you. And the hat?"

"It's in the box to protect it."

"That was very thoughtful of you," she told Sylas as she motioned the two of them over to a table. Sylas placed the box down and carefully removed the hat. "Oh, my," she said, her eyes instantly welling up. "I remember this one. It was from long ago. I made it for a man named Oliver."

"Not Brom?" Sylas asked.

"No, Oliver. Oliver Sprout. It would have been a hundred deathdays ago, or more. More. You stop counting after a while. You also stop striving for MLus." Something akin to melancholy traced across her eyes. "That was before they changed things."

"Before?" Tilbud asked. "Ah, you mean before the Crafting Laws."

"Yes, the Crafting Laws. I'm assuming your friend here doesn't know about them, so I will explain. People of the Underworld used to have more power when classing as a crafter, which allowed many, myself included, to exploit the system given to us by the Celestial Plains. People can still class this way, but its powers are much more limited."

"The Celestial Plains are responsible for the system?" Sylas asked. This was news to him.

Liza sighed. "They most certainly are, for better or worse. Who do you think created the Underworld?"

"I honestly never really thought about it. Should I tell her?" he asked Tilbud.

"Let her finish first."

"Yes, let an old lady say her piece before she learns new information that will likely trouble her." Liza smiled. "Hats like this, with Legendary Locks, are rare indeed. They cannot be created anymore, only destroyed at this point. You all are too young to remember true crafters, but they were a very powerful bunch, who practically ran the Underworld. As a type of crafter, a haberdasher, I had access to their powers. The types of basic crafters we have now, your cobblers, tailors, and haberdashers like me, can no longer bring an object to Legendary Locks status. There are smaller charms, but nothing like what we could do then."

"So Legendary Locks status would mean something with a powerful enough charm that it would need to be locked from others using it?" Sylas asked.

"Precisely."

"Do apothecaries work the same? They are a type of crafter."

"Yes, they are. A good one can be much more powerful than someone like me these days. Not as powerful as they were then. The Celestial Plains saw to that."

Sylas still had questions about this part, but he held them for now. Tilbud could explain later.

"There are collectors who would pay thousands of MLus for a good one, a good one like this. I will tell you what these charms do and then I will unlock them. But before I do, what did you have to tell me?"

"One of the reasons that I have taken a second class is because of an invasion message I've been getting. It comes to me every morning, a countdown letting me know I have one day less until the invasion."

It was a moment before she spoke. "And how many days do you have now?"

"Fifty-six."

"Oh, my. And you are trying to grow your powers exponentially in that time, yes?"

"Correct."

"Because you don't know what this invasion means or what you will be called upon to do?"

"That's right."

"What do you make of this, archlumen?" she asked Tilbud. Sylas couldn't remember Tilbud telling her that he was an archlumen, but this fact didn't seem to throw him off.

"I find it both troubling and fascinating."

"As do I. And I agree, you should do what you can to increase your MLus to the best of your ability. This hat will help you do that. It provides several charms. One, it will decrease harvest times by two days. Two, it will create a legendary yield, which is worth more than the normal amount. It will do this every time. You are growing what, exactly?"

"Corn. Between two and five MLus per bushel."

"This will always bring you the higher number. Finally, after I deal with the Legendary Locks, giving you access to the charms, the hat will serve as a warning sign that there are demons about. The charms will light up, which is helpful if you are hunting at night, or you are about to sleep and something decides to pay a visit to your farm. Put it in a place where you will see it. And take good care of it. One more thing."

"Yes?"

"Visit me closer to the day of the invasion so I can throw *my* hat into the ring as well. It's too early to speculate, but if it is what I think it is, I know others willing to join the cause. The Underworld will not be destroyed. Defending it will be our Hallowed Pursuit."

———

The pub was busy for a Thornsday, especially because of the impromptu quiz led by Tilbud. He changed things this time, going with neutral questions about the world the patrons had lived in before their deaths. Shamus and his assistant came later and paid for a round for everyone there, which brought cheers and bardly behaviors from Bart, Godric, and some of the people that lived around the volcano.

It was a joyous time for all.

Later that night, Quinlan did a stomping-and-singing-chant that soldiers used to do, one that the former people of the Shadowthorne Empire knew as well.

While he mostly saw to pouring pints and keeping an eye on everyone, Sylas also had a few important conversations that night. The first was with Nelly and Karn, who had finally emerged from the general store after being locked away in there together for some time.

"I think running an inn would be an excellent idea," Karn told him after Sylas explained the conversation he'd had with Tilbud. "I don't have a class, but I will get the merchant class on account of my relationship with Nelly, and together, we can expand. Anders would love the work."

"That he would. You'll need more than one carpenter, but he could head the team."

"Exciting, really. Ember Hollow is really starting to change," Nelly said, and by the look on her face, Sylas got the sense that she hadn't told Karn about the invasion message. "You are busier than ever and things remain steady at the store. Steady enough that there's room for more investment."

"Don't feel any pressure," Sylas told her.

Karn grabbed his ale and toasted Sylas. "I was wondering what to do around here aside from helping Nelly run the store. I didn't realize that sort of thing was an option. Wouldn't be much different from running the place we were running for the Aurumites, sans, well, you know."

"Yes, no poison this time around."

Karn tensed and relaxed. "Hard to imagine this is where we ended up."

"I know the feeling. But, like I said, Tilbud will get you squared away. He will know what to do, and I'm all for it. We need something like that in this town, a place for people to stay."

The other important conversation was the one Sylas had later that night as he walked Mira home. The two took their time, passing right by her house, headed in the direction of the Hexveil.

Sylas brazenly took her hand and she let him. "I'm glad you had a good night at the pub," she said. "It's nice to see things changing so quickly around here. They were so stale before."

"It is."

"And Azor brewing? That's brilliant too. She's truly an asset."

"Agreed. I couldn't do it without her. I was meaning to ask you back at the pub, but what do you know about the Crafting Laws? I learned about them today, from a haberdasher in Ghostford."

"A haberdasher in Ghostford? Why am I just hearing this now? I look away for one moment and you are into something else, something entirely unpredictable."

As they continued toward the Hexveil, Sylas detailed his trip with Tilbud to get new powers and to discover more about his hat.

"You mean the hat you were wearing at the farm with the little dangly things?"

"Yes, Legendary Locks, which Liza, the hat designer, was able to remove so I could use the charms. Amazing charms too. It will give me a top yield, reduce crop time by two days, and alert me to monsters."

"Monsters that feed off the mana your fields will be absorbing, yes?"

"Precisely. Mana Ghouls, I believe they're called, at least according to what Tilbud told me."

"Then you know more about the Crafting Laws than me. I've never encountered an object from one of the old crafters. I've heard about them, but that is quite different. Lucky you. I swear you arrived in the Underworld with more luck than any newcomer before. Crafted items like that are worth a fortune."

"Liza mentioned that."

"But you'd make more simply using it. Do you know what that would look like in the end?"

"Five days or less from planting to harvesting. Fifteen thousand MLus. There would be taxes, and the cost of planting, but they would be negligible compared to what I'd be bringing in."

"Clearly."

"The part about the Crafting Laws that took me by surprise was that they were initiated by the Celestial Plains. I always felt the Underworld, aside from the counties and towns, didn't really have that sort of managing force. I liked that part of it, actually, *not* being part of some kingdom set to operate at the whim of a king or queen that doesn't have my best interests at heart. To learn that there are structures here governing what we can do." Sylas stopped. "It sort of makes me wonder."

"Wonder about what?" Mira continued to hold his hand as she turned to him. He took her other hand.

"About a lot. Like the message itself. Maybe trying to get as much power as I can, while helpful, is an old thinking style. I mean, shouldn't I be trying to communicate with those who can speak directly to the Celestial Plains."

"From my knowledge, that isn't something that's possible. But you'd have to ask Tilbud, someone who knows more of the inner workings of the system here."

"I had an idea about that."

"What idea?"

Sylas glanced in the direction of the Hexveil. "I want to find Raelis, who I firmly believe will help fight off whatever invasion is coming."

"But you just said fighting might not be the best way forward."

"It might not, and that brings me to my father. He's from the Celestial Plains, currently on a Hallowed Pursuit. What if I were to find them both?"

Mira dropped Sylas's hands. "You are suggesting that you would actually journey into the Chasm? Have you gone mad?"

"If it is necessary, yes, yes, I would. And no, I haven't gone mad. Tilbud told me it's possible."

"You'd go on a Hallowed Pursuit?"

"Not exactly, more of a rescue mission."

"What if they don't need rescuing?"

"I'm certain Raelis will return if I fetch him. I don't know about my father, but if I did meet with him, I could perhaps get a message to my mother, who is in the Celestial Plains."

"This all sounds mental, Sylas. And we still don't know what Nuno has learned. Shouldn't we wait until we know?"

"We don't know when Nuno will return."

"All right, let me ask you this, then: What if he returns while you are in the Chasm?"

"I have to do something, Mira. I know I'm new here, and I know things can change, but this life, this *afterlife*, is better than any life I had back in our world. Just the fact that I met you alone, that's better than anything that happened to me back there."

"You mean that?" Mira took a step closer to him.

"I mean it. Sorry, if I'm being too forward."

Mira wrapped her arms around Sylas's neck. She had to stand on the tips of her toes to do it, but she did so gracefully, the apothecary clearly in charge.

Sylas smirked.

"What?" she asked, the confidence on her face replaced by surprise.

"Patches."

Mira let go and turned to find the pub cat sitting there. He mewed and approached. "Patches?"

"He certainly knows how to ruin a good moment."

The two laughed and turned back to Ember Hollow.

CHAPTER FOURTEEN

A BULL AND A TIGER

Sylas was up early the next morning, prepared to take the hit from both the Mana Lumens he'd spent the previous day and his loan payment. The damage wasn't too bad considering he'd grossed quite a bit at the pub last night, but like any sudden loss in money, or in the case of the Underworld, inherent power, it still stung.

And it wasn't the only thing that stung. Seeing that invasion message, especially after the incredible moment he'd shared with Mira last night, caused him to momentarily freeze up.

[You have 55 days until the invasion.]
[A loan payment of 75 has been deducted from your total Mana Lumens. Your total loan balance is 17361 Mana Lumens.]

Sylas let it go for now and glanced at his stats, aware that his new powers would populate after Tilbud transferred the abilities to him.

Name: Sylas Runewulf
Mana Lumens: 4217/4217
Class: Brewer
Secondary Class: Farmer
[Lumen Abilities:]
Flight
Quill

He yawned, and as he did Patches shifted closer to him. As always, the pub cat had replenished his Mana Lumens overnight. "You really are the best," he told Patches as Cornbread burst into the room barking, the dog joined by Azor.

"I came early with Tilbud," she said. "Wait. Sorry. Happy Fireday! I meant to say that first."

"Morning," Sylas told her.

"Also, I made biscuits and sausage gravy. I hope that's fine. Tilbud said it was one of his favorites." She flared up. "I used the peppers you found. It's spicy." Horns grew from her head. "Very spicy, according to Tilbud."

Cornbread barked.

"She's excited to get back to work. Isn't that right?" Azor twisted into the air and came down in front of Cornbread to pet her. "Isn't that right? Cute little farm dog, yes, you are."

The dog barked again. By this point, Sylas was out of bed and heading to the main room of the home, where he found Tilbud seated by the window, a half-finished plate of biscuits and gravy in front of him.

"It smells delicious."

"It was truly wonderful, Sylas. That spice. I'm not used to it, but I do enjoy it. I really do. Please, sit. The sooner we get your crops started, the sooner I can teach you your new powers."

"Apparently, one of your new powers involves me," Azor told Sylas as he made his plate.

"Yes, Soulfire. I'm glad you got that one," Tilbud said. "It's smart of you to listen to the recommendations of a friend and not choose something random and baffling, like some of Meldon's suggestions. A power that changes your voice into that of an orator? Great for telling stories, but not so useful if we need to battle our way through the Chasm. Although, having a great voice in the Chasm might make things easier there, especially if you are able to sooth others."

"It's true, then?" Azor's flames sank. "You really are planning to go to the Chasm?"

"That hasn't been decided yet. I need to talk to Quinlan."

"He's still asleep, last I checked," she said. "Has he decided how long he will stay?"

"Is he that bad?" Sylas spooned some of the spicy gravy into his mouth, his eyes watering at the sudden burst of heat. "I know he's rough around the edges."

"If he is *rough around the edges,* as you say, I'd hate to meet a human who is entirely rough."

"I don't mind the fellow," Tilbud said. "Loud, yes, but I've met rougher ruffians."

"I'll talk to Quinlan today or tomorrow," Sylas said. "But before we do anything, or make any big plans, we have to get these crops planted."

"And then, my friend, you'll need to be ready to protect your fields at night."
Azor glanced from Tilbud to Sylas, worry in her eyes.

"I will only stay here when I'm actively farming," Sylas told her. "My hat will reduce the days it takes for my crops to grow. So perhaps I'll do something like five days here and two days at the pub. Or, we can switch, if you'd prefer guard duty. If I leave my hat here, it will let us know if demons are present. Cornbread will help."

"But Patches goes where you go," she said.

"Yes, that would be ideal considering his ability. I hate using him in that way, though."

"You aren't using him, Sylas; he is designed for this, considering he came with the pub." Tilbud took a final bite of his biscuits and gravy. "I know I said I could, but I can't possibly eat any more. A pity, really. I wish I had the room in my stomach. Azor, my dear, most wonderful of fire spirits, this was bloody excellent, and I do hope you make it again sometime, preferably when I am around."

"You have been around a lot, recently."

"An astute observation. What can I say?" Tilbud grinned at the two of them, the corners of his mustache lifting. "I am a sucker for adventure, among other things."

———

Sylas stood at the top of one of his fields, holding the corn on the cob. Similar to the way he had first brewed, even though Sylas had already known about the process, his new farmer class gave him an instant understanding of what needed to be done next.

Now wearing his straw hat with charms, Sylas turned the cob over and removed some of the kernels from the top. Tilbud had already transferred the three farming skills he needed, which had been much easier than the process for flying. It had been a simple initiation, the archlumen glowing and that glow passing to Sylas.

It made instinctual sense and Sylas knew exactly what he needed to do next. He cast his hand out and the kernels hovered into the air and rapidly multiplied.

[Spend 500 Mana Lumens to seed your fields? Y/N?]

"Yes," Sylas said.
The kernels zipped toward the rows of soil and planted themselves.

[Add stakes and a line to manage your growth.]

Sylas understood the prompt and could see the stakes now with a line of rope to help keep the cornstalks straight.

He made a mental note to check the shed for some rope and turned to the next row. Sylas planted this one in the same way. As Azor and Tilbud stood back, he did this until all ten of his fields were fully planted, the soil suddenly fresh and turned, green buds already showing by the time he approached his front porch.

"We'll make a bloody farmer out of you yet," Tilbud said.

"I just need stakes and rope, but I'll get that later. Shall we?"

"Right. More powers to learn. Perhaps, yes, perhaps this isn't the right place to do it. Might I suggest we move to the woods, to that same meadow where I taught you to fly? It's not so far from here."

Cornbread, who was lying near Tilbud's feet, looked up at Sylas.

"Let's get them back to the pub."

The farm dog barked as if she understood him.

"I might be wrong, and I do wish there was a spell for animal communication, but I believe Cornbread might want to stay here now." Tilbud smiled down at her as she wagged her tail. "She has a role in all of this, you know. It's her duty to protect your fields."

"Right. In that case, we will leave Patches here for now as well, and we can take him back to the pub after I'm done. Quinlan will hopefully be up by then."

"Hopefully," Azor said, her arms crossed over her chest.

"Works for me." Tilbud stood and took a deep breath in through his nostrils. "I must say, there is something enjoyable about this farm life that I hadn't anticipated. A bit boring, yes, but that's only because the demons haven't come yet."

"And you're certain they will?"

"With a blossoming hub of mana like this? Yes, I'm certain. But that's what Cornbread and your new powers are for. Shall we?" He motioned to the forest. "It is a wonderful day to learn something new."

Patches remained invisible as he followed the big man, the magician, and the fire spirit into the forest. They flew overhead, easy enough to track, and the pub cat was curious as to what they could possibly be doing.

They sure left in a hurry . . . Cornbread had stayed behind, the farm dog saying something about watching the fields. Patches understood her desire to protect the Farmly Realm, and he would help her to the best of his ability. But he certainly wasn't going to sit around a boring farm all day.

I have my own realm to protect as well. Patches was itching to get back to the pub. It had been varmint-free for a while now, but that didn't mean they wouldn't come again. *When they do, I'll be ready.*

He traveled through a hollowed-out tree trunk hopped from stone to stone over a trickling stream, and carefully made his way around purple mushrooms with big blue dots on their caps, which smelled poisonous.

Patches paused.

He looked up again and spotted the magician, who twisted in the air, golden bits of mana spiraling around his legs. The fire spirit was next, accompanied by a *whoosh* of flames, and finally the big man, who was doing his best to keep up, his hands at his sides like it would make him fly faster.

The piebald pub cat took off yet again, still invisible. This time it was straight through the bramble, where he startled a rabbit feeding on a bit of grass. The rabbit raced away, Patches letting it go for now. It wasn't the kind of varmint he normally went after anyway.

But if you come anywhere near the Tavernly Realm . . .

Patches crept low to the ground as he came upon a meadow, where he found the two humans and the fire spirit standing together, discussing something. A golden glow engulfed the magician. It moved forward in a nebulous way until it completely surrounded the big man.

He looked down at his hands and nodded. The big man turned suddenly, his palm out, and pointed at a lone tree.

Patches nearly jumped backward as a bolt of mana struck the tree trunk. His ears flattened, whiskers pressing back as he watched the mana sizzle out.

That was strong . . .

The magician slowly clapped and offered the big man two enthusiastic thumbs up.

What followed was a lengthy explanation, Patches listening to the peculiarities of human speech. It was too bad he couldn't understand them. They could have been discussing anything, from having a picnic to taking down the entire forest using mana.

There was no real way to tell, although Patches didn't suspect they were looking to do that much damage. *The tree is smoldering, however . . .* Patches looked back to the trunk that the big man had blasted with mana.

The magician cast his hand toward the big man, floating him into the air. He continued explaining what was happening for a moment as the big man floated there. After cracking his knuckles, the magician then carefully sent this hand out wide, in the same gesture one would make if they were flinging something away.

The big man was lowered to the ground. He turned toward Patches, startling the cat. He approached, Patches doing his best to remain absolutely still. The big man picked up a large hunk of wood, which he balanced against his shoulder.

He returned to the magician and the fire spirit. The big man placed the log on the ground. He stepped back and performed the same gestures that the magician had just moments ago.

The log floated into the air.

With a grunt, the big man cast his hand out to the right, and the log hurtled away.

Whack!

It struck the same tree he had blasted earlier and splintered into sticks and twigs. The magician had him do this again, with one of the smaller pieces.

A new discussion started as the magician paced back and forth like some sort of professor. He instructed the fire spirit to come stand near him, and then twisted his finger up in a swirl, as if he were describing the way she should move. He touched his arm, and as he pulled his hand away, the water spirit took shape.

The water spirit swished forward, coating a swath of the forest and nearly getting Patches wet in the process.

Patches was so shocked by the sudden shower that he nearly turned visible again, stopping himself from doing so just in time. He was glad he did once the fire spirit turned to the big man.

She curved into the air and dove directly at him, merging into his form. Patches had seen her do something similar before, so this didn't startle him as much as the water spirit had moments before.

A purple flame flared and settled on the big man's shoulders.

He turned to the area of the forest that had just been dampened and sent one leg back, as if he were about to wield a weapon.

Further instruction from the magician had Patches twitching with anticipation, not certain of what was about to happen. He found out soon enough as the big man brought both hands back and practiced thrusting them forward.

More instruction. The magician swung his arm as if it were a club.

The big man nodded, focused again, and then said something under his breath to what Patches assumed was the fire spirit. He took another step back and charged forward.

Whoooompf!

What he released next was unlike anything Patches had ever seen before. The giant fireball was followed by an explosion, one that instantly ignited a large section of the forest. The water spirit surged into action to put the fire out.

What is he planning? Patches wondered as he started slowly to back away. He looked one more time at the entire scene, shuddered, and turned.

Patches ran as fast as he could back to the farm, where he found Cornbread waiting for him on the front porch.

What is it? the dog asked as she immediately sniffed Patches. She licked his face and he batted her away. *Are you—*

I'm fine! Get away from me. The big man, the magician, the fire spirit. They are learning new spells, but one of them was absolutely mental. You could burn the forest down doing something like that.

Is that what that explosion was?

You heard it from here?

Of course I did. I have excellent hearing and smelling. My eyesight isn't as good, but it is still decent. Are you telling me the big man made that explosion?

He did. I saw him do it with my own two eyes.

Cornbread nodded and looked out at the fields of what would soon be corn. *Whatever he's doing, he's doing it to protect us. I trust him. Don't you?*

I do. But I still didn't like it. I know you heard it, but you weren't there. An attack like that could be devastating. It could destroy the Tavernly Realm. Or the Farmly Realm.

Cornbread huffed. *I trust him. He's a good human. He would never do something like that.*

————

Sylas checked his status to see that his forest experiments had cost him nearly four hundred Mana Lumens. This wasn't great considering what he normally earned on a Fireday night, but it was important to be able to use the new powers. Even now, as he prepared to open for the night, Sylas's thoughts kept circling back to what he had done.

He looked down at his hand. The Field Warden power would be an added bonus on any hunt he joined in the future. Same with Whimsical Drift. But Soulfire would be the one that would likely save him at some point, at the expense of those around him if he wasn't careful with it.

He didn't know if he'd always be joined by Tilbud, who could deal with any fire because of Horatio. If Tilbud wasn't there, Sylas knew he would have to be extra careful.

"Just the man I was looking for," Quinlan said as he came down the stairs, his hair a mess. "I have decided to head back to Geist tomorrow. Been loving it here, though. I just don't want to wear out my welcome, and as you may have picked up on, I'm a bit sweet on the innkeeper there, Priscilla. Pretty Priscilla."

"Is that what you call her?"

"Sometimes. Why are you looking at me like that?"

"We really haven't talked much about what I'm going to say next, but I wanted to run it by you." Sylas glanced over to Azor, who was frantically sweeping, even though the place was dust free. "Care to join us?"

"Is this *that* kind of talk?" Quinlan asked.

"It might be."

"In that case, care to pour up a pint?"

"Only if it's on the house."

"You strike a hard bargain, mate."

Soon, Quinlan had a fresh pint of the flamefruit ale. "Go on, then."

"The Chasm."

"What about it?"

Azor flared up beside Quinlan. "Sylas is thinking about going there in search of your friend and his father."

"Azor."

"Sorry," she said, "I just got a bit ahead of myself."

"Going to the Chasm, eh?" Quinlan took a long sip of his pint. "It's dangerous."

"I'm aware. I spent today learning powers that would help me there."

"And they don't like us going there, you know."

"They?"

"The guards at the Hexveil, the people above."

"People from the Celestial Plains?"

"Those are the ones."

"I keep hearing more about them, and it makes me question whose side they're on."

Quinlan laughed. "They aren't on our side, I can tell you that much, mate. I saw some of them once, you know, some procession in Battersea. Bloody full of themselves, the lot of them. Parading around in white silk, gold, all things bright, really. The exact opposite of the cozy gloom we have here, which, if we're being honest, I much prefer."

"Tilbud says there are ways to get through without being detected."

"There are."

"I did," Azor said. "But that's because I was weak."

"That's one way to do it," Quinlan told the two of them. "You can practically pass through the Hexveil if you're down to your last MLus. The guards won't even see you. But if you try to cross with any more than that, they'll swarm you."

"I've seen that," Sylas said, recalling how they had all seemingly moved at the same time, the towering guards in their blackened armor, robotic in nature.

"There are other ways in, but you have to really want this, Sylas."

"I don't know just yet. But I think it's the right thing to do. I'd like to discuss it with Nuno the manaseer first, but there's no telling when he'll show."

"Yes, they can be mysterious, those types. Heh. Kael will be one in the future, if there is a future. I've been before, you know."

"To the Chasm?"

"Briefly. A hunt took me there."

"How?"

"There are some things that come from the Chasm that you can't let escape, things that will return to haunt you if you do. It was one of them. You don't want to see one of them."

"What is it?" Sylas asked. "I've seen my fair share by now."

"Yeah? Name them."

Sylas listed the demons that he had encountered from the Chasm.

"Not bad. Well, heh, all of them are bad, but you know what I'm saying here. For a newcomer like yourself, that's quite a bit. But you also live close to the Hexveil. It is to be expected, if we're being bloody honest. Anyway, this demon I was telling you about. Imagine if a bull and a tiger were somehow merged, and they had the same properties as a Voidslither, meaning they can become intangible. Same sort of sheet-in-the-beating-wind movement too, but a bull. And a tiger. They don't even want that thing in the Chasm." He took another sip from his pint. "It's called a Taurigraith."

"Taurigraith. I'll have to ask Tiberius about that one."

Quinlan laughed. "Yeah, do that, mate, and watch the Thorny bastard look at you dumbfounded. All high and mighty, our lord commander. I guarantee Tib hasn't encountered one of those. They are legendary monsters. The kinds that aren't ranked. The kind that our guild will give you a plaque and enough Mana Lumens to keep you high off life in Battersea from now until your next *next* deathday. You would have seen his plaque if he had one. All I'm saying."

"I saw the tracks from one," Azor said, and she showed with her hands how big they were. "About that big, and they don't have hooves like a bull, they have clawed feet like a tiger. Or Patches."

The cat, who rested on the windowsill, looked up at them, mewed sleepily, repositioned himself, and yawned.

"Sleepy cat, that one," Quinlan said with a chuckle. "Anyway, Taurigraith. You should ask Tiberius about that one, see if it makes him flinch. Probably will. Big bastard gave me a right fright, and to kill it, I had to head across the Hexveil. I had a permit, but even then, the guards at the gate gave me hell. They aren't human, you know."

"I knew they were something else."

"The guards are on assignment from the Celestial Plains. That bulky armor, you wouldn't believe it, but there's actually a smaller person in there. They're controlling it with mana. Strange stuff."

"So to get across, we would need a permit?"

"Yeah, but you aren't going to get a permit. Why would you need to go there? If it's for a Hallowed Pursuit, they'll have you join one of the coteries. They won't let you go to find a friend."

"And my father."

"That either."

"But you could find them, right? The same way you tracked Karn?"

Quinlan finished his ale. He placed it on the counter and Sylas filled up another before he spoke again. "I would be able to find Raelis. I briefly saw him before he left. We'd find his coterie through publicly available information. How do you know your father's there, again?"

"Catia, a lumengineer, told me."

"But he is from the Celestial Plains, right?"

"Right. My mother is there too."

"Aren't all our mothers, mate." Quinlan raised his mug to Sylas. The way that he held it let Sylas see *The Old Lamplighter* etching on its outer surface. This reminded him that he still needed to visit Battersea to order additional supplies.

"Maybe Tilbud would know."

"Could be. Where did he run off to anyway?"

"Back to Duskhaven. He'll come later for a pub quiz. He did one last night, but he traditionally does it on Fireday and he likes to make a show of it."

"I'm making fish-and-chips tonight," Azor said to Sylas. "I forgot to tell you."

Quinlan grinned. "Did I say I was leaving? I'm definitely leaving tomorrow. That is, if you don't mind me staying"

"You can stay as long as you want," Sylas said. "I could use you on the farm too, once I've used Mana Saturation."

"You're too kind, mate." Quinlan drank a bit of his ale. "Maybe we could speak to Tilbud about finding your father. But I know he can help us find Raelis, and that's who we want if we're going to head off some invasion. It's a bit crazy, if you think about it."

"What is?"

"Because of the way the Underworld is organized, there isn't really a central government that we can go to rally their help. We could speak to the places that have a city council, places like Battersea, but most of this will have to be by word of mouth. And you're the only one receiving the warning at the moment, and others can't see it. So I don't know if they will believe you."

"I was thinking that myself."

"But if we decide that it is Ember Hollow that we want to defend, that this is where we make our stand, that is more manageable. I'll bloody be there, and I know Kael will as well. Raelis too, once we find him."

"I'll speak to Tilbud."

"Good idea. He may have more insight, but once it's time to crack on, I'll be here, no question about it." Quinlan burped. "Sorry, Azor. That one was unexpected."

"Most burps are."

"Do fire spirits burp?"

"You'll know when we do."

"Fair enough. Sylas, mate, whatever you decide, I'm right there with you. If that involves going to the Chasm, we'll have to be clever about it. But it is doable, especially with a strong archlumen."

"Tilbud always has another trick up his sleeve. If there is anything I've learned about that man, it is that he is entirely unpredictable with what he can do. I would bet that he has only shown me a sliver of the powers he is capable of wielding. Plus, if there is something he really needs, he can get it from the Archlumenry. If it's something I need to fund, I will be able to do that pretty soon here as well."

"Because you're a bloody farmer now, yeah? Richie Rich over here."

"Something like that. I'll have my first batch of corn by next Tombsday."

"Next Tombsday. Heh. Maybe I'll stay until then. By that point, we should know if we're going to journey into hell itself. I'll tell you this though, mate, there isn't another man that I would do it with aside from Raelis and my brother."

"Same," Sylas said.

"As for these new powers of yours, when you're ready to put them to the test, let me know, yeah?"

"What do you mean?"

"We're close to the Hexveil. I get notices of demons daily around here, mostly low-level. But if a big one comes up, you and me, we can get it."

"And me," Azor said.

"The more the merrier. But maybe we keep Tiberius off that hunt."

"Yeah?"

"Yeah, I'll keep my eye on the notifications. If we get lucky, we get lucky." He raised his mug to Sylas. "Cheers."

————

Cornbread appeared at the door of the big man's bedroom at the farmhouse. She was just about to bark at Patches and the resting man but then decided otherwise. *Stealthy,* she said as she transitioned to a whisper. *Cat? Are you paying attention to me?*

Yes.

Something is out there, in the fields.

Patches hopped down from the bed. He stretched, yawned, and then joined Cornbread at the door, where he paused. *I don't hear anything, and I am certain my hearing is better than yours.*

Cornbread threw her head back and took a big whiff of the air. In doing so, a gridline of the farmhouse and its fields painted across her mind's eye. She could see it now, the spectral demon, a small one, right there on the edge of the property. *It's there.*

Your smell really is that good?

It's even better than this but I'm picking up your scent as well because you're so close to me.

Patches rubbed his body against Cornbread to annoy her. *Am I?*

This is serious.

The cat straightened up. *You're right. In that case, you lead the way. Unless you want to try to do it with stealth. Then I'll lead the way.*

Stealth won't work the same on these types. You can't sneak up on them. As soon as we're out the door, it will know. Then, we chase it.

And kill it.

Not tonight. Cornbread hung her head with shame for a moment. *Neither of us are fast enough to reach it before it disappears. They do this all the time, scouting.*

Patches nodded. *So that's what it is doing?*

Scouting, yes. Then the Mana Ghouls will come back in force. We might need to speak to the other dogs about cornering it.

I've only met the one, Patches told Cornbread as he was reminded of the white dog with its clipped ears, the one that protected the tomato farm.

Yes, him. Some of the others are nicer. The pepper dog is the nicest.

Pepper dog?

We'll go meet her after we deal with the ghoul. Come on. Cornbread approached the door of the farmhouse. She jumped a few times and used her feet to open it.

She took off as soon as it swung open, Patches bolting after her. Cornbread never barked, but she did gnash her teeth as she ran toward the ghoul. The Mana Ghoul swelled into the air in panic as she neared it.

Cornbread jumped to bite it. She managed to take a corner of the demon as it began its retreat, the tendrils of its black, billowy body whipping all around as it rushed toward the forest.

This should do, Cornbread said as Patches caught up. She now had a piece of its form in her mouth, the hunk reminding Patches of one of the rags the fire spirit used when she wiped down counters. *We don't have much time.*

We don't?

It will disappear, Cornbread said, the piece still in her mouth. *This way.*

She took off running, the farm dog hurtling down dirt road until the air filled with a new scent, one Patches was a bit unfamiliar with. The sharp, pungent fragrance caused Patches to sneeze. He sneezed so hard that he actually lost his balance.

Cornbread turned to him. *The peppers. They're strong. They will be harvested soon.*

Hey! A female voice called out. A dog just about the size of Cornbread but with gray flecks in her coat jumped onto the path. She approached Cornbread with her tail wagging. Like Cornbread, she had a collar with a name on it.

Hi! Cornbread said excitedly. *This is new.* She dropped the piece of demon onto the ground.

Patches approached and sniffed.

He did this for two reasons, the first being to know the scent of the demon and the second to let the other female dog know that he wasn't afraid of her, and that he was casual enough around dogs to choose when and if he wanted to greet them.

Who is the cat?

My owner had a cat before me. Now he has both of us, Cornbread told the other dog. *He owns a place where humans drink and eat.*

The Tavernly Realm, Patches said.

The other dog sat. *Interesting.* Her eyes narrowed on Patches. *Are you done yet?*

Patches hopped away from the swath of demon flesh.

Good. Let me get a smell of this. The new dog sniffed for a moment. *Yes, a new pack. This isn't a good sign.*

What do you mean? Patches asked. *Is this bad?*

It's bad. These demons travel in packs.

Like dogs?

They are nothing like us, she told him. *And since you have a new farm—*

Cornbread barked. *Our farm isn't new.*

I mean that you have a new crop, it will likely alert their pack.

Even if we attacked it? Patches asked.

Yes. They aren't smart, these sorts of demons. They're hungry. Very, very hungry. But now, I know what it smells like, and I'll be able to alert the others.

Should I go around with it to show them? Cornbread asked.

Patches hopped back again as the swath of demon flesh sizzled and popped. It quickly faded.

Too late, the other dog said.

So what do we do now, exactly? Patches asked the dogs.

Cornbread spoke after a long pause. *Now, we wait until tomorrow night and see what happens. The big man will need to saturate his fields the day after, which will likely be when they strike. But they may try it earlier. And next time, I'll alert him.*

Wake him up?

You said he was powerful, right?

He is. But he needs the fire spirit to be even stronger.

And she's back at the Tavernly Realm. I thought you said he had powers of his own as well.

Patches swished his tail back and forth. *He does, but I don't want him to get hurt.*

He won't get hurt, Cornbread growled. *But those nasty demons will.*

The other dog barked in agreement.

Must we all bark? Patches asked the pair.

You can't bark? Cornbread turned to Patches and tilted her head.

No.

Are you sure?

I'm sure.

Do you want to try?

Patches turned back toward the farmhouse. *Goodnight, both of you.*

———

Sylas's daily ritual of staring at the invasion message and his loan payment made him wish there was a way to be reminded later in the day, after he'd had a moment to process things:

[**You have 54 days until the invasion.**]
[**A loan payment of 85 has been deducted from your total Mana Lumens. Your total loan balance is 17276 Mana Lumens.**]

It also wasn't great to see that he had less Mana Lumens than he had the previous day on account of all the magicking he'd done, from his new spells to Mana Infusion. At least he had a nice list of new spells to make him feel like he was growing.

While he didn't have an active quest at the moment, he couldn't just relax the entire day. Knowing his life and the way things worked out, Sylas would probably get into something by the time The Old Lamplighter opened its doors that night.

Name: Sylas Runewulf
Mana Lumens: 4132/4132

Class: Brewer
Secondary Class: Farmer
[Lumen Abilities:]
Flight
Quill
Mana Infusion
Mana Saturation
Harvest Silos
Field Warden
Whimsical Drift
Soulfire

Cornbread burst into the room barking, which made Sylas miss Azor. He all but expected the fire spirit to materialize out of thin air and wish him a happy Specterday.

The dog hopped onto the bed, startling Patches, who jumped back and took off toward the other room. Cornbread got under the covers and popped her head out, panting wildly.

"What's got into you?" Sylas asked as he petted her. Cornbread barked. She looked to the other room, turned back to Sylas, and barked again. "I'll get up and then we'll go check the crops."

Sylas entered the kitchen, where he had a piece of bread he had carried with him from the pub last night. He still needed a bit of food here at the farmhouse, yet he also knew himself well enough to know the reason he hadn't stocked the place with food. The pub would always be his home, yet Sylas needed to be reasonable considering he would be spending four nights in a row here when he planted.

Cornbread circled him, the dog whining. "We'll get some food for both of us. Today. How about it, girl? I go to Battersea, get the bottles I need from the Ale Alliance, and pick up some food. Something we can easily store here. Just a bit of breakfast, some snacks. That's all."

Cornbread barked.

Patches, who had been resting in a corner, got back to his feet and rushed toward the bedroom.

"Are you and Patches getting along?"

Yet again, Cornbread barked.

"Good, good girl." He sat at the table and the dog hopped into his lap, even though she was a bit too large to be doing that. Sylas hugged her while he shared his piece of bread with the dog. "It's good to be dead, you know that?"

CHAPTER FIFTEEN

LANDLORDS

Mira made up her mind to visit Sylas.

She hadn't approved of his purchase of the farm at first, and she still felt like he was taking on more than he could handle, but she also wanted to support him. And maybe he was right after all. No, he *was* right, it had just taken her some time to work up to admitting it.

It got too busy at the pub last night with the quiz and the music that followed from Bart and Mary, the lutist who sometimes accompanied him. Mira had barely been able to get in a word, and, while he normally insisted on walking her home, she had snuck out on her own so Sylas could focus on the tasks that she knew he needed to handle at the pub.

Mira briefly scanned her status as she fixed her dress in front of the mirror.

Name: Mira Ravenbane
Mana Lumens: 1841/2696
Class: Apothecary
[Active Quest Contracts:]
Create Elixir of Easing for Evelyn Barrowsly
[Lumen Abilities:]
Flight
Lumen Beam
Mana Trace

The fact that Sylas had double-classed also made Mira want to do something to improve her powers. She'd never really thought about taking out a loan to buy some sort of property that would allow her to gain a new class, even if the option had always been available. This was due to the way she was raised: her father and mother were very strict with money, the type to never take on debt.

Now, as she examined herself, she realized how much this had set her back in the Underworld. Mira knew she *could* take on debt here, improve herself and her prospects, and she wouldn't die doing it, nor would she forever be indebted to a system.

"Off we go," Mira said to herself, rather than dwelling on the mistakes of the past. She knew how those could weigh someone down.

She grabbed a picnic basket that she'd already packed and didn't say good-bye to her uncle, who she could already hear was working out back with his militia.

After a brisk walk, Mira reached Nelly's General Store and entered to find Karn behind the counter. "Morning, Mira. You opening up?"

"I was planning to visit Sylas."

"Good to hear. I still feel like I haven't had a chance to properly thank him for what he did."

"Is Mira here?" Nelly called to Karn from upstairs.

"She sure is, love."

Nelly came waltzing down, the woman happier than Mira had ever seen her. She gave Mira a big hug and patted her on the shoulders before stepping back. "You look pretty. Is that a new dress?"

Mira blushed as she looked down at her dark purple dress. "No, I've had it. I just don't wear it very often."

"I like your boots too. You really have an eye for fashion."

"Stop it, Nelly."

"What? You do. Are you off to visit Sylas?"

"How did you know?"

Nelly took Mira by the arm and led her away from Karn, who turned back to the inventory he was taking. "I know," she told Mira. "I've seen the two of you together. It's quite obvious."

Mira went pale. "Is it?"

"What's wrong if it is? We're dead, Mira." Nelly smiled at her. "We might as well enjoy our lives, yeah?"

"We are both quite busy."

"Did you not hear what I just said? The part about being dead?"

Mira laughed. "You are quickly becoming a Nelly I hardly recognize."

Nelly placed her hand behind her head and struck a pose. "I'm the same Nelly, just a happier one. The way my life ended was bloody terrible. I wouldn't wish it upon anyone, and then to end up here without Karn." Her exuberance faded.

"Oh, Nelly, I'm sorry if—"

"No, it's fine, Mira. What I'm saying here is enjoy your afterlife. Even with the message."

"You mean Sylas's message?"

"Yes. I haven't even told Karn about it yet," she whispered. "I probably should. Or I should focus on the good things. We're meeting with the MLR Bank today about opening an inn. We'll need to construct the place as well, but I have already spoken to Anders about that, and such things go quite fast here."

"I've seen that. When will you start?"

"Today if we're lucky. We'll be up and running in a week."

"That fast, huh?" Mira knew how this was plausible, especially if someone had charms. Anders didn't, but he must have known someone who did.

"That fast."

"I need to visit a banker myself," Mira said.

"Are you expanding your annex?"

"No, not that. I'm quite happy with the space." Mira looked across the large space to the door, currently locked, which had a sign over the door that said *Ravenbane Apothecary*. "What else does Ember Hollow need?"

"You should be asking yourself what Ember Hollow needs that you would like to give it. There is the market."

"I believe Sylas is interested in that."

"You could go in on it with him, could you not?"

"A market?" Mira considered the abandoned structures. "I'd have to class as a landlord."

"If you did that, you could also buy up some of the property available—and I'm sure there's some because this place is half abandoned—and rent it out, yeah?"

"I think some of my uncle's men are just living in some of the places for free at the moment. I wouldn't want to run them out."

"How did they manage that? Don't all the doors unlock only with a deed?"

"The rules are much looser this close to the Chasm. There are plenty of abandoned structures that I could purchase without running them out. I would never do that."

"Of course not."

"Some of them are quite agreeable, especially Duncan and Cody."

"So, two of them are quite agreeable?" Nelly asked.

"I suppose you could say it like that. You know, that's actually not a bad idea. Ember Hollow might very well be up-and-coming, and to own some of the land here could prove beneficial. Plus, I could see to its upkeep and, you know, turn this whole place around."

"That's an incredible idea. Do ask Sylas about it."

"Ask him today?"

"Why not? I know it feels like we have all the time in the world here, but we don't have as much as we'd like, if his message is to be believed. Mira," Nelly placed a hand on her arm, "we'll turn this place around regardless, but I don't want to see it turn around without someone like you at the helm, someone who actually gives a damn."

"I do give a damn."

"Yes, you do. So ask Sylas. Make plans. And cheers."

"Cheers?"

"Yes, cheers to everything." Nelly hugged her again.

Mira took the portal to the Seedlands, the apothecary lost in her thoughts of what was to come. She didn't even notice Sylas moving through his fields until he called out to her, and she saw he was wearing his funny hat and had a pair of tinted glasses on his face.

"I brought breakfast," she said as she thrust the picnic basket forward.

Sylas, who held a pitchfork, stuck it into the ground. He wiped a bit of sweat from his forehead, the fields around him perfectly staked, the corn already at its full height. "How did you know I was hungry?"

"Lucky guess."

"Any big plans today?" he asked as Cornbread came around and rushed toward Mira.

"Just opening the shop."

"Any chance you'll open late? I was thinking of portaling to Battersea to pick up some things. I wouldn't mind the company."

"Sure," Mira said, "I wanted to talk to you anyway about an idea I had. But only if we can have some tea and pastries. I know of an adorable bakery near the water there."

"Deal. But I'm paying."

———

Mira was a bit hesitant to broach the subject with Sylas, even though Nelly was entirely right. It made sense. If both of them classed as landlords, they would be able to do much more than get the market up and running in Ember Hollow. That would be a perfect start, and acquiring some property afterward would allow them to manage the growth of the village.

Her head buzzed with the ideas, the potential, but she also felt like it would be asking too much, that Sylas wouldn't think it is a good idea. There was only one way to find out.

The two were now at the coffee shop and bakery she had recommended, not far from where they had first met Nuno. Sylas looked around like he was familiar with the area, like he knew where they were.

"We could visit Nuno's home?" she suggested once he mentioned their proximity to the place.

His eyes shifted to Mira and warmed immediately. "I would, but that place was strange. Too strange for my taste. He'll come to us when he's ready, no need to rush the man. The boy? He's a teenager, isn't he?"

"A teenager who is much older than us. We can't forget that," she said as flamefruit turnovers came, the pastries fresh out of the oven. "Those smell wonderful," she told the waitress.

"The best in Battersea, ma'am," the woman said. "I'll be back with your tea in a jiff. You wanted the cardamom tea, and you, the creamshade nectar, yes?"

"That's right," Mira said. "You'll like the creamshade," she assured Sylas once the waitress was gone. "Now, this idea I have."

"Yes, tell me what you're thinking, Mira. I'm interested. Always interested."

"So, you know how there is that abandoned market in Ember Hollow."

"Yes, what about it?"

"Are you still interested in it?"

"The village could use a market, but I'd have to take on an additional class to purchase it."

"The landlord class, and before you could do that, you would need to purchase the market to have the paperwork you needed for a lumengineer and the Landlord Guild to approve your class addition."

"Yes, same process with the farm."

"Exactly. Now, what I was thinking, and I hope I'm not being too forward about this, was that you and I purchase the market together. We both class as landlords, and we work with the Farm and Field Guild and the Merchant Guild to outfit the place. We could have a produce section, meat, antiques, and other items."

"What about the general store? We don't want to compete with Nelly."

"No, we don't. Nelly must know something I don't know because she was the one that suggested I ask you."

"They already sell different things at the store, household items, some food supplies, and clothing. We could specifically *not* sell those things at the market and focus on local produce and antiques, as you said. Produce and antiques."

"And meat."

"It would be a rather odd market, but if we were known for something, it would bring more people to Ember Hollow on account of the market," Sylas said as the tea came. Mira's was dark and his was a milky purple color. He tasted it.

"Well?"

"It's really good," he said, smacking his lips. "It reminds me of warm milk, with a bit of honey and something else, some sweet root. It's quite filling. But back to the market, and regarding competition with Nelly. If she suggested we go in this together, I think her overall plan is to bring more people to Ember Hollow, which will help the inn they are going to have. Soon, right?"

"In a week."

"That's fast."

"They're finalizing it today."

"Good for them. I've yet to spend any time with them since Karn came into the picture. I need to, I've just been so busy with the farm."

Mira took a sip of her tea, which had just a hint of spice to it. She enjoyed seeing Sylas in the bakery, the big man dwarfing his chair in an almost comical way. Sylas was eternally rugged, yet also soft. "The farm looked good, but I have to ask, what are you going to do with corn?"

"Aside from sell it? Maybe do something with it. Eat it. Corn isn't so bad. Not really common where I'm from, but I had it on the border."

"From my kingdom."

"Yes. Loads that can be done with it. And that gives me an idea. The market, *our* market—"

"So you like the idea?"

"I wasn't clear earlier?" Sylas ran his hand over his beard. "I suppose I wasn't. I love the idea. If we're both classed as landlords, there is a load we will be able to do in Ember Hollow."

"Yes, I was thinking the same."

"So, our market, what about this? What if we made it an antiques, relics, rare items type of market? Do you have something with Legendary Locks? Come get it appraised at our market. Do you have something with a slight enchantment, or do you have items that you'd like to trade that have historical value? Sell it at our market. Antiques, relics, rare items, things a bit off the beaten path—is there anything like that in the Underworld?"

"A market of oddities?"

"Not oddities, rarities. Face it, the market is already pretty junky as it is. We capitalize on that by focusing on the sale of these objects. It also has an additional effect?"

"What's that?"

"It brings these objects to Ember Hollow, and some are worth quite a bit, which brings more MLus into the village."

"Which can be used to improve it. But we don't have taxes."

"And we don't want them, they will drive people away."

"How do we improve it without taxes?" Mira laughed. "This conversation has certainly taken a twist. Here I was thinking about classing as a landlord and running a little market."

"It would be little, but it would also be grand. I think. I don't know. I will be the first to tell you I'm winging it, but I see value in Ember Hollow and making it better."

"Others may not see eye to eye with you. My uncle."

"Your bloody uncle. I promise you, Mira, he'll like it in the end. He's a stubborn one, Tiberius, but once he sees that people are enjoying Ember Hollow and that he has more authority as more join his militia, I believe things could change. Maybe I'm delusional, though."

Mira knew that Tiberius could be as stubborn as a mule, but he was easily persuaded in the way that most men were easily persuaded—through an appeal to their egos. Mira could see her uncle eventually happy for Ember Hollow to be populated with newcomers, even if he was reluctant at first. She also saw a scenario in which he used this newfound interest in Ember Hollow as a power grab, a way to secure the town in some militaristic way.

This thought brought a frown to her face.

"What is it?" Sylas asked.

"My uncle. That might not work out in the way you think it will. He might take the sudden interest in the town as a way to expand the power of the militia. He has always been an isolationist at heart. This could bring that out even more."

Sylas set his tea down, the look on his face souring. "I didn't consider that. Perhaps that is a bridge we face when we get there. By the time that could even start to happen, we'd be well past the invasion, whatever that may entail."

"You'd be surprised."

"What do you suggest then? We abandon the market idea?"

"Absolutely not. I'm not letting my uncle get in the way. This is my decision to make, and I brought it to you because I think we'd make a good team."

"I think we'd make a good team too. It should be clear how I feel about you by now."

Mira cleared her throat, the apothecary not at all expecting Sylas to be so forthcoming. "And I, you," she finally said.

He chuckled. "You look as if you've seen a ghost, which is appropriate considering we're all dead."

"It's nothing like that. I have similar feelings for you," she said carefully. "But right now, I feel like they could get in the way."

"So we wait?"

"Wait until what? The invasion? We don't know what will happen yet."

"No, we do not. I would say that is the excitement in all of this, but it is absolutely anything but. It is an idea, though."

"Maybe we don't fully wait, but we wait a bit longer," Mira finally said. "My feelings for you aren't going to change."

"I don't see how mine would change for you unless you did something terrible."

The smile that had been on her face earlier formed again. "Terrible like what?"

"Steal my cat or my dog?"

"Please, Sylas, I don't want a pet, although Patches is cute."

"Cornbread is equally cute. I never thought I'd be the type to end up a pet owner. I suppose that is neither here nor there. We can investigate the market, purchasing it as co-owners. I would like that."

"Yes, let's." She raised her teacup to him and laughed. "Cheers, I guess."

"Cheers, Mira. Before we go back, would you care to take a boat ride? We could go to Everscene."

"Why would we do that? Don't you need to go to the Ale Alliance anyway?"

"I thought it would be a nice trip, and you're right, I do need to go. I have plans to bottle and sell ale to that inn we stayed at in the Shadowstone Mountains. I should probably give myself a quest contract so I can just get it done. Endless tasks, you know."

"The never-ending to-do list."

"It's how you know you're still alive, right?"

"Or dead," Mira said. "As for a boat ride, next time. I need to open my store, and I'm sure you have things to do on the farm."

"Yes, and I'd like to check with Quinlan."

"Planning something, are you?"

Sylas shrugged. "Just looking for new opportunities."

———

Sylas checked his fields that afternoon and found everything to be in order. Before heading back to the pub, he decided to seek out the pepper farmer who lived down the lane. He'd heard enough about the man named Sterling to warrant a meeting.

He approached the pepper farm and was greeted by a dog with gray hair, one that seemed to get along with Cornbread. The two dogs sniffed each other, played, and then ran back and forth through Sterling's pepper fields as Sylas knocked on his door.

"Can I help you?" a man asked after he opened the door. He was dressed a bit like an undertaker, with a black hat, coat, boots, and even a thin black tie. The man had long dark hair and a pipe sticking out of his mouth. He puffed it as Sylas spoke.

"I just wanted to stop in and say hello. I am running the corn farm now, Brom's old place, and I also run The Old Lamplighter in Ember Hollow."

"I see. I've heard good things about the pub."

"You should stop by some time. We have a feast on Wraithsday and a pub quiz on Fireday."

"Do you, now? I heard people talking about the place. Sorry, where are my manners? The name is Sterling, and that's my farm."

The two shook hands.

"Sylas Runewulf. I hope you don't mind, I already sampled a few of your peppers the other day. They were lying in the road."

Sterling grinned. "Fair game, then."

"I was actually wondering about buying some of your peppers, not a huge amount, but I have several ideas of ways I could use them. The fire spirit I'm bonded with," Sylas said, showing the man the tattoo on his arm, "likes to cook. And adding your peppers could give whatever she makes a kick."

"It would certainly do that. Not a good idea for all dishes, but for the right one, it might be delicious."

"And I might experiment with a spicy ale. But I wouldn't do that too often, just novelty."

"A spicy ale." Sterling brought his pipe back to his lips and puffed it as he nodded. "It could work," he finally said.

"I think it would be interesting."

"It would be that. Could be a disaster too. Anyway, I was just planning to lay my head down for a nap. Didn't get enough naps in our world on the account of being on the front line."

"Aurumite?"

"Indeed. You?"

"Same."

The half grin on Sterling's face morphed to a full-on smile. "I thought you might be with a last name like Runewulf, but one can never tell, especially if someone is from the border regions. Anyway, if you need anything, let me know. Once it's harvest time, I'll bring you a basket of peppers to play around with. Consider it a farmwarming gift. And be sure to let me sample some of that corn. I haven't had corn in ages."

"Neither have I," Sylas said.

The two dogs barked as they continued chasing one another. "Cornbread and Sunflower have always been good friends," Sterling said. He whistled and the dog named Sunflower came running up to him. "Come on," he told her, "it's time for our nap. Sylas"—the man tipped his hat at him—"it's nice meeting you."

———

Quinlan pulled Sylas aside later that night. Throughout the evening, Sylas had noticed the Quinlan hadn't been drinking. He would soon learn why.

The pair stood outside in the glow of the lamp in front of the pub. Nelly's General Store was still open next door, and there were a few people inside. Sylas also noticed a pair walking through the main street of Ember Hollow heading in the direction of the portal.

"Mate, there's been a development."

"Yeah? You found something?"

"I did. But I heard Tiberius's men talking about it as well." He eyes flitted back and forth. "A C-Rank demonic Wolftiger."

"A what now?"

"Hard to kill, but doable with two people," Quinlan said. "Doable with one person, really. I'm sure Tiberius will be around here later to round his men up. I'm surprised he's not here now, but one of them, the big guy—"

"Duncan."

"He said Tiberius was in Battersea at the salt bath. That he goes for his skin. A lord commander at the spa."

Sylas started to laugh. "I suppose that does make sense. A spa would be nice."

Quinlan buried his head in his hand. "No, you don't need one of them here."

"I wasn't thinking that," Sylas assured his old friend.

"Heh, right, mate. Maybe we'll go after all this is said and done. Anyway, this hunt. The reward is a pretty good one. Three thousand MLus. I've seen Wolftigers go much higher, but that's normally the B-Rank and above. Fifteen hundred each will do."

"How far is it from here?"

Quinlan's eyes glazed over, as if he could actually see the beast. "It's moving in the woods at the moment, toward the Seedlands."

"So we get it now. Will Tiberius know?"

"Not if we're smart about it. Our system doesn't tell us which hunter took the kill; it only tells us that the kill is no longer available."

Sylas touched the fire tattoo on his arm, which signaled Azor. The door of The Old Lamplighter swung open and Azor appeared.

"Quinlan and I need to do something, and it has to be secret."

"Secret?" she asked Sylas.

"A hunt," Quinlan said, "not far from here. We don't want Tiberius's men knowing."

"What about your mace and your armor?" Azor asked.

Sylas took a step back and glanced at the window on the second floor of the pub. "We can hop up there and get the stuff. Quinlan?"

"Works for me." Quinlan hovered into the air. "No maces, though. Won't do."

"What do I tell Mira?" Azor asked. What she really wanted to ask was if she could go with them, but she knew that wouldn't be possible. Someone would need to close up the pub.

"Mira? Tell her Quinlan had someone he wanted to meet in—" Sylas shook his head.

Azor understood. She was bonded with Sylas, and the longer their bond lasted, the more she recognized subtle changes in his demeanor and what they meant. "You don't want to lie to her."

"No, I do not. She wouldn't tell Tiberius anyway."

"I agree. I don't think she would. She was already complaining about her uncle earlier, but not in a mean way. I probably shouldn't speak for her, but I don't think she likes him, only that she has learned to accept his behavior, maybe something like that. Oops, I'm saying too much, aren't I?"

"You're fine, Azor, really. Just tell Mira the truth, but do so quietly. For Tiberius's men, I would say give them a free round, but that would look suspicious. Not to them, but to Tiberius. So just tell them Quinlan got into something in Cinderpeak and we decided to go there, that I also wanted to check on Iron Rose and thank her again for the painting."

"It is a lovely painting."

"Yes, it is."

Cornbread came around the pub and barked, the dog wagging her tail with excitement.

"How did . . . ? Right," Sylas said, "the cat door."

Quinlan landed, the man now in his armor and armed with his club, which Sylas had noticed before was covered in protrusions. He'd have to ask Quinlan about that later. Sylas wondered if it did something to the attacking power of the club.

"Mate, we going or what?"

"I thought you said no weapons."

"Heh. Bad habits. Can you take it back up for me when you get changed?"

"Sure. What about Cornbread?" Sylas asked him.

"Bring her. We'll cut her part of the reward. Hunting with a dog will make this easier." Quinlan glanced down at Cornbread, who had been wagging her tail so hard it caused her entire body to swish. She sat obediently, looked up at him, and grew serious. "Demon hunters who have subclassed as trackers have a bond with dogs."

"Azor, you've got this," Sylas told the fire spirit. "I'll be back later and we'll brew. Then I'll head to the farm."

"Busy night, yeah?"

He smiled at her. "You know it. Good luck."

Quinlan turned away. The sleeve of his chainmail armor that had been tied tightly over his missing hand slapped against his leather faulds.

Azor steeled herself. She really hated to see Sylas leave without her, especially for something dangerous like a hunt. "Good luck to yourselves, then, yeah?"

CHAPTER SIXTEEN

WOLFTIGER

Sylas was reminded yet again of why Quinlan had been so impressive, both in their former lives and now in the Underworld. It was as if the jovial man had a switch he could flick, one that turned him from an ordinary bloke into a world-class soldier in a matter of seconds. It showed in the way Quinlan moved, his focus, his courage, and his sudden understanding of their environment.

A force to be reckoned with.

It was a wonder Sylas had been his commanding officer. Yet Quinlan's other side, the comical man fond of causing a stir and following his own rules, had often been to his detriment.

And it was through a mixture of these two traits Quinlan had lost his hand.

Sylas had been there during that critical battle, one in which Quinlan had broken away from the formation to attack what he thought was an exposed lord commander. Sylas had shouted for him to return to the line, but Quinlan had ignored him; the man had a one-track mind at that point, rage in his eyes, fueled by bloodlust.

The lord commander, who had been a better swordsman than most, parried Quinlan's first attack and took his left hand off with the next.

That fast. Bravado to disaster. A clean cut.

It had been Sylas who had dragged Quinlan out of that fight, Sylas who had later killed the lord commander as an act of vengeance, and Sylas who kept Quinlan in his ranks after several other leaders of the Royal Guard had wanted him to retire due to his disability.

That had been such a fight, but as Sylas had explained then, *Even if he has one hand, Quinlan is still a better soldier than half my regiment.*

All those memories were gone in a flash as Sylas tuned back in to what Quinlan was saying.

"We're close," he whispered, body low to the ground, eyes scanning the trees ahead. "The Wolftiger is going to spring out at us if we get any closer. We need bait. Sylas, mate, do you trust me?"

"I do. Do you trust me?"

"You bet your arse I do. I'm going to ask you to do something that sounds really stupid. Right now, we're downwind of the Wolftiger."

"There's a breeze?"

"Subtle, but yeah. I also have a compass I'm looking at that you can't see. Tracker skills. And the compass tells me the wind direction. The reason I asked if you trusted me is because I know how you feel about Cornbread, and I don't want you to think I'm putting her in harm's way. I would never do something like that, mate. That bloody Wolftiger won't get a single bite, I guarantee it. I'm going to ask Cornbread to move ahead and bait it out of the trees."

"I have so many questions."

"You said you got magical glasses, right? Put them on."

Sylas popped open a pouch on his armor and removed the tinted glasses. He had gotten so wrapped up in the hunt that he had forgotten about them. Once he had them on his face, he looked ahead and saw a faint glow in the trees beyond.

"Keep them on. Cornbread is going to go ahead of us to root the Wolftiger out. As soon as it's revealed, we'll both blast it from behind."

"So that's why we didn't bring our weapons."

"No maces or clubs. Weapons like that are a last resort with this sort of monster. It'll chomp your mace in half at a B-Rank. This one is C-Rank, but that doesn't mean it isn't strong. We only want the bludgeoning weapons for the finale, once our mana has done damage. Do whatever you can *not* to let that bloody Wolftiger get near us. If it does, plan B."

"Plan B? Run?"

"Nah, mate, fly. And that's bad for us because the Wolftiger will be agitated, and by the time it settles, Tiberius and his men will be in the area. Best we do this right the first time." Quinlan crouched in front of Cornbread. As he petted the dog, he stared deeply into her eyes.

She blinked a few times, grunted, and took off.

"Be ready."

"How did you—"

"I can't explain it, but it will work, Sylas. Cornbread and I are locked in. Keep your focus on the Wolftiger, and don't worry about the farm dog."

Now with his glasses on, Sylas could see Cornbread racing ahead, her body covered in a faint glow, mana rippling past her tail. She ran right past the tree with the Wolftiger in it. The beast, which was easily the length of a horse, turned to her. It reared back and hopped down to another branch as it stalked the dog.

"Come on," Quinlan whispered as he took the lead.

Sylas followed after him, the two creeping closer to the tree as Cornbread barked and did a few nervous circles.

Quinlan raised his hand just as the Wolftiger jumped down to the forest floor.

Whoosh!

He hit it with a crackling swell of mana that ignited everything in front of them as it struck the Wolftiger.

The beast let out an angry roar as it hit the ground. The monster staggered to its feet, its rugged brown coat smoldering. It turned to Sylas and Quinlan, seething, its head a fearsome fusion of wolf and tiger, the piercing eyes of a wolf coupled with the powerful jaw and razor-sharp canines of a tiger.

Zapp!

Sylas fired a much smaller yet equally powerful shot that went wide. The Wolftiger changed trajectory as it lunged toward them, clearing the distance in a matter of seconds.

Whoompf!

Quinlan hit it with another charge, but it was less powerful than his last.

"I've got it!" Sylas cast his hand out and used Whimsical Drift to hurtle the beast to the side. It struck a tree, the timber cracking as it brought it down. Cornbread came in barking, ferocious as ever, her bark amplified to the point that it pushed Sylas back. The sound was entirely disorienting, her subsequent barks erupting like sonic booms and causing a deep, throbbing pain in his head.

Sylas's ears rang as he tried to make sense of the sound. He gripped his mace with both hands, prepared for an inevitable that never came.

The blast of mana that followed, courtesy of Quinlan, put the Wolftiger down for good. The beast hit the ground, let out a death rattle, twitched, and stopped moving.

Quinlan said something to Sylas, his voice barely audible. The man smiled now. He approached Sylas and clapped him on the shoulders.

Cornbread came around, wagging her tail.

"Not bad," Quinlan said, his voice growing louder as the ringing in Sylas's head slowly subsided. "Cornbread to the rescue. We'll turn this one in, should only be a moment now, and get paid up. Ol' Tib will be none the wiser, and we'll be back to the pub so you can brew up some more ale. None the wiser. Any big plans for tomorrow?"

Sylas laughed, the adrenaline still racing through him as he caught his breath. "That was bloody insane."

"Another day in the life. And tomorrow?"

"Tomorrow. Right. Mana Saturation at the farm. If you're keen to do some more demon fighting, tomorrow night and the night after might have some serious paranormal activity at the farm. That's what I've been told."

"The ghouls come out toward the end, don't they?"

"That they do."

Quinlan grunted. "You know I'll be there, mate. Are there any trees nearby?"

"Trees?" Sylas thought about the farm, from the hill it sat on to the forest across from his fields. "If you're looking to put up a hammock, we could put one up on the front porch. There's a bit of space there."

"How'd you know?" Quinlan looked back at the Wolftiger as it began to glow. "Ah, looks like the hunt has been registered. Prepare to get paid, mate. And nice hunting."

"You and Cornbread did all the work."

Cornbread barked.

"She's a good hunter, and she definitely deserves a reward. What do you say? Five hundred MLus? Two-fifty each from our cut?"

"You don't have to."

"I insist." Quinlan smiled down at the dog. "I got this feeling that hunting with Cornbread will become a favorite pastime of ours."

The farm dog barked.

"You're lucky to have such a good dog."

Cornbread approached Sylas and he scratched her behind the ears. "I am, I really am."

———

Later, Cornbread told Patches everything that had happened as the two sat on the front porch of the farm. *That human can speak to us. I understood him!*

The warrior man can speak to animals? He barked at you?

Not exactly. But I understood what he wanted.

Patches's tail sashayed. *I don't like him.*

Why?

He has a peculiar scent.

All humans have peculiar scents. I just got used to it.

How long is he going to stay at the pub?

I don't know, Cornbread told Patches. She straightened up, as if she had seen something in the fields beyond. Cornbread took a big sniff of the air and settled back on the porch next to Patches. A dog barked in the distance.

Anything?

Nothing. But I should give a bark to confirm.

No barking, please.

It's how we dogs communicate. Remember the pepper dog?

How could I forget?

If you ever hear her bark a lot, it means something serious is coming. We help each other. Well, all of us aside from the tomato dog. He thinks he's in charge and he's not, so we ignore him.

I remember that one.

Did I tell you that the two big men gave me some power? I felt so much stronger after.

You got power too? Patches tensed his paws. *I need to go on one of these hunts.*

See? I told you that you should have come.

I was busy.

Doing what?

What cats do.

Cornbread laughed. *What do cats do?*

The Tavernly Realm needs protection at all times.

Yet you are here, in the Farmly Realm.

I already checked the pub for the night. And the fire spirit is there. Maybe I should be staying back more often.

Our big man will need to take the next step with his fields tomorrow, which will draw more demons out at night. I won't be able to leave.

I can help, Patches told the dog.

We'll both do the best we can, and that should be more than enough. We make a good team, Cat. Don't give me that look. It's true. No one will mess with either of our realms as long as we're banded together.

Patches stood. *I'm going inside. Someone has to make sure he has the power he needs.*

That's very thoughtful of you. I'll stay out here. If you hear me barking, get ready.

I'm always ready. Patches stopped in front of the door and slowly turned back to Cornbread. *Can you open it for me?* He curled his tail in the air and held his head high. *Thank you.*

[You have 53 days until the invasion.]
[A loan payment of 212 has been deducted from your total Mana Lumens. Your total loan balance is 17064 Mana Lumens.]

Gaining Mana Lumens from the hunt also meant Sylas had a larger loan payment. He was fine with this since he had still made a pretty big leap from the previous day, and was now at just over six thousand banked. He would need all the spare mana as well with what he planned to do today in his fields.

"Might as well get out there," he told Patches and Cornbread, who slept on either side of him. Once he was up, Sylas had a biscuit that Azor had made him while they were closing up the pub last night.

Cornbread barked, and for a moment Sylas thought that Mira had come for a visit. Instead, he opened the door to find Trampus, the thin, younger man who ran the fireberry farm. "Looking real nice," Trampus said of the cornfields. "Saturation today?"

"That's the plan."

"I figured. Want some tips?"

"I'd love some tips. Are you hungry? I have biscuits."

"And I have jam." Trampus produced a jar of jam. "Looks like we were reading each other's minds."

"Please, come in."

Trampus entered just as Patches came out of the bedroom to see what all the commotion was about. "You have a cat too?"

"He came with the pub and he follows me here every night."

Trampus chuckled as he approached Patches. "Is he friendly?" He crouched and reached his hand out to the cat, who sniffed it and then let Trampus pet him.

"Patches loves people. He was the talk of the pub until Cornbread showed up."

"Now they both get a lot of love, I bet," Trampus said as he petted both animals, Patches on his right and Cornbread on his left.

The two men had biscuits and fireberry jam. Once they were done, Sylas put on his farm hat and joined Trampus, who didn't even blink twice when he saw Sylas in the hat, outside. He began his explanation: "I'm sure you noticed with Mana Infusion that it came naturally to you, that you just sort of knew how to do it."

"I did."

"Saturation is similar but there is a tip that will help you." Trampus looked out at Sylas's fields, at the cornstalks that had reached their full height. "Right now, most of the mana that your field has absorbed is in the soil. When you used Mana Infusion, it might have seemed that you were infusing mana into the kernels you planted, but you were really infusing it into the soil. And it only works on your field before you get the wild idea of, I don't know, trying to plant a forest."

"How did you know that was what I was thinking?"

"Because I thought the same thing at first. Well, not exactly, but I did want there to be nice shade around my home. I kept trying to plant trees and grow them rapidly. It doesn't work that way, I'm afraid. It will only work within your sanctioned field. Look closely."

Sylas focused on his fields again. He noticed the stalks emitting a soft glow as the leaves rippled gently, as if a breeze had blown through.

"That mana is coming from the soil, and it is the soil we want to focus on now to evenly distribute the mana it has absorbed and will continue to absorb until harvest. These are quite large. When is harvest exactly?"

"Tombsday, according to my calculations."

"And where did you get these calculations?"

"The Farm and Field Guild," Sylas lied. His hat was a rare item and even if he liked Trampus, he didn't know the man well enough to tell him what it did.

"Makes sense." Trampus returned his focus to Sylas's fields. "Here's what you'll want to do to assure an evenly distributed saturation: Now, you'll see some farmers, or at least I have in the past, just cast their hand out and be done with it. That works too, but you want even saturation, and that's going to take a little more time than that. Imagine that, having to work for our crops." Trampus laughed at his own joke. "The real work begins tonight. Let me ask you, Sylas."

"Yes?"

"Do you enjoy sleeping?"

"As much as anyone else, but I'm not the type to, say, take a nap midday or anything like that."

"Well, for the next few nights you aren't going to be sleeping much at all. Saturation attracts monsters, ones that demon hunters deem too worthless to hunt."

"What do you mean?"

"Demon hunters prefer D-Rank and above. Some will go after E-Rank, but anything below isn't really worth their time. The payout is too low, and a normal person could easily kill the monster with your typical club if, and this is a very big if, the demon is actually tangible. They're here right now, actually." He pointed toward Lucille's leafy greens farm. "If you had certain powers, you'd be able to see them floating around, Mana Ghouls."

Sylas thought of his tinted glasses. Once Trampus left, he would put them on and take another look.

"Mostly harmless during the day, and you can't easily kill them at that time anyway. But they'll be out in force at night come Mana Saturation because it is the best time to feed. So that's what I mean when I say that you will be up the next several nights."

"Then so be it."

"That's the spirit, and that's why you have a farm dog."

Cornbread, who stood near them, seemed to intuit they were talking about her. She barked and wagged her tail.

"Do you have one as well? I noticed Sterling did, Edgar too, although I've never seen his."

"Edgar's is nasty. A big white dog named Bruno. But he gets the job done. Sterling has Sunflower, and she's a good one. My farm didn't come with a dog, it was too small at the start with just one field, but I got one later. She likes to stay inside during the day and sleep, but come night, Miranda is out in force."

"Miranda, huh?"

"Named her after my wife."

"Is she still alive? Sorry if that came out wrong."

"No, no, that's a normal question whenever you tell someone something like that. My beautiful Miranda is in the Celestial Plains watching down on us. I was able to get a message to her once, you know, told her I was happy and that she's welcome anytime. Of course, why would anyone want to go from heaven to the Underworld."

"You can send a message to the Plains?"

"You most certainly can. You'll need a lumengineer to do it and it isn't cheap. The cost is in the tens of thousands of MLus."

Sylas instantly thought of Tilbud and wondered if there wasn't some work-around the archlumen would know about. He would have to ask next time he saw him, which could happen at any time based on their conversation before Tilbud departed, a conversation in which he let Sylas know that *they would be in touch shortly.*

"You have someone up there?" Trampus asked.

"I do, two people, actually. My mother and father. Actually, my father is in the Chasm. Hallowed Pursuit."

"Ah, the only thing that levels the playing field between people like us and people like them."

"What do you mean?"

"An unnecessary desire to head into hell itself to see if one can't raise a little hell, themselves." Trampus grinned. "So for saturation, as I said, you'll want to walk through your fields and do so in an organized way. Know where you started and know where you'll end up. Don't be surprised if Cornbread starts barking. The animals can sense the mana as it stirs beneath the soil. Also, expect something that looks like little rain clouds to form over the fields. This is just part of the process as the mana is stirred in the soil and distributed to the clouds to better coat your plants. You'll be able to see some of it as well, but the true effects won't start until nightfall."

Sylas walked to the far end of his field and a prompt came to him.

[Mana Saturation cost is 75 Mana Lumens per field. Would you like to begin the process? Y/N?]

"Yes." He glanced down at the overturned soil that signaled the start of the first row and began, intuitively, mana pouring from his palm. The soil came alive, a gentle radiance glowing from the turned dirt. As Sylas continued on, he noticed a network of light starting to form between the stalks.

"That's it," Trampus said. "This is what I meant by evenly distributed. Keep it up."

As the other farmer had predicted, Sylas saturating his field also came with a response from Cornbread, who barked wildly as she ran through the stalks.

"Look at her go," Trampus said at one point. "And equally important, look who has joined us."

Patches was there now, the cat twisting through the stalks as well as he tried to keep up with Cornbread.

"They can recharge their MLus in this way. It doesn't take much, so don't let it worry you."

"I wouldn't," Sylas told Trampus as he continued, "even if it did. If they're charged, I'm charged. Ahem, I mean, if he's happy, I'm happy."

"There's a vet that comes around every now and then named Leah. She'll tell you how many MLus they have, just so you know. Not many like her."

"What do you mean?" Sylas asked as he continued saturating his field, the mana crackling all around them now.

"It was one of the classes that was removed by the Celestial Plains. They govern the Underworld, you know, not that you'd ever see any of the bloody bastards around unless you went to the Hexveil. The veterinarian class was *retired,* as it is known. There are still some, and there are charms that can help with the skill too. Most have roving practices, although if you looked hard enough and asked around, you'd be able to find one in Battersea."

"Why would they retire that class?"

"The Celestial Plains doesn't want us to have too many advantages. This is supposed to be a form of punishment, you know, being in the Underworld. And pets, especially magically inclined ones, make it much easier for us to game their system."

"So they are older ones then, the pets with powers?"

"They are, which is why it is good to find a vet. Luckily, as I said, Leah comes around regularly. Next time she comes, I'll be sure to tell her to stop by your farm."

"If I'm not there, please, send her to the pub. Drinks on me."

Trampus nodded. "I'll be sure to tell her that." He took a deep breath in. "I love Mana Saturation day. It always signals the start of excitement, from beating back the demons at night to finally getting paid. But that's not the part where we make MLus. What about that? What you plan to do with your corn?"

"Aside from sell it, not a lot. But I would like to see if Cornbread's namesake holds any potential. Azor—"

"Who now?"

Sylas showed him the tattoo. "The fire spirit I'm bonded with. She wants to try making cornbread and some other recipes. There might be an ale I can do as well, which I'll attempt. Maybe, yes, that would be quite a celebration for our upcoming Wraithsday feast."

"Corn-themed, huh?"

"That's what I'm thinking. Azor would enjoy it, and I could try to whip something up." Sylas nodded as a few ideas flitted across his mind. "Besides, after harvest, there would be cause for a celebration, anyway."

"In that case, I'll be there," Trampus said. "Been meaning to go to one of your feasts anyway. I'll try to bring some of the other farmers as well."

———

Once Trampus was gone, Sylas placed the tinted glasses over his face. He gasped as he looked out at the fields beyond. He could see ghouls floating over them, their mouths open, chins drooping toward the ground. They hovered in a lackadaisical way. Occasionally, one would swoop down, try to absorb energy, and fail.

The daytime looked almost like the nighttime in the Underworld, yet there was a subtle difference that Sylas had noticed. It did get slightly darker, but that didn't explain why they weren't able to absorb the mana now, while it was so fresh.

Sylas pondered this for a moment.

Was "fresh" the right word?

What he had done made no sense in terms of actual farming, at least to his knowledge. He had met plenty of farmers; he had never heard them say anything about infusion or saturation. Then again, he knew the actual steps in the brewing process from his previous life, and was still amazed at the fact that he could refill casks in what some would consider the blink of an eye. So there was some correlation there and the defining link was the magic, or the Mana Lumens of the Underworld.

Cornbread barked.

"I see them too, girl." he crouched and the dog approached, wagging her tail. She licked his hand and Patches showed up, the pub cat swishing his body against Sylas's leg and purring.

"You two are too cute, you know that?" Sylas scooped Patches into his arms and turned back to the house. Since the hat and the glasses were so valuable, and since he didn't have a great place to hide them, at least not yet, he kept them on as he then left the house to walk toward the portal, Cornbread following after him.

Sylas reached Ember Hollow and decided to pay a visit to Mira, happy as ever that he didn't have to do so at her home anymore. After dropping Patches and Cornbread off at the pub and greeting Azor, Sylas headed next door, where he struck up a conversation with Nelly and Karn while Mira helped a customer.

He waited until Mira was done and then stepped into her shop. It still felt recently moved into, yet there was a hint of organization to it, everything in its right place. Behind her counter were numerous glass jars with plants and roots in them. Mira sat on a stool, one leg crossed over the other, a smile on her face as she looked up at Sylas.

"Can I help you?"

"I like the new shop. Do you think there is anything you can do with corn? I might have a lot of corn soon."

She slowly rolled her eyes. "What am I supposed to do with that?"

"I don't know," he said as he tapped on the counter. "You're the apothecary. Are you stopping by the pub tonight? I have a pint with your name on it."

"Last I checked, your pints say *The Old Lamplighter*."

"Are you suggesting we get custom pints?"

"That would be nice for regulars. I never thought I would be a regular at a pub, yet here we are."

"I never thought I would own a farm, yet here I am."

"Saturation day, yes? How did it go?"

"Well. Everything is going to come to fruition soon, and then . . ." He couldn't help but bite his lip for a moment. "Things are going to have to change."

"You aren't seriously considering it, are you?"

"What choice do I have?"

"A lot of bloody choices, Sylas."

"I need to find Raelis, and perhaps my father."

Mira frowned. "How do you plan to do it? You can't just waltz in, you know. There are rules and regulations."

"How I plan to do it remains to be seen. But there have to be ways. I'm sure Quinlan and Tilbud know. Anyhow, I'll let you get back to it." He tipped his hat at her and the charms all bounced. "Hopefully, I'll see you tonight."

CHAPTER SEVENTEEN

WAYWARD DEMONS

Sylas didn't know what to expect that night as he returned to the farm early, leaving Azor to finish up and do the necessary brewing. Quinlan and his pets went with him, both men wearing their armor and had their weapons ready if need be.

Sylas was disappointed that Mira never came by the pub that night, but he understood why she didn't. It was her way of expressing her opinion on what he would soon attempt.

Hopefully, she would come around.

"The way I see it," Quinlan said as they reached the portal, "we should mostly be in the clear tonight. I might have to stir a few things up, but with me around, the demons won't be out in force."

"You're suggesting they can actually sense you, your presence?"

"Yes, they can. Just like any animal, they know when they're being hunted. It is when they get too large, when they themselves become hunters, that things can get a bit hairy. But I will be on the front porch, got me hammock already packed up." He patted his bag. "Found one in Cinderpeak earlier."

"How was it? Was The Ugly Duckling open?" Sylas asked.

"I stopped in for a pint and told Iron Rose I was an old mate of yours. She was interested in how we knew each other. A real looker, that one. But I always liked an artist."

"Really?"

"What, mate?"

"What about Priscilla? Forgot about her already?"

"Missy Prissy—don't tell her I called her that—she's an artist in her own way. But Rose, those paintings. I like the one you have in The Old Lamplighter, but seeing all of them in her pub there, it really pulls a theme together. I'd like to buy one from her, one of these days."

"To put where exactly?"

The large man laughed so hard that he bent over. "You got me good with that one, mate. Haven't had the chance to acquire any property yet, so maybe your pub? In the portal room?"

"I already have one of her paintings at the pub."

"Maybe at the inn, then."

"In Geist? Do you think Priscilla will like that?"

"What's not to like about a bloody swan?"

The two appeared in the Seedlands, mana fizzling around them. Patches grew restless and Sylas set him down on the ground, where he quickly caught up with Cornbread. The two raced ahead, leaving Sylas and Quinlan to take their time walking to the farm.

"Too quiet out," Quinlan said.

"Agreed." Sylas placed the tinted glasses over his eyes. He scanned the area and didn't see anything out of the ordinary. Still, it felt like something was set to happen. "You feel that?"

"I do. Some trouble brewing. No pun intended."

This had happened on the front lines before, especially with the people he was closest with. There were times that it seemed like they were reading each other's minds, privy to the innermost thoughts. They reached the farmhouse and Sylas helped Quinlan prepare the hammock.

He placed his hat inside the home but kept the glasses on.

"At night, these Mana Ghouls decide to get a bit cheeky, a little gutsy. They won't like seeing us," Quinlan said.

"I suspect not."

"But there's nothing like the hunt. I mean it. Clobbering a few wayward demons makes me feel alive, even though I'm anything but. I prefer fighting them over men. Just as nasty, but . . ." He trailed off, never finishing his sentence. "You know," Quinlan said once the hammock was set up.

"I get it."

"Heh. We sure pulled a fast one on bloody Tib last night. I saw that Thorny bloke today on my way to the portal. Didn't say nothing about missing his kill, but I could tell something was annoying him. I also got the feeling he didn't suspect us. He seemed more mad at his men for not being ready to go when he called upon them."

"That sounds like Tiberius. And it sounds like the old bastard would be mad at them for that, even if he was in Battersea enjoying a spa day."

"None the wiser. But hey, who doesn't like a good spa day? Look, mate, try to get some rest. I've got this. If you hear barking, sure, grab your mace, and come join me."

"You know that's not happening. If you're staying up, I'm staying up."

"You don't have to be the hero all the time, Sylas."

"You don't have to be the hero all the time either."

The two men laughed. They took their seats on the porch and leaned their weapons up against the railing. Another look out at the fields didn't show him anything different, no ghouls. Not yet anyway. But he did see the mana that now radiated off his plants.

"So what's your decision, mate?" Quinlan asked after he got settled.

"About what?"

"The Chasm. Are we going looking for Raelis and your father, or what?"

"I still want to see what the manaseer says before we do anything." Patches jumped into Sylas's lap and he petted the cat, who instantly started purring. "It may change what we do next."

"So you are chickening out then, is it?"

"That line of argument won't work against me and you know it."

"It was worth a shot though, yeah? We should have brought a few pints to go. Remember that time they had us on guard duty in Old Haven? Nothing to guard there aside from a pub. Best night of me bloody life out there on the front line. The owner wasn't too keen about us cleaning him out, but we did pay."

"That we did." An idea came to Sylas as he sat there in the dark with his old friend. "How about this? It's Soulsday. If Nuno hasn't come in a week, we leave for the Chasm. The crop will be ready come Tombsday morning, which means I can replant and harvest again before we go. Big payday."

"And who doesn't like that? Who are you thinking will go?"

"You, me, perhaps Tilbud. We'll keep the team small."

"And Cornbread." The dog looked at Quinlan and barked. "Good to have a watchdog, and I can communicate with her in subtle ways. Helpful. Wish I could tell you more about what she's thinking, but our communication doesn't work like that. It's more of a one-way street, if you get my drift. And it only applies to certain situations. But guarding, attacking, rooting out some demonic being—that's all possible. If I had classed differently, I could do more with her. Wait. What about Azor?"

"She would be helpful there. She knows her way around."

"But then the pub would be closed, and you'll do better with a source of incoming mana if you have one available. I don't have that advantage."

"You could always class again."

Quinlan cracked his knuckles. "Yeah, I suppose I could add a third class, but I'm lazy, and I like my life. And who wants to run a pub or a farm, no offense? I like the fact that I can just take random quests and hunts and get paid handsomely, that I can go wherever I want. Demon hunter and adventurer complement each other, you know. It's an exploit of the system, but the MLus I receive as a demon hunter are tripled because of my adventurer class. If I had gotten them the other way around, the reward wouldn't be as high, but all quests taken by adventurers come with a multiplier. So each demon contract I take, I set it as a quest."

"Brilliant."

"Raelis taught me that one. He's classed the reverse way, so he doesn't get as much, but his payout is still decent. Anyway, where the bloody hell were we?"

"Azor. If she stays here or if she goes. I'd personally like her to stay here, not because of the MLus or to keep the pub open, but because it seems like the Chasm traumatized her. I don't want her to go back, but I'll ask her and see what she says."

"Any kind of spirit like that would be helpful *if* we were getting into something more than a simple rescue mission."

"How will that work, anyway? How will you track Raelis down?"

"Already discussed that part with Tilbud. We need essence to find him, in our case, an essence of our memory of him. With Nelly, Tilbud borrowed her scarf that she had cried onto, right? Wiped her tears? That's what he said."

"Yes, and then he took it."

"The manaseer he knows got essence from Nelly's tears, her memories of her husband. That's what I used to find him."

"So you want us to cry about Raelis?"

Quinlan snorted. "Yeah, mate, I want you to sob like a wee little baby. No, that's not what we'll use to get essence. It will be something else."

"What exactly?"

"Can you draw?"

"Not well."

"Huh. I've seen that work before. Likely memories, then. Which means we may need to relive something, a time when we have a strong memory of Raelis."

"Night of Raining Arrows."

"That would be the one option. We'll go into a trance, relive it, and the manaseer will withdraw our memories."

"What about my father?"

"Do you have any foundational memories of him?"

"Most are just in his pub, The Old Lamplighter."

"You might need to remember some of them."

"And how will we get into the Chasm itself?"

"I'll discuss it with him some more, but that can be arranged without doing something foolish like a Hallowed Pursuit. The archlumen comes and goes as he pleases, yeah?"

"He does, and I'm fine with it. The money I paid him to teach me to fly remains the best funds I've ever spent."

"Yeah? How much did he charge you?"

"Two thousand."

Quinlan laughed. "You were done there, mate."

"At the time, maybe. But I got a spell called Quill out of it, and Tilbud has been by my side since, imparting wisdom and connecting me with people. So it was well worth it." Sylas yawned.

"Get some sleep. We'll take shifts. The hammock is yours. I'll stand guard. Better, I'll sit guard. No reason to stand when you have a chair."

CHAPTER EIGHTEEN

MANA GHOULS

Cornbread turned to the fields, her ears perked up, tail erect. *They have come,* she told Patches excitedly. She barked, but by this point, the warrior man was already moving toward the field, his hand glowing with mana, club at the ready.

Patches hopped out of the hammock, his ears flitted back. *This is bad . . .*

Let's go! Cornbread barked wildly.

The big man was out of the hammock in a matter of seconds. He grabbed his mace and took off after his companion, yelling something.

Patches watched him go, much less excited than Cornbread.

What are you waiting for? she asked.

I don't rush into things if I don't have to. Let's creep around the sides and provide support for the two of them. These Mana Ghouls don't seem too troublesome, not yet, but if more come, or if a bigger one comes, we can help.

I want to help now!

Then you go, I'll do the creeping.

Cornbread barked and raced after the two men.

Keeping low, Patches started at the portion of the field closest to the house. He doubled his size and then turned invisible. He glanced down one of the rows of corn to see a smaller ghoul bent forward and sucking the mana out of the ground.

Patches slowly produced his claws.

I've got you now!

He sprang onto the ghoul and dug in. The demon whipped to the right, Patches striking some of the cornstalks as the two tumbled into another row. Swift as ever, Patches brought the ghoul down and incinerated it.

A new flash of mana ahead caught his attention. He pressed low to the ground as a larger ghoul turned down the lane, which would allow it to come up behind Cornbread and the two men.

Not today, you don't. Timing his attack just right, Patches hit the ghoul with an amplified purr that caused it to pause momentarily, the demon disoriented just long enough for Patches to leap onto its back and steer it to the ground.

Another Mana Ghoul incinerated.

Patches remained low to the ground as he watched the two men fight off the largest of the group, both using swelling blasts of mana. Near them Cornbread dragged one by the place where its neck would be.

They seem to have this group. I'll move out farther. Still invisible, Patches crawled under the cornstalks as he headed toward the back of the fields, closer to the forest. He saw a group of the ghouls, small but formidable, and decided to wait for them to make the first move.

The first came. Patches rushed out from the cover of the cornstalks, grabbed it, and pulled it in, where he quickly killed the Mana Ghoul.

He rushed to the other side of the row just as the next ghoul came to investigate. Patches hit it with a disorienting purr and incinerated it.

Two remaining. Patches carefully moved into a position behind the first one as it swooshed forward, sucking up mana. He stopped it with a purr, incinerated the creature, and full-on charged the final one.

I've got you now!

Patches jumped for it, claws extended, clamped down in the space where its shoulders would be, and dug his teeth in. The two tumbled to the ground. Patches finished it with a blast of mana.

He heard Cornbread bark for him. *Cat! Cat!*

Rather than reply, Patches ran toward the sound and came up next to the dog, still invisible. *I'm here.*

Cornbread nearly bit him. *Don't sneak up on me like that!*

My apologies.

Did you get any? she asked, panting.

Five. No six. Maybe seven. I lost count.

Really? Wow. You're really good at that!

Patches held his head and his tail high. *I told you stealth would be better.*

We should be fine for now. I don't detect any more. Besides, tonight is not the night we need to worry about.

Oh?

Cornbread's lips curled, the farm dog baring her teeth. *They will be out in force tomorrow.*

———

Sylas awoke in the hammock. The prompts came as he glanced out at his fields, where he saw Quinlan building something.

[You have 52 days until the invasion.]
[A loan payment of 70 has been deducted from your total Mana Lumens. Your total loan balance is 16994 Mana Lumens.]

Sylas briefly skimmed his status to see that he was just a few Mana Lumens lower than the previous morning, mostly due to the cost of Mana Saturation and how this had broken even with last night's earnings. This was to be expected, and soon, his first farming payday would come.

"Is he really building scarecrows?" Sylas asked Patches, who purred next to him.

The two watched as Quinlan fashioned a pole in the ground and draped some fabric he'd found over it. The pole had stick arms attached to it and it held a shoddy wooden sword.

Quinlan glanced back to Sylas and saw that he was up. As soon as he noticed, he started arguing with the scarecrow. Quinlan shook his fist at his creation. He drew his club and pretended to suddenly be scared of his opponent.

By this point, Sylas was already walking over to him. "Found yourself a new friend now, yeah?"

"Yeah, Tiberius, here, is all right. A bit stubborn, and prone to drawing his blade and waving it around like he has an army of soldiers that he is prepared to needlessly send to their deaths, but a good bloke, good enough. And certainly good enough to protect your farm. I made another one as well." He motioned to another scarecrow. "These particular ghouls aren't that bright, and this may keep new ones away. Not tonight, mind you. Tonight is going to be their last stand for this crop. But in the future. How'd you sleep?"

"All right, I reckon. The hammock isn't so bad."

"I wouldn't know."

"Sorry about that. I sort of dozed off there."

Quinlan waved Sylas's concern away. "I can sleep all day and you cannot. I got a bit of an advantage there."

Cornbread came trotting over to them with a stick in her mouth. She dropped it in front of Quinlan.

"She's been helping?"

"She certainly has. Cornbread is the one that found the stick shaped like a sword. Big one too. As for the fabric, I found that out in the old shed. Lots of bits and ends in there. I'll dress them up a bit more." He pointed at the other scarecrow. "And they'll help us keep the ghoulies away. Maybe not. But I like to think so. So, mate, what's your plan for today? I ask because I'm about two seconds away from heading to that hammock and passing out."

"Today? Not yet decided. I'll head back to the pub, check in with Mira, and see what I get into from there."

"You really fancy her then, yeah?" Quinlan laughed. "You don't have to tell me. Your face says it all. And I get it. She's friendly, a bit standoffish but in a good way. Plus her uncle was a bloody lord commander and getting under his skin like that is something I should aspire to. But I have Priscilla, or at least, I have a room at her tavern."

"You keep saying that. Maybe you should give her a visit this week."

"Maybe I will," Quinlan said on the tail end of a yawn. "But first, a nap. You can leave Cornbread here if you'd like. I'll bring her around later."

———

Azor brimmed with excitement upon seeing Sylas come into the pub. A whirlwind of activity followed as she caught Sylas up on what had already happened that morning, from the construction of the inn next door to Cody and Duncan, who had shown up early, hungry after a night of patrolling Ember Hollow.

"I had to feed them. They're doing so much and it's always those two on patrol. I never see Henry or any of the others. It's not fair. I think they look up to you too."

"You think?"

"They always talk about you and ask questions when you're not here."

"Really?" An idea came to Sylas, one that he knew would ruffle feathers. He wasn't the type to ruffle feathers if it wasn't absolutely necessary, but he figured that both Cody and Duncan, the youngest of the militiamen, could use the MLus. He turned to the door. "I'll be right back."

"Are you hungry?"

Sylas turned back to her. "I'm fine, Azor. In fact, let's go to Battersea for food supplies. I want you to think of something that you could make with corn, because that's my plan for the Wraithsday Feast, a celebration of my first crop. A Cornday Feast, if you will. Sound good?"

"Sounds great!"

"We'll do some shopping too."

"Maybe we can get some more fireweave stuff."

"What are you thinking of?"

"I'll know it when I see it." She swelled with excitement, her fire dimming at Sylas's next words.

"We also need to talk about future plans. Azor."

"Yes?"

"Don't look at me like that."

Patches hopped up onto the counter and mewed at the fire spirit. "Like what?"

"None of it is as bad as it sounds. I just made a decision last night. But we'll talk. Is there anything you'd like to see in Battersea? I want to take a boat ride over Lake Seraphina."

"A boat ride for no reason?"

"Well, there would be a reason: just to enjoy it. Have you been on a boat before?"

"I stay away from huge bodies of water," she said. "But . . . it would be exciting. Sort of like how you were so close to the lava in Cinderpeak. It's dangerous, but safe because I was there. The boat is safe, right? What am I asking? I can just fly if it started sinking."

Sylas rubbed his hands together. "That settles it. Shopping in Battersea, a boat ride to Everscene, and then back here. Before we head out, I'll go talk to Cody and Duncan."

Not long after, a sleepy Duncan opened the door to his home to find Sylas smiling at him. "Morning," he said, straightening up, his short hair a mess.

"Sorry to wake you. Is Cody in there as well?"

"He's sleeping, but yeah. How can I help you, Sylas?"

"Are you and Cody on patrol for tonight?"

"Unfortunately. It seems like it's always us, but that's because Tiberius keeps assigning it to Henry, and Henry has us do it so we 'can learn something about something.' I don't know what we're supposed to be learning, if we're being honest."

"Would you be available to help at the farm tonight?"

"What would we tell Henry? That we're sick?"

Sylas smiled. "Telling him you're sick is an excellent option. Or just be honest and say you're taking the night off. What's Henry going to do? Quinlan and I are expecting a wave of demons because it's nearly harvesting time, and I figured some extra hands would be nice. What will it cost me?"

"Make it five hundred MLus split between the two of us and you have yourself a deal," Duncan said.

"Cody will be fine with that?"

"Yeah, he'll go ahead with it if I tell him it's a good idea."

"Works for me. I'll pay it out of the harvest."

Duncan shook hands with Sylas. "I really need to add a class."

"You should talk to Quinlan. He was an adventurer who took demon hunter as a second class. That would be the correct order. He makes a lot more doing it in that order than if he'd done it the other way around."

"Tiberius has asked us not to take the demon hunter class."

"Why?" The answer came to Sylas instantly, and it related to something Tiberius had said over a week ago about not wanting competition. "No need to explain, mate, I know why. And if you ask me, you should do what works best for you. Both you and Cody should. You can get a loan to class as demon hunters and go anywhere, not that I mind you all here. Or just head to other cities for hunts and stay here. What I'm saying here is not to let Tiberius hold you back. I'm not trying to cause a rift between us either. The afterlife is your second chance at life, and it's ridiculous that he wouldn't want the rest of you to class as demon hunters so he could reap all the rewards."

"I'll have to talk to Cody about it. We've been thinking of expanding lately, getting out and exploring. As adventurers, that's easy. If we double-class, we'll make even more."

"The two of you would make a fine team, in my opinion, and I say that having seen plenty of men. I don't wear the time I served as a badge of honor like others, but I spent enough of my life warring to say this with finality: I know a good soldier when I see one, and I see potential in both you and Cody. Anyhow, I'll let you get back to sleep. See you tonight at the pub. We can head over to the farm from there together."

————

Sylas and Azor appeared in Battersea and headed to the market from there.

"I have an idea," Azor told him, "and it involves cornbread."

"Our dog?"

"No, actual cornbread. I want to ask around, but I think I could make something like that. I will also make grilled corn slathered in butter and spices. Ooo, that gives me another great idea. I could use the flour from the cornbread to bake some sort of pastry. I could get some fish from Tartar, season it, wrap it in the corn husk, and grill it. So that means we need seasoning and some tools like a mortar and pestle. Ooo, an even better idea: I could get some fish from here, from Battersea. I hope Tartar won't mind. What I'm saying here is I don't have a menu just yet, but I'm close."

"I'm sure he won't. We'll put together a menu with a corn-based ale, sell it for thirty MLus split down the middle. We can put enough food there that it's good for two people to share, so two ales. Meaning I'll brew two casks. Yes, that should work. Two casks gives us forty pints, so that means food for twenty, but technically forty."

"Because they'll share. Like a chef's tasting menu."

"Yes, exactly. You know, since we are in Battersea, we should tell the Ale Alliance as well. Greta might be able to attract folks."

"Yes," Azor said with an enthusiastic nod.

"This is the best idea we've had in weeks. And by that, I mean that we could, in the future, partner with farmers to do the same and have a huge event, perhaps something with outdoor seating even, that brings people from across the Underworld." Sylas could see it, the tables full inside the pub, more in the back and in the front. "A real community feast."

"We could even do it to raise MLus for Ember Hollow since there's no tax there."

"Brilliant. We cover our costs; we introduce people to new food, something like Sterling's peppers; we fund something in Ember Hollow that needs work, like fixing up the town square. That's an option as well."

"This is all so smart!" Azor flared up to the point that she scared a pair of women walking by with baskets. She shrank immediately and disappeared into the tattoo on Sylas's arm. "Sorry. I'll stay here until I can get control of myself."

Later, after they had the supplies they needed and Azor had picked out a pair of fireweave gloves, short ones that stopped just at her wrist, the pair headed to the docks. They chose a boat that had seating on the top deck, which allowed for sweeping views of the lake.

The waiter that came by didn't blink an eye at the fact that Sylas was seated across from a fire spirit. He smiled, placed a menu down for Sylas, and returned with one made of fireweave.

"They have menus for me?" Azor asked. "Look, Sylas!" She showed him the menu made of fireweave metal, Sylas able to make out some of the options including a set menu with pastries and a special elemental tea.

"You should get that one," Sylas told her.

"But it's expensive."

"It's fine, Azor. I'll cover everything."

The waiter returned and Sylas ordered the set menu for Azor and a fireberry tea for himself, which came with a trio of small eclairs. The food came, Azor's made of wood. She laughed as she looked at the piece of wood that had been shaped into a scone. "I was wondering how they would pull this off." She looked up at the waiter. "And you have options for all elementals?"

"We most certainly do. Please, let me know if you need anything else."

Azor glanced from the waiter to the glistening water and finally back to Sylas. "This is so nice."

"Aren't you going to try it?"

"It's just wood, Sylas. And this beverage?" She looked down at the tea. "Wait, there's something in it."

"It looks like some sort of oil."

"I should try it." Azor brought the teacup to her lips and tossed some into her mouth, careful not to actually place her lips on the ceramic. The flames of her body flashed into various hues of green and blue. She let out a big gasp. "That was amazing. I could taste it, Sylas!"

"Really? Try the pastry."

Azor took a bite of the wooden scone. She placed the rest of it back on her plate, the flames dying out as she chewed. "How . . . ?" she asked. "It actually tastes like food." Azor waved the waiter over. "How is this possible?"

"Food for elementals? It is a new thing that has started up here in Battersea. We just hired a chef who is able to make the stuff. Would you care to meet him?"

"I would love to," she told the waiter.

"Let me check with him. I believe he's working on something at the moment, but he will likely be available when we dock."

"Thank you!"

Later, once they were halfway to Everscene, Sylas decided to discuss his recent decision with the fire spirit. "I want to wait for Nuno to visit, but I don't know when that will be, and the invasion gets closer every day. So here's what I've come up with: if he hasn't shown by Soulsday, I'll head out the following morning with Quinlan, Tilbud, and Cornbread."

She deflated to some degree. "Not me?"

"That's what I wanted to talk to you about. We have a very specific mission in visiting the Chasm, meaning Quinlan will be following a tracking line, and I'll be with people who know what they're doing. I wanted to see if you would run the pub in my absence because according to Quinlan, I will likely need the MLus while I am there."

"Time works differently there, Sylas," she said. "You know that, right?"

"I've been told, I'm not worried about the time; I'm worried about not being strong enough to come back through. I don't want you to have to experience it again if you don't have to."

"I hated the Chasm."

"I know."

"Do you trust Tilbud and Quinlan enough to handle things?"

"I do. I trust those two with my life, Quinlan more so, but Tilbud as well."

"And Cornbread?"

"That was Quinlan's suggestion, but it makes sense."

"I can stay behind, but I'm not going to like it."

"I'm not expecting you to."

"This is terrible. Just as we come up with new ideas, ways to grow The Old Lamplighter and build a solid community in Ember Hollow, you are also planning to go to the Chasm."

"We don't know if I'm going just yet. That really depends on Nuno. And our plans remain. We need Raelis, especially if we are to fend off an invasion."

"Is Raelis like Quinlan?"

"No, he's not. But together, and with Kael, they make a well-rounded team."

"And your father, you'll look for him too?"

"If time permits and they are part of the same Hallowed Pursuit, yes. Quinlan seems to think there's a good chance of this. If we have to go farther out of our way, deeper into the Chasm, then no. But having a direct line to the Celestial Plains could prove beneficial."

The waiter came by to announce that they would dock soon. "The chef will see you now," he told Azor.

————

Sylas liked the idea. He thought about it that night as he sold pints, the pub much busier than he had expected. He ended up brewing three casks, a regular, a flamefruit, and a fireberry ale, before leaving the pub with Azor and Cornbread. They left Patches behind this time to protect the place, the cat not at all happy about it.

"I double-checked all the windows," Azor said. "He won't be getting out. Anders helped me board up the cat door for the night. At least now the pub is protected."

Cornbread's tail was tucked between her legs as she looked up at the pub. Patches remained at his perch, watching them with anger in his eyes. He mewed once he saw that people were looking at him.

"You'll be fine," Sylas told him. "It's just for the night. Shall we?"

Azor let out a deep breath, which lessened the brightness of her form. "I don't like leaving Patches in there."

"He was in that pub long before we came."

"What about your power levels?"

"I'll come back tonight, but later. Much later. I can't have you and Quinlan taking care of the farm without me."

"Why not?"

"Because I want to be helpful. Come on." Sylas rested his mace on his shoulder and turned to the portal. He reached it, and after Cornbread circled a few times sniffing at the ground, he portaled to the Seedlands.

Sylas came to his farmhouse to see Quinlan already waging war with a particularly large demon, the large man firing waves of mana at it and beating back smaller Mana Ghouls with his club.

"Let's do it!" Sylas told Azor as he jumped into the fray and delivered his first strike, his mace cracking into the side of one of the ghouls.

Sylas used Field Warden to blow back another.

He looked up at the large monster, not quite a Voidslither, but equally terrifying.

Azor surged into action, her flames whooshing overhead, encircling the large demon. She concentrated this into a fiery downstrike that broke through the demon's outer shell and conducted the movement of the fire within its form, the flames curling and fanning out, yet always controlled, always moving with awareness of the crop.

The crop itself was glorious, and Sylas was doubly inspired to protect his harvest as he cracked another Mana Ghoul across its face and beat back two more that rushed toward him.

Cornbread took one down, the dog tearing it to shreds. When she wasn't fighting demons, she was running in a circle barking. Sylas only understood her intent *after* a couple other dogs came charging into the fray.

"Where the hell did they come from?" Quinlan yelled.

"From the other farms!"

It wasn't the time to wonder, to contemplate some of the things that had already happened. Yet seeing the dogs sparked a thought that Sylas couldn't let go. *How* had the Voidslither killed Brom in the first place? He was certain Cornbread wouldn't have let Brom die. Brom didn't have fields when he died, so how would he have attracted the monster anyway?

A Mana Ghoul lunged for Sylas. It would have taken a bite out of him had it not been for Quinlan, who blasted it back.

"Where's your head at, mate? Let's keep this going!"

"Right! I'm back in." Sylas rushed up beside Quinlan and struck another one of the Mana Ghouls.

They continued to beat them back, the dogs helping, the tide of the battle turning until another swell of darkness from the forest signaled that their fight was far from over.

"A Voidslither," Quinlan said as he took a step back, mana swelling around him. "We're going to need to torch this one, mate."

"I have just the thing. Azor!"

The fire spirit came to Sylas. She spun around him, flames flaring, crawling like liquid fire over his body as he charged up a blast that he knew would level the monster. He released it just as the Voidslither broke free of the forest.

Whoosh!

The flames engulfed the demon, causing it to squeal with pain.

The dogs all barked, their barks louder and louder until Sylas's head was ringing. Now separated from Azor, he dropped down to cover his ears, Quinlan doing the same as the Voidslither swelled until the point it took up a large swath of the sky.

The demon exploded, bits of burned-out mana falling toward the crops.

Sylas used Whimsical Drift to blow them away, where they fizzled out. He glanced over to Quinlan.

"That was unexpected." Quinlan got to his feet and some of the dogs approached. "Must belong to the neighbors."

"It's so cute," Azor said. "They all help each other here."

"It's cute until you wonder what happened to Brom."

Azor and Quinlan turned to Sylas. "What do you mean?" Quinlan asked.

"I mean there's something off about all of this. Brom, the guy who owned the farm before me, was killed by a Voidslither. Why did it kill him if he didn't even have a crop?"

"Ah, that makes sense to me," Quinlan said with a huff. "Voidslithers are like Noxes in certain ways."

"Possession?"

"Well, not in the same way. They would like to possess their host, but it never goes that easily for them. They're too powerful. So they possess and the host usually goes overnight. Was he covered in spiderwebs?"

"Yeah."

"He was probably walking home one night and a Voidslither that was escaping from another field hit him. Maybe one of the other farmers chased one away and it ran into him. Either way, there's nothing off about any of this from what I can tell. It's one of the risks of having a farm. As for why Cornbread didn't help, she found you, didn't she? I think that's what you told me."

Cornbread looked up at Sylas and wagged her tail.

"She did," Sylas told Quinlan, "and I'm glad for it."

"I would be too if I had a pup like that. Best you get back to the pub and let Azor and me handle whatever comes next. We'll be ready. Cornbread too."

The farm dog barked.

"In that case," Sylas told them, "I'll see you in the morning. And Quinlan, Azor? Thanks."

————

Patches paced back and forth.

They think they can trap me in here? That they can contain me?

He turned to the cat door and sighed miserably at the fact it had been boarded up.

Patches took the stairs to the window he had climbed out before and found that it was also shut tight, locked. There was an exit he had used in the cellar before, but the big man had fixed this several weeks ago.

Patches continued to pace. *You're in the Tavernly Realm. It needs protecting. That is fine.*

But he couldn't shake this feeling that he was missing out on something, that there was more he could be doing. Where was the dog? The fire spirit and the big man? They seemed like they were ready for battle.

And I want to battle with them!

He doubled in size and stalked back and forth, as if this would somehow spawn an idea that he could use to escape the pub. He could always blow the window out, but that would cause trouble for the big man, and it would leave the Tavernly Realm wide open for an enemy to enter.

Curses, he said.

Patches produced his claws and scratched them against a wooden post. He felt his own power; he knew he could bring the post down and cause some damage, but he didn't want that for the Tavernly Realm.

He just wanted to know what was going on out there.

Where are they?

Patches tried to busy himself by searching around for mice. There were none. He found some food that the fire spirit had left out and ate it angrily. He continued pacing back and forth until he spotted a pint glass that hadn't been washed out. There was some ale inside.

Patches stuck his head in the cup to lick up the ale. He felt like drinking something, and while he didn't like the smell of the human drink, he knew it made them feel better.

He pushed his head farther into the glass pint trying to get the ale at the bottom. He finally reached it and extended his tongue forward.

Patches lapped some up, and instantly disliked the taste. He tried to pull his head out of the pint and couldn't.

No.

He moved backward, the pint glass stuck to his head, Patches's face covered with what was left in the glass as he titled his head back.

No!

Patches thought about jumping onto the ground, but he was afraid the glass would break, that it would hurt him.

The inside of the pint glass started to fog up.

Patches felt like he was going to suffocate.

And then the big man opened the door. He stepped in and set his mace down, only to notice that Patches was behind the bar with his head stuck in a pint glass.

Don't laugh at me!

The big man laughed even harder. But then he came forward cautiously and brought the cat into his arms. He set him down on one of the tables and pried the pint glass off his head.

He said something to Patches, hugged him, and then placed him on the ground.

Patches instantly bolted away, embarrassed. He found a place in the shadows and turned invisible. The big man continued to laugh as he headed upstairs.

Later, after he was certain that the big man was asleep, Patches headed up the stairs too. The Tavernly Realm was secured, he had cleaned himself to the best of his ability, and it was time to get to work refilling the big man's power.

[You have 51 days until the invasion.]
[A loan payment of 85 has been deducted from your total Mana Lumens. Your total loan balance is 16909 Mana Lumens.]
[Your fields are ready to harvest.]

Mana Lumens: 6435/6435

Sylas liked the sound of that.

"Stay here again," he told Patches. The cat joined him at the door and circled between his legs. "Fine, fine." Sylas scooped the piebald pub cat into his arms and headed to the portal. He appeared in the Seedlands, and after a short walk, Sylas reached his farm to find Quinlan seated on the front porch, a haggard look on his face.

"Morning, mate." Quinlan motioned toward the door. "Azor is whipping up something to eat. Borrowed some eggs and whatnot from a neighbor, tall, thin guy."

"Sterling, likely."

He yawned. "Didn't say. We fought off another wave last night. It might have been tough had it not been for those two militiamen. They're inside now."

"Duncan and Cody. I'll get them paid up. I need to pay you as well."

"You don't need to pay me, Sylas."

"Didn't you say that any payment you get is tripled because of your class?"

"That's right, if it's payment for successfully hunting a demon."

"And I need you to be as strong as possible when we head to the Chasm."

"That's also right."

"So let me pay you. One thousand MLus."

"Five hundred."

"Nine hundred."

"Seven fifty." Quinlan laughed. "Pretty wild to think I'm bargaining against myself. No more than seven fifty, Sylas."

"You have yourself a deal."

[Transfer 750 Mana Lumens' to Quinlan Ashdown? Y/N?]

Sylas nodded. He felt a small tug in his chest as the power vacated his body. "And I'll pay you the same next go-around." He placed Patches on the ground. The cat rushed to the door, looked back at him, and mewed.

"Looks like he missed Azor and Cornbread. They're inside."

"I can tell." Sylas had already heard Cornbread bark twice. He opened the door and the dog rushed out. She first came to Sylas, but quickly turned away from him so she could greet Patches, which she did by licking his face.

Quinlan burst out laughing. "Look at that miserable cat!"

"But he's letting her lick him anyway."

"Happy Tombsday, Sylas!" Azor called from inside.

"Hey, Azor, gentlemen," Sylas said as he saw Duncan and Cody seated at the table. He transferred Mana Lumens to them and sat down as well. "Thanks again."

Duncan wiped his mouth with his arm. "Bloody wild, last night. Sorry we were a little late. We still had to patrol Ember Hollow, at least until Henry went to sleep. He won't know the difference."

"You all should talk to him about that, or Tiberius. Because I'll need you on Soulsday as well for the next harvest. If something happened, well, we'd all be in trouble."

"I'll talk to him," Duncan said.

"Breakfast," Azor said as she slid a plate in front of Sylas. "Runny eggs and grilled peppers, plus a side of greens."

"Wonderful, thank you."

After he ate, and after Duncan and Cody headed back to Ember Hollow, Sylas prepared to harvest his first crop. While Quinlan rested in the hammock on the front porch, Cornbread and Patches cuddled in the shade, and Azor hovered nearby, nervous as ever, Sylas cracked his fingers and waited for the system prompts.

Sylas put on his hat with the dangling charms, which would give him a legendary yield. With the three thousand bushels he expected, the payout was set. There would be the harvesting cost, which would come from his current MLus, and the tax, which would come out of the payout, but the only other thing he'd need to worry about from there was the loan payment in the morning.

[**Your Harvest Silos are ready.**]

The floating silos appeared, rimmed in golden mana. They floated over the fields, sucking up the corn as a number in the air tallied Sylas's yield and payment. The process took all of ten minutes.

Once the silos finished, they turned back to Sylas, awaiting his responses.

[You have yielded 15000 Mana Lumens' worth of corn. Pay tax now? Y/N?]

"Yes, but before I do, fill this bucket." He held up a large wooden bucket, which soon filled with corn until it was overflowing. "That enough?" Sylas asked Azor. "Remember, I need a little for Trampus and Sterling too."

"That's plenty."

[A payment of 1050 Mana Lumens has been deducted from your yield. Transfer to the guild now for distribution? Y/N?]

"Do it," Sylas said, surprised that the system didn't make him pay tax for the sample it had given him. Perhaps that was a baked-in cost.

He tensed up as the silos disappeared in an epic golden flash. For a moment, Sylas felt a flutter in his chest that made him wonder if it had worked, if he was about to be paid. But then the prompt came.

[You have received 13950 Mana Lumens.]

Sylas realized the error in his ways almost immediately. As he looked at his Mana Lumens, he cursed himself for *not* transferring the payment to Quinlan and the militiamen until after he received his payout. The harvesting fee didn't matter, but had Sylas waited to transfer, he would have nearly thirteen hundred *more* Mana Lumens than he currently did due to the way the system worked.

Then, he could have transferred.

Still, Sylas had more Mana Lumens than he had ever had before. He looked at the number again and simply shook his head.

"Everything fine?" Quinlan asked as he approached. He looked out at the dormant field and whistled. The corn and all of their stalks were gone.

"Everything is fine, I just need to change the order in which I do things next time. I thought you were going to rest?"

"How can I rest with all the excitement in the air? As for the order of operations, with MLus, yeah, it matters, mate, it really does." He rubbed his hands together. "What now?"

"Now, I prepare to replant tomorrow. And then, I head to the pub and figure out the rest of my day." Sylas grinned at his old friend.

"In that case, while you dig about the dirt, I think I'll sleep on the hammock. It's nice out."

CHAPTER NINETEEN

QUIZ AND HARVEST

Patches watched the big man that night as he experimented with new brews.

He sure is good at this, Cornbread said, who sat near the cat, wagging her tail. *I really like watching him work. So focused. Such an expert.*

He's the best. The Tavernly Realm wouldn't be the same without him. It wouldn't be anything, really. Patches slipped over to the big man and twisted between his legs. The big man said something and eventually reached down to pet him.

Patches continued rubbing his body against his leg until the big man picked him up and took him over to Cornbread. He pointed at the dog and said something again, still chuckling.

I think he needs to focus and he wants you to hang out with me.

Oh, bother, Patches said.

Are you angry now?

I'm not angry. Patches puffed his tail up and made a dramatic show of heading up the stairs.

Cornbread followed. *Wait. Where are you going?*

Away from you.

The fire spirit rushed forward and greeted Patches with a big grin, which caused him to nearly double his size in anticipation of a fight. He regained his composure, turned to the cat door, and ran out.

Once again, Cornbread chased after him. *Hey!*

Can't I be alone?

You don't like me? Cornbread sat on the back step and looked at Patches, who jumped up onto the well.

Earlier that day, someone had been by to check the well. Patches remembered the man now. He had all sorts of tools that looked like they would be fun to play with.

Cornbread barked. *What's wrong?*

I don't always have to be around you to like you.

We aren't always around each other.

Are you sure about that? Dogs like being around people and other animals. You like having packs. Cats are solitary. We like being alone.

You don't enjoy my company?

I never said that.

I try not to lick or sniff you too much.

Patches looked down at the dog. He relaxed to some degree and hopped down to move closer to her. *I'm not going to apologize.*

Apologize for what?

Nothing. What happened last night? You never told me. The big man came back looking pretty exhausted, Patches said, not mentioning that he'd gotten his head stuck in a pint glass. How embarrassing that had been.

Last night? We fought so many demons. After he left, two other men came and helped us. It was me, the warrior one, and the fire spirit. Plus these two others. They are the ones that patrol at night. I smell them now. Cornbread took a big sniff of the air.

And the big man got his crop today. That was why he had the corn.

Cornbread barked and started wagging her tail. *It's a celebration!*

Patches relaxed even further. *Maybe it really is.*

Trust me, it is. Everything is going to get better from here.

Sylas expected a pretty big hit that next morning with his loan payment. It turned out, he was right.

[You have 50 days until the invasion.]
[A loan payment of 1468 has been deducted from your total Mana Lumens. Your total loan balance is 15441 Mana Lumens.]

Sylas checked his Mana Lumens next.

Mana Lumens: 17577/17577

It was still more than he had ever had, and at this rate, he would be able to pay off his loan relatively quickly. At least, until he took on another loan to become a landlord.

As he sat up and rubbed the sleep out of his eyes, Sylas saw a message shimmer into existence across from his bed.

Dearest and most sincerest Sylas,

Why not have a feast and a quiz? A grand idea! I will be by tonight to celebrate your crop and deliver the most quizliest of pub quizzes. We will also talk about the future. There is a future for those that passed, right? I do hope so!

Cheers,

Archlumen Octavian Tilbud

Sylas slowly shook his head just as Azor burst into his room. "Happy Wraithsday. Can you smell that? I already have cornbread in the oven."

"You did what to Cornbread?"

Azor laughed. "Not Cornbread the dog, cornbread *the food*. Mira is down there now. Nelly and Karn are there too. Quinlan came by early as well, but he went back to sleep. Are you coming?"

"I guess, I am."

Sylas headed downstairs to find everyone seated around the bar, having a lively conversation about the Shadowthorne Empire. Cornbread, who was being cuddled in Nelly's arms, looked up at Sylas and started wagging her tail. Rather than interrupt them, he continued on to the cellar, where he joined Azor as she continued working on breakfast.

He put on his apron and started helping.

"You don't want to talk with them?"

"They're all from the Empire. I wouldn't know much of what they are talking about. Some, yes, but I don't want to interrupt. Besides, you look like you could use some assistance." He smiled at the fire spirit and she seemed to soften to some degree.

"Want to taste the cornbread? It should be ready any moment now. I want you to taste it before I bring it up there, just in case it's not good."

"I'm sure it will be fine."

Azor pulled the pan out to reveal a golden cake. "Do the honors, please," she told Sylas as she nodded to a knife.

He cut a piece of the cornbread and added a bit of butter. The outer edge was slightly crisp, its interior moist and full of the sweet, hearty flavor of corn. After adding the butter, Sylas chewed the piece, noticing the crumbly texture and how the flavor profile matched perfectly with the butter.

"Amazing."

"Really?"

"You're making this tonight, right? This will go perfectly with the corn ale I made."

"I can if you think it's good."

"I think it's great. Thirty MLus a plate, as discussed. But the plate is big enough for two people. I brewed enough for forty pints and that's it. Did you finalize your menu yet?"

"Yes. I'm planning a corn chowder soup with crumbled bacon; soft-boiled eggs encased in a mix of sausage meat and sweet corn kernels, breaded and fried; fish-and-chips, but I wanted to use cornbread crumbles to make the batter; grilled corn; and some kind of pudding. I'm thinking cornbread pudding with caramelized apples and a custard. I would make something for elementals as well, but I don't think there will be any."

"Horatio will be here."

"Will he?" she asked.

"Tilbud left me a message."

"Maybe I could make something for him as well. I think that would surprise him."

"I'm certain it would. Let's bring some of this bread up." Sylas sliced more pieces of cornbread, put a piece of butter on each, and brought them up.

"I've been waiting for this all morning," Mira said. "It's been ages since I had cornbread."

"Same," Nelly said as she licked her lips.

"I hope it's good," Azor told the group.

"I'm sure it will be perfect," Mira said.

As Nelly and Mira started eating and complimenting Azor's dish, Sylas asked Karn about the inn. "More things are going up today," Karn told him. "Anders should be here soon."

"I'll bring up some more cornbread, then," Sylas said.

"I'm sure he would like that."

"And how long do you think framing will take?"

"Anders said we'll be up and running by next Tombsday. So not long. I'm looking forward to it as well. Helping with the construction and planning out the inn has been fascinating. You know, it's not often that we get to build something from the ground up. Many things that we got in our lives, or past lives, were already there in some way. But this is all new, and I enjoy that aspect of it. I really do. It's nice here."

"The Underworld?"

"Yes, even with the, ahem, demonic possession I had to deal with. A fresh start. Who doesn't deserve that?"

———

The food that night was spectacular, and the pub was packed to the brim with everyone from the Seedlands farmers to Shamus and some bankers, Greta and some of the Ale Alliance people to Ember Hollow locals. The most surprising appearance was from Catia, the lumengineer from The Distinguished Society of Lumengineers and Etheric Constructs.

Tilbud showed up at the very last moment, scarfed down a plate that Azor had waiting for him, and took his place in front of the crowd. He bowed graciously, and looked out at the crowd as pieces of paper flew out of his back pocket and landed on each of the tables. "State your team name. There are many here tonight, and it will be too loud if everyone shouts at the same time. So keep it down, people. Let's see what we have here," he said as walked over to Godric's table.

"The Lava Boys!"

"Ah, yes. And your team, Mira?"

Mira was teamed up with Nelly, Karn, Catia, and Quinlan, a team Sylas was pretty sure would win the quiz. "We are the Cornbreads."

Cornbread, who stood near Quinlan, threw her head back and barked.

"Awww, that's pandering," Edgar the tomato farmer said with a laugh.

"And your team name?" Tilbud asked him.

"The Good Seeds." Edgar and his team, which consisted of Lucille, Sterling, Trampus, and May, the bean farmer Sylas hadn't officially met, all grunted in agreement.

Tilbud turned to Shamus, who was partnered with Elena the banker, the Brassmeres, and John, their shop assistant. "And yours?"

"The MLus, because that's what we're going to win tonight."

Mr. Brassmere leaned to the side and kissed his wife on the cheek.

The team that consisted of members of the Ale Alliance, plus Meldon from the Archlumenry, chose the name Gilded Gents and Ladies. The group of militiamen, which included Leowin the constable, went with the Defenders, and a team out of Cinderpeak led by Iron Rose went by the name Troll-eyed Tricksters. Finally, there was a group of people that had come from Douro, who went by the name the Underwinners.

Aside from the cost of the Wraithsday Feast, each team paid ten Mana Lumens per person, to be distributed along with two free rounds of pints to the winners.

"Right, we have all of our teams," Tilbud said as Azor distributed some pints. "Now, I decided not to go with the theme for tonight's questions. I wanted it to be a little unpredictable, and increasingly challenging. You all have three sheets of paper. For each round, you will write your answers, legibly. Once we have finished, we will exchange our answers and grade them. Those will all be passed up to me. Now," he said as he produced a note card. "Let's begin, shall we? Ah, yes, one more thing: do not call out answers, and if you are going to discuss among yourselves, do so with whispers. This is a competition, you know. May the best team win!"

Tilbud started with a question about the creation of the Underworld. Sylas, who wasn't on a team, knew the correct answer was that it was created by the people of the Celestial Plains. Sylas continued to listen and guess the answers in his head as he filled up pints, cleaned glasses, and brought dishes down to the cellar.

"These questions are too easy," Shamus said after a question about death-days.

"The first round is always easy," Tilbud told him. "This is by design. My goal is to fill you with confidence early on, inflate your egos so I can crush them later. How am I doing?"

"I'm confident we're going to win," Shamus said, the man a little drunk. A few at his table laughed. Elena gave Tilbud an awkward look.

The archlumen straightened up and smiled briskly at the people before him. "Moving on. Name a demon that consists of a collected group of Mana Ghouls, one that travels in the form of a flock of birds. Continuing on the demon front, name a demon that can possess someone and develop acolytes. Yes, another demon question, a trilogy of sorts: What are the known cures for the curse known as Witherbone?"

"Witherbone?" Sylas said under his breath as he continued working on pints. He knew the answer to the first two questions, but he had never heard of witherbone.

After a few more, Tilbud ended the round with a question about geography: "Name the town nestled in the mountains near Wraithwick, home of the famous haberdasher known as Liza."

This one was a stumper, which led people that had been beyond Everscene to quietly discuss the mountains in the region.

The teams graded the questions, some of them making fun of each other before they passed the papers to Tilbud, who plowed ahead with the second round. "Name two types of wood common to the Underworld, known for their dark nature when cut and used in construction."

Sylas had no idea what the answer to this question was but he saw several faces light up.

From there, Tilbud moved to a question about the Gloomflower Meadow and a rare bloom that only happened on special occasions. Mira seemed to know this one, but no one else. A question about spiders and their lairs had the

Lava Boys all whispering to one another. Same with the question that started with the first lyrics of a song that was apparently popular in the dive bars on the outskirts of Battersea. A question about common loans and interest rates had Shamus's table buzzing with excitement. And one about common guild laws had the Gilded Gents and Ladies frantically writing answers.

It got complicated, however, when Tilbud asked the county tax for a large northern city known as Lilihammer.

"We still haven't visited there," Sylas told Azor, who had just come up from the cellar with a dish that she'd made for Horatio.

It was a soup of sorts, yet there were bits of the same wood-like material in it.

"For after," she told Sylas. "The quiz should end soon anyway."

The final questions for the second round were also geography based. With all the flourish he was known for, Tilbud traced up a glowing map and pointed at a number one floating on it. "Name this city." He then pointed at a number two. "This city." Number three was to the far east and Sylas was almost certain it was Geist. "This city. And finally, this city," he said as he pointed at the number four.

Tilbud had the groups exchange papers. They graded the results, and he prepared for the third and final round. Sylas was downstairs for most of the round, dealing with dishes and bringing up casks. The plan for the two rounds to the winning team was to use fireberry ale, so he brought that cask up and also a cask of strong ale, both of which he balanced on his shoulders.

"You good?" Azor asked.

"Yes, chef," he told her with a grin as he tuned back into Tilbud's next question.

"Legendary Locks is the name given for locks on an enchanted object that can only be unlocked by their creator. Someone who has taken a crafter subclass is able to break the locks, but to do so will reset the enchantments. What is the highest level of enchantment available to an object that once had a Legendary Lock?"

"How the bloody hell are we supposed to know that?" Godric asked. Bart the bard, who sat next to them, burst out laughing.

"We aren't meant to know all the answers, gentlemen. If we were, well, life would be much different for most of us." Tilbud clapped twice. "Come on then, lads and ladies, write down what you know. There is no wrong answer, but there is only *one* right answer. Next question."

"We're still bloody writing," Shamus growled.

"Indeed you are. Next question. Gloombra had a name change after the Crafting Laws were introduced. What was its original name?"

"Blimey," Quinlan said as he threw his hands up in the air. Mira spoke quickly to Catia and they wrote something down.

Sylas laughed. He felt joy in seeing the others have fun. He also felt a sense of contentment rolled down his shoulders in knowing that his pub was full of people, that it was a third place, where denizens of the Underworld could gather and enjoy each other's company.

Yet again, he was reminded that it was worth protecting.

Still no word from Nuno.

Sylas knew this wasn't a good thing. His next crop, which he had planted earlier that day, would be ready on Soulsday. By that point, things would be set in motion. A journey to hell itself was something Sylas had yet to process.

For now, he would let it go, well aware that dwelling on it wouldn't help. And who knew, maybe Nuno would turn up soon.

Later that night, after the quiz was over and the Cornbreads had won, Sylas and Mira talked to Shamus and Elena about purchasing the abandoned market. Near them, Horatio tried Azor's elemental food, a big smile on his face as he tasted his soup.

Shamus, who was even drunker than he had been earlier, leaned back and placed his hands across his belly. "My apologies, Sylas. I remember you mentioning something about that market, but I didn't realize how interested you were in it. And you," he told Mira. Shamus hiccupped and covered his mouth. "Excuse me. Now, the abandoned market. I do believe it's available. And if it's not, I can head to Battersea and see about making it available considering it has been abandoned for . . . who knows how long, yeah?"

Elena nodded. "And the two of you would like to cosign a loan, take it out together?"

"That's right," Sylas said. "I was thinking of doing the credit union in Cinderpeak considering I pay taxes, but Mira says it will be easier to keep my loan with MLR."

"She is correct. Especially because you already have a loan, we can couple it together and you can pay one installment every morning for both of them. Otherwise, you'd have two separate loan payments." Her eyes glowed for a moment. "I see you are making good on your payments on the farm. The paperwork should be rather easy, and because you are earning so much, you will be the one we will use to qualify for the loan. Just visit me in Duskhaven tomorrow, or the next day."

"Would there still be an auction?" Sylas's eyes narrowed on Shamus. "And next time someone is bidding against me, let me know ahead of time."

"Yes, that, well, the bid was placed anonymously. And it was done just so the field didn't sit fallow for too long. I have your best interest at heart. I know you may not believe that, but I assure you that this is the case. And I will know tomorrow how much it will cost. No auction necessary for something like this considering it has been abandoned for so long." Shamus shook his head. "None necessary. Once I know the cost, I will let you know, and I will be in touch with Elena as well. You can purchase the market, and then take your landlord class."

"Were you this entrepreneurial in our previous world?" Elena asked Sylas.

"No."

Tilbud approached at just the right moment. "A word," he told Sylas as he looked right past Elena.

Sylas soon joined the archlumen out back, where they found Quinlan crouched at the bottom of the steps.

"What's going on?" Sylas asked.

"It has come to my attention that the two of you are in need of a manaseer, one able to tap into the essence of a memory. You are planning to go to the Chasm, yes?"

"Likely," Sylas told Tilbud.

"I assumed as much, and asked myself, why not? Why not go with them, Tilbud?" he said to himself. "Kidding, you already knew I would come. I have been a handful of times, and it was always an interesting experience, to say the least. But before we could do that, we need to better understand where your father and your friend may be. And to do that, we need the services of a manaseer."

"How much will it cost us?" Quinlan asked.

"I'll cover everything," Sylas said.

"No, no, mate—"

"I mean it," Sylas said. "And I want to know what other powers I should learn before we go," he told the archlumen.

"About that. Well, let's discuss the manaseer first and then we can come back to the powers you may need and what they will cost. One thing at a time, no?"

Sylas looked back to the pub to see Azor handling things. It was less lively now, just a handful of people left. They would close the place soon.

"What else do I need to know?" Sylas asked.

"You know how I was able to locate Karn?"

"Through Nelly's tears, which she wiped on Mira's scarf."

"Correct," Tilbud said. "There are other ways to find the essence of someone. If you don't have memories that could bring you to emotion, emotion that would create something like tears, the manaseer I know can extract the essence in a different way."

"This is the part I don't like," Quinlan said.

"That's what you're discussing then, yeah?"

"That is precisely what we were discussing," Tilbud told Sylas. "The manaseer—"

"Do they have a name?"

"Yes, her name is Inesh. She can extract the essence necessary from a memory. Because there are two of you, it would need to be a shared memory. But for her to do this, you will both have to relive what happened."

"The Night of Raining Arrows, the worst part of the Battle of Willcrest." Quinlan threw his hands up in the air. "There, I said it. I have other strong memories of Raelis, but that one, we were both there. We saw what he did."

"We were."

"So that would be the first part of this," said Tilbud. "Inesh would need for the two of you to remember this together. I don't know what you're envisioning, but I can tell you what that will look like. She will put you both in a trance, and you will be transported back to that memory, this Night of Raining Arrows. Once she has the essence, she can then give it to Quinlan, who will use it to track Raelis in the Chasm."

"When would this take place?" Sylas asked.

"Tomorrow. We can leave for Duskhaven early in the morning."

"I would like to go," Mira said.

Sylas had been so focused on Tilbud that he hadn't sensed the apothecary standing behind him.

"We have to go to Duskhaven anyway to visit Elena about the market," she told Sylas.

"Right."

"But I'm not talking about that. Well, I am talking about that, but I'm talking about the Chasm. I want to go there as well with you all. You did say I would get to go next time." Mira placed a hand on Sylas's arm. "You said that, right?"

"I did. And you're more than welcome."

"We are getting a bit ahead of ourselves," Tilbud said. "First, we need to find where Raelis is. And your father. So you will need to think of a memory you have of him, a very strong one."

"I can do that."

"Good. Now, about future powers. You might not like this next bit, but it's better I tell you now. There is a gauge when it comes to MLus, one that is created to keep things fair and to stop someone from completely controlling the entirety of the Underworld. Once you pass the twenty thousand MLu range, buying becomes more expensive. There is also a real estate component to this once you get more, but you haven't reached that threshold yet. What I'm trying to tell you here, dear Sylas, is that I would love to teach you more abilities in the future, but they're going to cost more than they once did. Unfortunately for me, I get the same cut as before."

"So it costs more for you to buy them for someone who is high-powered."

"That's right," Tilbud said. "I thought you should be aware of that. Once you dip below ten thousand, things can change."

"Can I buy powers for other people?"

"You can, but these same rules apply. And remember, not all powers are for everyone. That said, many classes have an equivalent skill." Tilbud looked past Sylas. "Ah, Catia. She seems to be waving me over. I should say hello. Talk more in the morning, yes? And tomorrow, the manaseer."

[You have 49 days until the invasion.]
[A loan payment of 107 has been deducted from your total Mana Lumens. Your total loan balance is 15334 Mana Lumens.]

Name: Sylas Runewulf
Mana Lumens: 18040/18040
Class: Brewer
Secondary Class: Farmer
[Lumen Abilities:]
Flight
Quill
Mana Infusion
Mana Saturation
Harvest Silos
Field Warden
Whimsical Drift
Soulfire

Sylas scratched Patches behind the ear as he scrolled through his status. He was at his farmhouse, and he could already hear Azor talking to Quinlan, who had slept out in the hammock. Mira was there too, his heart fluttering slightly at the sound of her voice.

Sylas got to his feet. He heard Cornbread outside his bedroom door, panting, the dog's snout in the threshold. "I'm coming," he said as she started to whine.

"Top of the bloody morning to you," Quinlan told Sylas. He lifted a little teacup, which looked way too big for his hand.

"Where did you get that?"

"Mira brought the cups for you. In case you didn't know, you could use some bloody dishware around here."

"Hi, Sylas," Mira said, unable to hide the grin on her face.

"Morning."

"Happy Thornsday!" Azor said, Cornbread barking alongside her.

"It won't be that." Quinlan looked down into his teacup. "We're going to have to relive something today."

"We are, mate." Sylas sat next to his friend. "But we'll get through it."

"Aye."

"And where's Tilbud? Please tell me he is already in Duskhaven with the manaseer."

"He's somewhere, all right," Quinlan said.

Azor flared up. "Can you believe it? He spent the night with Catia!"

"Did what now?"

Quinlan laughed. "I've got to hand it to the man, he knows what he's doing. A bit mad, yes, but he can be quite charming."

Sylas slowly shook his head. "He can be *very* charming. So he's at the pub with Catia?"

"He was," Azor said, "but then she left, embarrassed, and he went back to sleep. Tilbud said he set an alarm—"

"He can do that?"

"That's what he said. Tilbud promised to meet us in Duskhaven at his home. So that's where we're going next, right?" Azor asked the others.

"I think we should go to the bank first," Mira said.

"Tilbud said you would say that," Azor told Mira matter-of-factly, "and he wants to go with you to the bank as well because of some previous relationship he's had with Elena. So, meet him first."

Quinlan laughed even harder at Azor's statement.

Mira was less amused.

"It's fine," Sylas told her. "Best we do this the right way."

CHAPTER TWENTY

THE NIGHT OF RAINING ARROWS

G o!" Sylas shouted. The soldiers all around him moved forward with their shields overhead, everyone crouched, calves screaming, their boots heavy in the mud as they neared the long trench where they would be able to shelter for the night.

Thunk! Thunk!

The sound of arrows hitting metal never ceased.

Thunk! Thunk! Thunk!

There must have been a thousand Shadowthorne archers, more than earlier scouts had indicated. They protected the pass that Sylas had been tasked with gaining control of, one that was crucial for their future supply chain.

It would be an uphill battle.

Literally.

In the rain, and against an army of archers.

"Mind your shields, lad!" Sylas called to one of the younger recruits on the outer edge of the formation. He brought his shield back toward the center, where he clanked it against Quinlan's. "Watch him," Sylas called to Quinlan, who responded with a grunt.

On the other side of the formation, Raelis barked orders at several of the younger men. At the front, Kael maintained the most complicated part of the formation, the forward-facing shields at a ninety-degree angle, their holders hunched over so they could be covered by the men behind them.

"Almost there!" Sylas called from the center of the formation, where he had been counting steps. He couldn't see in front of him; but he had been told how many steps it would take to reach the trenches, and he knew better than to question his intel.

"Keep it steady, lads!" Quinlan yelled to the men on his right.

"Halt!" he shouted a bit later, as arrows continued striking the shields. He waited until there was a gap in the attack. "Now, mates! First wave!"

The front line moved into the trench, followed by the others, a line at a time, all protecting one another. As soon as Sylas was in, he approached Raelis, who screamed at one of the recruits.

"You almost got me killed there. Pay attention." Raelis slapped the younger man's face. "An arrow will hurt much worse than that. Get it together, mate. Protect your brothers!"

"Raelis," Sylas said. "Enough of that. The fire arrows will start soon; we need to make sure the coverings are coated."

"On it."

Sylas stopped Raelis before he could walk away and clapped his hands on his shoulders. "Focus, mate, we'll get through it."

Raelis looked up at Sylas from the cover of his helmet, his eyes bloodshot. "Right."

Kael and Quinlan approached. "We're set for the night. Going to be a long one, though," Quinlan said. "I suspect the first wave can move forward in the wee hours."

"A scouting mission."

"I volunteer my regiment," Kael said. He looked just like Quinlan. The two were often mistaken for twins although they were not. Like his older brother, Kael had a scruffy beard, yet he was smaller and thinner.

"You and Raelis can lead one," Sylas told Kael. "Moving at different times. Best that way. Quinlan, you'll stay here and keep the men—"

"Bloody hell, I will, Sylas. If Kael—"

"Quinlan."

"Right," Quinlan said as he dipped his chin some. "In that case, I'll support Raelis."

"Yes. Good."

Thunk! Thunk!

"The Thornies and their arrows," Quinlan growled. "They will run out at some point."

"That's also the plan. We're here now. Smart of Amilcar to build this trench last summer during the dry season."

"I still don't know how he did it with the archers along the pass."

"Slowly," Sylas told Quinlan. "Very slowly."

"And nightly," Kael added. "A couple shovelfuls a night. The archers were far enough away that they didn't see it. At first. Only problem now, aside from the bloody arrows, is the mud."

"Good point. I'll have some of the men use their shields to scoop mud out and shore up the walls. Gents"—Sylas grinned as best he could—"it's going to be a horrible night, especially if we get more rain. Which we will. But we'll make it out the other end."

The casualties began later, once the Shadowthorne Empire used the cover of night to send dagger-wielding rogues into the trenches. They were hard to find, and the rogues killed several of Sylas's men before they were rooted out by Raelis's unit.

"No one in, and only approved regiments out," Sylas said. His head pulsed now, the sound of arrows nonstop. He had known they would be fired upon all night, but he didn't expect that the sound of the arrows would have such an effect, not only on general morale, but also on his nerves.

Thunk! Thunk! Thunk!

Their protective ceilings helped, but the constant flare of fire and the cacophony of arrows was brutal. The rain grew stronger, giving them a sudden break in the arrows. This was what they had waited for, and if Sylas secured the pass, it would allow future waves of Aurumites to turn the tide of an endless war.

Later that night, Quinlan, Kael, and Raelis gathered around Sylas. Raelis and Kael prepared to move out with their units. "Who goes first?" Raelis asked, his voice cutting through the occasional sound of flaming arrows.

"Up to you, mate," Kael told him.

"We will go first then. Clear the way."

"All," Kael called to his men. "Shields behind. We make our stand after Raelis and be done with this."

"We will not die here tonight," Raelis said boldly. "But others will."

Sylas was about to tell him not to be too confident, when he stopped. He had served with Raelis long enough to know that the man had a unique way of encouraging himself, which translated to how others interpreted his words. It could sound cocky, but it was actually done out of fear for the safety of his peers. Like Sylas, Quinlan, and Kael, Raelis cared more about the people around him than he did himself.

Sylas gave the signal. "Let's move out."

It worked, their advance allowing them to secure the pass despite the pouring rain, yet it would be a while before Sylas processed that part of what they had done, how it had changed the tide of the war for the better.

Raelis was missing that next morning, and a frantic search for the man began until both Quinlan and Sylas saw someone limping toward them.

Raelis had been struck by three arrows, and the infections he would get from these wounds would later cause his death.

The memory faded and Sylas gasped.

He let go of the hand he was holding, only then realizing it belonged to Mira.

She pulled it away from him and shook it out.

Sylas was in a bed across from Quinlan, who had just come out of the trance as well, his brow covered in sweat, his only hand over his heart. Seated between them was the manaseer, who turned to Sylas and smiled faintly. "Now, your father. Unless there is a better time for us to do that."

"No," Sylas said, "now is fine. Did you get what you need."

"I did. The essence has been captured." Inesh produced a small vial and gave it to Quinlan. "It is yours when you need it."

———

The memory of his father was much shorter.

It felt so long ago, Sylas looking up at him at The Old Lamplighter, helping his father every day as his youth blazed by, all culminating into the last night before he was conscripted.

"You're going to do great," his father said as he stood behind the bar, Sylas seated in front of him.

The memory was clear enough that Sylas could see the similarity in their faces: the same blue eyes; his father's beard with specks of gray in it; the shape of his face, only a bit filled out, older, cheeks a bit puffy.

Sylas didn't know what to say, so he didn't say anything.

He merely sat there looking at the man, in awe of his presence. So much had happened since that moment. The rest of his life he had been at war, and had he known that this would be the last time he would see his father, the last time he would be able to enjoy the relative peace and quiet of the place he grew up, maybe he would have tried to cherish it more.

But as moments often did, they passed before they could be fully appreciated. It was the next day and Sylas was sitting on the back of a wagon, waving goodbye to his father, never to see him again.

Sylas woke with a strange sense of calm, like all of this had been a pleasant dream and his day was just starting. Even though it had been brief, Sylas had seen his dad, the man's image still vivid in his mind's eye.

It brought a smile to his face, even if the memory was both pleasant and surrounded by regret. Sylas had never been able to leave the front line long enough to travel back to the village to visit his father.

"Good," the manaseer said as a puddle of golden mana hovered in the air before her, defying gravity. She bottled this and gave it to Quinlan. He left without saying much else, still troubled by what he had experienced with Sylas.

———

The manaseer's services were well worth it.

"Two thousand fixed MLus," Mira later said as they headed toward the bank with Tilbud.

"A small price to pay for memory," Tilbud told her.

"I hope it works."

"It will work. But now, we will have to work on getting into the Chasm," he said.

"You have a trick up your sleeve, don't you?"

"I always do," Tilbud told her. "Because we can't go as part of a Hallowed Pursuit. Or can we?"

"What would we have to do to qualify?" Sylas asked.

"We would need to join one, to start. So that could complicate things. And the option of lowering our MLus to dangerous levels to pass through like Azor did, is, as you can both imagine, an absolutely terrible idea. No, there is another way. Actually, there are several other ways, but I think one will work best. It will cost a lot, likely between eight and ten thousand fixed MLus, but it will be worth it."

"Steep."

"Indeed."

"What are you thinking?" Sylas asked as they came to a large brick building, surrounded by well-manicured bushes and featuring several statues that reminded Sylas of Aurumite statesmen. He saw the MLR Bank's sign and noticed that the letters were carved into the stone trim as well.

"Let me worry about that. You know how I am," Tilbud said with a twist of his mustache. "I like to keep you guessing. Just be ready to pay that amount."

"I will, and you certainly kept me guessing with Catia."

Tilbud chuckled. "Ah yes, that. *That*. Rather unexpected, but it isn't what you think. We had a lot to discuss, from shared relations to your new class."

"We haven't bought the market yet," Mira reminded him.

"But you will. I think the two of you will make excellent business partners. Excellent afterlife partners as well, if we're being honest. Now, don't look at me like that. I can sense when love is in the air."

"Are you coming or not?" Mira said as she opened the door.

"Ah, yes, Elena. I should say hello, but only briefly, and only so she knows that I will be the one teaching you class powers."

"Do you even know the powers?"

"Of course I do not. That is what Elena is for, my dear. Or should I say, that's what the loan you are going to get is for. Come, come. Let's see what she has to say."

The news turned out to be better than Sylas had expected. The loan amount would be for twenty thousand MLus, and with the 10 percent added on, this brought it to twenty-two thousand, Sylas and Mira planning to split it down the middle.

"It truly is a steal," Elena assured them. "A market like this could easily bring in ten thousand MLus in a week depending on what is sold there. And with the class, which is what you're mostly paying for here, you can start to purchase plots of land and abandoned buildings. So even if the market doesn't do so well, you will have other options in growing your portfolios. There won't be any taxes in Ember Hollow, but you will pay dues to the Landlord Guild."

"How much is that exactly?" Mira asked.

"It is based on gross revenue at the end of the week, when landlord bills are paid. That amount would be ten percent."

"Not too bad," Sylas said.

"And even better with the first-time landlord discount of five percent, which both of you would qualify for. This would apply to everything within your territory that you purchase."

"So five percent."

"That is correct, Mr. Runewulf."

"All of Ember Hollow?" Tilbud asked.

"Also correct. If you purchased something outside of the village, or its vicinity, you would face the ten percent guild fee."

"Five percent isn't bad," Mira said. "And the loan payment would be ten percent every morning, yes?"

"And to be clear, that number would be ten percent of your previous day's net revenue. Because you already have a loan, Sylas, your payment will remain ten percent. That is the advantage of not going to another bank, how we're able to consolidate your loan here at MLR. I should also note that like your previous loan, there is no down payment necessary. With afterlife spans, and a system that automatically withdraws MLus, it isn't something that is necessary. Your leverage, however, remains what you are able to already bring in and your current amount of MLus. I see you harvested."

"I did."

"And it looks to be quite the harvest," Elena said, her eyes suddenly gold as she took Sylas in. "Now, as for the skills that you will need, it varies based on location. The guild will have further options, but at the very least you will need a version of Structural Reinforcement, similar to what a carpenter might have. You won't build properties as much as you will strengthen the ones you already own."

"Anders will come in handy."

"Who?" Elena asked Sylas.

"He is classed as a carpenter. Right now, he's working on the inn that Nelly and her husband are adding to their shop."

"I see, a good move on their part. I was part of those negotiations, you know."

"I figured."

Elena shuffled some papers, even though it seemed like she really didn't need to. "A landlord and a carpenter working together create a beneficial situation in which they work faster, and they are able to uncover future issues before they arise. You will need that skill. You will need tenants for your market, so something like Bargain Binding would be beneficial. This is a spell cast weekly on Moonsday that ensures fair dealings within the market boundaries. Being so close to the Hexveil, you'll also need to have a Ward of Welcome in place, which casts a protective barrier around the market that repels those with ill intent."

"And what you quoted us, all those are covered in this cost?" Mira asked.

"That is correct. The purchase of property, the class additions, and the three spells." Elena smiled at them. "You will also have access to Magical Ledger, which is something that merchant and landlord classes can utilize. This keeps an accurate ledger of all vendor agreements and transactions, updated in real time. What do you say?"

Mira and Sylas exchanged glances. He cleared his throat. "I'm for it, if you are."

CHAPTER TWENTY-ONE

PATCHES TRIUMPHANT

Sylas had to laugh. With all he had already taken on, now was *not* the time to add a third class and pick up an abandoned market, yet that was where he found himself later that day, clearing out some of the debris and piling it for Azor to torch. Mira moved around the market as well, confirming the vendor booth count and making notes on a little pad she carried.

They still needed to buy the actual landlord class at the guild in Battersea, but that would be easy, and Tilbud had already gone ahead and obtained the initial landlord skills they would need. Things were falling into place much faster than he had anticipated.

"Should we charge a fee to come to the market?" Mira asked. "Something small, like five MLus?"

"So we'd collect on people visiting, vendor fees, and a small percentage on revenue over a thousand MLus."

"That's what Elena said was standard, but I don't know about the fee to get in. We want more people to come. Most markets I've been to are free."

"Agreed. I can't recall paying to come to a market yet in the Underworld." Sylas ran the math in his head. He hadn't taken the landlord class just for the market. That wouldn't be worth his time, considering it might only bring him five thousand Mana Lumens a week when split with Mira. He'd taken the market for the *class*, which would allow Sylas to buy up other properties in Ember Hollow and help revitalize the village.

If he was able to bring in up to thirty thousand Mana Lumens through his farm weekly, depending on when he harvested, and his pub brought an average of eight hundred a night, all of it stacking with additional rental incomes, Sylas would soon have enough power to do . . .

What?

That, he didn't quite know, but Tilbud had mentioned there were spells that cost tens of thousands of Mana Lumens. And before they signed their paperwork, Elena revealed something else to Sylas regarding the cost of a fourth class, which was astronomical:

"You can switch out your class once your total loan is paid, or you can buy out your loan to switch a class. At three classes, you have reached the Threshold of Affordability, as we bankers like to call it. To add an additional class, your fourth class, the cost starts at a hundred thousand Mana Lumens. Steep, but that is by design to prevent anyone from becoming too overpowered."

Now, as he turned back toward the pub to open for the night, Sylas thought about that cost. He had been interested before in classing as an adventurer, and being a demon hunter would give him access to available hunts, which as he already had learned was a great way to bring extra Mana Lumens.

But a hundred thousand was quite the haul.

"Hey," Mira said as she caught up with him. Cornbread, who had been trotting alongside Sylas, turned to the apothecary and looked up at her, tail wagging. "Are you doing all right? You have been quiet."

"I'm fine. It's just been one of those days."

"Yes, I can imagine. Reliving the memories."

"That and taking on more debt, although I don't know why that part bothers me."

"You'll be fine," Mira told him. "I'm the one that should be worried. It will take me forever to pay off the loan."

"Not when we get the market up and running it won't. And once you acquire more property."

"Tiberius is going to light into me when he hears what I have done."

"Then don't tell him."

She crossed her arms over her chest as they continued walking. "He's not supposed to notice a market suddenly sprouting up in Ember Hollow?"

"Yes, I suppose he will notice that."

"We'll need a name for the market."

"Whatever you'd like to call it, Mira, works for me."

"Something bespoke would be nice. Something instantly explains what it is to people who hear the name." She bit her lip. "Ember Hollow Market just doesn't do it for me."

"Same, although that might work for now. As for the market itself, I will continue searching the grounds tomorrow."

"You don't really think you'll find something with Legendary Locks on it, do you?"

"I don't know. Patches came with the pub, and the hat and tinted glasses came with the farm." Cornbread barked. "Yes, you came with the farm too," Sylas told her. "If we can find something with high-powered charms, we will be able to reap even more from the market."

"Wouldn't it be funny if that was the exact kind of antique one of our vendors sold at the market?"

"It would." Sylas stopped in front of The Old Lamplighter and looked up at the sign. Nelly's General Store was bustling, as always. A pair exited carrying sandwiches and a few food supplies, heading toward the opposite side of town, toward the Hexveil. An idea came to Sylas as he observed the market. "Maybe we are going about this the wrong way."

"A little late for that, yeah?"

"I don't mean buying the market or taking the loan, I mean not fully roping Nelly and Karn in. We can have our antique market, but what if they helped run a food vendor and merchant market? If we do that, our market expands to something that we didn't even think about earlier on, vendor fees go up, more in attendance, and the market brings in more than Elena suggested. This would also help our other businesses through spillover to the pub and the store."

"Wait, I see what you're saying," Mira said. "And that would make it so we aren't competing with them, because they are managing the food market and other goods side, leaving you and me to manage the antiques side."

"Exactly. It will bring in more people and ease the burden of running the market. We're getting ahead of ourselves, I know."

Mira took Sylas's hand, stepped back, and smiled at him. "We do tend to do that, don't we?"

"Or, I do."

"Yes, you do, but it's contagious, exciting. And sometimes necessary. How about this? What would you say to selling ale at the market?"

"I can only have eight casks. However, that might be a per location thing. I will have to check with the Ale Alliance."

"Tasks galore, yes?" Mira turned back to the general store. "Let's see what Nelly and Karn have to say. The worst they can say is no."

"Exactly."

"But I think they will see value in this, I really do. And it will make the market even better."

"Speaking of which, tomorrow, Battersea, you and me, we'll get the class, meet with Tilbud, get the powers we need, and then I have to prepare for Mana Saturation. I guess I should stop by the Ale Alliance as well and ask about opening a branch of The Old Lamplighter at the market. I hadn't considered that, but it's a brilliant idea."

"I'd like to see what the Mana Saturation part is like."

"Then you're invited, but come ready to fight."

Mira dropped Sylas's hand and playfully lifted her fists. "I'm always ready to fight."

———————

The alarm rang out later that night. Cornbread was just getting comfy at the foot of the bed when she heard the dog named Sunflower howling in the distance.

The pepper farm. She hopped off the bed and raced to the door, where she stopped and turned back to look at Patches. *Are you coming or not? She helped us; that's what we do around here.*

Just give me a moment. Patches yawned. The pub cat was tired after he had just finished giving the big man energy, and now he was being called away.

Even so, he hopped off the bed and caught up with the farm dog, who was already jumping at the door to open it. Once she was out, Cornbread took off.

I'm almost there. She took a shortcut that put her right past the tomato farm.

As she was coming around, Bruno, the white dog with clipped ears, charged directly at her. He would have hit her had it not been for Patches, who collided with the dog.

What the . . . ? Cornbread swiveled midsprint.

Patches quadrupled in size, his claws growing into razor-sharp talons. He was hunched up now, prepared to do everything he could to stop the white dog from advancing.

You wouldn't dare! the white dog barked.

We are trying to help her, Cornbread told him in her most reasonable voice. She heard the way that the Sunflower barked in the distance. Cornbread didn't want to fight now, not if she didn't have to.

But Patches saw things differently. *Go on,* he told Cornbread. *I have it from here.*

Are you sure?

Patches nodded.

Bruno laughed. *This is going to be fun.*

I can't—

Go, Patches told her. *Help your friend. I'll try not to kill him.*

Cornbread hated to do it, but she heard Sunflower cry out again and knew that things were going to be desperate soon. She took off, and ran through Bruno's fields this time, which she knew would infuriate him, perhaps even confuse him for a moment, giving Patches the time he needed to attack.

She reached Sunflower and found her fighting off several Mana Ghouls. Cornbread launched into action, her jaw enlarging as she ripped into one of the demons. Another dog was fighting alongside them, a cute, smaller one that helped out at the bean farm.

Where's the cat? Sunflower asked Cornbread.

He stayed back to fight the mean dog!

He did? Why would he do that?

Because he's a cat and, apparently, he thinks he is a lot larger than he actually is. She took a bite out of a demon and brought it to the ground. *I have to help him!*

But you came here.

I have to help you too!

The smaller dog barked. *They're getting away!* He took off after the Mana Ghouls.

Let's go, Cornbread told Sunflower. The two quickly caught up with the smaller dog and they chased after the fleeing Mana Ghouls together.

Mana swirled around the smaller dog's form as he released a beam of concentrated energy, one that cut straight through two of the ghouls. *Take that!*

Cornbread moved into action next, barking so loudly that a ghoul instantly froze in midair.

Once she was ready, Sunflower exploded forward with a series of quick bites, almost jab-like, which destroyed several more of the Mana Ghouls.

The three dogs finished off what was left, and then gathered around one another, Cornbread panting. *I have to go back to the cat.*

I will help you, Sunflower said.

The smaller dog barked. *I hate that big white dog! Let's go!*

He took off again, faster than the other two, the dogs making a beeline straight through the fields. They came onto a scene that Cornbread wasn't expecting.

Patches stood over Bruno, whose coat was covered in blood. The pub cat swayed back and forth, also bleeding profusely. *See?* Patches said. *I told you not to worry.*

He tried to turn away, but in doing so ended up falling off to the side.

Cornbread rushed to him and began licking the cat, healing him instantly. Her friends joined in, but none of them helped Bruno until he started to yelp.

Please, he said. *I'm sorry. I was wrong.*

Why should we help you? Sunflower asked. *You always torment us.*

I won't do it anymore. We should work together. Even the cat.

The three dogs turned to Patches, who now sat licking his paw, glaring at Bruno defiantly.

The smaller dog sniffed the bigger canine. *His wounds are pretty bad. He may die.*

Once again, Cornbread and Sunflower glanced over to Patches. The cat finally spoke: *We have to think of the big man. Dogs are owned, and we don't want this dog's owner angry at the big man. Heal him. But if you ever try anything again, against anyone around here, we won't be as gracious next time.*

Patches turned, thrust his tail up into the air, and strutted away to the best of his ability.

CHAPTER TWENTY-TWO

RANDOMS AND ODD FELLOWS

[You have 48 days until the invasion.]
[A loan payment of 65 has been deducted from your total Mana
Lumens. Your total loan balance is 26269 Mana Lumens.]

Sylas briefly scanned his Mana Lumens and saw that he had well over six-teen thousand. It had been a slow night at the pub, but he had still brewed five casks, two regular, two strong, plus a flamefruit. There had also been the fixed cost of the manaseer, and he could now see the increase in his loan amount.

Still, he was happy. Seated in his bed at the farmhouse, staring out at his fields, Sylas felt joy in knowing that he was getting closer. To what exactly, remained to be seen. But he could tell he was progressing.

"Happy Fireday!" Azor called from the living room.

Sylas entered the living room to find Azor using flame from her hand to toast a piece of bread. "When did you get here?"

"Earlier. The front door was open and Cornbread was on the front porch with Patches."

"I was wondering where he was this morning," Sylas said as he scratched the back of his head.

"They are so cute. Always seated next to one another now. I think they just go around playing all night with their friends from the other farms. Must be nice."

"I'm sure they do something. I did hear some barking, but it was in the dis-tance." Sylas cracked his knuckles. "Have you heard anything from Mira?"

"I did. She was opening her shop and said she would be over later so the two of you can go to Battersea and get your new classes."

"I could just go to Ember Hollow."

"She said you would say that. She said she wanted to take a walk later, and that she would join you here, and you both could go back and portal from the pub." Azor shrugged. "I don't know what goes on in her mind, but I am excited for whatever it is the two of you will do next. Landlords. Soon enough, you will own most of Ember Hollow."

"That's not exactly the plan, but we would like to revitalize it." Sylas sat at the table and Azor brought him a plate of scrambled eggs and toast.

"Flame-kissed," she said.

Sure enough, each side of the toast had a set of lips burned onto it.

Sylas laughed. "That sure is something." he scooped some of the scrambled eggs onto the toast and ate it. Once he was finished, he put on his hat with its charms and headed out to the fields.

"Mana Saturation time," Azor said as she joined Sylas.

"Indeed. I guess Mira won't make it this time, but there will be others." Sylas turned to his fields and noticed the soil radiating with golden mana. The prompt came:

[**Mana Saturation cost is 75 Mana Lumens per field. Would you like to begin the process? Y/N?**]

"Let's do it."

He moved through his fields. The ground glowed with mana that soon rose and formed clouds over his plants. As he reached the end of the row, these clouds sprinkled glittery bits of mana onto the row upon row of cornstalks. The stalks straightened, flourished, and gave his fields a sudden glow that gave Sylas a warm feeling.

He continued, back and forth, everything around them vibrant with life even if he was dead.

"It's crazy how easy it is," Sylas told the fire spirit after he was done with Mana Saturation. "Even though we still have to defend it tonight and tomorrow night."

"Right, that will be fun." This time, Azor produced several rows of devil horns, all of which popped out of her head, lit with purple flames.

Cornbread raced up and down the rows, barking. Patches chased her for a moment, but then gave up as he rolled onto his back, absorbing some of the mana.

"Look at Patches," Azor said with a laugh. "So bloody adorable!"

"How was Quinlan last night?"

"Aside from snoring—snoring that was loud enough to rock the pub, mind you—he was fine. I'm getting used to him being around. It doesn't really bother me as much as I may have let on earlier."

"He can be rough, but he always means well. He would do anything for a friend. That's an important trait in my book."

Sylas approached the front porch. He sat and stared out his fields as he waited for Mira to come.

"Maybe I should head back with Patches," Azor said. "And are you sure Cornbread will be fine here by herself?"

"She will be great. Don't worry about her." Sylas relaxed, the brim of his hat low enough to cast a shadow over his eyes. Soon, he was sleeping again, lightly, like he used to do on the front lines when he was given a moment of rest. There wasn't a sound, whether a slight creak in the old home or Cornbread rustling through the fields, that didn't draw his attention.

Later, when Mira arrived, she found Sylas on the porch smiling at her, even though his eyes were closed.

"You are such a strange man," she told him.

"Am I?" he stood and removed his hat. Once it was locked up in the box that Rufus had given him, he joined Mira outside. "Back to Ember Hollow then, yeah?"

"I know, it is nonsensical for me to come all the way here for us just to go back there. But I like the walk to the portal, and I like the little stroll from the portal here in the Seedlands to your farm. What can I say? A nice walk is a nice walk."

"It is indeed. And while we are in Battersea, any chance we can take a boat to Everscene?"

"Right, you mentioned that last time."

"I've been twice now. Once with Tilbud and once with Azor. She actually learned to cook for elementals on that last trip."

"Did she?"

"But we don't really have many around here, aside from Horatio."

"I feel like I saw him eating something the other night."

"Yes, that was Azor's doing."

"She is so clever, you know. I need a spirit that helps me keep it all together. Maybe they could run interference with my uncle."

"I don't wish that upon any bonded spirit."

"Perhaps not." Mira turned to Sylas and smiled. Soon, her arm was looped in his, the two of them taking their time as they walked to the portal.

———

Getting the approvals they needed from Catia at The Distinguished Society of Lumengineers and Etheric Constructs was a breeze. The scholarly woman hardly made eye contact with them as she used mana to stamp the paperwork that Mira and Sylas presented. She said goodbye and didn't bother inviting them into her office.

"That was . . . odd."

"Yeah, about that," Sylas told Mira as they left the Society. She was in the lead now, moving in a way that told Sylas she had used a quest contract to make directions easier. "I don't know the details, but she might or might not have had a fling with Tilbud."

Mira laughed. "That would explain so much."

They reached the Ale Alliance, where Sylas learned from Marty that he would be able to open a second branch of his pub.

"There is a fee, however, of eight thousand fixed MLus to supply the casks needed for a secondary location."

"So they are tied to the market, then?"

"*Tethered* would be the right word, Sylas, but yes, they are tethered to their location. I've heard of people bringing ale over pint-by-pint, but that would be tedious."

"So I would have up to sixteen to fill each night."

"That is correct. You could also see how the business goes at the market and only sell ale on certain nights."

Sylas ran his hand over his beard. "Maybe that would be the best idea. Perhaps the second location would only be open on the weekends and Moonsday at first."

"Whatever works best for you. And don't forget, you will want custom mugs for the market. Branding is everything."

"Well, this is all good information. It gives me something to think about."

"Indeed," Marty said. "I keep hearing good things about Ember Hollow. It's really up-and-coming, you know."

Mira and Sylas visited the Landlord Guild next, which was set in one of the nicest buildings Sylas had seen yet. The salmon-colored building was several stories tall, with an observation deck up top. Surrounding it were numerous gardens being enjoyed by the people of Battersea. Leading up to the entrance was a grand pathway made of white marble, currently being cleaned by a team of men in green tunics, rags wrapped around their knees.

"The landlords are doing well for themselves, it seems," Sylas said as the double doors opened on their own. They were greeted by a well-dressed man who brought them over to a seating area while he handled the paperwork. Soon, they were called into an office, where a woman sat on the ground, legs crossed beneath her, her lower half covered by a wool blanket.

"Please," she said as she motioned to a set of pillows. Sylas took the one on the left, Mira the one on the right.

The prompt came moments later.

[Class as a landlord? Y/N?]

"Yes," Sylas said as Mira squeezed his hand and said the same thing.

"And it says here that the two of you have an archlumen who will be transferring the skills, Archlumen Octavian Tilbud, A-Rank Sovereign of Arcane Mysteries and Paramount Luminary of the School of Echelons and Enchantments, yes? My, that is quite the title."

"That's his full title?" Mira asked. "That's worse than the name for my uncle's militia."

"I've heard Tilbud say it before," Sylas told her. "Rolls right off the tongue. For him, anyway. And yes, that is our plan. He will provide the spells."

"I see. In that case, your classes have been added and you can start landlording." The woman laughed to herself. "Sorry, they ask me to say that, and I still find it a bit baffling."

Sylas accessed his stats.

Name: Sylas Runewulf
Mana Lumens: 15189/15939
Class: Brewer
Secondary Class: Farmer
Tertiary Class: Landlord

"Everything in order?" the woman asked.

Sylas and Mira exchanged glances and nodded at each other.

"Good. Congratulations, you are now landlords. You now have access to our library and legal services should you want to use them. Your dues are to be paid once you start collecting rents. This will automatically be deducted from payments you receive, so there's never a need to calculate anything."

"Understood," Sylas said, used to the system by now. "And thank you."

"What now?" Mira asked as they left the guild.

"I have an idea . . ."

"Everscene?"

"Yes, that, but something else. Let's head to the Archlumenry first, though. There's someone I would like to visit there."

———

Meldon, who sat in his high chair, looked down at Sylas and Mira as they entered the Archlumenry.

"Welcome back, Sylas," he said as the chair magically shrank until he could stand. Meldon placed his hands together and stretched them in front of his body. "I see you have come without Tilbud."

"I'm sure he will want to be involved with this. He did say that there was a way for archlumens to contact one another. I figured you would be able to do that."

"You are correct, how may I help you?"

"Can you call him?" Sylas asked. "It would be doing us a favor, one that we would greatly appreciate."

"It doesn't exactly work like that, but yes, I can. Let me ask you before I do that, what is it you are looking to do?"

"Yes," Mira said as she turned to Sylas. "Why are we here?"

"Because of what we are planning to do in the future, I know that you could use some more abilities. Without a guild for apothecaries, there isn't really a central place for you to get them. I figured that I could buy some for you."

"You mean it, Sylas?"

"I do. But I'd need Tilbud to transfer the powers, and I figured I would ask you what she could benefit from," he told Meldon.

The archlumen rubbed his hands together. "Oh, this is wonderful news. Shopping for powers. Who doesn't like that? And while you haven't technically come to the right place, it is exactly the right place considering the people you know, and what we are capable of. Now, as for apothecaries, there is a reason that they do not have a guild, and that is because of the Crafting Laws. Are you familiar with them?"

"I am," Sylas told the man.

"Long story short, because I should be contacting Tilbud in a moment, the Crafting Laws did away with the The Alchemical and Arcane Apothecarium because it was manufacturing pills and other medicines used to augment powers. These medicines, potions, and powders were able to do miraculous things; it threatened the order that the Celestial Plains has maintained over the Underworld. Anyway, it will take a moment for me to contact Tilbud. Please, wait here."

"You don't have to," Mira told Sylas as soon as Meldon left.

"I insist."

"Sylas."

"Mira."

By this point, they were turned to each other, holding hands, a grin forming on Sylas's face.

"Why do you have to be so stubborn?"

"I'm not the one who is stubborn," he told her. "If we are going to go to the Chasm together, you are going to need more powers. Now that you have classed as a landlord, there are probably other options for you, similar to the ability I have called Field Warden that lets me fire mana like a demon hunter."

"I can already do something like that."

"And I need to spend these MLus now. Once I hit the twenty thousand MLu threshold, things become more expensive. Right now, I'm at nearly sixteen thousand total. After I harvest again, that number will be well over thirty thousand unless I do something now. What I'm saying here is I need to spend some today. Besides, I owe you. I don't remember how much I owe you, but I definitely owe you for all that you've done."

"You act like I saved you."

"You did save me. And if you really are planning to go to the Chasm, then you should be prepared."

She let go of his hands. "You can be very motivating, you know that."

"It was sort of my job. Someone had to rally the troops. It wasn't always me. Quinlan was good at it as well."

"I can see that."

Meldon returned. "Ah, Tilbud. He shall be here shortly."

"What was he doing exactly?" Mira asked.

"It's funny you ask that. He said that he was having a conversation with a few friends about elementals for hire, if that means anything to you. He will be here shortly because he felt that this was an important interruption."

"Elementals?" Mira turned to Sylas. "Do you know anything about this?"

Sylas suspected something, but he didn't say anything. For the next hour, the two sat in the waiting area of the Archlumenry, while Meldon and Andrea went about their business, which seemed to involve clearing out one room of books and scrolls and transferring them to another.

It was only on their fifth or sixth time opening one of the doors that Sylas realized they were portaling to another location and retrieving the documents from there. Not only were they doing that, the room they were moving them to also had a portal.

"I wonder where it goes," he told Mira, whose head now rested on his shoulder.

"There really is no telling."

Finally, after another thirty-minute wait, Tilbud stepped out of one of the doors, the archlumen in a periwinkle suit with a yellow flower in his breast pocket that matched the brim of his hat. "Sylas, Mira, dears. It appears I have been summoned." He grinned at the two of them. "But that is quite all right. And I think this is a wonderful idea, especially as you push toward that next threshold, Sylas, where everything starts to cost more. Best to spend cheaply while you can."

"I thought it would be smart."

"It is, indeed. Now that you have your new classes, you are already set to learn Bargain Binding, Ward of Welcome, and Structural Reinforcement, which you will need for the market. Have you thought of a name for your market? No? Well, I suppose with all that you have going on—Mana Saturation day, yes?—and the fact that you haven't taken the class until now, you wouldn't have a name for it."

"We don't have a name," Mira told the archlumen, "but we have an agreement with Nelly and Karn to create an even larger market, one that has antiques and food, a way to supplement what they already sell at the general store and inn. They are going to be running that portion of it and dealing with all the merchants. We will also open a branch of The Old Lamplighter there."

"A second location?" Tilbud nodded, the man clearly impressed. "That, my dears, is the kind of brilliance I was hoping you'd be able to conjure up in a partnership. Now, all you have to do is collect rent. Am I understanding this correctly?"

"Yes, and pay our guild dues," Mira told him.

"And brew."

"Yes, those tasks. Always something. Who would have thought we would be so busy in death? You will benefit, however, being in Ember Hollow and only paying five percent. How will the Redgraves' cut work out, if you don't mind me asking?"

"That's one thing Nelly was excited about," Sylas said. "There are small vendor fees that are available for merchants who have partnered with someone that owns the market. These are fractional, but they do add up."

"On the sale of all goods?"

"Exactly."

"And you aren't charging a fee to come in the market, so while you may lose a little off the top there, there will be more people if the booths are curated correctly, which will mean more foot traffic, which helps both you, by your tenants wanting to stay in the market, and Nelly and Karn. Have you decided when the market will be open?" Tilbud asked.

"I suggested we have a daily market for food and daily items, and a weekend market for antiques," Mira told him. "We still don't know how that part is going to work yet, or how popular it will be. But we can have that, and we can also do something like have a night market during the Wraithsday Feast."

"Well, I'm all for it. I will certainly be there for the feast, for the market, and for the pub quiz, which seems to do best when it takes place on Fireday. Maybe best to set that in stone and make it a weekly occurrence." He stroked his mustache. "I do hate committing." Tilbud looked to the two doors. "Where are Andrea and Meldon?"

"Your guess is as good as mine," Sylas told him. "They said that you were dealing with elemental spirits. Is that what took you so long?"

"I'm not normally called to the Archlumenry, so, yes, while I was dealing with that, I also had a few other little, ahem, *situationships* I needed to handle in Duskhaven. And then there is this bloody pub quiz. It's hard, you know, coming up with such clever questions. But I do have them for tonight, and it should be a stellar time. Perhaps we make an announcement about the market? No time like the present to get the buzz going."

"I can make an announcement." Sylas turned to Mira. "If you're fine with that."

"That works for me. I already see how this can work between us, you know. You are much more sociable than I am, but I can handle things on the back end, such as the curating."

"I would love to assist you in any way with that," Tilbud told her. "I do know random and odd fellows all across the Underworld. Oh, drat. I just realized I had a quiz a few days back. Perhaps every Fireday going forward. Next Fireday? No, we will be in the Chasm then."

"It will take us that long?" Sylas asked.

"No one told you? Time moves differently there. As for tonight, perhaps we do something that will certainly get the blood pumping. An arm wrestling competition? A storytelling competition? A dice game? Perhaps Hoodman's Blind."

Mira raised an eyebrow at the archlumen. "What now?"

"Hoodman's Blind can be played several ways. One of my favorite ways to play it is for the blindfolded person to try to guess what an object is in their hand. The drunker, the better. Also, there is the Hoodman's Duel, where the hoodman holds a wooden spoon and their opponent, also blindfolded, a pot. The game relies on the person with the spoon locating the person with the pot, who must then defend themselves."

"That sounds like it will get out of hand."

"It most certainly would, Mira. I suppose we could scratch that one then. A talent competition could be nice. Yes, a talent competition. But I think we should keep those other ideas on the table as well, arm wrestling, and storytelling. Let's see what the crowd is like. They will be there tonight, I'm certain of it. The Old Lamplighter is a destination, you know. What do you say, Sylas?"

"A talent competition is fine by me. Explain what you said before all that, about time moving differently in the Chasm. I love how you brush over the most important details sometimes."

"I do that just to make sure people are listening to me. Or, because I'm a bit scatterbrained. Learn enough spells and cause enough trouble, you will be scatterbrained as well. I don't wish it upon anyone." He playfully blew a bit of hot air on his knuckles. "Now, time. It looks like we have time to talk about time, considering Andrea and Meldon have decided to take an extended break. It is hard to quantify."

"Time in general, or time in the Chasm?" Mira asked.

"Both, really, but I'm referring to the Chasm at the moment. We will do our best to find your father and your friend, Sylas, but we don't know what this will look like when we return here, the day, I mean. I'm surprised Quinlan didn't mention it. When I last entered the Chasm, I entered on Moonsday and returned to the Underworld on Soulsday. But only a couple hours actually passed, to my knowledge. Hard to tell, really. Another time, an acquaintance went in on a Moonsday and came out on Thornsday, and that was a longer trip, or it felt that way, according to them. I might have a solution, though. Let me ask around."

"Either way, we'll need to hurry," Sylas said.

"Yes," Tilbud told him, his eyes suddenly serious. "We will need to hurry, especially with the message you continue to receive. You received it today, yes?"

"I did."

"How many days, again?"

"Forty-eight."

Tilbud's brow furrowed. "Right. In that case, we best get a move on, yes?"

CHAPTER TWENTY-THREE

DISPUTE

The pub opened later that night, Sylas pouring pints while he thought about what they had decided back at the Archlumenry. Tilbud would teach Mira and him the new spells in the morning alongside their basic landlord class skills.

The new ones were powerful enough that Sylas had opted for all of them as well, which doubled the cost. Ten thousand fixed Mana Lumens was quite a bit, but he would replenish his supply in two days, and the spells were certainly worth it.

Mira, who sat at the bar sipping from her ale, grinned at Sylas. Every time he looked over at her she was smiling, content. It made him feel good, but a part of him also felt a tinge of fear about what they were planning to do.

As Sylas watched Tilbud host the talent competition, Azor flit about with pints, Patches curl up in Duncan's lap, and Cornbread sit next to Quinlan, he started to feel that same sensation he had once felt in his world. It was this notion that he was about to be pulled away, sent to the front lines. It happened every time he would get a short reprieve, be it a few days, or up to a week.

Just as he was getting comfortable, change would rear its ugly face on the horizon.

As the talent show continued, a group of farmers entered the pub. Edgar, Sterling, Trampus, and Lucille were joined by a young woman in a straw hat. Long earrings dangled from her ears, the right one shaped into a parrot, and the left one a tropical tree.

Trampus approached Sylas. "This is who I was telling you about, Leah. She can take a look at your pets and tell you how many MLus they have."

"Please." Sylas motioned for the veterinarian to sit.

"Nice to meet you." Leah had a glow about her, like she had been outside all day. It was different from anyone currently in the pub.

Sylas poured up a pint of fireberry ale for the woman. "On me. Anything you want is on me."

As if he had been summoned, Patches hopped up onto the bar. The pub cat immediately approached the woman, stepping right past Mira.

He started purring and Leah placed her hand on his head. "You have yourself quite the defender here," she told Sylas.

"Can you speak to him? Quinlan—he's my mate, over there—has a bond with Cornbread."

"Your second animal, yes? Trampus was telling me you had two."

Sylas whistled and Cornbread came running. She also joined the woman, putting her two front paws on the chair as she looked up at Leah, who continued to pet Patches.

"This cat is a defender," she said again. "Would you like to know how many MLus he has?"

"I would. He restores my power nightly."

"Yes, I've seen that before." Even though Leah seemed younger, much younger than Sylas, she spoke with true wisdom. It was a reminder that a person's age in the Underworld didn't match the way they appeared. "Your Patches has other powers, yes?"

"I've seen him do several remarkable things, if that's what you're asking."

"He is a very old cat."

Sylas examined the purring cat. "He is?"

"Perhaps one of the oldest that I have encountered. Patches has been in this very pub for ages, and every time a new owner comes, he forgets more and more of the people who have owned it in the past. In that way, he is born anew. He gives you power, but he feeds off what you have done. This is why he is alive and doing so well. Now, the dog." Leah placed her hand on Cornbread's head. "The dog . . ."

"Are you able to tell Patches things?" Sylas asked.

"What do you mean?"

"I just want him to know that I appreciate what he has done around here. He helps keep the place tidy, and I have a feeling a lot more goes on behind the scenes than I'm seeing. Patches and Cornbread, actually. I want to thank both of them."

"Unfortunately, I don't communicate directly with them the way we speak. But I can see through them, if that makes sense, through their past experiences. With Patches, I see that he is very curious and dedicated to stopping anyone and anything that gets in your path. To him, this means protecting the pub. It is his obsession and his life's calling."

"He hunts," Azor said, who now hovered nearby with an empty tray of pint glasses.

"Yes, as most cats do. But his hunting is different." Leah scratched Patches behind the ear. "His goal is to hunt things that are either directly going to disrupt what you are doing here at the pub, or demonic beings. Cornbread is similar in that regard, but she isn't as old as Patches. Much younger, in fact. Like him, she has dedicated her life to protecting her owners' property, which just so happens to be your farm. While Patches does it because he gains power, Cornbread does it because she is loyal. Not that Patches isn't loyal. I'm sure if you asked him how he felt he would tell you that he cared deeply for you."

"He really is a good cat."

"And so cute too, when he's nice," Azor said.

"Not many people get a pet in the afterlife that has the potential of yours, Sylas. There are regular animals, you know. And to have two of them is something I've only seen a handful of times. You are very lucky in that regard. Very lucky."

"I keep telling him he's lucky," Mira said as she joined the conversation.

"He is that. As for MLus, Patches has just under three thousand now. Cornbread has around nineteen hundred. Patches uses his more often because of what he does for you, but his gauge refills faster. They always say a catnap is good for the soul. This is doubly true for Patches. Either way, these two will protect you, and I'm certain that you will protect them," Leah told Sylas. "As it should be."

The crowd beyond laughed at Godric, who was hopping around like a chicken.

"I should fill some more pints," Sylas told Leah, "but before you join the others, I know there are more like you. Those who have had classes that have been discontinued. If you know any of them, or encounter any in your travels, invite them here to Ember Hollow. Soon, we will have a market that sells rare items, perhaps things with Legendary Locks. Mira and I are looking to change the place, breathe new life into the village. And sometimes, the best way to do that is to understand what was here before."

"Good to know," she said after a careful pause. "I wish you both well."

———

Sylas was just thinking about doing his nightly *last call* announcement when the door of The Old Lamplighter swung open. Tiberius stomped in, the lord commander in full armor, a nasty look on his face. "Runewulf! You have gone far enough!"

"Uncle." Mira hopped off her stool and approached the man. "How dare—"

"Out of my way, Mira. This isn't about you." Tiberius pointed an angry finger at Sylas. "Too far!"

Quinlan stood. The sound of his chair legs scraping against the ground was a sign of how angry he was at the lord commander's sudden appearance. It also had a way of silencing anyone still murmuring. "Sylas," he said as he stepped past the bar, tension heavy in the air. "I'll deal with this. Tib won't be the first bloated blustering lord commander I've tossed out of a place."

Sylas, who had been fiddling with the spout on one of his casks, brought his hands back, rubbed them together, and casually stepped around the bar. Quinlan reached Tiberius, the former soldier nearly two heads taller than the lord commander.

"I think—" before Tilbud could finish whatever it was he was going to say, Tiberius pushed forward and bumped his chest into Quinlan.

"Well, mate?" he growled. "You ready to lose that other hand of yours?"

Quinlan bent over and got in his face. "I'll pluck your other eye out, you useless sack."

Sylas pushed between the two of them. "Not in the pub." He did so in a way that wouldn't result in either Tiberius or Quinlan swinging at him. This wasn't the first fight he had broken up, especially one in which Quinlan was a main player. "Tiberius, there's no need to storm in here making accusations. I won't have it. And this is your final warning on that front. If you have something to say, mate, just come up to the bar and we'll talk."

Flustered, irate to the point that he was red in the face, Tiberius barked "Outside," turned, and left.

Duncan and Cody, who had been seated at the back of the pub, rushed after him. The other militiamen joined them, all aside from Henry, who finished his pint, wiped his mouth, grumbled, and finally got to his feet and hobbled to the exit.

By this point, Cornbread was rushing around, the dog sensing the nervous excitement.

"Well?" Quinlan asked Sylas. "Should we give them a bloody stomping, or what?"

"Let's not go that far. Yet." Sylas locked eyes with Quinlan. In a single glance, he indicated that if it came to that, he was ready, but that they would try to compromise first.

Other patrons began filing out.

"That's right," Quinlan said. "Pub is closed for tonight. But stop by tomorrow night—the first round is on me! Don't mind the lord commander, he gets his knickers in a twist from time to time."

A few of the patrons clapped Quinlan on the back as they left. Sterling, who was the only farmer still at the pub, stepped up to the bar. "Do you want me to stick around?" the pepper farmer asked Sylas.

"Not necessary."

"Lot of Thornies out there," Sterling said calmly. "You are outnumbered."

Quinlan instantly recognized that the man had been a soldier by the term he'd used. The slur was common among Aurumites along the border. "You're with us, mate. What was your name again?"

"Sterling."

"Quinlan."

Mira turned to Sylas. "Aren't you going to do something? Should I go next door and get Nelly? We can't have a bloody street fight in Ember Hollow!"

"It won't come to that, but sure, get Nelly and Karn. Although, I'm going to assume they have heard the crowd gathering outside now. We will talk some sense into Tiberius, and by talk sense, I mean we need to hear him out first," Sylas said, mostly for Quinlan, but also to let Mira know that he planned to maintain his composure.

Tilbud approached Sylas. "You know, there might be a way to use a spell I have to either put everyone to sleep or, yes . . . that could work as well. A little Charm?"

"No, not necessary. Not just yet. Let's see how this goes first."

"Well, are we ready?" Quinlan asked. "They're out there waiting for our response."

Azor flared up, bright enough that it looked as if a comet had landed in the pub. "That's . . . it!" She rushed out the door.

Sylas chased after her. "Azor, no!"

The fire spirit grew in size until she was a wall of hulking flames taller than the two-story pub itself, Azor radiating heat as purple flames raced through her form. She was large enough now that she would easily be able to engulf several of the buildings.

"You think I'm scared of a little fire?" Tiberius asked as he produced his mace, the tip of which glowed with mana.

"Azor, to me." Sylas touched his tattoo and she disappeared. His tattoo blazed with an intensity that made the people standing in front of him look away. "Everyone needs to relax."

Tilbud, Sterling, Quinlan, and Mira joined Sylas.

"Yes," the archlumen said, "I'm sure there's a perfectly logical answer to whatever it is that has infuriated you, Tiberius."

"You want to know what has infuriated me? I'll tell you what has infuriated me! One, you are using my men *without* my permission. Two, you continue to create more interest in Ember Hollow, which is not what this village needs." He glared Quinlan. "Three, you have started taking my hunts!"

"Your hunts?" Quinlan burst out laughing. "Mate, I swear you're more delusional by the day. Hunts don't belong to anyone. If you can't get your men rallied, or you, yourself, are too busy getting your bum scrubbed in Battersea to give a damn."

"Getting my what?!"

"He means the bathhouse you go to, Uncle. Really, you are making a fool of yourself with these accusations," Mira said. "Go home. Everyone was having a good time until you showed up."

To her right, Nelly and Karn stepped out of the general store and began discussing how they could possibly intervene. By this point, Tiberius was shaking with anger to the point that Duncan approached him.

"Maybe—"

"Get away from me!" He slapped his hand at the larger man.

"To address your points," Sylas said. "Hunts don't belong to anyone. That's been covered. It is sort of an early bird gets the worm situation, no? To your second point, get used to Ember Hollow growing. Mira and I both just classed as landlords."

"You did what?" he asked his niece, true pain in his voice. "But that would mean you went into debt."

"Debt isn't necessarily a bad thing," she told him. "I will be able to earn more and change things around here with this class."

"But Ember Hollow doesn't need change. It's cozy, isn't it?" Tiberius glanced around. "Right?"

No one responded. Sterling cracked his knuckles.

"Have all of you lost your damn minds?" Tiberius asked.

"Now, as to your first point, using your men without permission. I paid them for their help, Tiberius. Are you paying them to patrol Ember Hollow?" Sylas asked.

"It is their duty. They do get residuals from—"

"And you have told them not to class, which is another issue. It seems to me like you think Ember Hollow is your little domain, where you can do things as you please. I suppose, to you, it seems like I am the enemy trying to change that. I'm not, Tiberius, but your hold over the village isn't helping anyone."

"My hold? What do you suggest then?"

"What do I suggest?" Sylas took a step closer to him. "I suggest that you . . ."

"That I what?"

Sylas grinned at the former lord commander.

"Get on with it, then? What do you suggest I do?"

"I suggest that you patrol the village yourself, Tiberius. Sure. That would work. Or pay them to do it, much more than you are paying them now. You have enough militia members that others can patrol Ember Hollow while Duncan and Cody are helping me, if that is what this is about."

He touched his chest. "Me?"

"Yes, you. Has it never occurred to you that you can do the same work that your men can do? This can't be the first time you've ever even considered something like that." Sylas motioned up and down the street. "Patrol tonight and see how it goes. You already have your armor on. Maybe you will learn something."

"I'm not . . . I'm not the one that patrols!"

"Why not?"

"Yeah?" Henry asked Tiberius. "Why not? You have us patrolling every night, two or three at a time. You haven't come out with us once, not once."

"That is not—"

"—What a lord commander does?" Quinlan howled with laughter. "Really, mate, you've lost the plot. We're dead. In case you didn't get the memo, you're *not* an actual lord commander anymore. You're a sad bloke whose only claim to fame is that he died by the hands of an Aurumite. In that regard, we're all sad blokes who died at the hands of someone, or some disease. So you aren't remarkable for that either."

"You know nothing of my death!" Tiberius brought his weapon up.

Sylas stepped in front of Quinlan. "We're not the enemy here. The enemy is there, toward the Chasm. The unknown. If we band together, we'll get much further. If we remain at each other's throats, whatever is set to happen in under fifty days will happen."

"Oi, what do you mean?" Henry asked Sylas.

"This isn't how I wanted to reveal this information to everyone, and I'm still waiting for a manaseer to provide more detail, but . . ." Sylas gave them a brief explanation of the invasion message that he'd been getting every day since arriving in the Underworld.

The crowd murmured.

Duncan spoke: "You think someone is coming here to Ember Hollow?"

"I don't know."

"He doesn't know anything," Tiberius said. "And he certainly doesn't know if he can trust the message."

"Do you trust your prompts?" Sylas asked Tiberius. "When you're told there is a hunt in the vicinity, do you trust it?"

"Why wouldn't I?"

Quinlan shook his head. "I'm done trying to reason with this Thorny bastard. I'm off to the farm." He whistled. "Cornbread, you're with me, love. Sterling, you can join me if you'd like. The lord commander isn't going to do anything."

Sterling nodded. "I believe I will."

The dog looked at Sylas as if she were awaiting confirmation. "Go on," he told her.

"Uncle, I think you've made your point, and I think Sylas has made a good point as well. Why don't you patrol tonight and tomorrow night so you know what it is like?"

"I think that is a grand idea," Nelly said, echoing Mira. "It is important for leaders to lead from the front, and in this case, the streets of Ember Hollow are the front. Tiberius, I realize you're upset about things, but I believe all of this has been solved."

He gave her a confused look, like she had betrayed him somehow.

Nelly continued: "You don't own the hunts, so anyone can take them. You should encourage your men to take more classes if it will make them stronger. If you aren't able to pay your men, you can't expect them to be loyal to you. And what was your other point? Yes. The village. The village is changing, I'm part of that change, and you can either be part of it, or, and I'm not trying to be rude here, get out of the way. There are plenty of villages scattered across the Underworld that could use someone like you. That one village in Windspeak Valley, Solyphia, I believe, comes to mind."

Tiberius bowed his head in shame. "You want me to pack up and leave, Lady Redgrave?"

"I absolutely do not want that, but if you think it would be best for you to have the kind of control you seek, perhaps it is a good option. Because Ember Hollow is changing for the better, it will only get livelier from now, and your militia will be helpful once the town repopulates. Now is a perfect time to take a step back and be a part of the change, rather than a stone in the road trying to thwart its advance. I've said what I need to say. Karn?"

"That covers it from us, dear."

"Right. In that case, I'll be getting to bed now." Nelly walked over and turned off the light in front of the pub. "The pub is closed, and we're closed, so I believe it's safe to say that there won't be a fight here, people, and all should go home. Good night."

Tiberius turned back to Sylas. He huffed, seemed like he was about to say something, but then turned in the opposite direction. The crowd watched him march to the end of the lane and stop. He turned around and headed back in their direction.

"What?" Tiberius growled to anyone that would look at him. "Someone has to look after the place."

CHAPTER TWENTY-FOUR

NEW SPELLS

Patches and Cornbread never fully understood what the humans were so worked up about.

The one-eyed warrior . . . I'm pretty sure it was his fault, Cornbread told the invisible cat as they followed Quinlan and Sterling to the Seedlands. The humans had decided to walk rather than portal. *It has to be.*

I really thought he was going to try something there. It would have been a bad move on his part.

You'd fight for the big man?

Wouldn't you?

Of course I would.

We're no different, Patches told the dog, *aside from the fact that you are owned, and I am not. It felt like everything would work out, though. People were on the big man's side.*

That makes sense. He's not bad for a human.

[You have 47 days until the invasion.]
[A loan payment of 81 has been deducted from your total Mana Lumens. Your total loan balance is 26188 Mana Lumens.]

Sylas skimmed over his Mana Lumens to see that he was just over the sixty-six hundred mark with what he had spent the previous day. He rolled to his side and yawned. The hammock swayed, and he would have fallen back asleep had it not been for Quinlan, who came to him with a cup of hot tea.

"Mira just made it. Bloody fun sleepover last night, yeah?" Quinlan smirked.

"Something like that."

"You sure are a gentleman."

Sylas returned Quinlan's smirk. "Something like that," he repeated.

Not wanting to go home, where she assumed she would have to deal with her irate uncle at some point, Mira had joined Sylas and Quinlan at the farm. She patrolled alongside them for a few hours before calling it a night. Naturally, Sylas had offered her the bed, considering he would be dealing with Mana Ghouls anyway.

They chased off several and killed eight, Sylas and Quinlan taking shifts through the night.

He was fading a little, but then he took a sip of the tea that Mira had made. "Wow," Sylas said, the world around him growing brighter for a moment. "Amazing."

"Good, right?" Quinlan asked. "It's made of lumeberry leaf, which Mira says makes a person more alert. I could have used this stuff on the border."

Sylas drank a bit more. "It's certainly doing something."

Soon, he joined Mira inside, where she poured up another tea.

"Already had three cups myself," Quinlan said as he plopped down into one of the chairs. "We'll need this stuff in the Chasm."

"You were saying that," Mira told him.

"If we can get by without resting, we'll do better. I know that might sound crazy, but you don't want to sleep over there if you can help it."

"In that case, I'll see what I can do."

"How was my bedroom?" Sylas asked. "Did Patches sleep next to you?"

"For a little bit, but then he went back out, and I have no idea where he is now."

"I haven't seen him all morning either," Quinlan said. "I reckon he's out there with Cornbread, though. She keeps barking playfully at an invisible friend."

"That would be Patches." Sylas finished his tea. As he approached the front door, Patches came running in, mewing wildly. The cat rubbed his body up against Sylas's leg and purred. He scooped him into his arms. "There you are."

Cornbread was next to enter, the dog barking and wagging her tail, joy in her eyes.

Sylas placed Patches down on the table. "Right, then. I should probably cook something up. Tilbud will be here shortly."

"New spells, yeah?" Quinlan asked on the tail end of a yawn.

"Correct."

"In that case, I'll probably just rest in the ol' hammock. Seems like a nice day to do that, and I want to be ready for tonight."

———

Tilbud showed up an hour later in a lime green suit that had embroidered snakes on its lapels, a big grin on his face. "I see the two lovebirds finally spent the night together," he said.

"Ha," Sylas said.

"Mind yourself," Mira told Tilbud. "How was the pub after we left?"

"It was quiet, nice, even. I do like sleeping there. I'm starting to consider it my home away from home."

"Would you care for some lumeberry tea?"

"Azor already made me breakfast and tea. I couldn't resist, you know. Especially that cornbread." He patted his stomach. "Most excellent."

"In that case, where are we going to do this?"

Tilbud pointed his finger in the air. "Ah, I know a spot in the forest. I should name that spot, you know, it has been most beneficial in teaching new powers. I would also like to add, *welcome to the family, Mira,* considering you have decided to finally learn some spells with me. Congratulations. The following spells are landlord class spells that Meldon and I, upon close consultation, thought would be best for the two of you. You are lucky, you know."

"People keep telling me that," Sylas said.

"If you had passed the twenty thousand MLu threshold, these spells would have cost a lot more. I was able to swing a discount as well by buying two of each at a time."

"Could I put spare MLus in an account at the MLR bank?" Sylas asked. "You know, to avoid the threshold? I was wondering about that."

"You used to be able to, yes, but the threshold is meant to keep our power levels fairer. This was also a part of the Crafting Laws, sadly."

"It almost makes me think I shouldn't aim for some high number."

"No, you should. It gives you access to even better powers, more classes, property, and communication methods."

Sylas nodded. "Like sending a message to the Celestial Plains."

"Where did you hear about that?"

"From someone. I've been meaning to ask you about it, actually."

"Come, let's head to our training grounds for the day." They took the lane that ran to some of the other farms, and from there, directly into the forest. "It is expensive to do such a thing, but not entirely impossible. It can take time, but I believe it would be a worthwhile endeavor, if that is something we must do."

"But first we should try to find my father."

"Correct. We're already going to the Chasm anyway."

"Nuno could still show up," Mira said.

"He could, he very well could. But, Mira, my dear, it is Specterday, and the deadline we have decided upon is Soulsday. So he should hurry, if that is what he plans to do. Now. These new spells." Tilbud clapped his hands together. "How bloody exciting, and, if I dare say, *clever,* on behalf of Meldon and yours truly."

"You sure are proud of yourself," Mira said.

"I sure am. Pride, while often toxic, can be a good trait as well, you know. But you're not paying me to be your life coach and/or your spiritual advisor, you're paying me, or you have already paid me, to teach you some amazing new spells. In going over my notes last night, I believe each of these will come with benefits that will improve your odds during a battle. We will begin with Territorial Domain."

Sylas remembered the explanation for this one. It allowed him to temporarily expand his control over an area to disrupt a fight and create obstacles. It was fueled entirely by Mana Lumens, meaning they could modify entire landscapes if they so desired, but only on a temporary basis.

"Do be aware," Tilbud said after gifting Mira and Sylas the power, "while you can change the landscape, to maintain it indefinitely would require a continuing supply of MLus. As an example: Sylas, perhaps you would like another hill next to your home, maybe for a second home, or a place for visitors to stay when they have worn out their welcome. You could do this, but maintaining the hill would require a constant stream of mana. The upgraded version, which costs fifty thousand MLus, would allow you to permanently modify the landscape."

"So that's why having more MLus could work out in my favor."

"Correct, Sylas. Go on, then. Try. Mira, you first."

Mira focused on the meadow. The ground rippled. At first, it seemed like all she would be able to do was slightly disrupt the landscape. But then a great mound grew from the soil. Rocks burst out of it.

Tilbud gave her two thumbs up. "Not bad. Adding a projectile nature to this sort of attack could prove beneficial."

"How did you do that?" Sylas asked her.

"I wish I could tell you better. I sort of just did it. I thought it, and it happened."

"Sylas, try for a hole in the ground."

Sylas imagined a hole. The trees and plants were sucked into it, the branches actually cracking. As soon as he released his hold over the area, the ground swelled and righted itself, yet the trees remained uprooted.

"And we have learned another interesting thing about this particular power. You can do great damage with it. The ground will reform to however it was before, even if you move the soil somewhere else. But the damage you do will remain. I'll let the two of you play with this a bit longer and then we'll learn the next spell."

Mira and Sylas moved the soil, uprooting plants and rearranging the terrain. "This could actually be helpful," Mira said as she used the power to uncover a mushroom that grew deep in the ground. "These are hard to find."

"Soil shrooms," Tilbud said. "Correct me if I'm wrong, but these can be used to replenish MLus. They absorb MLus and don't release them like normal dirt."

"They can. And they can replenish quite a bit. I'll have to collect more. They have other properties when mixed with other things as well, like the lumeberry leaf."

"You could make a pastry with Azor for us to bring to the Chasm," Sylas suggested.

"Yes, that would be a great application," Tilbud said. "A bonus, if you will. This next one will be a bonus as well. Architect's Arsenal is meant to be a spell for someone that has double-classed as a landlord and a carpenter. It would be even stronger in that form, and usable more than once per day. But it will still work well without the carpenter class as a last resort kind of attack."

"I'm looking forward to seeing this one," Sylas said.

"I thought you might be. Architect's Arsenal allows you to summon a temporary hammer of sorts that lasts for thirty seconds. It is meant to take down walls, as I said yesterday, but you could also take down a demon if and when you are in a pinch." Tilbud granted them the spell. "To summon the weapon, stick your hand out and imagine it appearing. Your imagination is key here because you are going to use the dormant MLus in the air to create it. It will be hammer shaped, but its actual size and power are really up to your imagination. That's what I meant earlier when I said 'of sorts.' Brilliant, yes?"

"Let me try it first before we talk about how brilliant it is," Mira said.

"By all means. Please, conjure your arsenal. Wait, better idea. Horatio?"

The water spirit appeared. "Yes?"

"I need an enemy made of water, a big, burly fellow, or perhaps a version of Tiberius that isn't too lifelike, something that Mira could really sink her teeth into. Do you mind?"

"Not at all."

Horatio floated to the side and formed a cloud of mist, which soon thickened until it was a fully contained entity made of water. Tilbud flicked at it, nodded, and smiled at Mira.

"Give it your worst, Mira."

"I just conjure something to hit it with, yes?"

"Conjure to your heart's content, my dear."

Mira closed her eyes. She opened them again, and lifted both arms as if she were holding up a great mallet. It appeared in her hands, made of golden energy. She bashed it into her watery enemy.

"Fun, right?" Tilbud asked.

"This is incredible." She struck the water construct again and seemed a bit disappointed once the hammer started to fade away.

"Look at you," Sylas said, laughing. "It's like a child had their toy taken away."

"It's not often that I get to pull a golden mallet out of the air." She stuck her tongue out at him. "Well? Are you going to give it a go?"

"I certainly will." Sylas waited for Mira to step aside. Once she was clear, he imagined an even larger mallet in his own hands. He could see it in his mind's eye, Mana Lumens radiating off its head, the back end of the mallet with a spike on it.

It formed in his hands, and he swung it at the water construct. Water sprayed out the back of the hovering form. Sylas brought his mallet in again and was able to hit it a third time before his weapon faded away.

"New spells," Tilbud told the two of them, his hands proudly on his hips, "and dare I say they are good spells? I know there were other options, and there will be more options in the future. This should be helpful in the Chasm." He peered up at the sky, the Celestial Plains beyond. "Not much longer now."

"Will you be joining us tonight at the pub?"

"Not tonight, I'm afraid," he told Sylas. "I need to deal with something in Battersea, a quick visit with Catia, *not* for those reasons. Although, if they do arise, I won't deny my most primal of urges. Where was I? Yes, Catia. Our dear lumengineer just so happens to know a freelance elemental that is keen to our cause. But I will be there on Moonsday."

"At The Old Lamplighter?" Sylas asked.

"Correct. Unless you want to meet at the farm."

"No, we are closer to the border in Ember Hollow." He extended his hand to the archlumen. "Thanks, for all you do."

"Please, Sylas," Tilbud said with a little chuckle as he took his hand. "You know flattery will get you somewhere. Good luck tonight, and try not to fight Tiberius if he shows up. That poor man. To be so misinformed . . ." He shook his head. "But what can we do?"

CHAPTER TWENTY-FIVE

THE DAY BEFORE THE STORM

Tiberius never showed up at the pub that night, but Duncan and Cody did, ready to go to the Seedlands to help defend the farm.

"We have officially decided to double-class," Duncan told Sylas. "Come next week, we're going to take the trek to Battersea and double-class there. It's going to be an incredible trip. I've heard so many things about the big city."

"I can't wait to go," Cody chimed in. "Been a long time coming. Didn't you say we could take a boat there? Was that you?"

"You can't take a boat to the city, but you can take one once you get there. And good for both of you." Sylas finished cleaning the bar. It had been a decent night at the pub; he estimated that he had made close to eight hundred Mana Lumens in sales. Sylas had certainly spent some power learning his new skills, and if the night was anything like he expected it to be, he would use more mana in the fight to defend his fields.

Sylas also reminded himself to pay his companions *after* harvesting this time, which would allow him to save additional Mana Lumens. He also planned to pay Mira, who was insisting on going to help defend the farm that night.

"I'll head down and brew now," he announced to his companions. "It shouldn't be much longer now."

"What about Patches?" Azor asked. "Is he coming to the farm or staying?"

"Eh, we should probably bring him. Last time he stayed, I came back to find him with his head stuck in a pint glass."

"You never told me that," Mira said she looked over to Patches.

For a moment, it seemed like the pub cat knew that they were talking about him. Patches stiffened, then strutted toward the place that he liked to perch on the window. But then he relaxed, and Cornbread barked.

"Come on," Sylas told the farm dog as he headed down to the cellar, where he brewed four casks while Cornbread sniffed around.

Once he was finished, Sylas found her a piece of sausage, which she readily ate. Somehow, the thought of Cornbread being fed without him summoned Patches down to the cellar, so the pub cat also received a piece of sausage. "You two are really spoiled, you know that?"

After getting his armor on and grabbing his mace, Sylas joined the others outside of the pub. Mira now held Patches in her arms, and Cornbread happily circled Azor, who kept teasing the dog.

"Are we ready?" Sylas asked.

"Yes, sir!" Cody and Duncan said at the same time.

"No need for that, mates," he said as the group started off toward the Seed-lands, to his farm, where Quinlan had already set up shop.

As soon as they stepped out of the portal, Sylas heard barking in the distance, which he took to mean that the local dogs had joined Quinlan.

"We'd better hurry," he said as he took to the air in the direction of his farm. Mira and Azor joined him, while Cody and Duncan ran toward the hill with Sylas's pets.

They came upon quite the fight, Quinlan beating back several Mana Ghouls as more raced toward them. Sylas blasted one, landed, and swung his mace into another. Some of the local dogs continued shredding any bit of ghoul they could get as Cornbread came around, barking wildly as she jumped into the fray.

Patches, who was nowhere to be seen, appeared out of thin air and took one down while Mira used bolts of mana to fry a Mana Ghoul that had joined with another to form an even larger monster.

"'Bout time you all show up!" Quinlan said as he used both hands on his club to swing into a Mana Ghoul.

"I thought you'd said you had it," Sylas told him. He beat back one of the creatures, and stepped aside as Cornbread finished it off.

"I thought I did! Too many of the buggers!"

"Are they always this strong?" Mira fired on another, its body disintegrating into golden motes.

"Cody and I are running to the other end of the farm," Duncan announced. "Two of the dogs took off that way. I think they're chasing something."

"We want to help them," Cody said.

"Good luck. Do it." Sylas continued to fight the Mana Ghouls, the creatures hell-bent on getting to the power radiating from the soil. It turned into an all-night battle, with little time to rest. Later, a low-tier Voidslither came over one of the fields, its body consisting of raven-like creatures. Sylas and Azor were able to handle it with Soulfire just as they had the last time.

As its body burned, its form disappearing into mana, Sylas was well aware of the fact that he wouldn't be able to do an attack like that in the Chasm without Azor by his side. But he had his new powers, he had strong companions, and that they would find Raelis and hopefully, his father.

It was only a matter of time.

[You have 46 days until the invasion.]
[A loan payment of 79 has been deducted from your total Mana Lumens. Your total loan balance is 26109 Mana Lumens.]
[Your fields are ready to harvest.]

And later, as his corn was being placed in silos.

[You have yielded 15000 Mana Lumens' worth of corn. Pay tax now? Y/N?]

"Do it."

[A payment of 1050 Mana Lumens has been deducted from your yield. Transfer to the guild now for distribution? Y/N?]

"Yes," Sylas said as he looked out at his fields at Cornbread as she trotted down one of the lanes.

[You have received 13950 Mana Lumens.]

He checked his updated status:

Name: Sylas Runewulf
Mana Lumens: 20865/20865
Class: Brewer
Secondary Class: Farmer
Tertiary Class: Landlord
[Lumen Abilities:]
Flight
Quill
Mana Infusion
Mana Saturation
Harvest Silos
Field Warden

Whimsical Drift
Soulfire
Bargain Binding
Ward of Welcome
Structural Reinforcement
Territorial Domain
Architect's Arsenal

From there, Sylas transferred Mana Lumens to everyone who had helped; Mira got a thousand because she didn't have a multiplier; Quinlan got seven hundred and fifty; Cody, Duncan, Patches, and Cornbread got five hundred a piece, an upgrade for the two militiamen and a bonus for his pets. He tried to give Azor her cut, but she refused it to the point that Sylas realized he wasn't going to be able to break through to her.

"I have plenty," she said yet again. "Worry about yourself and the others."

"Only if you're sure."

"I'm sure. Now," Azor said as the flames that had grown off her form settled. "Is there anything in particular that you would like to eat?"

"Everything you make is good."

She puffed up with pride. "I'm aware of that."

"Fish-and-chips, if you're taking requests," Quinlan said, who stood near one of his scarecrows adjusting its wooden sword. "Yeah? And extra Tartar sauce."

"Fish-and-chips, extra sauce. We have corn as well."

Mira, who held Patches, set the cat down. "That corn pudding you made was amazing, Azor."

"Fish-and-chips, extra sauce, corn pudding, what else?"

Cody and Duncan exchange glances. "We both liked the cornbread," Duncan said.

"Fish-and-chips, extra sauce, corn pudding, and crisp, buttery cornbread. Do you think there's something Tilbud will like?"

"If the bloody archlumen shows," Quinlan said.

"He'll be there," Sylas told him.

"And then we'll be *there.*" Quinlan turned back to the farm. "I'm going to take a long nap. See you all tonight. Mira, Azor, boys."

Duncan and Cody looked like they were going to salute Quinlan in the way they saluted Tiberius but thought better of it.

Cornbread barked.

Quinlan tipped an invisible hat at the dog. "It's been a pleasure, love, but I need to get some rest, so keep quiet."

CHAPTER TWENTY-SIX

CHANGE OF HEART

It was a slow night at The Old Lamplighter and Sylas was fine with that. When not slinging ale or enjoying the wonderful food, he had long conversations with Nelly, Karn, Mira, Quinlan, and Azor.

Since he hadn't publicly announced his plan to go to the Chasm, Sylas didn't expect anyone to show up and wish him goodbye, and he certainly didn't expect to see a former lord commander of the Shadowthorne Empire come through the door later, when he and Azor were close to closing up.

"Tiberius," Sylas said as a greeting. "Take a seat."

Instead of taking the single seat on the far end of the bar next to Karn, Tiberius simply approached the bar near where Mira was sitting. "I won't be having a pint."

"Fair. Then how can I help you?"

Sylas caught Quinlan looking over at the two of them. He waved away the other man's concern and leaned in closer to Tiberius.

"Could we speak about this outside?"

"Uncle, why are you being so mysterious all of the sudden?"

"A man can't talk in private?" he asked his niece.

"It's fine," Sylas said as he came around the bar. Cornbread joined him just as he was about to follow Tiberius outside. "Let's head out."

"Actually, I'd like to hear this," Nelly said. "We're all friends here, Tiberius. Let us know what's on your mind."

"But, my lady . . ." A frown formed on the lord commander's face.

Yet again, Sylas was impressed by how much control Nelly had over him due to her old title, especially as Tiberius turned to her, brought his hands together, and stiffened up.

"Yes?" she asked.

"It has come to my attention that Sylas and a few others, including my niece, are planning a bit of an excursion to the Chasm. I have come to volunteer my services." Tiberius stood defiant, his chest deflating some once Quinlan spit out some of his ale.

"Really, Tib, you've got some nerve coming here to invite yourself on a trip you know nothing about." Quinlan laughed and Cornbread barked, the farm dog not quite certain what all the fuss was about.

Tiberius gathered his composure. "As you know, someone classed as a demon hunter in the Chasm has a debuff effect on certain demonic creatures, lowering their boldness. With two, this effect would be quite profound, at least on lower-level monsters. That is not all. I have been before, you know. I do not wish to discuss my time there, but if I must—"

"You know why we're going there, right?" Sylas asked as another thought came to him. "Wait, how did you find out we were going in the first place?"

"Tilbud. He caught up with me after our little conversation the other night to explain why you were trying to get stronger and, well, you are friends with the bloody archlumen, you know how convincing he can be. Charming, even. While I certainly don't agree that making Ember Hollow the hottest village to move to this side of Battersea is a good thing, I do understand your desire to protect it and our way of life. We might have our differences, but I want to protect Ember Hollow just as much as any of you."

"To the point that you won't let your men advance, yeah?" Quinlan joined Sylas, arms crossed over his chest. "Tib, I've got to be honest with you, I find everything about the way you behave and how you've run your life in the Underworld to be—"

"Quinlan."

"Now, hold on," he told Sylas, "I need to get this off my chest."

"Maybe you don't," Nelly said firmly. "Maybe the two of you need to cast your egos aside here while we work to deal with something that could very well change the course of our afterlives."

"Nelly is right," Mira said. "You two can behave like boys later, once we know that there isn't some invasion set to happen."

"Like boys?" Quinlan turned to Mira, a smirk on his face.

"Yes, like boys measuring your clubs. Why did Tilbud tell you, anyway?"

"Because he thought I could be of service to the cause," Tiberius told his niece. "He asked if I had been to the Chasm before. I have, as you know, and then he told me what was being planned. If we're being honest, at first, I questioned why I shouldn't just go looking for my mates that may or may not be in the Chasm, but then I realized . . ." He swallowed hard. "Then I realized that perhaps I don't have any. At least any worth finding."

"Are you saying you don't have any friends?" Quinlan asked.

"It can be lonely at the top," Tiberius said carefully. "I haven't really thought of finding any of the other lord commanders I served with because many of us were competing with one another for the Crown's favor. It could be quite ruthless, you know, and there were plenty of duels that stemmed from this scramble to look best."

Sylas had heard this before about the Shadowthorne leadership, how cutthroat it could be, and how it had this strange effect on most of their campaigns, the competitive nature of the upper echelon changing the very course of their battles.

It hadn't been the same in the Aurum Kingdom, which had a much more egalitarian way of managing its campaigns. The Aurumites considered themselves all in it together, where the Shadowthorne Empire operated in an every-man-for-himself frenzy that made them difficult to defeat.

Another thought came to Sylas as he observed Tiberius, who had an almost pleading look on his face. The man wanted to redeem himself, but how had Tilbud convinced him to visit the pub with his suggestion? The only way Sylas could think of was the archlumen's Charm spell. This also told him something else: Tilbud thought Tiberius would be helpful in the Chasm, and even if Tilbud could be unorthodox, Sylas knew he had everyone's best interest in mind.

"If you are willing to join us, to put your ego aside, then you are welcome," Sylas said, cutting Tiberius off from continuing to explain how the Shadowthorne leadership worked. "But you must understand we're going there for Raelis and for my father due to his connection to the Celestial Plains."

"Yes, Tilbud briefed me. I'm aware."

"And that we will share leadership between all of us. Different situations call for different types of leaders. Since Quinlan is our tracker, he will keep us on the right path. Tilbud will have insight and spells that will likely help us. He'll also get us past the Hexveil. Mira has learned new spells and will work as a healer and a combatant. I will be there doing all I can to assist in any way I can, and we will have Cornbread with us too."

Tiberius gave Sylas a puzzled look. "You're not bringing Azor?"

"No," the fire spirit said, "I will stay here. But Horatio will be there."

"A water spirit, right. That could be helpful. There's only one piece left to this puzzle then, aside from finding your people."

"Yes?" asked Sylas.

"How will we get through the Hexveil? Tilbud wasn't clear on that part. He just assured me that he would be here on Moonsday with a solution, and that you would pay for it."

"I don't know."

"He didn't tell you?"

"He did not. But I trust him," Sylas said, "I trust all my friends."

―――――――

They are planning something, Cornbread told Patches later that night, after everyone had went to bed.

Patches, who sat near the cat door, looked over at the fire spirit resting in the hearth. *I can feel the same thing.*

Something big. Their tones. They made an agreement with the one-eyed man. They shook hands.

Humans shake hands when they agree to something.

What do you think it is?

Patches swished his tail against the ground. *How would I know?*

You've known these people longer than I have.

True, but they could be planning anything. Last time they got together like this, we went into the well.

Do you think they'll do that again?

I don't see why they would.

Cornbread glanced around nervously. *What will you do if they do something like that?*

I will go with them. I have to protect the big man. You?

I . . . will go with them too. I have to protect him too.

Then we will go together. They will likely bring you because you're a dog and more agreeable to travel with humans. But I will be there.

Cornbread wagged her tail. *Invisible.*

Exactly. You'll know I'm there, wherever "there" may be.

And the Tavernly and Farmly Realms?

If he's going somewhere, he won't be planting. The fire spirit often stays here when he travels, and I trust her enough to look after the place.

Then I do too. Cornbread came forward and licked Patches's face.

What did I tell you about doing that!?

Sorry, I'm just so excited!

[You have 45 days until the invasion.]
[A loan payment of 1458 has been deducted from your total Mana Lumens. Your total loan balance is 24651 Mana Lumens.]

Sylas skimmed over his Mana Lumens and saw a number that could be cut severely by the cost of getting to the Chasm, at least according to what Tilbud had told them.

And he still didn't know how they would pull it off.

Rather than get out of bed, Sylas lay there for a long spell, Patches purring next to him, Cornbread still asleep at the edge of the bed. He stared out the window of his room at the pub, to the golden sky beyond. "Well," he finally said to his two pets, "let's see what the day brings."

Sylas was surprised to go downstairs and find Tiberius and Quinlan already in their armor, the two men seated at the bar eating porridge. He heard Mira and Azor in the cellar, and assumed by the smell of cornbread that they were baking.

"Morning," Quinlan said with a grunt. "Where's the archlumen?"

"Tilbud will be here."

"He bloody better," Tiberius said, like he truly knew the guy.

Sylas laughed. He laughed hard enough that he had to lean a hand on the railing of the stairs to support himself.

"What?" Quinlan asked.

"Just thought of something funny, that's all." He continued down to the cellar to find Mira and Azor talking, the apothecary leaning against a table.

"Happy Moonsday," Azor said. "Food should be ready in a few minutes."

"And still no sign of Tilbud," Mira noted.

"Everyone worries too much about him. When has he ever led us astray?" Sylas smiled at her. "Don't answer that question. Also, nice armor."

Mira wore the same kind of leather armor that the militiamen wore, hers just a bit oversized. She had tried to fix this by pulling her britches up and adjusting how the belt was tied, but there wasn't much one could do with the armor. "I know it looks bad, but Uncle insisted I wear it. He gave me a club too."

"If it does its job, it doesn't matter how good or bad it looks."

"You sound like him."

"Please, Mira, never say that again."

She approached Sylas and smiled. "I guess I'll head up to check on the boys. Besides, I want to rearrange the herbs I'm bringing. I got a good number of those soil shrooms, you know. And lumeberry leaf, which is steeping now."

"That will come in handy, I'm sure."

Mira placed a hand on his arm, kept it there for a moment, and moved on.

"Ooo, I told you she liked you," Azor said once Mira was gone.

"When did you say that?"

"What day is it today?"

"Moonsday."

"Right, I told you that already. Maybe Moonsday a few weeks ago. Time flies when you're running a pub." She winked at him.

"And you're sure you will be able to do this, because you don't have to."

"I want to make sure you have enough power while you are there, Sylas. This is something I'm entirely capable of doing, and you know that. Nelly already said she'd help out in her downtime."

"I only wish we could have got the market up and running before we set out, but there's no time."

"There's plenty of time."

"Forty-five days' worth of time."

"Right, maybe not so much," Azor said as she got the cornbread out of the oven. "I made porridge if you'd like some."

"That sounds wonderful, sure."

"There he is!"

Sylas squinted up at the ceiling upon hearing Quinlan's voice. "I guess Tilbud has arrived."

"It sounds like it. I'll bring everything up. And Sylas."

"Yes, Azor?"

"Please be careful in the Chasm."

"In and out. That is our plan. And I'll be as safe as I can. I can't promise anything, but I can tell you I'll do my best to stick to the plan and return to Ember Hollow in one piece."

Sylas took the stairs up to find Tilbud out of his trademark suit. Instead, he wore black armor that looked even nicer than the set Tiberius had on. He was joined by a golem of a man completely covered in stone.

"I was just introducing Matthew to everyone," Tilbud said once he spotted Sylas. "In any case, here he is, the terra elemental that will be helping us get to the Chasm."

"Hello," Matthew said in a gravelly voice.

"You plan to burrow there?" Tiberius asked the archlumen with an arched eyebrow.

"Indeed. I figure we can take the same route that the possessed cinderspiders were trying to take. Shrink ourselves first, of course, and come up in the Chasm. We find Raelis and Sylas's father, and then we return the way we came."

"And you can't track from here, right?" Mira asked Quinlan. "Meaning, you don't know if they are near each other."

"Because Raelis is from the Underworld, I'm already able to pick up his scent, if you want to call it that. We will be relatively close if we enter from Ember Hollow, lucky us."

Azor floated up with a tray of sliced cornbread. "Another elemental? I can make something."

"You know how to make elemental food?" Matthew asked her.

"I certainly can! Does Horatio want something as well?"

The water spirit appeared. "That would be most excellent, Azor. Thank you, my love."

Sylas and Mira exchanged glances. Before he could return his gaze to Azor, she rushed back down to the cellar. "Now," Tilbud said, "I have another bit of information that we should all be aware of, some highly secret information that I was able to get from Catia in Battersea. It relates to timing. As we all know, time in the Chasm is different from time here. It's not an exact science, but Catia claims that new tests indicate that an hour there is the same as a day passing here. With a spell I have that I normally use to set alarms, I will be able to keep track of each hour that passes."

"Which represents a day here," Mira said. "Wild."

"Wild, indeed. But at least we can have a better understanding of how long we've been there, and how long we have before we should return." Tilbud grinned nervously at all of them. "Exciting and frightening, yes? Another day in the life. I suppose there is nothing left to do aside from head out."

"Well then, what are we waiting for? Sylas, get your armor on," Tiberius said. "The Chasm waits for no man."

CHAPTER TWENTY-SEVEN

CAMPAIGN CITY #1

Sylas and the others stood before the well as Tilbud explained once again what he was planning to do, and more importantly, and how it would work. After a brief diversion into his Shrink power and how he had recently upgraded it to accommodate more people and more castings per day, Tilbud had everyone gather in front of him, including Cornbread.

"Remember," he told Matthew the terra elemental. "The hole has already been started. We just need to continue it in the direction of the Chasm."

"In that case, someone toss me in." Matthew shrank until he resembled a stone, his face still visible across its rough surface.

"I was wondering about that part," Quinlan said as he scratched the back of his head.

The terra elemental gruffed a response: "I can resize myself at will. Now, who wants to throw me in the well? I'll fix the tunnel."

"I'll do the honors." Tilbud picked Matthew up and dropped him into the well. Sylas heard a *plunk* somewhere near the bottom. He listened carefully but didn't hear anything else.

"We'll just give dear Matthew a moment to get it all together. I collapsed some of the passageway last time, so it will take him a little bit to get that all in order. But he'll manage, and you all will soon see that Matthew is worth his weight in MLus."

"Let's hope so." Sylas had already transferred eight thousand fixed MLus to Matthew, as previously agreed upon.

It certainly felt strange doing so for a smuggling operation, but he knew that Raelis would have done the same for him. Once Sylas got back, he could get another crop going. By then, he would also have the market running and a second branch of the pub. As he continued to learn about the Underworld, it cost Mana Lumens to make Mana Lumens.

Azor floated up next to him. "I would hug you, but that wouldn't be pleasant for you. Ugh. I'm so sad to see you all go."

"We're coming back," Sylas told her. "It will feel like a few days, but I promise we are coming back. And if Nuno shows up, convince him to stick around. Also, let him know that we waited an additional week hoping that he would come with some news. I think he'll understand. Make sure that Duncan and Cody are fed every time they come in, and if anyone gets too rowdy, have them throw the person out."

"People don't get too rowdy around me," she said as her flames brightened. "They know better."

"I don't doubt it."

"Are we all ready?" Tilbud asked a few minutes later, after Nelly and Karn had shown up to see them off. You will all feel a slight tingling sensation. Then, we will be small, and we will go from there. Here we go!"

The sensation of shrinking was still something Sylas couldn't quite describe. He certainly felt it in his arms and legs, this sudden contraction. But it was magic, and in a flash, he stood there in his miniature form, nothing much different from how he had been before, aside from the sheer size of everything around him.

"Good, away we go." Tilbud hovered into the air, the others all doing the same, Cornbread tucked under Tilbud's arm.

As Azor, Nelly, and Karn waved goodbye, the group headed down into the well, where they swooped into the tunnel that was already there, well above the waterline.

Rather than take it on foot, the group zipped ahead in the air, Tilbud in the lead. "What a way to travel, yes?" he called back to Sylas.

Tiberius answered. "We need to focus. Things are about to change."

"That, they are," the archlumen told them as they reached the terra elemental.

Ahead, Matthew continued to burrow in the direction of the Hexveil, the terra elemental able to enlarge the tunnel yet keep the debris from kicking up dust into the air. It was a smooth process, one that continued until he arced upward.

Sylas felt a sudden jolt of electricity that passed as soon as he noticed it.

"We're getting close," Matthew announced.

"Have we passed the Hexveil?" Mira asked.

"You didn't feel it?" Tiberius asked him.

"The buzzing sensation, right. I was wondering what that was."

Sylas glanced to his left to find Mira with a determined look on her face, her arms beside her body, a small mace in one of her hands, and leather bag of herbs and supplies strapped to her back. She looked tough, but he could see a hint of fear in her eyes.

He felt this as well, the feeling only deepening as they paused so Matthew could make a proper exit. Once he was finished, he called down to them and they floated up.

The first thing that struck Sylas as he observed the enormous world beyond, the golden sky above, was that it reminded him of the Underworld. But then he remembered he was viewing it at a microscopic level, that its appearance could very well change by the time he was his regular size again.

"You are clear to change," Matthew told them as he stepped aside, the elemental large again.

"Right, let's make the best of this. Horatio, please join us after we are properly sized again."

Tilbud returned to his normal form and stretched his hand above his head. As Sylas stabilized, he saw that they were at the edge of a forest, not unlike the one outside of Ember Hollow. The landscape differences beyond were dramatic, great rock formations curled in the distance like skeletal fingers, the stone formations grotesque, as if they had been conjured by a dark mage.

Yet the woods beyond almost resembled what Sylas had grown used to around Ember Hollow, which reminded him of something he had learned earlier on: the Underworld had been carved out of the Chasm. It made sense the two looked similar along the border and got stranger the farther one traveled.

Cornbread barked. She sniffed something at her side and barked again.

"Put your glasses on if you want to see what she's barking about," Quinlan told Sylas.

He did just that and saw what Cornbread was barking about. "Patches."

"We have a cat with us as well?" Tiberius asked. "Why is your cat always getting involved in things that he shouldn't be involved in?"

"I could ask you the same thing, Uncle."

He turned slowly to Mira like he was going to say something. Ultimately, Tiberius kept his mouth shut. By this point, Sylas had scooped Patches up into his hands, the cat visible again.

"You really weren't supposed to come with us, you know," he told the cat.

Patches mewed and began to purr.

"That's on us. We really should have seen that coming," Quinlan said. "But, I think it will be fine. Cornbread and Patches seem to get along quite well. They'll look after each other. Now, are we ready to track Raelis down?"

"What about my father?" Sylas asked, a sudden lump in his throat.

Quinlan shook his head. "I don't think it's going to be possible, mate. He is in the same direction as Raelis, but much farther in. I don't know how far we want to go, but we've got a time limit considering your invasion message."

"I see."

"Sorry, mate."

"There is another option to reach him. We can focus on Raelis."

"Yes, and speaking of timing, thanks for reminding me to set it." Tilbud's eyes lit up, mana fizzling in the air before him. "Our timer has been set. I will announce when it has been one hour. Remember, one hour here will be roughly equivalent to a day back in the Underworld."

―――――

I still don't understand how he spotted me, Patches told Cornbread as they trekked through the forest. Cornbread had started by going ahead and circling back, but then she had sensed from the hammock-loving warrior at the head of the group that he wanted her to stay back.

So that's what she did now, moving alongside Patches, her ears alert. *The big man is powerful,* she reminded Patches.

So many threats here. I don't understand where we are, but there is danger all around. I can sense and smell it.

Cornbread tilted her snout up. She could smell them as well, demonic beasts tracking them the same way she was tracking them. A deep inhale gave her a vision of the monsters, which were humanlike but hunched over, moving on all fours, spines lifted off their backs. She was certain they wanted to attack, yet they didn't.

The reason why dawned on Cornbread as they came to a small stream, where the humans huddled for a moment. She noticed the scent immediately, her fur standing at attention with fear. *Something terrible lives here. We're not being attacked because they would be taking another's kill.*

Patches sat and scanned the forest beyond. *I think you're right. Do you sense what it is?*

No, but it looks like they have noticed. Cornbread approached the big man, who was deep in conversation with the hammock-loving warrior and the one-eyed guy who only came around occasionally, but often in agitation.

Patches tensed. *I wish I knew why we were here.*

I don't understand it myself. We traveled underground to come here. It looks like home, but something is different about it.

We have to trust the big man.

We have to protect him too.

―――――

"It's a Taurigraith," Quinlan said as he pointed at the track print visible in the mud. "Definitely a Taurigraith."

"Isn't that the one you were telling me about?" Sylas asked. "Big beast of a thing?"

"It is. A bull and a tiger mixed, one that can become intangible. It's why none of the Norakes have attacked us."

"That checks out," Tiberius said.

"Norakes?" Tilbud asked. "Ah, wait, I do know what they are. Stuff of nightmares, really. Human-looking demons walking around on all fours. I've only seen a sketching of one before."

"Ugly buggers, yes, but easy enough to deal with," Quinlan said. "The Taurigraith will prove difficult. You can't see anything, mate?"

Sylas did a slow circle. Beyond the trees, he spotted the Norakes watching them, their bodies glowing due to his glasses. They were all hunched over, poised to strike, yet seemed to be held back by an invisible force. "I see them, but nothing else. Nothing bull-sized."

"We will know when it comes for us," Mira said.

"Hopefully, it doesn't."

"Huh." Sylas turned to Tiberius, surprised to hear him say this.

The lord commander continued, "I'd prefer *not* to fight a legendary demon on this trip if we can help it. It does make me worry that it is so close to the Hexveil. It will become our problem at some point because the guards and the barrier itself usually cannot contain these sorts of demons. You'd think they would be able to, but they do get through from time to time. Curious, if you ask me."

Quinlan cast his hand forward and the footprints lit up. They continued along the water, his eyes flicking left and right as he considered something. "We might be good, for now. The tracks are old. But it has marked its territory."

"That would explain the smell," Mira said.

"Which is why the Norakes have yet to attack. Once we leave its territory, they will move on us." He turned in a different direction. "Raelis is this way."

"How much farther?" Tilbud asked Quinlan.

"We're through the rougher part of the woods, meaning we can take to the air now."

"If we do that, we stay low," Tiberius said. "There are nasty dragons and fiery drakes and all sorts of flying beasts in the Chasm. I've already seen a few fly overhead."

"So that's what that was," Sylas said, recalling a few times in which a shadow passed over them. He thought it was just a trick of light, or perhaps some effect of the Celestial Plains.

"It will be faster if we take to the air, but I don't think any of us are equipped to handle dragons," Tiberius said, "aside from me. I have a power known as Flame Wings. I've rarely used it, though."

"Gentlemen, my lady, dearest pets," Tilbud began, "what if we shrank ourselves again and flew in miniature form?"

Tiberius considered this with a short nod. "That is certainly a solution. We will be much harder to spot at that size."

"Unless the flying demons can see dispersed mana," Quinlan noted.

"Bah, I hadn't thought of that." Tilbud hung his head in shame. "I'm sorry, mates, we could have been dragon chow if we had gone with my idea. Although, at that size, we might be able to pass through the dragon's digestive system. I should say, that would be quite interesting. I've heard there is dormant mana there."

Mira shared a baffled glance with Sylas. "Let's not," she said. "And there are still trees ahead. So we continue on foot a bit more until the trees are smaller."

"She's right," Quinlan said. "Once we're out of the Taurigraith's territory, expect trouble."

"I expect trouble anyway. Just because it hasn't attacked us, doesn't mean it won't soon." Tiberius squinted around again with his one good eye. "You can't always trust relics like those glasses of yours."

A flash of mana startled all of them. Tilbud laughed nervously. "And just like that, a day has passed in the Underworld. Shall we?"

A day. Sylas thought about this as they crossed the stream and continued on. He thought about Azor, his farm, the future market, all the advances he had made in a relatively short amount of time. He then thought about the sacrifices those around him were making, even Tiberius, who could be a nuisance at times.

He had to remind himself that he was doing this for a reason.

A bit later, as they reached the end of the Taurigraith's territory, Sylas was actually glad to see a dozen Norakes, even with how hideous they were. It gave him a moment's reprieve, a chance to think of something else for a brief spell.

"Weapons first, mana only if necessary," Tiberius told them as the seething Norakes prepared to attack. "Once we're out of the woods, this will change."

"Agreed," Quinlan said as he readied his club. "Conserve mana."

"Horatio, drown as many as you can," Tilbud said.

"I'll take the Norakes at the back. They have scouts moving to summon more of their clan."

"Good, go."

The water spirit swished forward. One of the Norakes snarled. The humanoid demon shot forward, where it was taken down by Cornbread.

"Bloody right!" Quinlan swooped in with a strike that crushed the skull of another.

It had already been agreed upon that Sylas, Quinlan, and Tiberius, would be the enforcers, the front line, so to speak. But the way the Norakes had surrounded them complicated this.

One of the beasts lunged for Mira, who managed to beat it back. It caught her mace in its mouth, only to find itself with an angry pub cat on its back, claws digging in.

Mira pried her weapon away as Patches incinerated the Norake. "Thanks, Patches!"

The cat moved on and joined Cornbread as the two cornered another of the demons.

Tiberius clobbered one and gave it a second strike once it hit the ground and rolled onto its side. Another jumped onto his back. Tiberius rammed it into a tree and Sylas finished the job with a well-timed blow.

"Nasty things," the lord commander said as Quinlan grabbed two by the necks and rammed their heads into one another. "Bloody show-off!"

Quinlan beat one down and Sylas managed the other. A great pillar of water collapsed onto some of the trees, where it swirled around the Norakes, drowning a few and burying others in a pit of mud.

Soon, the group of Norakes were no more, but that didn't mean they were in the clear.

"We need to move," Quinlan said. "Their bodies will attract other predators, even if we bury them all. The trees are smaller now. We can fly, but keep toward the canopy. It should be tickling your stomach is what I'm saying here. Stay low. We'll come back down at the start of the Hallowed Pursuit."

———

Sylas didn't know what the Hallowed Pursuit would actually look like.

He imagined it would be set up like a military campaign, with tents, horses, siege weapons, and whatever else was legal to use in the Chasm. What he found instead was an entire city that had been carved out of the landscape by what he assumed were archlumens and terra elementals. It was walled in, and there were watchtowers equipped with weapons capable of killing dragons every hundred feet or so.

"The Hallowed Pursuit has . . . a city?" Sylas asked after they touched down.

"Yes, indeed," Tilbud said, "one of many cities that the Celestial Plains have carved out of the Chasm. They are known as Celestial Campaign Cities, and they are numbered."

"But why? I'm still unclear what they are attempting to do."

"With the demonic warlords and the other terrible things in the Chasm, it is important for them to maintain control. The people from the Underworld that take part in a Hallowed Pursuit do so with the faith that they will be looked upon favorably by the Celestial Plains. Why didn't you ask these questions earlier?" Tiberius asked Sylas.

"It's quite all right," Tilbud told him. "It's best that questions come up naturally, in my humble opinion."

"So we made it here to this city. And we just . . . find Raelis?" Mira asked. "Why did we learn all these spells if that's all we had to do? It can't be this easy."

"Because finding Raelis will mean going to whatever front line he is currently fighting for," Quinlan explained, "where the spells will come in handy. There is an old saying, though. Well, maybe not that old, but I've heard it thrown about from time to time. *The best spell is one you never need to use but know you have at your disposal.* Something like that."

Cornbread barked.

"See? She gets it."

"First, we enter the Campaign City to locate your friend. Then, we retrieve him," Tilbud said. "As for your father, I would say he is at one of the other Campaign Cities deeper in the Chasm, considering he came here from the Celestial Plain. This is why we won't be able to find him this time around."

"I don't get it," Sylas admitted.

Tilbud spoke: "The Celestial Plains are above all of it, the Underworld and the Chasm, as you know. They can beam down a Campaign City if they'd like. The people there have a direct link between the city and the Plains—heaven— while people from the Underworld have their own cities. It is a rite of passage to many. By starting in an outer city, they can work their way to an inner city where they will potentially be cleansed of their past sins."

"But it's all nonsense." Tiberius threw his hands up in the air. "Nonsense."

"You act like you tried, Uncle."

"That's because I did, Mira. Before you came to the Underworld. I made it to one of the inner cities. And they portaled me back to the Underworld, near Geist. I moved to Ember Hollow soon after. It was a sham, all of it. Anyone attempting it is either a fool, or they are simply trying to grow stronger."

"You must have gotten something out of it," Mira said. "How come you never told me about this?"

"I didn't tell you because you didn't ask. And as for my reward, yes, MLus, a good many of them that allowed me to completely change my class."

"Hold on. What were you classed as before?"

"Before? I was classed as a butcher." Tiberius laughed bitterly. "The only thing good about that class is that it came with a proficiency in using blades, which, as you know, are illegal in the Underworld. But they aren't here, in the Chasm. And I was able to use my class to amplify my strength and speed with the swords I later acquired." Something akin to fondness came over his face. "You all should have seen me. I was truly a marvel."

"Right," Quinlan said. "Keep patting yourself on the back, Tib."

"No, let him finish," Sylas told his friend.

"There's not much more to say other than the fact that the goal of reaching one of these cities is a sham, that one *will not* be gifted a free trip to heaven by fighting back the demon hordes between here and the other Celestial Campaign Cities, as they are known."

"So the outer ones, the cities created by people from the Underworld, are basic Campaign Cities, and the ones created by the people from the Plains are Celestial Campaign Cities?" Mira asked. "Just trying to understand the terminology here."

"That is correct. And the reason we don't often speak of it is because there is sort of this unwritten rule for people who have survived a Hallowed Pursuit. We don't talk about it." Tiberius shrugged. "I don't know why that is."

"But you knew all along what we were getting into," Sylas said. "So there is that."

"Of course I did. Why do you think I bloody came along? The last thing I need is for my niece to get swept up into some senseless pursuit spearheaded by an overambitious Aurumite. So I am here to speed this along. Speaking of which, are we done? Has it been another day in the Underworld yet?"

"He's not wrong," said Tilbud, "even if he is both blunt and grumpy—blumpy, no, grumpty, yes, that could work—we should continue on to one of the leaderboards."

"This is all so new to me," Sylas told Mira as the group headed toward one of the entrances. They were given a bit of flack by a pair of guards but were quickly let through after Tiberius revealed some credentials Sylas didn't know he had.

"Another reason I came," Tiberius told the group proudly as he marched on.

"You really didn't know any of this about him?" Sylas asked Mira as they reached a square populated with what Sylas assumed were other Underworldians.

"No. I showed up in the Underworld after him, and he had already been here for a while. We didn't actually die that far apart timewise in our world. But things are different here."

"Same as the Chasm and the Underworld."

"And the Plains."

"I'm confused about something else. If Brom passed on to the Chasm, could he simply live in a city like this?" Sylas gestured around. "It honestly doesn't seem that bad."

"No, he cannot," Tilbud said. "Unfortunately for Brom, he won't be allowed in the Campaign Cities, meaning he will have to go to one of the cities where demons live. Even if he made it inside one of the Campaign Cities, he would be portaled away to the outer walls. There is powerful magic in the air, I'm afraid. People here are here for a Hallowed Pursuit. They are either preparing for another one, training for their first one, or they have portaled here from another Campaign City, similar to what we can do in the Underworld."

They stepped around a woman pushing a cart filled with blades. Sylas eyed the weapons.

"You won't be able to bring it with you, mate," Quinlan said. "And I'd say to stock up before we head out again, but that's not necessary with our clubs and magic. Besides, to buy a good sword would cost quite a bit. And we need to preserve our MLus."

"But you could buy a single dagger," the woman with the cart said as she overheard their conversation. She looked up at them with a pair of pleading eyes.

"We could, but we won't," Quinlan told her. "Oi, Tiberius, remember you have people following you!" he called to the lord commander who was far enough ahead that it was hard to pick him out of the crowd.

"Try to bloody keep up. I'm not here to babysit."

"That's literally why you came, Uncle," Mira told him. "You just said as much."

Rather than respond, Tiberius shouldered through the gap between a pair of large, armored women.

One started to say something but Sylas apologized: "Sorry, ladies, we've got an irritable lord commander here."

The two laughed. The woman on the right spoke. "A Thorny is true to his nature even in hell, yeah?"

"That's right," Quinlan said. "Which Campaign City is this, by the way? I didn't catch the number at the gate."

"Campaign City #1," the woman said. "Welcome."

They moved on, Tiberius grumbling under his breath until they reached a series of buildings that resembled large stone churches. Each of the buildings had a station out front where people could check in. It took them a few attempts, but they soon found the building that had Raelis Sund's name posted on the leaderboard within.

"Ah, the plot thickens," Tilbud said as a bit of mana fizzled in front of him. "It appears that two days have now passed in the Underworld. Chop-chop, team, we must find Raelis soon!"

CHAPTER TWENTY-EIGHT

THE HORDES

Sylas and his group were given multiple warnings once they reached Campaign City #1's exit, where they found more guards with huge shields that had strange runes etched into them. The visual warnings continued as they headed down a lane away from the walled in city, where they encountered people moving away from the front lines, many of them injured.

"What a sorry bunch," Tiberius said. "Clearly bit off a bit more than they can chew, yeah? You don't take a Hallowed Pursuit unless you are absolutely ready."

"Were you absolutely ready, Uncle?"

"No, I was not," he admitted to Mira. "But I spent a lifetime preparing for the sort of battles that were to come."

Quinlan laughed but didn't say anything.

Mira continued, "I'm sure you did. Should we take to the air yet?"

Tiberius motioned to a sign that said no flying. "They do this to keep the skies clear around Campaign City #1. We'll be able to fly soon, Mira. Perhaps now would be a good time for us to eat some of the pastries you and Azor made." He smacked his lips. "I'm certainly hungry. Anyone else?"

"Count me as hungry," Quinlan said. Sylas nodded as well.

"Not a bad plan. We should have some tea as well. It will be cold, but the effects will be the same." Mira turned the bag she had slung over her shoulder to the front.

Huddled together now, the group passed a leather waterskin around. Each of them ate one of the pastries and they shared the lumeberry tea.

Sylas gave some of his pastry to Cornbread and Patches, who continued to get plenty of attention from people that passed them, to the point that both animals had taken center stage, strutting in their own ways.

"They would be cute if the situation wasn't so dire," Mira said after a man supporting his weight on a crutch motioned for Cornbread to come to him. She did so, and he carefully reached down to pet her head. She licked his hand, and his posture straightened some, the man not fully healed, but certainly better.

———

"Here we are," Tiberius said a few minutes later, once they reached a glowing sign that told them that they were no longer protected by Campaign City #1's outer defenses. "Quinlan, take the lead."

Quinlan hovered into the air. Tilbud joined him after using his powers to float both of Sylas's pets, even though this was something Sylas could technically do with Whimsical Drift. He had yet to try that aspect of the power and Sylas was glad for Tilbud's help as they continued their journey away from the city.

Cornbread was used to flying, but Patches didn't seem to like it.

"Poor Patches," Mira said, unable to contain her laughter.

At that moment, Patches was suspended upside down, wind blowing past him, the cat clearly not happy but tired of struggling.

"We're going to have to lower soon anyway," Quinlan called to them. "Trust me, none of us want to deal with a dragon. Not even a lord commander."

———

Sylas didn't expect enemies to move on them so quickly. The monsters swarmed toward their group as soon as they touched down onto a stretch of land covered in craters. Sylas and the others beat them back with their clubs. Horatio joined the fight as well, lashing at the monsters with watery arms that he had shaped into blades.

"A raid is incoming," Tiberius told Quinlan.

"Did you see them?"

"I get raid warnings for taking part in a Hallowed Pursuit."

"What's a raid?" Sylas yelled over to Tiberius.

Quinlan struck one of the demons across the head. Near him, Tiberius beat another demon back, while Sylas used both hands on his mace to deliver a finishing blow.

He stepped back as Horatio whooshed forward, the water spirit forming a doorway of water that crashed down on the several of them.

Tiberius spoke after they'd cleared out the few that had surrounded them: "There are warring demon factions here in the Chasm. They tend to raid the badlands between Campaign Cities in order to gain territory and capture new wards. They're not going to be easy."

"But we are close to Raelis now," Quinlan said.

"And just like that," Tilbud said as a bit of mana fizzled in front of him, "three days have passed." The archlumen moved ahead and formed a sphere of light over the group. "That should give us a moment to prepare for the raid. Horatio, strengthen it as best you can."

"Will do."

"A shield?" Tiberius asked. "We don't need a bloody shield." As soon as he said this, mana-tinged arrows struck the protective barrier. "How did you know?" he asked the archlumen.

"I didn't, but it's best to be prepared. Quinlan, how much farther do we have to go?"

"Raelis is in the vicinity. I'd say we'll be to him within the hour."

"We'll likely run into him dealing with the raid," Tiberius said. "These things can be massive."

"We have company," Quinlan said as humanoid demons wearing armor appeared at the top of the crater. They were mounted on bone horses with long barbed tails.

Sylas had a brief flashback of the last battle of his life, as he came face-to-face with mounted cavalry. This was nothing like that; now, he wasn't simply a man standing his ground, he was a man standing his ground with access to a host of powers that would help him and his companions.

"Keep the shield up for a bit longer," he told Tilbud as the mounted demons trotted down into the crater.

A flourish of anger came to Sylas as he took control of the landscape using Territorial Domain. Sylas was able to smash one of the riders down as he formed a pair of wedges that trapped the others. He released his hold over the soil, which caused the sudden mounds he had created to collapse, burying their adversaries.

"Can you do that on a larger scale?" Tiberius shouted to him.

"I can use it as long as I have mana."

"Check!"

Sylas accessed his stats to see that he had plenty. He also noticed that he had received several boosts from Azor to the tune of over two thousand Mana Lumens.

"I can help as well," Mira said.

"We're going to need it. I say, yes, that would work." Tiberius turned to Quinlan. "What do you think about doing this?" The archlumen explained his plan. Sylas watched as Quinlan got that crazed look in his eyes, the one that signaled something just might work.

"It's bloody brilliant," Tilbud said. "Sylas, Mira, we're going to use your power to create a small valley, which we will then travel up until we reach Raelis. We get him, head back to Campaign City #1, and to the border from there.

If we hurry, only two more days will pass on the outside. Three at the most. No, four at the most."

"How will we travel if we're casting Territorial Domain?" Mira asked the archlumen.

"I failed to mention that part. I will handle travel management. Tiberius, Horatio, Quinlan, and, I suppose, Cornbread and Patches, you are in charge of defending us."

More of the raiding demons appeared. These ones carried large pikes covered in black scales that matched their menacing armor.

"Well? What are we waiting for?" Quinlan asked. "Let's go!"

Sylas began splitting the ground ahead, a single palm outstretched, all of his concentration on the soil beyond. Mira did the same next to him, the two so focused that neither noticed they had started to move forward.

The ripple they caused continued to thwart foes, making it easy for Tiberius and Quinlan to handle any that broke through the water-strengthened shield, as they tore through the landscape toward Raelis.

———

I hate flying!

I know you do. But we're going somewhere! Just hang on, Cat!

There's nothing to hang on to!

The ground ruptured, parting like water as the group hurtled through the cratered landscape.

Cornbread barked. The world around her sped up and it was frightening, but she trusted the big man and his friends. She knew they wouldn't let harm come their way.

Patches didn't seem to feel the same way. As soon as he was able, he reached the big man and drove his claws into the man's armor. He held on there, now positioned near the big man's neck, the cat yowling until the big man was able to send a hand up and pet his head. Even as he petted Patches, he continued to clear the ground in front of them, his hand charged with mana.

He's a good person, Cornbread thought as a demonic being made it through the barrier.

Cornbread leaped toward the demon and took it down. She latched on to its neck and shook her head out, her teeth tearing into its flesh.

Cornbread was soon stripped away from the demon as she flew forward, her movement outside of her control. *Wait, I got it!* It made sense now, how she was flying, her limitations. She engaged any demon that the two warriors and the water spirit didn't pick off.

What they were doing in such a terrible place didn't matter.

The big man knew best.

———

Patches didn't feel the same way.

As he clung to the big man's shoulder, he tried to remind himself that the big man would never lead him astray. Yet here they were, in hell itself, pummeling forward as rocks ripped from the ground and skull-masked demons continually attacked their group.

Watching Cornbread changed his opinion.

Seeing the farm dog take hold of her destiny and fly back and forth biting demons lit something deep within Patches. It wasn't courage as much as it was trust, and he still didn't know why they had come all this way, but he would no longer fight any apprehensions he might have.

Patches loosened his grip. He changed positions on the big man's shoulder and pounced at the next demon to break through, this one wielding an enormous sword that would have struck the big man had Patches not wrapped himself around the demon's face.

Patches grew in size, and they slammed into the ground together.

The demon tried to pull Patches off.

It sunk its fist into Patches's back again and again as the two struggled. Patches maintained his grip and bit into the demon's face, claws digging into the side of its head and neck, the demon delivering pummeling fist after pummeling fist.

I'll help! Cornbread collided with the demon and clamped down on its side with her enlarged jaw, which allowed Patches to use his incineration power on the demon's head.

The two were pulled forward by an unknown force. Yet again the world raced around them as Cornbread licked Patches's face, healing the cat. *You'll be fine . . .*

Patches lashed his tail against Cornbread in thanks.

The two human warriors shouted and pointed ahead. The upturned stones slowed as the group lowered to the ground, where they quickly surrounded a man with long dark hair in full armor who was holding a nasty demon sword.

Cornbread was just about to move ahead to sniff and greet the man when Patches stopped her. *Wait! Something is wrong . . .*

CHAPTER TWENTY-NINE

BENEFITS OF AN APOTHECARY

Demon Fevre," Tiberius said as he kept his weapon at the ready. Sylas saw it then, the way that Raelis twitched like his body was being controlled by some unknown force. The former soldier held an absolutely massive sword, with a hilt made from the petrified claw of a demon, the black blade covered in pulsing purple veins.

"Is it like dealing with a Nox?" Sylas asked the lord commander.

"Nothing like that. We're going to have to fight him until he naturally tires. We'll need to rush him over the border at that point. The Hexveil will break the spell."

Tilbud considered this. "I do have an ability that can put one to sleep, but he'll need to be closer to exhaustion first. And it looks like he is anything but that. We could have Horatio drown him, or sink him into the soil, but that could be difficult. And we need Horatio to protect us from the other demons." While he was maintaining their protective barrier, it was clear that some of the horde were close to breaking through.

Raelis seethed, his lips curling into an evil smile. *"Join me,"* he said, his tone garbled and scratchy, nothing like the Raelis that Sylas once knew. *"Join me and be free."*

"We can't kill him either," Quinlan said. "Not that I want to. If he dies, he will be sent to the Chasm. Since he's already here, he'll only grow stronger and will never be able to return to our world."

"Even if we take him through the tunnel?" Sylas asked.

"He's not like your fire spirit," Tiberius said as Raelis continued to size the group up, "something born of the Chasm. If he comes through the tunnel and appears on the other side, the Hexveilian Guard will come for him. You'll be taken into custody as well for bringing him."

"Can I reason with him?" Quinlan asked Tiberius.

"No. We must beat him into exhaustion and bring Raelis across the border. Mira can help at that point."

"I might have something that can help now," Mira said.

"Argh!" Raelis exploded forward with an opening strike, one that Quinlan blocked.

Clank!

"Blimey, he's strong! But you're going to have to be stronger than that to get a lick in on me, Raelis!" Quinlan pushed forward with his own strike, Tiberius brazenly doing the same. Raelis was able to parry both of their attempts.

"What do you have?" Tilbud asked Mira.

"I brought something I thought we might need to use if one of us was injured. It has a numbing effect, but enough of it can be used to temporarily paralyze a person."

"How do I administer it?" Sylas asked.

"He'll need to ingest it."

Sylas glanced over to Raelis, who continued trading blows with Quinlan and Tiberius. Raelis was incredibly fast; his attacks strong enough that they left a trail of mana in the air. If he could somehow get behind Raelis, Sylas could perhaps shove the small packet of herbs Mira now held into his mouth.

But how would I make him ingest it? Sylas wondered.

As if she could interpret his thoughts, Mira continued: "You just need to get it in his mouth and keep his jaw shut for a moment. The packet the herbs are in will dissolve."

"Right. Tilbud? Your thoughts?"

"Deliver the herbs and I'll put him to sleep after. In the meantime, I can keep the pets back. Mira and Horatio, deal with the hordes. We've got this!"

Sylas stuck his hand out to Mira. "Give me the herbs and I'll get it done."

———

"What's the plan?" Quinlan asked Sylas as he joined them. Tiberius swung his weapon at Raelis, only for Raelis to respond with an epic slash that forced all of them to defend. Luckily, Sylas had his buckler, which he used to his advantage as he blocked the attempt.

Clank!

"I need you two to distract him!" was all Sylas managed to say as he tried for a wide berth around Raelis.

Quinlan blasted their friend with a bolt of mana. He would have come in with another strike had it not been for the appearance of several demonic fighters, all stocky brawler types. Mira moved to the offensive, blasting one with mana and taking out the largest of the group using a magical hammer with her Architect's Arsenal ability.

Tiberius defeated another, while Quinlan took the brunt of Raelis's next attack. "Come on, Raelis, snap out of it!" Quinlan yelled, even though this wouldn't help.

"Join me or die!" Raelis kept pivoting, preventing Sylas from doing what needed to be done. The need to watch his back was making it even harder. He could see the actions he needed to take to pull it off, but he would only have one shot.

Once Raelis realized they were trying to shove something in his mouth, his strategy would change.

While a demon may have been possessing Raelis at the moment, it was clear in his stance and the sheer power he put behind his strikes that he was well trained. Even Tiberius, who Sylas assumed would be more forthright in a situation like this, seemed to hold back.

That could have also been because of Raelis's sword, which was a monster of a weapon capable of doing more damage than any of them could likely take head-on. Sylas had blocked it with his buckler, but had he been closer, had Raelis's blade actually reached him, he would have been severely injured.

Quinlan and Tiberius exchanged quick glances.

They charged Raelis, the pair simultaneously batting away his incoming strike and causing Raelis to bend forward slightly as he delivered it.

Sylas saw his chance and took it.

He abandoned his mace and buckler and launched forward, both arms going around Raelis's neck.

As the man struggled to buck him off, Sylas shoved the packet of herbs into his mouth.

He held them there, even as Raelis bit down onto his hand, drawing blood.

Quinlan grabbed Raelis's sword arm, preventing him from stabbing his blade upward. Tiberius managed to grab his other arm, while Horatio, who was still fighting back some of the demon horde on the periphery, took hold of his legs. The four anchored Raelis until he finally fell forward into a heap.

Sylas scrambled off him. He held his hand, which bled profusely, Raelis's teeth marks visible in his flesh.

As soon as Tilbud released Cornbread she pushed forward.

"Easy, girl!" Sylas said as she jumped at him and immediately began licking his wound. "Hey—"

"She'll heal you, mate," Quinlan said as he stood over Raelis. "She did it to me the other night when one of the Mana Ghouls gave me a nasty slash. Just let her do her thing."

Sylas lowered to his knees and noticed a sensation in his hand as his wound healed. "Thanks, girl." His focus turned to Raelis, who was quickly put under Tilbud's sleeping spell. While Horatio, Tiberius, and Quinlan stood guard, the archlumen hovered Raelis's limp body in the air.

The ground beyond cracked.

At first, Sylas thought they were about to face off against a new enemy, but then he saw the path they had cleared reforming.

"The landscape is changing and we need to move to higher ground," Mira said. "Gather your things."

Sylas retrieved his weapon and his buckler. "Patches." The cat approached. Once his mace was sheathed, Sylas placed the cat on his shoulder. "Think you can stay there?"

Patches flexed his claws and purred as a response.

"What about Raelis's weapon?" Mira asked after they'd all floated into the air, Quinlan with Cornbread tucked under his arm. "Won't he want it?"

"That blade won't make it through the Hexveil," Tiberius reminded her. "Best to leave it behind. A blade like that deserves to be buried, anyway."

Sylas looked down at the massive weapon. "Where do you think he got it?"

"If you're asking if you can buy one of those in one of the Campaign Cities, you can't, which is probably a good thing. It belonged to the demon that continues to possess him, but these sorts of demons can't traditionally pass through the veil. So we'll bury it, and the Hexveil will fry the demon as we bring his body through."

The weapon quivered.

The purple veins on it pulsed and a yellow, reptilian eye blinked open. Just as it started to move, the soil came crashing, rocks spilling forward. The ground hardened immediately, the barren landscape back to its original form.

"We could put a sign up that says something like *Here Lies the Demon Sword*, but something tells me that thing will only bring trouble to its wielder." Quinlan smirked. "It was a bloody good-looking weapon, though. Hate to see it buried."

"Good-looking?" Mira raised an eyebrow at him. "That's not how I would describe it."

"What can I say? I like sharp swords, and I cannot lie. Tilbud, what's our timing looking like?"

Mana fizzled into the air in front of Tilbud. "Five hours have passed now. I got the fourth notification just a little while ago. It will take us another one or two hours to get to the border. Moving through Campaign City #1 could prove difficult with Raelis's floating body."

"Not necessarily," Tiberius said. "People come to retrieve those who have fallen all the time. No one will bat an eye, but we should cover him in some way." He removed his black cape, the one normally worn by a lord commander. "Place this over him, and if anyone says anything, I'll do the talking. I highly doubt we will run into trouble."

"And after we're out?" Mira asked. "Won't we have to go through that forest again that has the Taurigraith?"

"Yes, we will. And we will need to do so as quickly as possible. We can fly at first, but then the trees are too tall, meaning we'll have to move on foot." Tiberius shook his head. "Tilbud."

"Yes?"

"Shrink Raelis and put him in your pocket."

The archlumen grinned. "That would make this much easier, but it would cost more mana. We'll float him behind us now and shrink him once we reach Matthew at the tunnel."

"Could you Shrink him twice?" Sylas asked.

"You mean Shrink him, and then Shrink myself while he is in my pocket? No, Sylas, I've yet to try a double shrinkage, and something tells me I shouldn't. But once should be enough. And when we get to the forest, we'll hurry to the best of our abilities."

"I might have something for that as well," Mira said.

"Yes?" Tilbud asked her.

"Just get us to the forest first. Let me think about how it would work."

———

They had no problem passing through Campaign City #1, Sylas and his group walking through the crowds of those brave or foolish enough to come to the Chasm, while Raelis floated behind them covered by Tiberius's cape. Just as the lord commander had said, nobody asked any questions.

They reached the outer gate and were able to fly again.

"We need to head around the site where we killed those Norakes," Quinlan said. "Look ahead."

Sylas saw them in the distance, giant trolls with withered faces and bloated bodies. They had feasted on the buried Norakes, and they now patrolled the area, enormous clubs resting across their shoulders.

"Those things are hideous," Mira said as the group started to curve around them. One of the trolls spotted them. It produced a giant horn made of bone, brought it to his lips, and blew it.

Sylas had assumed that this would call more of the trolls. Instead, its action created a giant gust of wind that struck his group and would have knocked several of them out of the air had it not been for Tilbud.

Still maintaining his hold over Raelis, the archlumen was able to temporarily stop the force of the wind.

"If they get any closer, Whimsical Drift!" he told Sylas once his group was traveling again.

For a moment, it seemed like the trolls were going to pursue them. One even started charging through the trees. But they soon gave up because Sylas and his group were moving fast enough that they were no longer of interest.

"Ever fought something like that?" Quinlan called to Tiberius.

"I did. Came across a sleeping one. When they sleep, their backs harden and they look like a giant rock. It surprised me."

"To say the least."

"But it was drowsy, so I cut at its heels and managed to topple it."

Quinlan turned to Tiberius, impressed. "You killed a troll by yourself?"

"What was I supposed to do? Let it kill me?" Tiberius's laugh was short and stilted, but it soon had Quinlan laughing as well.

"I can't believe they are getting along," Mira said, who hovered next to Sylas.

"You aren't the only one. It's crazy what being in a dangerous situation can do to people, the way it can bring us together."

"But we are not out of the woods yet," Tilbud said. "Literally. We're going to have to go it on foot now. Mira, you said you may have something?"

"I don't know if it will work, but I think it will. You know I brought lumeberry tea? I brought some of the leaves and stems as well because, when ground with soil shrooms, they create a pungent odor that is said to act as an animal deterrent. I thought it might come in handy."

"You've tried this before?" Sylas asked.

"No, I haven't, but as an apothecary, I have access to a full system of known plant properties. Not just that, other items as well, such as boiled mare bone. But I don't have that. What I'm trying to say here is that we have lumeberry leaves and there are several more pastries left. I can try to make the deterrent, but only if we find a flat stone where I can grind the ingredients together and put the stuff on our exposed skin. It won't take much. We'd also put it on Patches and Cornbread."

"Just rub it into their fur, yeah?"

"Exactly," she told Sylas. "Unless Horatio can do something to it."

"My power levels are lower than they should be," the water spirit said.

"Then return to me and restore your strength for a bit," Tilbud told Horatio. "Mira, I think your idea might work. Maybe."

"Well?" she asked as Quinlan and her uncle gathered around them, the group just about to head down to the forest floor. "What do you think?"

"It is certainly worth a try," Tiberius said. "But we have two animals with us, and they are not going to like it. I'll say this too: getting the stuff off might be hard as well."

"Nothing a trip to the spa won't handle," Quinlan said. "You know a good place, right, Tib?"

A genuine grin spread across Tiberius's face. "That I do, yes."

"If it keeps a Taurigraith off our arses, then I think it's worth a shot. All we need to do is get to Matthew's tunnel. We do that, and we're good."

CHAPTER THIRTY

THE CELESTIAL PLAINS HAVE SPOKEN

I *can't take it any more,* Cornbread said. She started to hack.

Why have they put this stuff on us? It smells so horrible!

The big man said something to Patches. He petted the cat. Patches could tell by the tone of his voice that he wasn't trying to hurt him. He knew it instinctively. But the smell. It was the foulest thing that ever reached his nostrils. And to make matters worse, Patches was confronted with it everywhere he turned.

All of them now smelled this way.

Cornbread seemed to be having an even harder time now, the dog no longer able to walk. The hammock-warrior carried her, also assuring the dog of something. But what? What could possibly warrant smelling like this?

What's that? Cornbread froze, Patches doing the same as he noticed something beyond.

If we value our lives, we need to remain still, the cat said carefully. *That's what I think the big man is trying to tell.*

Do you see it?

I do. Be ready.

———

"Remain still," Quinlan said as the trees ahead shifted. Cornbread quivered. "Don't bark," he told her, the dog seeming to understand what he was saying.

"Only move if it approaches you," Tiberius whispered.

All the hairs on the back of Sylas's neck stood as a towering beast appeared, the monster pushing through the underbrush. He had already seen it with his glasses, but closer to it now, he could see how it was the combination of a bull and a tiger, with bovine horns, a tiger's face and teeth, and sinewy brown flesh.

If he were to estimate its height, Sylas would guess that the beast was easily as tall as his two-story pub.

The Taurigraith took a step closer to them and examined the group, Tilbud so freaked out that Sylas would later swear that his mustache stood to attention. Soon, disgust filled the Taurigraith's face. The beast shook its head and moved on.

Or at least it seemed that way.

Sylas thought they were in the clear when the beast stopped and turned back to his group. Rather than address them, it kicked its legs back, sending some mud, leaves, and sticks into the air. With that, the Taurigraith took off, leaving over-turned trees in its wake, its stomps heavy enough to shake the ground.

Sylas let out a deep breath once it was gone. "How did that work? Why didn't it attack us?"

"The same way a skunk often survives. It didn't trust our smell," Quinlan said, the man also relieved. He wiped a bit of sweat from his brow, smelled his hand, and made a disgusted face. "And it didn't know if eating us would transfer the stink, or if we were poisoned in some way. That would be my estimate. Either way, this close to the border, I wouldn't be surprised if it comes through at some point. That's not the last we have seen of that bastard."

"Brilliant. That was utterly brilliant," Tiberius told Mira. "How did you know that would work?"

"I had no idea if it would work or not." Mira, who had been pinching her nose, finally released her hand. "It's so bad."

"It's absolutely foul," Sylas said as he rubbed Patches behind the ear, the cat perched on his shoulder.

"Don't worry, Horatio will be able to help clean us off," Tilbud said. "It won't be pleasant, will it?"

"No, it won't," Horatio said, the water spirit hovering nearby. "But it will work."

"I believe I'll just go to the spa."

"I'm with the lord commander here," Quinlan said. "It shouldn't be much longer now."

Mana fizzled in front of Tilbud. "Good. Six days have passed. By the time we get there, it should be night if we're lucky."

———

As soon as they passed the invisible border representing the Hexveil, Raelis, who floated behind the group, began to twitch.

A demon stripped away from him, one that would have rushed back to the Chasm had it not been for Horatio and Matthew, who were able to deal with it by burying it deep within the underground tunnel.

"Let's hurry," Tilbud said as Raelis moaned in pain.

Their group burst out of the well and instantly grew in size.

Sylas let out a sigh of relief as he looked over to see The Old Lamplighter, its inside emitting a soft, orange glow. They had done it. They were back in the Underworld.

Before any of them could say anything, the back door of the pub swung open and Azor came rushing out. There were several patrons inside, many of whom were shocked to see the fire spirit move so quickly.

"You're back? You're back! Oh, I would hug you if I could!" she said with a big smile, her flames brightening.

"We smell right now," Sylas warned her. "It's a long story."

"I need to treat Raelis." Mira lowered in front of the long-haired man, who now lay on the ground, breathing softly, a dazed look on his face. She looked up at Sylas. "Do you think we could put him in your spare bedroom?"

"I think that would be fine. Azor. Clear everyone out of the pub. We are closed for the night. Any questions can wait until later. Quinlan, Tiberius, thank you."

The two exchanged glances. "The spa is open all night," Tiberius told Quinlan. "They have sauna rooms with mats to sleep on."

"Our armor is going to stink too."

"Leave it all here and I'll handle it," Horatio said as he took place. "Hi, Azor."

"Hi, Horatio!"

"You mean strip down?" Tiberius asked Horatio. "Do it right here?"

"I mean just that."

"I suppose I don't mind."

Mira spoke: "Let's not do that just yet, Uncle. There are a lot of moving pieces here, but you're both right, we do need to get cleaned up."

"My services are still available," Horatio said. "I can use the water from the pub to create a shower, and Matthew can wall it in."

"And I can warm the water," Azor said. "How does a piping hot shower sound?"

"I think that would work perfectly. Let's test it on Patches and Cornbread," Sylas said.

Quinlan roared with laughter. "Not a bad idea, mate."

———

This is great! Cornbread told Patches as she was sprayed with warm water, which soon washed the stink away. The two were in a stone tub behind the pub, the water draining out of the bottom.

Patches didn't like it, but he also didn't like the smell, and he knew that this would wash it off. What was most annoying was that humans were all laughing at them. *I wish they would stop . . .*

It's fun! Cornbread snapped her teeth at the water. As soon as she was out, she shook her old body, spritzing the air with more water. She barked wildly. *I'm clean!*

Oh, bother.

What? This is great!

We're still sopping wet!

The fire spirit said something to them. *I don't know what she's saying, but I bet it has to do with food.* Cornbread licked her lips. *It better have to do with food.* She looked back and forth between the fire spirit and the big man, who had gone from happy to serious. *I wonder what they're saying.*

I really don't care at the moment. I'm wet, and I'm not happy.

But we're back. And we survived. The big man is safe as well. Cornbread licked Patches's face.

Enough. Patches said, but his heart wasn't in it. He finally relaxed to some degree. *I suppose you are right. The big man is safe, the Tavernly Realm is secure, and everything is where it should be. I guess I'll dry off at some point.*

Just get close to the fire spirit. She'll dry you.

Huh. I think I'll do just that.

———

"So Nuno came?" Sylas asked Azor as Tiberius took his shower behind the stone wall.

"He did. He's staying at Nelly and Karn's inn for the night. Nuno said he would check in the morning and if you weren't here by then, he would head back. So that's good, right? You are here."

"I suppose I could walk over there now. But . . ." Sylas ran his hand through his hair as he briefly checked his stats. "I'm exhausted. It was only six hours, but it truly felt like six days. I didn't use as much power as I thought I would, but I'm still ready to call it a night."

"You should. I can handle everything." Her flames brightened with fret. "I was so worried. I thought I was going to have to run the pub by myself forever."

"Anything I should know about?" Sylas asked as Tiberius barked about the water being too hot.

"Sorry!" Azor said. "Not everyone should multitask. As for the pub, nothing out of the ordinary. People missed you, but everyone knew that you were doing something important. I wouldn't be surprised if they don't have a celebration once they know that you're back. But none of that matters." She swooned with joy. "All that matters is that you are finally back!"

[You have 38 days until the invasion.]
[A loan payment of 48 has been deducted from your total Mana Lumens. Your total loan balance is 24603 Mana Lumens.]

Name: Sylas Runewulf
Mana Lumens: 8158/8158
Class: Brewer
Secondary Class: Farmer
Tertiary Class: Landlord

Later, after he spoke to Nuno, Sylas would get a new crop going at the farm and start the process again. He also needed to meet with Mira and Nelly about the market. They still needed a name and it was time to look for venders.

Sylas meant it when he said last night that he hadn't expected to come out of the Chasm with a healthy amount of Mana Lumens. But seeing it all topped off . . .

"Patches?" Sylas ran his hand under his blanket, expecting to find the pub cat. He listened carefully for a moment and could hear voices downstairs. He also heard the sound of Cornbread's nails tapping against the floor as she moved around below. Someone had stopped by, likely Nuno, but where was Patches?

Sylas went to his spare bedroom to find Mira sleeping with her back against the wall, Patches in her arms. Raelis lay on the bed, his eyes partially open.

"Mira," Sylas crouched in front of her. She yawned and a smile formed on her face. "You should have come to my bed, I mean, *used* my bed. I can't have you sleeping on the floor."

"I just dozed off," she said as she hugged Patches. "I wasn't planning on sleeping."

"There is bedding as well—"

"Quinlan's bedding? Where would he sleep?"

"I thought he went to Battersea with Tiberius."

"He did, and that was certainly unexpected. Next time, I'll find a proper bed." Mira nodded at Raelis. "He's doing better, by the way. He will need another day of rest to fully recover, I believe. This Demon Fevre is mostly a mind thing. He just needs to rest, and apparently, so do I. Although I feel quite refreshed. Yes," Mira said as her eyes flashed, an indication she was accessing her stats. "My MLus have been partially refilled."

"Patches."

"Apparently so."

"Mine are topped off as well. The poor guy must be tired." Sylas realized something else upon saying this. The reason he currently had more MLus than he had expected wasn't because of Patches, it was because of Azor.

Now that he thought about it, he recalled seeing the fire spirit sometime in the middle of the night, after he'd laid down. She had transferred some MLus to him, and he was pretty sure she said it was to cover the cost of brewing, which still drew from his power.

Sylas slowly shook his head.

"Yes?"

"Nothing. Just feeling blessed to be away from the Chasm."

"Yes. May we never return. You know, I have just a bit more of the soil shrooms. Let's chop them up and give them to him." She lifted Patches, who mewed softly. "Such a tired cat."

Sylas offered Mira his hand. She took it, and the two were just stepping out of the room when Raelis coughed. Sylas rushed to his bedside.

"Mate," Raelis said, his eyes twitching.

Sylas patted him on the shoulder. "Just get some rest. I'll explain everything later."

"Thank you." Raelis turned his head to the side, allowing him to see the golden sky outside. "Thank you."

———

Sylas and Mira went downstairs to find Nuno standing at the bar, Azor nervously trying to speak to the manaseer. "You're here," she said, relief rippling through her form. "I didn't want to wake you."

"Sylas, Mira," Nuno said as he looked over at them with his large, hazel eyes. The manaseer wore beige robes, his hair tied into a bun at the back of his head. He motioned for them to follow him out back.

"And you're sure you're not hungry?" Azor asked him.

"I'm fine, Azor. Thank you."

"Then . . . then I'll whip something up for Sylas and Mira."

"Can you make something for Patches?" Mira asked as she produced the soil shrooms. "Something with this in it. He's exhausted."

"Can do!" Glad to have a task, Azor whooshed over to Mira, grabbed the shrooms, and headed down to the cellar before Sylas could thank her for topping off his Mana Lumens.

"I hear you have visited the Chasm," Nuno said once they stepped outside, Cornbread joining them. The manaseer brought both legs up and crossed them under his body, allowing him to hover into a seated position in the air.

Sylas nodded. "We waited for you, and you never came. So we went ahead and made the trip. I had to find someone."

"A warrior like yourself?"

"Yes." Sylas was grateful that Nuno finally came, but part of him was annoyed as well, especially with how long it had taken.

The manaseer seemed to interpret how he was feeling. "It wasn't easy, you know. While the Underworld has been mostly mapped out, there are regions that are still dangerous to venture to, places you wouldn't expect. That's where I had to go to get a second interpretation of the message you receive daily. As I said the last time we met, I can confirm that the message isn't in relation to the Chasm. The Chasm, and monsters and demons within, do not have the collective power to invade the Underworld. No, it is something else."

"But this other manaseer confirmed that there is indeed an invasion coming?" Mira asked.

"Yes, she certainly did. And it is one that has been prophesied before. It nearly happened, but the Crafting Laws delayed it. Eons ago, the Underworld was a staging ground for people that were not yet ready for the Celestial Plains, but not iniquitous enough for the Chasm. Now, the Celestial Plains no longer desire this staging ground."

"Wait, are you saying that it is the Celestial Plains that will invade the Underworld?" Sylas asked.

"I'm saying exactly that."

"Why?" Sylas shook his head. "Before we get to that, how? How am I the only one receiving this message?"

"That we do not know. But I have my suspicions, which we will try to confirm in the coming days."

"Is there anything we can do?" Mira asked the youthful manaseer. "Anything to protect ourselves and the Underworld."

"I believe there are, but it will be an uphill battle against an incredible force. How many people know about the message?"

"Just some of the locals and a few close friends," Sylas said.

Nuno titled his head back and looked up at the shining clouds above. "That might need to change. The Celestial Plains have spoken. And our reply will be shaped by how we interpret the invasion message. It will become our legend, forge our legacy, and if we're unlucky, herald our demise. I know this isn't the message any of us wanted to hear, but now that we understand what is happening, we can act."

"I'm ready." Sylas looked back at The Old Lamplighter, instantly recalling all the joy the place brought him. "We're not going down without a fight."

"Good, I was hoping you'd say something like that." Nuno smiled at the two of them. "I feel the same way. And the Underworld will respond."

Cornbread, who had been sniffing near the well, turned to them and barked.

Mira took Sylas's hand and squeezed it. "Let's make these final days count."

ABOUT THE AUTHOR

Harmon Cooper is a bestselling author of LitRPG and progression fantasy, including the Pilgrim, Sacred Cat Island, Cowboy Necromancer, and War Priest series. Born and raised in Austin, Texas, he lived in Asia for five years before moving to New England and then finally settling in Portugal.

DISCOVER
STORIES UNBOUND

PodiumAudio.com

Printed in the USA
CPSIA information can be obtained
at www.ICGtesting.com
JSHW020822100824
67891JS00002B/4